Praise for

Colin Dexter's Inspector M...

'No one constructs a whodunit with more fiendish
skill than Colin Dexter'
Guardian

'Traditional crime writing at its best; the kind of book
without which no armchair is complete'
Sunday Times

'A character who will undoubtedly retain his place
as one of the most popular and enduring of
fictional detectives'
P. D. James, *Sunday Telegraph*

'Dexter has created a giant among fictional detectives'
The Times

'The writing is highly intelligent, the atmosphere
melancholy, the effect haunting'
Daily Telegraph

'Colin Dexter is the crime writer of
perfect pitch and perfect pace'
Jonathan Gash

'What construction! What skill! Why isn't this author
ever on the Booker shortlist?'
Beryl Bainbridge

THE WAY THROUGH THE WOODS

COLIN DEXTER graduated from Cambridge University in 1953 and has lived in Oxford since 1966. His first novel, *Last Bus to Woodstock*, was published in 1975. There are now thirteen novels in the series, of which *The Remorseful Day* is, sadly, the last.

Colin Dexter has won many awards for his novels, including the CWA Silver Dagger twice, and the CWA Gold Dagger for *The Wench Is Dead* and *The Way Through the Woods*. In 1997 he was presented with the CWA Diamond Dagger for outstanding services to crime literature, and in 2000 was awarded the OBE in the Queen's Birthday Honours List.

The Inspector Morse novels have been adapted for the small screen with huge success by Carlton/Central Television, starring John Thaw and Kevin Whately. Spin-offs from Dexter's much-loved novels also include the popular series, *Lewis*, featuring Morse's former sergeant, Robbie Lewis, and *Endeavour*, a prequel starring the young Endeavour Morse.

Colin Dexter's Inspector Morse Mysteries

Last Bus to Woodstock

Last Seen Wearing

The Silent World of Nicholas Quinn

Service of All the Dead

The Dead of Jericho

The Riddle of the Third Mile

The Secret of Annexe 3

The Wench Is Dead

The Jewel that Was Ours

The Way Through the Woods

The Daughters of Cain

Death Is Now My Neighbour

The Remorseful Day

Also available in Pan Books

Morse's Greatest Mystery and Other Stories

COLIN DEXTER

THE WAY THROUGH THE WOODS

PAN BOOKS

First published 1992 by Macmillan

First published in paperback 1993 by Pan Books

This paperback edition published 2016 by Pan Books
an imprint of Pan Macmillan
20 New Wharf Road, London N1 9RR
Associated companies throughout the world
www.panmacmillan.com

ISBN 978-1-4472-9925-7

1 3 5 7 9 8 6 4 2

A CIP catalogue record for this book is available from the British Library.

Printed and bound by CPI Group (UK) Ltd, Croydon, CR0 4YY

Visit **www.panmacmillan.com** to read more about all our books
and to buy them. You will also find features, author interviews and
news of any author events, and you can sign up for e-newsletters
so that you're always first to hear about our new releases.

To Brian Bedwell

The author wishes to record his gratitude
to the authorities of both Wytham Woods
and Blenheim Park for the information and
help they so readily gave him.
Also to Detective Inspector John Hayward,
of the Thames Valley Police, and to
Simon Jenkins, Editor of *The Times*.

ACKNOWLEDGEMENTS

The author and publishers wish to thank the following who have kindly given permission for use of copyright materials:

Extract from *A Portrait of Jane Austen* by David Cecil, published by Constable Publishers;

Extract from *The Rehearsal* by Jean Anouilh, published by Methuen London;

The Observer, for a quote by Aneurin Bevan © *The Observer*;

Faber & Faber Ltd for the extract from 'La Figlia Che Piange' in *Collected Poems 1909–1962* by T. S. Eliot;

Oxford University Press for the extract from 'AUSTIN, Alfred (1835–1913)' from the *Oxford Companion to English Literature* edited by Margaret Drabble (5th edition 1985);

Don Manley for the extract from the *Chambers Crossword Manual* (Chambers 1992);

Extract from *Marriage and Morals* by Bertrand Russell, published by Unwin Hyman;

Kate Champkin for the extract from *The Sleeping Life of Aspern Williams* by Peter Champkin;

Extract from *Further Fables of Our Time*, published by Hamish Hamilton, 1956, in the UK and Commonwealth and Simon and Schuster in the US. Copyright © 1956 James Thurber. Copyright © 1984 Helen Thurber;

Maps of Wytham Woods and Blenheim Park drawn by Graeme James.

Weather and rain have undone it again,
And now you would never know
There was once a road through the woods
Before they planted the trees.
It is underneath the coppice and heath
And the thin anemones.
Only the keeper sees
That, where the ring-dove broods,
And the badgers roll at ease,
There was once a road through the woods.

From *The Way Through the Woods*
by Rudyard Kipling

WYTHAM WOODS
OR THE WOODS OF KAZEL

1 Mile
(approx)

3/4

N

1/2

Woodland
Boundary

Forest rides &
footpaths

1/4

Wytham

White
Hart Inn

All Saints
Church

Oxford Western Bypass

Wytham
Abbey

0
Scale

Marley
Lodge

Woodland Boundary

Pond

HARP

MARLEY
WOOD

PASTICKS

THE
FOLLIES

Marley
Wood Plantation

WAY

Botley
Lodge

Boundary

CAR
PARK

Higgens's
Copse

PROLEGOMENON

Though your sins be as scarlet, they shall be whiter, yea whiter, than snow

(Isaiah, ch. 1, v. 18)

Whereof one cannot speak, thereof one must be silent
(Wittgenstein, *Philosophical Investigations*)

'I MUST speak to you.'

'Speak on, my child.'

'I've not often come to your church.'

'It is not my church – it is God's church. We are all children of God.'

'I've come to confess a big sin.'

'It is proper that all sins should be confessed.'

'Can all sins be forgiven?'

'When we, sinful mortals as we are, can find it in our hearts to forgive each other, think only of our infinitely merciful Father, who understands our every weakness – who knows us all far better than we know ourselves.'

'I don't believe in God.'

'And you consider that as of any great importance?'

'I don't understand you.'

'Would it not be of far greater importance if God did not believe in *you?*'

'You're speaking like a Jesuit.'

1

'Forgive me.'

'It's not you – it's *me* who wants forgiveness.'

'Do you recall Pilgrim, when at last he confessed his sins to God? How the weight of the great burden was straightway lifted from his shoulders – like the pain that eases with the lancing of an abscess?'

'You sound as if you've said that all before.'

'Those self-same words I have said to others, yes.'

'Others?'

'I cannot talk of them. Whatever it is that men and women may confess to me, they confess – through me – to God.'

'You're not really needed at all, then – is that what you are saying?'

'I am a servant of God. Sometimes it is granted me to help those who are truly sorry for their sins.'

'What about those who aren't?'

'I pray that God will touch their hearts.'

'Will God forgive them – whatever they've done? You believe that, Father?'

'I do.'

'The scenes of the concentration camps . . .'

'What scenes have you in mind, my child?'

'The "sins", Father.'

'Forgive me, once again. My ears are failing now – yet not my heart! My own father was tortured to death in a Japanese camp, in 1943. I was then thirteen years old. I know full well the difficulties of forgiveness. I have told this to very few.'

'Have you forgiven your father's torturers?'

'God has forgiven them, if they ever sought His forgiveness.'

'Perhaps it's more forgivable to commit atrocities in times of war.'

'There is no scale of better or of worse, whether in times of peace or in times of war. The laws of God are those that He has created. They are steadfast and firm as the fixed stars in the heavens – unchangeable for all eternity. Should a man hurl himself down headlong from the heights of the Temple, he will break himself upon the law of God; but never will he break the universal law that God has once ordained.'

'You *are* a Jesuit.'

'I am a man, too. And all men have sinned and fallen short of the glory of God.'

'Father . . .'

'Speak on, my child.'

'Perhaps you will report what I confess . . .'

'Such a thing a priest could never do.'

'But what if I *wanted* you to report it?'

'My holy office is to absolve, in the name of our Lord and Saviour, Jesus Christ, the sins of all who show a true repentance. It is not my office to pursue the workings of the Temporal Power.'

'You haven't answered my question.'

'I am aware of that.'

'What if I *wanted* you to report me to the police?'

'I would be unsure of my duty. I would seek the advice of my bishop.'

'You've never been asked such a thing before?'

'Never.'

'What if I repeat my sin?'

'Unlock your thoughts. Unlock those sinful thoughts to me.'

'I can't do that.'

'Would you tell me everything if I could guess the reasons for your refusal?'

'You could never do that.'

'Perhaps I have already done so.'

'You know who I am, then?'

'Oh yes, my child. I think I knew you long ago.'

CHAPTER ONE

A perpetual holiday is a good working definition of Hell
(George Bernard Shaw)

MORSE never took his fair share of holidays, so he told himself. So he was telling Chief Superintendent Strange that morning in early June.

'Remember you've also got to take into consideration the time you regularly spend in pubs, Morse!'

'A few hours here and there, perhaps, I agree. It wouldn't be all that difficult to work out how much—'

'"Quantify", that's the word you're looking for.'

'I'd never look for ugly words like "quantify".'

'A useful word, Morse. It means – well, it means to say how much . . .'

'That's just what I said, isn't it?'

'I don't know why I argue with you!'

Nor did Morse.

For many years now, holidays for Chief Inspector Morse of Thames Valley CID had been periods of continuous and virtually intolerable stress. And what they must normally be like for men with the extra handicaps of wives and children, even Morse for all his extravagant imagination could scarcely conceive. But for this year, for the year of our Lord nineteen hundred and ninety-two, he was resolutely determined that

5

things would be different: he would have a holiday away from Oxford. Not abroad, though. He had no wander-lust for Xanadu or Isfahan; indeed he very seldom travelled abroad at all – although it should be recorded that several of his colleagues attributed such insularity more than anything to Morse's faint-hearted fear of aeroplanes. Yet as it happened it had been one of those same colleagues who had first set things in motion.

'Lime, mate! Lime's marvellous!'

Lime?

Only several months later had the word finally registered in Morse's mind, when he had read the advertisement in *The Observer*.

THE BAY HOTEL
Lyme Regis

Surely one of the finest settings of any hotel in the West Country! We are the only hotel on the Marine Parade and we enjoy panoramic views from Portland Bill to the east, to the historic Cobb Harbour to the west. The hotel provides a high standard of comfort and cuisine, and a friendly relaxed atmosphere. There are level walks to the shops and harbour, and traffic-free access to the beach, which is immediately in front of the hotel.

For full details please write to The Bay Hotel, Lyme Regis, Dorset; or just telephone (0297) 442059.

'It gets tricky,' resumed Strange, 'when a senior man takes more than a fortnight's furlough – you realize that, of course.'

6

'I'm not taking more than what's due to me.'

'Where are you thinking of?'

'Lyme Regis.'

'Ah. Glorious Devon.'

'Dorset, sir.'

'Next door, surely?'

'*Persuasion* – it's where some of the scenes in *Persuasion* are set.'

'Ah.' Strange looked suitably blank.

'And *The French Lieutenant's Woman*.'

'Ah. I'm with you. Saw that at the pictures with the wife . . . Or was it on the box?'

'Well, there we are then,' said Morse lamely.

For a while there was a silence. Then Strange shook his head.

'You couldn't stick being away that long! Building sand-castles? For *over a fortnight?*'

'Coleridge country too, sir. I'll probably drive around a bit – have a look at Ottery St Mary . . . some of the old haunts.'

A low chuckle emanated from somewhere deep in Strange's belly. 'He's been dead for ages, man – more Max's cup o' tea than yours.'

Morse smiled wanly. 'But you wouldn't mind me seeing his *birth*-place?'

'It's gone. The rectory's gone. Bulldozed years ago.'

'Really?'

Strange puckered his lips, and nodded his head. 'You think I'm an ignorant sod, don't you, Morse? But let me tell you something. There was none of this child-centred nonsense when I was at school. In those days we all had to learn things off by heart – things like yer actual Ancient Bloody Mariner.'

'My days too, sir.' It irked Morse that Strange, only a year his senior, would always treat him like a represent-ative of some much younger generation.

But Strange was in full flow.

'You don't forget it, Morse. It sticks.' He peered briefly but earnestly around the lumber room of some olden memories; then found what he was seeking, and with high seriousness intoned a stanza learned long since:

> 'All in a hot and copper sky
> The bloody sun at noon
> Right up above the mast did stand
> No bigger than the bloody moon!'

'Very good, sir,' said Morse, uncertain whether the monstrous misquotation were deliberate or not, for he found the chief superintendent watching him shrewdly.

'No. You won't last the distance. You'll be back in Oxford within the week. You'll see!'

'So what? There's plenty for me to do here.'

'Oh?'

'For a start there's a drain-pipe outside the flat that's leaking—'

Strange's eyebrows shot up. 'And you're telling me *you're* going to fix *that?*'

'I'll get it fixed,' said Morse ambiguously. 'I've already got a bit of extra piping but the, er, diameter of the cross-section is . . . rather too narrow.'

'It's too bloody *small*, you mean? Is *that* what you're trying to say?'

Morse nodded, a little sheepishly.

The score was one-all.

CHAPTER TWO

Mrs Austen was well enough in 1804 to go with her husband and Jane for a holiday to Lyme Regis. Here we hear Jane's voice speaking once again in cheerful tones. She gives the news about lodgings and servants, about new acquaintances and walks on the Cobb, about some enjoyable sea bathing, about a ball at the local Assembly Rooms

(David Cecil, *A Portrait of Jane Austen*)

'IF I MAY SAY SO, sir, you really are rather lucky.'

The proprietor of the only hotel on the Marine Parade pushed the register across and Morse quickly completed the Date – Name – Address – Car Registration – Nationality columns. As he did so, it was out of long habit rather than any interest or curiosity that his eye took in just a few details about the half-dozen or so persons, single and married, who had signed in just before him.

There had been a lad amongst Morse's fellow pupils in the sixth form who had possessed a virtually photographic memory – a memory which Morse had much admired. Not that his own memory was at all bad; short term, in fact, it was still functioning splendidly. And that is why, in one of those pre-signed lines, there was just that single little detail which very soon would be drifting back towards the shores of Morse's consciousness . . .

'To be honest, sir, you're *very* lucky. The good lady who had to cancel – one of our regular clients – had booked the room as soon as she knew when we were opening for the season, and she especially wanted – she *always* wanted – a room overlooking the bay, with bath and WC *en suite* facilities, of course.'

Morse nodded his acknowledgement of the anonymous woman's admirable taste. 'How long had she booked for?'

'Three nights: Friday, Saturday, Sunday.'

Morse nodded again. 'I'll stay the same three nights – if that's all right,' he decided, wondering what was preventing the poor old biddy from once more enjoying her private view of the waves and the exclusive use of a water-closet. Bladder, like as not.

'Enjoy your stay with us!' The proprietor handed Morse three keys on a ring: one to Room 27; one (as he learned) for the hotel's garage, situated two minutes' walk away from the sea front; and one for the front entrance, should he arrive back after midnight. 'If you'd just like to get your luggage out, I'll see it's taken up to your room while you put the car away. The police allow our guests to park temporarily of course, but . . .'

Morse looked down at the street-map given to him, and turned to go. 'Thanks very much. And let's hope the old girl manages to get down here a bit later in the season,' he added, considering it proper to grant her a limited commiseration.

'Afraid she won't do that.'

'No?'

'She's dead.'

'Oh dear!'

'Very sad.'

'Still, perhaps she had a pretty good innings?'

'I wouldn't call forty-one a very good innings. Would you?'

'No.'

'Hodgkin's disease. You know what that's like.'

'Yes,' lied the chief inspector, as he backed towards the exit in chastened mood. 'I'll just get the luggage out. We don't want any trouble with the police. Funny lot, sometimes!'

'They may be in your part of the world, but they're very fair to us here.'

'I didn't mean—'

'Will you be taking dinner with us, sir?'

'Yes. Yes, please. I think I'd enjoy that.'

A few minutes after Morse had driven the maroon Jaguar slowly along the Lower Road, a woman (who certainly looked no older than the one who had earlier that year written in to book Room 27) turned into the Bay Hotel, stood for a minute or so by the reception desk, then pressed the Please-Ring-For-Service bell.

She had just returned from a walk along the upper level of Marine Parade, on the west side, and out to the Cobb – that great granite barrier that circles a protective arm around the harbour and assuages the incessant pounding of the sea. It was not a happy walk. That late afternoon a breeze had sprung up from the south, the sky had clouded over, and several people now promenading along the front in the intermittent drizzle were struggling into lightweight plastic macs.

'No calls for me?' she asked, when the proprietor reappeared.

'No, Mrs Hardinge. There's been nothing else.'

'OK.' But she said it in such a way as if it weren't OK, and the proprietor found himself wondering if the call he'd taken in mid-afternoon had been of greater significance than he'd thought. Possibly not, though; for suddenly she seemed to relax, and she smiled at him – most attractively.

The grid that guarded the drinks behind reception was no longer in place and already two couples were seated in the bar enjoying their dry sherries; and with them one elderly spinster fussing over a dachshund, one of those 'small dogs accepted at the management's discretion: £2.50 *per diem*, excluding food'.

'I think I'll have a large malt.'

'Soda?'

'Just ordinary water, please.'

'Say when.'

'"When"!'

'On your room-bill, Mrs Hardinge?'

'Please! Room fourteen.'

She sat on the green leather wall-seat just beside the main entrance. The whisky tasted good and she told herself that however powerful the arguments for total abstinence might be, few could challenge the fact that after alcohol the world almost invariably appeared a kinder, friendlier place.

The Times lay on the coffee table beside her, and she picked it up and scanned the headlines briefly before turning to the back page, folding the paper horizontally, then vertically, and then studying one across.

It was a fairly easy puzzle; and some twenty minutes later her not inconsiderable cruciverbalist skills had coped with all but a couple of clues – one of them a tantalizingly half-familiar quotation from Samuel Taylor Coleridge – over which she was still frowning when the lady of the establishment interrupted her with the evening's menu, and asked if she were taking dinner.

For a few minutes after ordering Seafood Soup with Fresh Garden Herbs, followed by Guinea Fowl in Leek and Mushroom Sauce, she sat with eyes downcast and smoked a king-sized Dunhill cigarette. Then, as if on sudden impulse, she went into the glass-panelled telephone booth that stood beside the entrance and rang a number, her lips soon working in a sort of silent charade, like the mouth of some frenetic goldfish, as she fed a succession of 20p's into the coin-slot. But no one could hear what she was saying.

CHAPTER THREE

Have you noticed that life, real honest-to-goodness life,
with murders and catastrophes and fabulous inheritances,
happens almost exclusively in the newspapers?

(Jean Anouilh, *The Rehearsal*)

MORSE found his instructions fairly easy to follow. Driving from the small car park at the eastern end of Marine Parade, then turning right, then left just before the traffic lights, he had immediately spotted the large shed-like building on his left in the narrow one-way Coombe Street: 'Private Garage for Residents of The Bay Hotel'. Herein, as Morse saw after propping open the two high wooden gates, were eighteen parking spaces, marked out in diagonal white lines, nine on each side of a central KEEP CLEAR corridor. By reason of incipient spondylosis, he was not nowadays particularly skilled at reversing into such things as slanting parking bays; and since the garage was already almost full, it took him rather longer than it should have done to back the Jaguar into a happily angled position, with the sides of his car equidistant from a J-reg Mercedes and a Y-reg Vauxhall. It was out of habit as before that he scanned the number plates of the cars there; but when about a quarter of an hour earlier he'd glanced through the hotel register, at least *something* had clicked in his mind.

Now though? Nothing. Nothing at all.

There was no real need for Morse immediately to explore the facilities of Room 27, and the drinks-bar faced him as he turned into the hotel. So he ordered a pint of Best Bitter, and sat down in the wall-seat, just by the entrance, and almost exactly on the same square footage of green leather that had been vacated ten minutes earlier by one of the two scheduled occupants of Room 14.

He should have been feeling reasonably satisfied with life, surely? But he wasn't. Not really. At that particular moment he longed for both the things he had that very morning solemnly avowed to eschew for the remaining days of his leave: cigarettes and newspapers. Cigarettes he had given up so often in the past that he found such a feat comparatively simple; never previously however had he decided that it would be of some genuine benefit to his peace of mind to be wholly free for a week or so from the regular diet of disasters served up by the quality dailies. Perhaps that was a silly idea too, though . . .

His right hand was feeling instinctively for the reassuring square packet in his jacket pocket, when the maîtresse d'hotel appeared, wished him a warm welcome, and gave him the menu. It may have been a matter of something slightly more than coincidence that Morse had no hesitation in choosing the Seafood Soup and the Guinea Fowl. Perhaps not, though – and the point is of little importance.

'Something to drink with your meal, sir?' She was a pleasantly convivial woman, in her late forties, and

Morse glanced appreciatively at the décolletage of her black dress as she bent forward with the wine list.

'What do you recommend?'

'Half a bottle of Médoc? Splendid vintage! You won't do much better than that.'

'A bottle might be better,' suggested Morse.

'A bottle it shall be, sir!' – the agreement signed with mutual smiles.

'Could you open it now – and leave it on the table?'

'We always do it that way here.'

'I, er, I didn't know.'

'It likes to breathe a little, doesn't it?'

'Like all of us,' muttered Morse; but to himself, for she was gone.

He realized that he was feeling hungry. He didn't often feel hungry: usually he took most of his calories in liquid form; usually, when invited to a College gaudy, he could manage only a couple of the courses ordained; usually he would willingly exchange an entrée or a dessert for an extra ration of alcohol. But this evening he was feeling hungry, quite definitely; and just after finishing his second pint of beer (still no cigarette!) he was glad to be informed that his meal was ready. Already, several times, he had looked through the glass doors to his left, through to the dining room, where many now sat eating at their tables, white tablecloths overlaid with coverings of deep maroon, beneath the subdued lighting of crystal chandeliers. It looked inviting. Romantic, almost.

As he stood by the dining-room door for a moment,

the maîtresse was quickly at his side, expressing the hope that he wouldn't mind, for this evening, sharing a table? They had quite a few non-residents in for dinner . . .

Morse bade the good lady lose no sleep over such a trivial matter, and followed her to one of the farthest tables, where an empty place was laid opposite a woman, herself seated half-facing the wall, reading a copy of *The Times*, an emptied bowl of Seafood Soup in front of her. She lowered the newspaper, smiled in a genteel sort of way, as though it had taken her some effort to stretch her painted lips into a perfunctory salutation, before reverting her attention to something clearly more interesting than her table companion.

The room was almost completely full, and it was soon obvious to Morse that he was going to be the very last to get served. The sweet-trolley was being pushed round, and he heard the elderly couple to his right ordering some caramelized peaches with nuts and cream; but – strangely for him! – he felt no surge of impatience. In any case, the soup was very soon with him, and the wine had been there already; and all around him was goodwill and enjoyment, with a low, steady buzz of conversation, and occasionally some muted laughter. But the newspaper opposite him, for the present, remained firmly in place.

It was over the main course – his only slightly after hers – that Morse ventured his first, not exactly original, gambit:

'Been here long?'

She shook her head.

'Nor me. Only just arrived, in fact.'

'And me.' (She *could* speak!)

'I'm only here for a few days . . .'

'Me, too. I'm leaving on Sunday.'

It was the longest passage of speech Morse was likely to get, he knew, for the eyes had drifted down again to the Guinea Fowl. Stayed on the Guinea Fowl.

Bugger you! thought Morse. Yet his interest, in spite of himself, was beginning to be engaged. Her lower teeth – a little too long maybe? – were set closely together and slightly stained with nicotine; yet her gums were fresh and pink, her full mouth undoubtedly attractive. But he noticed something else as well: her mottled, tortoise-shell eyes, though camouflaged around with artificial shadow, seemed somehow darkened by a sadder, more durable shadow; and he could see an intricate little criss-cross of red lines at the outer side of either eye. She might have a slight cold, of course.

Or she might earlier have been weeping a little . . .

When the sweet-trolley came, Morse was glad that he was only halfway down the Médoc, for some cheese would go nicely with it ('Cheddar . . . Gouda . . . Stilton . . .' the waitress recited); and he ordered Stilton, just as the woman opposite had done.

Gambit Number Two appeared in order.

'We seem to have similar tastes,' he ventured.

'Identical, it seems.'

'Except for the wine.'

'Mm?'

'Would you, er, like a glass of wine? Rather good! It'll go nicely with the Stilton.'

19

This time she merely shook her head, disdaining to add any verbal gloss.

Bugger you! thought Morse, as she picked up *The Times* once more, unfolded the whole broadsheet in front of her, and hid herself away completely – together with her troubles.

The fingers holding the paper, Morse noticed, were quite slim and sinuous, like those of an executant violinist, with the unpainted nails immaculately manicured, the half-moons arching whitely over the well-tended cuticles. On the third finger of her left hand was a narrow-banded gold wedding ring, and above it an engagement ring with four large diamonds, set in an unusual twist, which might have sparkled in any room more brightly lit than this.

On the left of the opened double-page spread (as Morse viewed things) her right hand held the newspaper just above the crossword, and he noticed that only two clues remained to be solved. A few years earlier his eyes would have had little trouble; but now, in spite of a sequence of squints, he could still not quite read the elusive wording of the first clue, which looked like a quotation. Better luck with the other half of the paper though, held rather nearer to him – especially with the article, *the quite extra-ordinary article*, that suddenly caught and held and dominated his attention. At the foot of the page was the headline: 'Police pass sinister verses to Times' man', and Morse had almost made out the whole of the first paragraph –

THE LITERARY correspondent of *The Times*, Mr Howard Phillipson, has been called upon by the Oxfordshire police to help solve a complex riddle-me-ree, the answer to which is believed to pinpoint the spot where a young woman's body

– when the waitress returned to the table.

'Coffee, madame?'

'Please.'

'In the bar – or in the lounge?'

'In the bar, I think.'

'You, sir?'

'No. No, thank you.'

Before leaving, the waitress poured the last of the Médoc into Morse's glass; and on the other side of the table the newspaper was folded away. To all intents and purposes the meal was over. Curiously, however, neither seemed over-anxious to leave immediately, and for several moments they sat silently together, the last pair but one in the dining room: he, longing for a cigarette and eager to read what looked like a most interesting article; wondering, too, whether he should make one last foray into enemy territory – since, on reflection, she really did look rather attractive.

'Would you mind if I smoked?' he ventured, half-reaching for the tempting packet.

'It doesn't matter to me.' She rose abruptly, gathering up handbag and newspaper. 'But I don't think the management will be quite so accommodating.' She spoke without hostility – even worse, without interest, it seemed – as she pointed briefly to a notice beside the door:

IN THE INTEREST OF PUBLIC HEALTH, WE
RESPECTFULLY REQUEST YOU TO REFRAIN FROM
SMOKING IN THE DINING AREA. THANK YOU FOR
YOUR CO-OPERATION.

Bugger you! thought Morse.

He'd not been very sensible though, he realized that. All he'd had to do was ask to borrow the newspaper for a couple of minutes. He could *still* ask her, of course. But he wasn't going to – oh no! She could stick her bloody paper down the loo for all he cared. It didn't matter. Almost every newsagent in Lyme Regis would have a few unsold copies of yesterday's newspapers, all ready to be packaged off mid-morning to the wholesale distributors. He'd seen such things a thousand times.

She'd go to the bar, she'd said. All right, *he* would go to the lounge ... where very soon he was sitting back in a deep armchair enjoying another pint of bitter and a large malt. And just to finish off the evening, he told himself, he'd have a cigarette, just one – well, two at the very outside.

It was growing dark now – but the evening air was very mild; and as he sat by the semi-opened window he listened again to the grating roar of the pebbles dragged down by the receding tide, and his mind went to a line from 'Dover Beach':

But now I only hear its melancholy, long withdrawing roar.

Much-underrated poet, Matthew Arnold, he'd always thought.

In the bar, Mrs Hardinge was drinking her coffee, sipping a Cointreau – and, if truth be told, thinking for just a little while of the keen blue eyes of the man who had been sitting opposite her at dinner.

CHAPTER FOUR

The morning is wiser than the evening.

(Russian proverb)

MORSE rose at 6.45 the following morning, switched on his room-kettle, and made himself a cup of coffee from one of the several sachets and small milk-tubs provided. He opened the curtains and stood watching the calm sea, and a fishing boat just leaving the Cobb. Blast! He'd meant to bring his binoculars.

The gulls floated and wheeled across the esplanade, occasionally hanging motionless, as if suspended from the sky, before turning away like fighter-aircraft peeling from their formation and swooping from his vision.

The sun had already risen, a great ball of orange over the cliffs to the east, over Charmouth – where they said someone had discovered a dinosaur or a pterodactyl, or something, that had lived in some distant prehistoric age, some figure with about twelve noughts after it. Or was it twenty?

Deciding that he really ought to learn more about the world of natural history, Morse drained his coffee and without shaving walked down to the deserted ground floor, out of the hotel, and left along Marine Parade – where his search began.

The newsagent on the corner felt pretty sure that he

hadn't got a previous day's *Times*: *Sun*, yes; *Mirror*, yes; *Express*, yes . . . but, no – no *Times*. Sorry, mate. Turning left, Morse struggled up the steep incline of Broad Street. Still out of breath, he enquired in the news-agent's shop halfway up on the left. *Telegraph, Guardian, Independent* – any good? No? Sorry, sir. Morse got another 'sir' in the newsagent's just opposite – but no *Times*. He carried on to the top of the hill, turned left at a rather seedy-looking cinema, then left again into Cobb Road, and down to the western end of Marine Parade – where a fourth newsagent was likewise unable to assist, with the chief inspector reduced in rank to 'mate' once more.

Never mind! Libraries kept back numbers of all the major dailies; and if he were desperate – which he most certainly *wasn't* – he could always go down on his knees and beg Mrs Misery-guts to let him take a peek at her newspaper. If she'd still got it . . . Forget it, Morse! What's it matter, anyway?

What's *she* matter?

Strolling briskly now along the front, Morse breathed deeply on the early-morning air – cigarettes were going to be *out* that day. Completely out. He had, he realized, just walked a sort of rectangle; well, a 'trapezium' really – that was the word: a quadrilateral with two parallel sides. And doubtless he would have told himself it wouldn't be a bad idea to brush up on his geometry had he not caught sight of a figure in front of him, about two hundred yards distant. For there, beneath the white canopy of the buff-coloured Bay Hotel, with its yellow two-star AA sign, stood Mrs

Hardinge, Mrs Crabcrumpet herself, dressed in a full-length black leather coat, and searching in a white shoulder-bag. For a purse, probably? But before she could find it she raised her right hand in greeting as a taxi drew up along the lower road, its driver manoeuvering 180 degrees in the turning area, then getting out and opening the near-side rear door for the elegant, luggageless woman who had just walked down the ramp. Morse, who had stopped ostensibly to survey the ranks of fruit machines in the Novelty Emporium, looked down at his wrist-watch: 7.50 a.m.

The ground floor was still deserted, and as yet no delicious smell of fried bacon betrayed the opening of the hostelry's daily routine. Morse passed by the giant potted-palm, passed by the statue of a maiden perpetually pouring a slow trickle from her water-jug into the pool at her feet, and was starting up the stairs when his eye fell on the reception desk to his right: a jar of artificial flowers; a tray of mineral water; a yellow RNLI collecting box; and below a stack of brochures and leaflets – the hotel register. He glanced around him. No one.

He looked swiftly along the linear information once again:

3.7.92 – Mr and Mrs ¢ A Hardinge – 16 Cathedral Mews, Salisbury – H 35 LWL – British – Rm 14

It had been the Oxfordshire letter-registration, LWL, which had caught his eye that previous evening. Now it was something else: that ¢. It was her all right though, for he'd seen the room number on her key-ring at dinner. And frowning slightly as he mounted the stairs, he found himself wondering how many married women were unable to write out the accepted formula for their wedded state without getting the wrong initial. Perhaps she was only recently married? Perhaps she was one of those liberated ladies who had suddenly decided that if only *one* initial were required it was going to be hers? Perhaps ... perhaps they weren't 'Mr and Mrs' at all, and she had been momentarily confused about what names they were going under *this* time?

The latter, he thought – a little sadly.

Breakfast (8.45 a.m.–9.30 a.m.) was for Morse a solitary affair, yet he was finding it, as ever, the biggest single joy of any holiday. After some Kellogg's Corn Flakes and a mixed grill, he strolled along the edge of the sea once more, feeling pleasantly replete and (he supposed) about as content as he was ever likely to be. The weather forecast was good, and he decided that he would drive out west to Ottery St Mary and then, if the mood took him, north up to Nether Stowey, and the Quantocks.

As he reached the second-floor landing after his return to the hotel, Room 14 was almost directly in front of him; and with the door slightly ajar, as one blue-uniformed room-maid came out with a hoover, he could see another maid inside the room replenishing the sachets of coffee and tea and the little tubs of milk. He took his chance. Knocking (not too hesitantly), he put his head round the door.

'Mrs Hardinge in?'

'No, sur.' She looked no more than eighteen, and Morse felt emboldened.

'It's just that she promised to keep yesterday's news-paper for me – we had dinner here together last night. *The Times*, it was.'

The maid gave Morse a dubious look as he cast a swift glance over the room. The bed nearer the window had been slept in – the pillow deeply indented, a flimsy black negligée thrown carelessly over the duvet. But had *Mr* Hardinge slept in the other? The bed could have been made up already, of course ... but where was his case and his clothes and his other impedimenta?

'I'm afraid there's no newspaper as I can see 'ere, sur. In any case, I wouldn't—'

'Please, please! I fully understand. I mean, if it's not in the waste-paper basket ...'

'No, it's not.'

'There'd be another basket, though? In the bath-room? It's just that she *did* say ...'

The young girl peered cautiously round the bath-room door, but shook her head.

Morse smiled affably. 'It's all right. She must have left it somewhere else for me. Probably in *my* room. Huh! Sorry to have bothered you.'

Back in Room 27, he found his own bed made up, the floor hoovered, and his coffee cup washed and placed upside-down on its matching saucer. He stood for several minutes looking out at the sea again, telling himself he must re-read *The Odyssey*; and soon, almost unconsciously, finding himself smoking one of his forbidden cigarettes and wondering why the brown leather suitcase he had just seen lying closed on the set of drawers in Room 14 bore, in an attractive Gothic script, the gilt letters 'C S O'. The only thing he knew with such initials was Community Service Order – but that seemed wholly unlikely. Must be *her* initials, surely. But whatever the C stood for – Carole? Catherine? Claire? Celia? Constance? – it was going to be obvious even to an under-achiever in the new seven-year-old reading tests that the O didn't stand for 'Hardinge'. It may reasonably have been the lady's surname before she got married. But the case was a new one – a very new one . . .

So what, Morse! So bloody *what*!

He sat down and wrote a note.

Dear Mrs H, I shall be most grateful if you can save yesterday's Times for me. Not the Business/Sport section; just the main newspaper – in fact I only really want to look at the bit on p. I (and probably a continuation on an inside page) about the 'Sinister Verses' article. Your reward, which you <u>must</u> accept, will be a drink on me at the bar before dinner, when I promise to adhere religiously to every one of the management's ordinances.

Room 27

Leaving this innocent, if rather pompous, communication with the proprietor, Morse walked along to the private garage, pondering the reason why the female half of Room 14 had not made use of car H 35 LWL instead of ordering a taxi. Pondering only briefly though, since he thought he now knew why Mrs C.

Something (Hardinge?) had been acting so strangely. Well, no – not 'strangely', not if you looked at it from *her* point of view. Forget it, Morse! Get your road atlas out and trace the easiest route to Ottery St Mary.

Soon the Jaguar was on its way, with the sun growing warmer by the minute, and hardly a cloud in the bluest of skies. By the time he reached Honiton, Morse had almost forgotten the rather odd fact that when he had looked just now around the other cars in the hotel's garage, there had been no sign whatsoever of any vehicle with the registration H 35 LWL.

CHAPTER FIVE

Extract from a diary dated 26 June 1992 (one week
before Morse had found himself in Lyme Regis)

Words! Someone – a Yank I think – said you can stroke
people with words. I say – sod words! Especially sod the
sight of words. They're too powerful. 'Naked's powerful.
'Breasts' are powerful. Larkin said he thought the most
splendid verb in the language was 'unbutton'. But when
the words are a joke? Oh God, help me! Please God,
help me! Yesterday Tom wrote me a letter from his new
house in Maidstone. Here's part of what he wrote

> I've got a pair of great tits in the garden here. Now
> don't you go and think that when I look down from
> my study window with the binocs you bought me
> there's this bronzed and topless and vasty bosomed
> signora sunning herself on a Lilo. No! Just a
> wonderfully entertaining little pair of great tits
> who've taken up residence – a bit late aren't they? –
> in the nesting-box we fixed under the beech tree.
> Remember that line we learned at school?
> Titvre tu patulae recubans sub tegmine fagi...

Those are Tom's words. Wouldn't you think that any
normally civilized soul would be delighted with the
thought of those little blue black white yellow birds (my

31

speciality!!) slipping their slim little selves into a nesting-box? Wouldn't you think that only a depraved and perverted mind would dwell instead upon that picture of a woman on a sunbed? Wouldn't you think that any sensitive soul would rejoice in that glorious Virgilian hexameter instead of seeing another 'tit' in the opening word? Christ, it was only a pun wasn't it! The Greek term is 'paronomasia'. I'd forgotten that but I just looked it up in my book of literary terms. And still the words follow me. Looking through the p's I found 'pornography' again. Words! Bloody hell. God help me!

> 'Common subjects of such exotic pornography are
> sadism, masochism, fetishism, transvestism,
> voyeurism (or scoptolagnia), narcissism, pederasty,
> and necrophilia. Less common subjects are
> coprophilia, kleptolagnia, and zoophilia.'

Should it be a fraction of comfort that my tastes don't yet run to these last three 'less common' perversions – if that's the right word. What does the middle one mean anyway? It's not in Chambers.

(Later) Dinner in SCR very good – 'Barbue Housman'. I phoned C afterwards and I almost dare to believe she's really looking forward to next weekend. I just wish I could go to sleep and wake up on the 3rd. But I seem to spend half my time wishing my life away. I have drunk too much. Oh God, let me sleep well!

CHAPTER SIX

> ... and hence through life
> Chasing chance-started friendships
>> (Samuel Taylor Coleridge,
>> 'To the Revd George Coleridge')

IN MID-AFTERNOON Morse looked back on his Coleridge pilgrimage with considerable disappointment.

Half a dozen miles west of Honiton he had turned left off the A30 for the little market town of Ottery St Mary. Parking had proved a virtually insuperable problem; and when he finally got to the Information Office he learned only that 'Coleridge was born here in 1772 at the Rectory (gone), the tenth child of The Revd J. Coleridge, vicar 1760–81, and master of the Grammar School (gone). The rapidly growing family soon occupied the old School House (gone) ...'. St Mary's was still there though, and he walked around the large church consulting some printed notes on 'Points of Interest', fixed to a piece of wood shaped like a hand-mirror. He began to feel, as he read, that it was high time he re-familiarized himself with 'corbels' and 'mouldings' and 'ogees'; but it was something of a surprise that the author of the notes appeared never to have heard of Coleridge. Indeed it was only by accident that as he was leaving the church he spotted a memorial plaque on the churchyard wall, with a low-relief bust of the poet beneath the outspread wings of an albatross.

An hour and a half later, after a fast drive up the M5, Morse was equally disappointed with the village of Nether Stowey. 'The small thatched cottage, damp and uncomfortable' wherein Coleridge had lived in 1796 was now enlarged, tiled, and (doubtless) centrally heated, too. More to the point, it was closed to the public – on Saturdays; and today was Saturday. Inside the church the leaflet available for visitors ('Please take – quite free!') was a singularly uninformative document, and Morse felt no inclination to heed the vicar's exhortation to join the church fellowship – 'emphasis ever on joyous informality'. He put 50p in a slot in the wall and joylessly began the drive back to Lyme Regis.

Perhaps Strange had been right all along. Perhaps he, Morse, was the sort of person who could never really enjoy a holiday. Even the pint of beer he'd drunk in a rather dreary pub in Nether Stowey had failed to satisfy, and he didn't really know what he wanted. Or rather he did: he wanted a cigarette for a start; and he wanted something to engage his brain, like a cryptic crossword or a crime – or the previous day's issue of *The Times*. But there was something else too, though he was hardly prepared to admit it even to himself: he would have wished Mrs Hardinge (or Mrs Whatever) to be beside him in the passenger seat.

A voice in his brain told him that he was being quite extraordinarily foolish. But he didn't listen.

*

At 3.45 p.m. he parked the Jaguar in the hotel garage: only three other cars there now – none of the three with the Oxon registration.

At the Corner Shop on Marine Parade, he succumbed to two temptations, and resisted a third. He bought twenty Dunhill International, and a copy of *The Times*; but the magazine with the seductively posed, semi-clad siren on its glossy cover remained on the top shelf – if only because he would be too embarrassed and ashamed to face the hard-eyed man behind the counter.

Back in the hotel, he took a leisurely bath and then went down to the residents' lounge, where he unfolded the cover from the full-sized billiard table, and for half an hour or so pretended he was Steve Davis. After all, didn't *The Oxford Companion to Music* devote one entire page to 'Mozart on the Billiard Table'? Morse, however, was unable to pot virtually anything, irrespective of angle or distance; and just as carefully as he had unfolded the cover he now replaced it, and returned to his room, deciding (if life should allow) to brush up on his cuemanship as well as on that glossary of architectural terms. This was exactly why holidays were so valuable, he told himself: they allowed you to stand back a bit, and see where you were going rusty.

It was whilst lying fully clothed on his single bed, staring soberly at the ceiling, that there was a knock on the door and he got up to open it. It was the proprietor himself, carrying a Sainsbury's supermarket carrier bag.

'Mrs Hardinge wanted you to have this, Mr Morse. I tried to find you earlier, but you were out – and she insisted I gave it to you personally.'

What was all this to Morse's ears? Music! Music! Heavenly music!

Inside the carrier bag was the coveted copy of *The Times*, together with a 'Bay Hotel' envelope, inside which, on a 'Bay Hotel' sheet of note-paper, was a brief letter:

For 27 from 14. I've seen a paperback called The Bitch by one of the Collins sisters. I've not read it but I think it must be all about me, don't you? If I'm not at dinner I'll probably be in soon after and if you're still around you can buy me a brandy. After all these newspapers do cost honest money you know!

For Morse this innocent missive was balm and manna to the soul. It was as if he'd been trying to engage the attention of a lovely girl at a dinner party who was apparently ignoring him, and who now suddenly leaned forward and held her lips against his cheek in a more than purely perfunctory kiss.

Strangely, however, before reading the article, Morse picked up the bedside phone and dialled police HQ at Kidlington.

CHAPTER SEVEN

I read the newspaper avidly. It is my one form of continuous fiction

(Aneurin Bevan, quoted in *The Observer*, 3 April 1960)

POLICE PASS SINISTER VERSES TO TIMES' MAN

THE LITERARY correspondent of *The Times*, Mr Howard Phillipson, has been called upon by the Oxfordshire police to help solve a complex riddle-me-ree, the answer to which is believed to pinpoint the spot where a young woman's body may be buried.

The riddle, in the form of a five-stanza poem, was sent anonymously by a person who (as the police believe) knows the secret of a crime which for twelve months has remained on the unsolved-case shelves in the Thames Valley Police HQ at Kidlington, Oxfordshire.

'The poem is a fascinating one,' said Mr Phillipson, 'and I intend to spend the weekend trying to get to grips with it. After a brief preliminary look I almost think that the riddle has a strong enough internal logic to be solvable within its own context, but we must wait and see.'

According to Detective Chief Inspector Harold Johnson of Thames Valley CID the poem would fairly certainly appear to have reference to the disappearance of a Swedish student whose rucksack was found in a layby on the northbound carriageway of the A44, a mile or so south of Woodstock, in July 1991. Documents found in the side-panels of the rucksack had identified its owner as Karin Eriksson, a student from Uppsala, who had probably hitchhiked her way from London to Oxford, spent a day or so in the University City – and then? Who knows?

'The case was always a baffling one,' admitted DCI Johnson. 'No body was ever found, no suspicious circumstances uncovered. It is not unknown for students to be robbed of their possessions, or lose them. And of course some of them run away. But we've always thought of this as a case of potential murder.'

At the time of her disappearance, Miss Eriksson's mother informed the police that Karin had phoned her from London a week or so previously, sounding 'brisk and optimistic', albeit rather short of cash. And the Principal of the secretarial college where Karin was a student described her as 'an attractive, able, and athletic young lady'. Since the discovery of the rucksack, no trace whatever has been found, although senior police officers were last night suggesting that this new development might throw fresh light on one or two possible clues discovered during the earlier investigation.

The poem in full reads as follows:

Find me, find the Swedish daughter –
    Thaw my frosted tegument!
Dry the azured skylit water,
    Sky my everlasting tent.

Who spied, who spied that awful spot?
    O find me! find the woodman's daughter!
Ask the stream: 'Why tell'st me not
    The truth thou know'st – the tragic slaughter?'

Ask the tiger, ask the sun
 Whither riding, what my plight?
Till the given day be run,
 Till the burning of the night.

Thyme, I saw Thyme flow'ring here
 A creature white trapped in a gin,
Panting like a hunted deer
 Licking still the bloodied skin.

With clues surveyed so wondrous laden,
 Hunt the ground beneath thy feet!
Find me, find me now, thy maiden,
 I will kiss thee when we meet.

A. Austin
(1853–87)

The lines were typed on a fairly old-fashioned machine, and police are hopeful that forensic tests may throw up further clues. The only immediately observable idiosyncracies of the typewriter used are the worn top segment of the lower-case 'e', and the slight curtailment of the cross-bar in the lower-case 't'.

'To be truthful,' admitted Chief Inspector Johnson, 'not many of my colleagues here are all that hot on poetry, and that's why we thought *The Times* might help. It would be a sort of poetic justice if it could.' Final word with Mr Phillipson: 'It might all be a cruel hoax, and the link with the earlier case does appear rather tenuous, perhaps. But the police certainly seem to think they are on to something. So do I!'

Morse read the article at his own pace; then again, rather more quickly. After which, for several minutes, he sat where he was, his eyes still, his expression quite emotionless – before turning to the back page and reading the clue he hadn't quite been able to see the evening before:

'Work without hope draws nectar in a—' (Coleridge) (5).

Huh! If the poem was a 'riddle', so was the answer! A quotation from Coleridge, too! Half smiling, he sat back in his chair and marvelled once more at the frequency of that extraordinarily common phenomenon called 'coincidence'.

Had he but known it, however, a far greater coincidence had already occurred the previous evening when (purely by chance, surely?) he had been ushered into the dining room to share a table with the delectable occupant of Room 14. But as yet he couldn't know such a thing; and taking from his pocket his silver Parker pen, he wrote 'I' and 'V' in the empty squares which she had left in S-E-E – before reaching for the telephone again.

'No, sir – Superintendent Strange is still not answering. Can anyone else help?'

'Yes, perhaps so,' said Morse. 'Put me through to Traffic Control, will you?'

CHAPTER EIGHT

Extract from a diary dated 2 July 1992 (one day before
Morse had found himself in Lyme Regis)

I must write a chapter on 'Gradualism' in my definitive
opus on pornography, for it is the <u>gradual</u> nature of the
erotic process that is all important, as even that old
fascist Plato had the nous to see. Yet this is a factor
increasingly forgotten by the writers and the film-
directors and the video-makers. If they ever knew it.
'Process' is what it should be all about. The process
typified in the lifting of a full-length skirt to a point just
above the ankle, or the first unfastening of a button on
a blouse! Do I make things clear? Without the skirt,
what man will glory in the ankle? Without the blouse,
what man will find himself aroused by the mere button?
Nudity itself is nothing: it is the intent of nudity which
guarantees the glorious engagement. Never did nudity in
itself mean very much to me, even when I was a young
boy. Never did I have any interest in all those Italian
paintings of naked women. Likewise it seems to me that
few of our licentious and promiscuous youth take
overmuch notice of the women who flaunt their bodies
daily in the tabloid press. Such young men are more
interested in back-page soccer stories. Is there a moral
here?

I've just read through all that shit I've just written

41

and it makes me sound almost sane. Almost as if I'd laugh outright at any quack who suggested that I ought to go along and see somebody. But in truth there's not much to laugh about considering the wreck I've now become — I've always been perhaps. These others are bloody lucky. Christ, how lucky they are! They have their erotic fancies and imaginings and get their fixes from their filthy mags and porno flicks and casual sex. But me? Ha! I study those articles in the quality press about the effects of pornography on the sex-crime statistics. That's what the civilized sex maniacs do. Does then pornography have the effect that is claimed? I doubt it. Yet I wish it did. Yes! Then almost everyone would be committing some dreadful sex-offence each day. I know — of course I do! — that such a state of affairs wouldn't be all that bloody marvellous for the goody-goody girls who've been guarding their virginity. But at least I would be normal! I would be normal.

Come on Time! Hurry along there! It is tomorrow that I see her and I can hardly wait to watch the hours go by. Why do I wait? Because although I have never really loved my wife (or my children all that much) I would sacrifice almost everything in my life if by so doing I could spare her the despairing humiliation of learning about my own shame.

(Later) I picked up The Guardian in the SCR and read about a Jap who murdered a young model and feasted off her flesh for a fortnight. They didn't keep him in jail very long because he was manifestly crackers. But when they transferred him to a loony asylum he kicked up such a fuss that they didn't keep him there long either. Why? Because the authorities became convinced that he was normal. After they'd let him go he said to a newspaper reporter: 'My time in the mental ward was like Hell. Everyone else in there was real crazy, but the doctors saw that I wasn't like the rest of them. They saw I was normal. So they let me go.' I wasn't too upset about what this weirdo said. What really upset me was what the <u>reporter</u> said. He said the most distressing aspect of this strange and solitary cannibal was the fact that he really believed himself to be normal! Don't you see what I'm saying?

CHAPTER NINE

And I wonder how they should have been together!
(T. S. Eliot, *La Figlia Che Piange*)

HE MADE his way from the dining room to the bar.
The meal had been a lonely affair; but Morse was never
too worried about periods of loneliness, and felt himself
unable to appreciate the distinction that some folk
made between solitude and loneliness. In any case, he'd
enjoyed the meal. Venison, no less! He now ordered a
pint of Best Bitter and sat down, his back to the sea,
with the current issue of *The Times*. He looked at his
wrist-watch, wrote the time (8.21) in the small rectangle
of space beside the crossword, and began.

At 8.35, as he struggled a little over the last two clues,
he heard her voice:

'Not finished it yet?'

Morse felt a sudden rush of happiness.

'Mind if I join you?' She sat down beside him, to his
right, on the wall-seat. 'I've ordered some coffee. Are
you having any?'

'Er, no. Coffee's never figured all that prominently
in my life.'

'Water neither, by the look of things.'

Morse turned towards her and saw she was smiling at
him. 'Water's all right,' he admitted ' – in moderation.'

44

'Not original!'

'No. Mark Twain.'

A young bow-tied waiter had brought the coffee, and she poured an almost full cup before adding a little very thick cream; and Morse looked down at those slim fingers as she circled the spoon in a slow-motion, almost sensual stir.

'You got the paper?'

Morse nodded his gratitude. 'Yes.'

'Let me tell you something – I'm not even going to ask why you wanted it so badly.'

'Why not?'

'Well, for one thing, you told me in your note.'

'And for another?'

She hesitated now, and turned to look at him. 'Why don't you offer me a cigarette?'

Morse's new-found happiness scaled yet another peak.

'What's your name?' she asked.

'Morse. They, er, call me Morse.'

'Odd name! What's your surname?'

'That *is* my surname.'

'As well? Your name's Morse Morse? Like that man in *Catch 22*, isn't it? Major Major Major.'

'Didn't he have *four* Majors?'

'You read a lot?'

'Enough.'

'Did you know the Coleridge quotation? I could see you looking at the crossword last night.'

'Hadn't you got the paper twixt thee and me?'

'I've got X-ray eyes.'

Morse looked at her eyes, and for a few seconds looked deeply *into* her eyes – and saw a hazel-green concoloration there, with no sign now of any bloodshot webbing. 'I just happened to know the quote, yes.'

'Which was?'

'The answer was "sieve".'

'And the line goes?'

'Two lines actually, to make any sense of things:

> "Work without Hope draws nectar in a sieve,
> And Hope without an object cannot live."'

'You *do* read a lot.'

'What's your name?'

'Louisa.'

'And what do you do, Louisa?'

'I work for a model agency. No, that's wrong. I am a model agency.'

'Where are you from?'

'From a little village just south of Salisbury, along the Chalke Valley.'

Morse nodded vaguely. 'I've driven through that part once or twice. Combe Bissett? Near there, is it?'

'Quite near, yes. But what about you? What do *you* do?'

'I'm a sort of glorified clerk, really. I work in an office – nine-to-five man.'

'Whereabouts is that?'

'Oxford.'

'Lovely city!'

'You know Oxford?'

'Why don't you buy me a large brandy?' she asked softly in his ear.

Morse put the drinks on his room-bill and returned with one large brandy and one large malt Scotch. Several other couples were enjoying their liqueurs in that happily appointed bar and Morse looked out from the window at the constantly whitening waves before placing the drinks side by side on the table.

'Cheers!'

'Cheers!'

'You're a liar,' she said.

The three words hit Morse like an uppercut, and he had no time to regain his balance before she continued, mercilessly:

'You're a copper. You're a chief inspector. And judging from the amount of alcohol you get through you're probably never in your office much after opening time.'

'Is it *that* obvious – I'm a copper, I mean?'

'Oh no! Not obvious at all. I just saw your name and address in the register and my husband – well, he happens to have heard of you. He says you're supposed to be a bit of a whizz-kid in the crime world. That's all.'

'Do I know your husband?'

'I very much doubt it.'

'He's not here—'

'What are *you* doing in Lyme?'

'Me? I dunno. Perhaps I'm looking for some lovely, lonely lady who wouldn't call me a liar even if she thought I was.'

'You deny it? You deny you're a copper?'

Morse shook his head. 'No. It's just that when you're on holiday, well, sometimes you want to get away from the work you do – and sometimes you tell a few lies, I suppose. Everyone tells a few lies occasionally.'

'They do?'

'Oh yes.'

'Everyone?'

Morse nodded. 'Including you.' He turned towards her again, but found himself unable to construe the confusing messages he read there in her eyes.

'Go on,' she said quietly.

'I think you're a divorced woman having an affair with a married man who lives in Oxford. I think the pair of you occasionally get the opportunity of a week-end together. I think that when you do, you need an accommodation address and that you use your own address, which is not in the Chalke Valley but in the Cathedral Close at Salisbury. I think you came here by coach on Friday afternoon and that your partner, who was probably at some conference or other in the area, was scheduled to get here at the same time as you. But he didn't show up. And since you'd already booked your double room you registered and took your stuff up to your room, including a suitcase with the initials "C S O" on it. You suspected something had gone sadly wrong, but as yet you daren't use the phone to find out. You had no option but to wait. I think a call did come through eventually, explaining the situation; and you were deeply disappointed and upset – upset enough to shed a tear or two. This morning you hired a taxi to take you to meet this fellow who had let you down, and I think you've spent the day together somewhere. You're back here now because you'd booked the weekend break anyway, and your partner probably gave you a cheque to cover the bill. You'll be leaving in the morning, hoping for better luck next time.'

Morse had finished – and there was a long silence between them, during which he drained his whisky, she her brandy.

'Another?' asked Morse.

'Yes. But I'll get them. The cheque he gave me was more than generous.' The voice was matter-of-fact, harder now, and Morse knew that the wonderful magic had faded. When she returned with the drinks, she changed her place and sat primly opposite him.

'Would you believe me if I said the suitcase I brought with me belongs to my mother, whose name is Cassandra Samantha Osborne?'

'No,' said Morse. For a few seconds he thought he saw a sign of a gentle amusement in her eyes, but it was soon gone.

'What about this – this "married man who lives in Oxford"?'

'Oh, I know all about him.'

'You *what*?' Involuntarily her voice had risen to a falsetto squeak, and two or three heads had turned in her direction.

'I rang up the Thames Valley Police. If you put any car number through the computer there—'

'—you get the name and address of the owner in about ten seconds.'

'About *two* seconds,' amended Morse.

'And you did *that*?'

'I did that.'

'God! You're a regular shit, aren't you?' Her eyes blazed with anger now.

'S'funny, though,' said Morse, ignoring the hurt. 'I know *his* name – but I still don't know *yours*.'

'Louisa, I told you.'

'No. I think not. Once you'd got to play the part of Mrs Something Hardinge, you liked the idea of "Louisa". Why not? You may not know all that much about Coleridge. But about Hardy? That's different. You remembered that when Hardy was a youth he fell in love with a girl who was a bit above him in class and wealth and privilege, and so he tried to forget her. In fact he spent all the rest of his life trying to forget her.'

She was looking down at the table as Morse went gently on: 'Hardy never really spoke to her. But when he was an old man he used to go and stand over her unmarked grave in Stinsford churchyard.'

It was Morse's turn now to look down at the table.

'Would you like some more coffee, madame?' The waiter smiled politely and sounded a pleasant young chap. But 'madame' shook her head, stood up, and prepared to leave.

'Claire – Claire Osborne – that's my name.'

'Well, thanks again – for the paper, Claire.'

'That's all right.' Her voice was trembling slightly and her eyes were suddenly moist with tears.

'Shall I see you for breakfast?' asked Morse.

'No. I'm leaving early.'

'Like this morning.'

'Like this morning.'

'I see,' said Morse.

'Perhaps you see too much.'

'Perhaps I don't see enough.'

'Goodnight – Morse.'

'Goodnight. Goodnight, Claire.'

When an hour and several drinks later Morse finally decided to retire, he found it difficult to concentrate on anything else except taking one slightly swaying stair at a time. On the second floor, Room 14 faced him at the landing; and if only a line of light had shown itself at the foot of that door, he told himself that he might have knocked gently and faced the prospect of the wrath to come.

But there was no light.

Claire Osborne herself lay awake into the small hours, the duvet kicked aside, her hands behind her head, seeking to settle her restless eyes; seeking to fix them on some putative point about six inches in front of her nose. Half her thoughts were still with the conceited, civilized, ruthless, gentle, boozy, sensitive man with whom she had spent the earlier hours of that evening;

51

the other half were with Alan Hardinge, Dr Alan Hardinge, fellow of Lonsdale College, Oxford, whose young daughter, Sarah, had been killed by an articulated lorry as she had cycled down Cumnor Hill on her way to school the previous morning.

CHAPTER TEN

Mrs Kidgerbury was the oldest inhabitant of Kentish Town, I believe, who went out charing, but was too feeble to execute her conceptions of that art

(Charles Dickens, *David Copperfield*)

WITH A sort of expectorant 'phoo', followed by a cushioned 'phlop', Chief Superintendent Strange sat his large self down opposite Chief Inspector Harold Johnson. It was certainly not that he enjoyed walking up the stairs, for he had no pronounced adaptability for such exertions; it was just that he had promised his very slim and very solicitous wife that he would try to get in a bit of exercise at the office wherever possible. The trouble lay in the fact that he was usually too feeble in both body and spirit to translate such resolve into execution. But not on the morning of Tuesday, 30 June 1992, four days before Morse had booked into the Bay Hotel . . .

The Chief Constable had returned from a fortnight's furlough the previous day, and his first job had been to look through the correspondence which his very competent secretary had been unable, or unauthorized, to answer. The letter containing the 'Swedish Maiden' verses had been in the in-tray (or so she thought) for about a week. It had come (she thought she remembered) in a cheap brown envelope addressed (she *did* almost remember this) to 'Chief Constable Smith (?)'; but the cover had been thrown away – sorry! – and the stanzas themselves had lingered there, wasting as it were their sweetness on the desert air – until Monday the 29th.

The Chief Constable himself had felt unwilling to apportion blame: five stanzas by a minor poet named Austin were not exactly the pretext for declaring a state of national emergency, were they? Yet the 'Swedish' of the first line combined with the 'maiden' of the penultimate line had inevitably rung the bell, and so he had in turn rung Strange, who in turn had reminded the CC that it was DCI Johnson who had been – was – in charge of the earlier investigations.

A photocopy of the poem was waiting on his desk that day when Johnson returned from lunch.

It had been the following morning, however, when things had really started to happen. This time, certainly, it *was* a cheap brown envelope, addressed to 'Chief Constable Smith (?), Kidlington Police, Kidlington' (nothing else on the cover), with a Woodstock postmark, and a smudged date that could have been '27 June', that was received in the post room at HQ, and duly placed with the CC's other mail. The letter was extremely brief:

Why are you doing nothing about my letter?
Karin Eriksson

54

The note-paper clearly came from the same wad as that used for the first letter: 'Recycled Paper – OXFAM ● Oxford ● Britain' printed along the bottom. There was every sign too that the note was written on the same typewriter, since the four middle characters of 'letter' betrayed the same imperfections as those observable in the Swedish Maiden verses.

This time the CC summoned Strange immediately to his office.

'Prints?' suggested Strange, looking up from the envelope and note-paper which lay on the table before him.

'Waste o' bloody time! The envelope? The postman who collected it – the sorter – the postman who delivered it – the post room people here – the girl who brought it round – my secretary . . .'

'*You*, sir?'

'And me, yes.'

'What about the letter itself?'

'You can try if you like.'

'I'll get Johnson on to it—'

'I don't want Johnson. He's no bloody good with this sort of case. I want Morse on it.'

'He's on holiday.'

'First I've heard of it!'

'You've been on holiday, sir.'

'It'll have to be Johnson then. But for Christ's sake tell him to get off his arse and actually *do* something!'

For a while Strange sat thinking silently. Then he said, 'I've got a bit of an idea. Do you remember that correspondence they had in *The Times* a year or so back?'

'The Irish business – yes.'

'I was just thinking – thinking aloud, sir – that if you were to ring *The Times*—'

'Me? What's wrong with *you* ringing 'em?'

Strange said nothing.

'Look! I don't care what we do so long as we do *something* – quick!'

Strange struggled out of his seat.

'How does Morse get on with Johnson?' asked the CC.

'He doesn't.'

'Where is Morse going, by the way?'

'Lyme Regis – you know, where some of the scenes in *Persuasion* are set.'

'Ah.' The CC looked suitably blank as the Chief Superintendent lumbered towards the door.

'There we are then,' said Strange. 'That's what I reckon we ought to do. What do you say? Cause a bit of a stir, wouldn't it? Cause a bit of interest?'

Johnson nodded. 'I like it. Will *you* ring *The Times*, sir?'

'What's wrong with *you* ringing 'em?'

'Do you happen to know—?'

'You – can – obtain – Directory – Enquiries,' intoned Strange caustically, 'by dialling one-nine-two.'

Johnson kept his lips tightly together as Strange continued: 'And while I'm here you might as well remind me about the case. All right?'

So Johnson reminded him of the case, drawing together the threads of the story with considerably more skill than Strange had thought him capable of.

CHAPTER ELEVEN

Nec scit qua sit iter
(He knows not which is the way to take)
(Ovid, *Metamorphoses II*)

KARIN ERIKSSON had been a 'missing person' enquiry a year ago when her rucksack had been found; she was a 'missing person' enquiry now. She was not the subject of a murder enquiry for the simple reason that it was most unusual – and extremely tricky – to mount a murder enquiry without any suspicion of foul play, with no knowledge of any motive, and above all without a *body*.

So, what *was* known about Miss Eriksson?

Her mother had run a small guest-house in Uppsala, but soon after the disappearance of her daughter had moved back to her roots – to the outskirts of Stockholm. Karin, the middle of three daughters, had just completed a secretarial course, and had passed her final examination, if not with distinction at least with a reasonable hope of landing a decent job. She was, as all agreed, of the classic Nordic type, with long blonde hair and a bosom which was liable to monopolize most men's attention when first they met her. In the summer of 1990 she had made her way to the Holy Land without much money, but also without much trouble it appeared, until reaching her destination, where she may

57

or may not have been the victim of attempted rape by an Israeli soldier. In 1991 she had determined to embark on another trip overseas; been determined too, by all accounts, to keep well clear of the military, wherever she went, and had attended a three-month martial arts course in Uppsala, there showing an aptitude and perseverance which had not always been apparent in her secretarial studies. In any case, she was a tallish (5 foot 8½ inches), large-boned, athletic young lady, who could take fairly good care of herself, thank you very much.

The records showed that Karin had flown to Heathrow on Wednesday, 3 July 1991, with almost £200 in one of her pockets, a multi-framed assemblage of hiking-gear, and with the address of a superintendent in a YWCA hostel near King's Cross. A few days in London had apparently dissipated a large proportion of her English currency; and fairly early in the morning of Sunday, 7 July, she had taken the tube (perhaps) to Paddington, from where (perhaps) she had made her way up to the A40, M40 – towards Oxford. The statement made by the YWCA superintendent firmly suggested that from what Karin had told her she would probably be heading – in the long run – for a distant relative living in mid-Wales.

In all probability K. would have been seen on one of the feeder roads to the A40 at about 10 a.m. or so that day. She would have been a distinctive figure: longish straw-coloured hair, wearing a pair of faded-blue jeans, raggedly split at the knees à la mode. But particularly noticeable – this from several witnesses – would have been the yellow and blue Swedish flag, some 9 inches by 6 inches, stitched across the main back pocket of her rucksack; and around her neck (always) a silk, tasselled scarf in the same national colours – sunshine and sky.

Two witnesses had come forward with fairly positive sightings of a woman, answering Karin's description, trying to hitch a lift between the Headington and the Banbury Road roundabouts in Oxford. And one further witness, a youth waiting for a bus at the top of the Banbury Road in Oxford, thought he remembered seeing her walking fairly purposefully down towards Oxford that day. The time? About noon – certainly! – since he was just off for a drink at the Eagle and Child in St Giles'. But more credence at the time was given to a final witness, a solicitor driving to see his invalid mother in Yarnton, who thought he could well have seen her walking along Sunderland Avenue, the horn-beam-lined road linking the Banbury Road and the Woodstock Road roundabouts.

At this point Johnson looked down at his records, took out an amateurishly drawn diagram, and handed it across to Strange.

'That's what would have faced her, sir – if we can believe she even got as far as the Woodstock Road roundabout.'

With little enthusiasm, Strange looked down at the diagram and Johnson continued his story.

Karin could have gone straight over, of course – straight along the A40, a road where it would be very much easier for a hitchhiker to get a lift than along the motorways and dual-carriageways she'd already negotiated successfully. In addition, the A40 would lead pretty directly towards the address of her third cousin, or whatever, near Llandovery. But it had not seemed to the detectives who considered the matter that she had taken the 'Witney' option – or the 'Wolvercote' – or the 'City Centre' one; but had taken the road that led to Woodstock . . .

CHAPTER TWELVE

Sigh out a lamentable tale of things,
Done long ago, and ill done
(John Ford, *The Lover's Melancholy*)

AT ABOUT 7.15 (Johnson continued) on the sunny
Tuesday morning of 9 July 1991, George Daley, of 2
Blenheim Villas, Begbroke, Oxon, had taken his eight-
year-old King Charles spaniel for an early-morning walk
along the slip-road beside the Royal Sun, a roadside
ale-house on the northern stretch of the A44, a mile or
so on the Oxford side of Woodstock. At the bottom of
a hawthorn hedge, almost totally concealed by rank
cow-parsley, Daley had spotted – as he claimed – a
splash of bright colour; and as he ventured down, and
near, he had all but trodden on a camera before seeing
the scarlet rucksack.

Of course at this stage there had been no evidence
of foul play – still wasn't – and it was the camera that
had claimed most of Daley's attention. He'd promised
a camera to his son Philip, a lad just coming up for his
sixteenth birthday; and the camera he'd found, a heavy,
aristocratic-looking thing, was a bit too much of a
temptation. Both the rucksack and the camera he'd
taken home, where cursorily that morning, in more

detail later that evening, he and his wife Margaret had considered things.

'Finders keepers', they'd been brought up to accept. And well, yes, the rucksack clearly – and specifically – belonged to someone else; but the camera had no name on it, had it? For all they knew, it had no connection at all with the rucksack. So they'd taken out the film, which seemed to be fully used up anyway, and thrown it on the fire. Not a crime, was it? Sometimes even the police – Daley had suggested – weren't all that sure what should be entered in the crime figures. If a bike got stolen, it was a crime all right. But if the owner could be persuaded that the bike hadn't really been stolen at all – just inadvertently 'lost', say – then it didn't count as a crime at all, now did it?

'Was he an ex-copper, this fellow Daley?' asked Strange, nodding his appreciation of the point.

Johnson grinned, but shook his head and continued.

The wife, Margaret Daley, felt a bit guilty about hanging on to the rucksack, and according to Daley persuaded him to drop it in at Kidlington the next day, Wednesday – originally asserting that he'd found it that same morning. But he hadn't really got his story together, and it was soon pretty clear that the man wasn't a very good liar; and it wasn't long before he changed his story.

The rucksack itself? Apart from the pocket-buttons rusting a bit, it seemed reasonably new, containing, presumably, all the young woman's travelling possessions, including a passport which identified its owner as one Karin Eriksson, from an address in Uppsala, Sweden. Nothing, it appeared, had been tampered with overmuch by the Daleys, but the contents had proved of only limited interest: the usual female toiletries, including toothpaste, Tampax, lipstick, eye-shadow, blusher, comb, nail-file, tweezers, and white tissues; an almost full packet of Marlboro cigarettes with a cheap 'throwaway' lighter; a letter, in Swedish, from a boyfriend, dated two months earlier, proclaiming (as was later translated) a love that was fully prepared to wait until eternity but which would also appreciate a further rendezvous a little earlier; a slim money-wallet, containing no credit cards or travellers' cheques – just five ten-pound notes (newish but not consecutively numbered); a book of second-class English postage-stamps; a greyish plastic mac, meticulously folded; a creased postcard depicting Velasquez's 'Rokeby Venus' on one side, and the address of the Welsh relative on the other; two clean (cleanish) pairs of pants; one faded-blue dress; three creased blouses, black, white, and darkish red . . .

'Get on with it,' mumbled Strange.

Well, Interpol were contacted, and of course the Swedish police. A distraught mother, by phone from Uppsala, had told them that it was very unusual for Karin not to keep her family informed of where she was and what she was up to – as she had done from London the previous week.

A poster ('Have you seen this young woman?') displaying a blown-up copy of the passport photograph had been printed, and seen by some of the citizens of Oxford and its immediate environs in buses, youth clubs, information offices, employment agencies, those sorts of places.

'And that's when these people came forward, these witnesses?' interrupted Strange.

'That's it, sir.'

'And the fellow you took notice of was the one who thought he saw her in Sunderland Avenue.'

'He was a very good witness. Very good.'

'Mm! I don't know. A lovely leggy blonde – well-tanned, well-exposed, eh, Johnson? Standing there on the grass verge facing the traffic ... Bit odd, isn't it? You'd've thought the fellow would've remembered her for *certain* – that's all I'm saying. Some of us still have the occasional erotic day-dream, y'know.'

'That's what Morse said.'

'Did he now!'

'He said even if most of us were only going as far as Woodstock we'd have taken her on to Stratford, if that's what she wanted.'

'*He'd* have taken her to Aberdeen,' growled Strange.

The next thing (Johnson continued his story) had been the discovery, in the long grass about twenty yards from where the rucksack had been found – probably fallen out of one of the pockets – of a slim little volume titled *A Birdwatchers' Guide*. Inside was a sheet of white paper, folded vertically and seemingly acting as a bookmark, on which the names of ten birds had been written in neat capitals, with a pencilled tick against seven of them:

HOBBY ✓
RED KITE
LESSER SPOTTED WOODPECKER
BREADED TIT ✓
CORN BUNTING ✓
TREE PIPIT ✓
REDSTART ✓
NIGHTINGALE ✓
GRASSHOPPER WARBLER ✓
NUTHATCH

The lettering matched the style and slope of the few scraps of writing found in the other documents, and the easy conclusion was that Karin Eriksson had been a keen ornithologist, probably buying the book after arriving in London and trying to add to her list of sightings some of the rarer species which could be seen during English summers. The names of the birds were written in English and there was only the one misspelling: the 'breaded tit' – an interesting variety of the 'bearded plaice' spotted fairly frequently in English restaurants. (It had been the pedantic Morse who had made this latter point.)

Even more interesting, though, had been the second enclosure within the pages: a thin yellow leaflet, folded this time across the middle, announcing a pop concert in the grounds of Blenheim Palace on Monday, 8 July – the day before the rucksack was found: 8 p.m.–11.30 p.m., admission (ticket only) £4.50.

That was it. Nothing else really. Statements taken –

enquiries made – searches organized in the grounds of Blenheim Palace – but . . .

'How much did Morse come into all this?' asked a frowning Strange.

Johnson might have known he'd ask it, and he knew he might as well come clean.

CHAPTER THIRTEEN

He that reads and grows no wiser seldom suspects his
own deficiency, but complains of hard words and obscure
sentences, and asks why books are written which cannot
be understood

(Samuel Johnson, *The Idler*)

THE TRUTH was that Morse had *not* figured on the
scene at all during the first few days of the case – for it
was not a case of homicide; and (as was to be hoped)
still wasn't. Yet the follow-up investigations had been
worrying, especially of course the steadily growing and
cumulative evidence that Karin Eriksson had been a
responsible young woman who had never previously
drifted into the drink-drugs-sex-scene.

Only after the case had grown a little cold had Morse
spent a couple of hours one afternoon with Johnson, in
that late July, now a year ago – before being side-
tracked into a squalid domestic murder out on the
Cowley Road.

'I reckon he thought it all a bit – a bit of a joke, sir,
quite honestly.'

'Joke? *Joke?* This is no bloody joke, Johnson! Like
as not, we shall be opening a couple of extra lines
on the switchboard once these bloody newspapers get
hold of it. It'll be like an air disaster! And if the

public come up with some brighter ideas than the police ...'

Johnson gently reminded him: 'But it's *your* idea, sir – this business of sending the letters to *The Times*.'

'What did you mean – about Morse?' asked Strange, ignoring the criticism.

'What I meant, sir, is that he, well, he only skipped over the details with me, and he sort of said the first things that came into his head, really. I don't think he had time to think about things much.'

'He'd have *ideas* though, wouldn't he, Morse? Always did have. Even if he'd been on a case a couple of minutes. Usually the wrong ideas of course, but ...'

'All I'm saying is that he didn't seem to take the case at all seriously. He was sort of *silly* about things, really—'

Strange's voice sounded suddenly thunderous: 'Look here, Johnson! Morse may be an idiot, you're right. But he's never been a fool. Let's get *that* straight!'

For Johnson, the differentiation between what he had hitherto regarded as virtual synonyms – 'idiot' and 'fool' – was clearly beyond his etymological capacities; and he frowned a guarded puzzlement as his superior officer continued:

'Some people are occasionally right for the wrong reasons. But Morse? He's more often than not wrong for the right reasons. The *right* reasons ... you understand me? So even if he sometimes drinks too much ...'

Johnson looked down at the file in front of him: he knew, alas, exactly what Strange was saying. 'Would you rather Morse took over the case, sir?'

'Yes, I think I would,' said Strange. 'So would the CC, if you must know,' he added cruelly.

'So when does he get back from leave . . .?'

Strange sighed deeply. 'Not soon enough. Let's see what happens with this newspaper angle.'

'He's pretty sure to see it – if they print it.'

'What? Morse? Nonsense! I've never seen him reading anything. He just spends half an hour on the crossword, that's all.'

'Ten minutes – last time I watched him,' said Johnson honestly, if somewhat grudgingly.

'Wasted his life, Morse has,' confided Strange, after a pause.

'Should've got married, you mean?'

Strange began to extricate himself from his chair. 'I wouldn't go as far as that. Ridiculous institution – marriage! Don't you think so?'

Johnson, himself having married only six months previously, forebore any direct response, as Strange finally brought his vertebrae to the vertical, from which vantage point he looked down on the papers that Johnson had been consulting.

'Isn't that Morse's writing?' he queried presbyopically.

Yes, it was Morse's handwriting; and doubtless Johnson would have preferred Strange not to have seen it. But at least it would prove his point. So he picked out the sheet, and handed it over.

'Mm.' Chief Superintendent Strange held the piece of paper at arm's length, surveying its import. Unlike Morse, he was an extremely rapid reader; and after only ten seconds or so he handed it back to Johnson: 'See what you mean!'

Johnson, in turn, looked down again at the sheet Morse had left him – the one he'd found on his desk that morning a year ago now, when Morse had been transferred to what had appeared more urgent enquiries:

I never got to grips with the case as you know but I'd have liked answers to the following half-dozen qq:

(a) Had Daley or his missus owned a camera themselves?
(b) What was the weather like on Tuesday 9th July?
(c) 'It's striped: what about ze panties?' (5)
(d) What's the habitat of 'Dendrocopus Minor'?
(e) What beer do they serve at the Royal Sun (or at the White Hart!)?
(f) What's the dog's name?

Strange now lumbered to the door. 'Don't ignore all this bloody nonsense, Johnson. That's what I'm telling you. Don't take *too* much notice of it; but don't *ignore* it, understand?'

For the second time within a short while the etymological distinction between a couple of unequivocal synonyms had completely escaped Inspector Johnson's reasonably bright but comparatively limited brain.

'As you say, sir.'

'And, er, and one other thing ... the wife's just bought a new dog – little King Charles, lovely thing! Two hundred pounds it cost. Pisses everywhere, of course – and worse! But he's, you know, he's always glad to see you. More than the wife sometimes, eh? It's just that we've only had the bloody thing a fortnight, and we still haven't christened it.'

'The dog's name was "Mycroft". Good name – be a good name for *your* dog, sir.'

'Imaginative, yes! I'll, er, mention it to the missus, Johnson. Just one little problem, though . . .'

Johnson raised his rather bushy eyebrows.

'Yes. She's a *she*, Johnson!'

'Oh.'

'Anything else Morse said?' pursued Strange.

'Well, yes. He, er, thought – he said he had a gut-feeling—'

'Huh!'

'—that we'd been searching for a body in the wrong *place*.'

'In Blenheim, you mean?'

Johnson nodded. 'He thought we ought to have been looking in Wytham Woods.'

'Yes. I remember him saying that.'

'Only after we'd drawn a blank in Blenheim, though.'

'Better wise after the event than never.'

Augh, shut up! Johnson was becoming a little weary of all the innuendos: 'If you recall, sir, it wasn't just Morse who was in favour of a wider operation. But we hadn't got the personnel available for a search of Wytham Woods. You said so. I came to ask you myself.'

Strange was stung into retaliation. 'Look, Johnson! You find *me* a body and I'll find *you* all the bloody personnel you need, all right?'

It was the chicken-and-egg business all over again, and Johnson would have said so – but Strange was already guiding his bulk downstairs, via the hand-rail on the HQ wall.

CHAPTER FOURTEEN

> Only the keeper sees
> That, where the ring-dove broods,
> And the badgers roll at ease,
> There was once a road through the woods
> (Rudyard Kipling, *The Way Through the Woods*)

IT WAS to be Morse's last breakfast at the Bay Hotel, that morning of Monday, 6 July 1992, six days after the long meeting just recorded between Strange and Johnson at Kidlington HQ in Oxfordshire. He would have wished to stay a further couple of days – but there were no vacancies; and, as the proprietor reminded him, he'd already had more than his share of luck.

As he waited for his mixed grill he re-read the article, again high-profile page-one news – the article promised the previous Friday by Howard Phillipson, literary editor of *The Times*:

A PRELIMINARY ANALYSIS

INTEREST in the 'Swedish Maiden' verses printed in these columns last week (Friday, July 3) has been sweeping this newspaper's offices, but I am myself now somewhat more diffident than I originally was about solving the fascinating riddle-me-ree presented by the five stanzas. I had earlier assumed that there might well be sufficient 'internal logic' in the information received by the Thames Valley Police to come to some firm conclusions. I am no longer so strongly of this opinion.

Only with considerable hesitation therefore do I offer my own amateurish analysis of the riddle, in the fairly certain knowledge that very soon the cryptologists and cabbalists, criminologists and cranks, will be making their own considerably more subtle interpretations of these tantalizing lines.

For what it is worth, however, I suggest that the parameters of the problem may be set, albeit rather vaguely. In modern mathematics (as I understand the situation) pupils are asked, before tackling any problem: 'What roughly do you think the answer might be? What sort of answer might you logically expect?' If, say, the problem involves the speed of a supersonic jet flying the Atlantic, the answer is perhaps unlikely to be 10 m.p.h., and any pupil coming up with such an improbable answer is advised to look back through his calculations and find out where he might have dropped a couple of noughts. If we are set to discover the time taken by those famous taps to fill the family tub, the answer is still rather more likely to be ten minutes than ten hours. Permit me then to make a few general comments on what would appear to be the sort of solution we might expect. (The verses are reprinted on page 2.)

Clearly the poem is cast in a 'sylvan' setting: we have 'woodman'; 'stream'; 'riding' (sic!); 'Thyme flow'ring'; 'trapped'; 'hunted deer'; etc. There will be no prizes, I realize, for such an analysis, but the neglect of the obvious is always the beginning of unwisdom.

The setting of some wood or forest therefore must be our donné, and my suggestion to the Thames Valley CID would be to concentrate their doubtless limited resources of manpower within two of the local areas which seem to hold the greatest promise: the forested area around Blenheim Palace, and the Wytham Woods – the latter becoming increasingly famous for its fox and badger research.

Let us now turn to the more specific import of the stanzas. The speaker of the poem, the 'persona', is clearly no longer a living being. Yet her dramatic message is quite unequivocal: she has been murdered; she has been drowned (or perhaps just dumped) in one of the lakes or streams situated in the wood(s); if such waters are searched and dredged her corpse will be found; finally the police may have been (somewhat?) remiss in not pursuing their enquiries with rather greater perseverance.

What can be gathered from the nature of the verses themselves? Their composer is certainly no Herrick or Housman, yet in terms of technical prosody the writer is more than competent. Vocabulary ('tegument', 'azured', etc.) is more redolent of the Senior Common Room than the Saloon Bar; and the versification, punctuation, and diction, all point to a literate and well-read man – or woman!

Can anything more specific be said about the writer? For some while, as I read and re-read the verses, I toyed with the idea of their author being a relative of the dead girl. The reason for my thinking was the continued emphasis, throughout the poem, of the 'find me' motif; and I was reminded of the Homeric heroes of the *Iliad* where death in battle was a fully expected and wholly honourable end – but where the most terrible fate of all was to die unrecognized, unburied, *unfound*, in some unknown and far-off land. Is the poem then above all a desperate cry for the Christian burial of the body? This would be most understandable. We have seen in recent years so many tragic instances (in the Middle

East, for example) where the simple return of a dead body has paved the way for some peace initiative.

But I no longer believe this to be the case. My firm conviction now is that the verses have been sent to the police by a person for whom the period – now a year – between the murder of Karin Eriksson and the present time has become an intolerable Hell. A person who is very near to breaking point. A person who wishes the crime at last to be uncovered, and who is now prepared to pay the penalty. In short, the murderer!

Dare I go any further? I learned two further (hitherto unpublished) facts from Detective Chief Inspector Johnson. First, that the letter-writer was able to spell, correctly, the not very easy or obvious 'Eriksson'; second, that the writer was aware of the previous Chief Constable's surname, but not that of the current incumbent. On the old adage then that one might just as well be hanged for a sheep as a lamb, I reckon the murderer to be male; to be between thirty and thirty-five years old; to have a degree in English literature; to have lived until about six or nine months ago in Oxfordshire; to have revisited the scene of his crime during the last month, say, whilst staying at one of the more upmarket hostelries in Woodstock, Oxon.

I rest my case, m'lud!

'Hi!' she said. 'Mind if I join you?'

'Please do,' said Morse, carefully mounting the last segment of his fried egg on the last square of his fried bread.

'You ever read about cholesterol?' Her voice was very cultured, the two 't's of her simple question affectedly exaggerated.

Morse swallowed his latest mouthful and looked at the slim, expensively dressed woman who now sat opposite him, ordering black coffee and a croissant – nothing more.

'They say we've all got to die of something.' He tried to make it sound reasonably cheerful.

'Ridiculous attitude!' The lips, expertly outlined in some pale-crimson shade, looked severe, yet the grey eyes in the delicate, oval face might almost have been mocking him.

'I suppose it is,' he said.

'You're overweight anyway, aren't you?'

'I suppose so,' he repeated lamely.

'You'll have high blood pressure in your mid-fifties – unless you're there now? Then you'll probably have a stroke in your early sixties; and like as not die of a heart attack before you're seventy.' She had already drained her coffee cup, and held up an elegant, imperious hand to the waitress. 'What's your job?'

Morse sighed, and considered the last piece of toast in the rack. 'I'm a policeman, and I come from Oxford, and I'm on holiday here until about ten o'clock this morning. I'm single and maybe I'm not much of a catch, but if I'd known I was going—'

'—going to meet a beautiful girl like me! Surely you can be more original than that?' The eyes were mocking him again.

Morse took the toast and started buttering it. 'No, I can't. I can't do much better than that.'

'Perhaps you underrate yourself.'

'What about you? What do you do?'

'Why don't *you* tell *me*. You're a policeman, you say?'

For half a minute or so Morse looked at her, cocking his head slightly to the right. Then he gave his judgement: 'You're a beautician, possibly a dietitian too, which you probably spell with a "t" and not a "c"; you're in your late twenties, and you went to school at Cheltenham Ladies'; you're married but you sometimes leave off your wedding ring – like now; you're fond of pets but you tend to think children are something of an exaggerated pastime. And if you come for a walk with me along the prom, I'll try to fill in a few more of the details as we go along.'

'That's much better.'

'Well? How did I do?'

She smiled and shook her head. 'Is your name Sherlock Holmes?'

'Morse.'

'Am I *that* transparent?'

'No. I, er, saw you come in with your husband last night – when you went straight to bed and he—'

'He stayed at the bar!'

'We had one or two drinks together, and I asked him who the beautiful woman was—'

'And he said, "That's not a beautiful woman: that's my wife!"?'

'Something like that.'

'And he talked about me?'

'He talked nicely about you.'

'He was drunk.'

'He's sleeping it off?' Morse pointed to the ceiling.

She nodded her dark curls. 'So he won't mind much if you take me on that walk, will he, Mr Morse? When you've finished your toast, of course. And wouldn't *you* spell dietitian with a "t"?'

CHAPTER FIFTEEN

At the very smallest wheel of our reasoning it is possible for a handful of questions to break the bank of our answers

(Antonio Machado, *Juan de Mairena*)

ON THE same morning that Morse was packing his single suitcase ('On the day of their departure guests are respectfully requested to vacate their rooms by 10.30 a.m.') Sergeant Lewis knocked on Johnson's door, soon seating himself opposite the chief inspector, and beside Sergeant Wilkins.

'Good of you to spare a few minutes.'

'If I can help in any way . . .' said Lewis warily.

'You know Morse better than most.'

'Nobody knows him all *that* well.'

'You've got a reasonable idea how his mind works though.'

'He's got a strange sort of mind—'

'Not many'd disagree with you.'

'He's good at some things.'

'Such as?'

'He's not bad at catching murderers for a start.'

'And you do realize the odds are we're trying to catch another murderer now, don't you, Sergeant?'

'If it *is* murder.'

'Did Morse think it was murder?'

'As I remember, sir, he was only on it with you for a day or so.'

'Less than that.' (Wilkins had made his first contribution.)

'You're following this – this newspaper business, I presume, Lewis?'

'Everybody reads *The Times* before the *Sun* now.'

'What do you make of this?' Johnson handed a photocopy of Morse's 'half-dozen qq.' across the desk.

Lewis looked down at the list and smiled. 'Bit of a joke – some of this, isn't it?'

'Take my advice, Lewis, and don't try telling that to the Super!'

'I don't know the answer to any of 'em,' admitted Lewis, 'except (e) – well, part of (e). It's a "Morrell's" pub, the Royal Sun. I've brought quite a few pints there, I reckon.'

'What, for Morse, you mean?'

'Who else?'

'But has he ever bought *you* any, Lewis? That's the real question, eh, Wilkins?'

The two men sniggered. And suddenly Lewis hated them both.

'What about the White Hart?' continued Johnson.

'Lot of "White Harts" about.'

'Yes, we know that!' Johnson gestured to Wilkins, the latter now reading from his notes: 'Headington, Marston, Wolvercote, Wytham, Minster Lovell, Eynsham . . .'

'I expect Morse could probably add to the list,' ventured Johnson.

Lewis, determining henceforth to be as minimally helpful as possible, made only a brief comment: 'She'd've got past the first two.'

Johnson nodded. 'What about Eynsham and Minster Lovell? Just off the A40, both of them – if she ever travelled along the A40, that is.'

Lewis said nothing.

'What about the other two: Wolvercote and Wytham? Which would you put your money on?'

'Wytham, I suppose.'

'Why's that?'

'The woods there – easy enough to hide a body.'

'Did you know that Morse asked the Chief Super about a search of Wytham Woods last year?'

Lewis did, yes. 'Only after the search in Blenheim didn't come up with anything.'

'Do you know how big Wytham Woods *is*, man?'

Lewis had a good idea, yes. But he merely shrugged his shoulders.

'Why would Morse be interested in the dog?'

'Don't know. He told me once he'd never had any pets when he was a lad.'

'Perhaps he should get one now. Lots of bachelors have dogs.'

'You must suggest it to him, sir,' replied Lewis, with a note of confidence in his voice, and a strange exhilaration flooding his limbs, for he suddenly realized that it was Johnson who was on the defensive here, not himself. They were trying to pick his (Lewis's) brains because they were envious of his relationship with Morse!

'What about the camera?' continued Johnson.

'You can ask the Daleys, can't you? If they're still there.'

'Odd question though, wouldn't you say?'

'I just don't know, sir. I think Morse told me he had a "Brownie" given him once, but he said he never really understood how to work it.'

Sitting back in an almost relaxed manner now, Lewis looked down at the questions again. 'Should be easy to check on (b) – about the weather . . .'

Again Johnson waved a hand, and Wilkins consulted his notes: 'According to Radio Oxford . . . the ninth of July . . . "Dry, sunny, seventy-two to seventy-four degrees Fahrenheit; outlook settled; possibility of some overnight mist".'

'Nice, warm day, then,' said Lewis blandly.

'What about (c)?'

'Crossword clue, sir. He's pretty hot on crosswords.'

'What's the answer?'

'No good asking me. Sometimes I can't even do the *Mirror* coffee-break one.'

' "Ze-bra" – that's the answer.'

'Really? Well that's another one crossed off.'

'What about this "Dendrocopus Minor"?' There was a note of exasperation in Johnson's voice now.

'Pass,' said Lewis with a gentle smile.

'For Christ's sake, man, we're on a potential *murder* enquiry – not a bloody *pub*-quiz! Don't you realize that? As a matter of fact it's the Lesser something bloody Woodpecker!'

'We learn something new every day.'

'Yes, we do, Sergeant. And I'll tell you something else, if you like. Its habitat is woodlands or parklands and there are a few pairs nesting in Wytham!'

Lewis's new-found confidence was starting to ebb away as Johnson glared at him aggressively. 'You don't seem all that anxious to help us, Sergeant, do you? So let me just tell you why I asked you along here. As you probably know, we're starting searching Blenheim all over again today, and we're going to search and search until we're blue in the bloody face, OK? But if we still don't find anything we're going to hand over to Morse – and to *you*, Sergeant. I just thought you might like to know what we're *all* up against, see?'

Lewis was conscious of a sinking sense of humiliation. 'I – I didn't know that, sir.'

'Why should you? They don't tell even you everything, do they?'

'Why might they be taking you off?' asked Lewis slowly.

'They – "they" – are taking me off because they don't think I'm any fucking good,' said Johnson bitterly as he rose to his feet. 'That's why!'

CHAPTER SIXTEEN

Between 1871 and 1908 he published twenty volumes
of verse, of little merit
('Alfred Austin', *The Oxford Companion to English Literature*,
edited by Margaret Drabble)

MORSE was spending the last three days of his West
Country holiday at the King's Arms in Dorchester
(Dorchester, Dorset). Here he encountered neither
models nor beauticians; but at last he began to feel a
little reluctant about returning to Oxford. On the
Wednesday he had explored Hardy's Dorchester on
foot (!) a.m., and spent the whole p.m. in the Dorset
County Museum. Nostalgic, all of it. And when finally
he returned to 'the chief hotel in Casterbridge' he sat
drinking his beer in the bar before dinner with the
look of a man who was almost at ease with life.

On the Thursday morning he drove out through the
countryside that provided much of the setting for *Tess
of the d'Urbervilles*, along the A352 to the east of Dorchester, following the Vale of the Great Dairies, past Max
Gate and Talbothays towards Wool. As he was driving
through Moreton, he wondered whether there was any
follow-up to the Phillipson analysis (there had been no
mention in the Tuesday or Wednesday editions), and
he stopped and bought the last copy of *The Times* from

the village newsagent's. The answer was yes – yes, there was; and he sat for a while in the sunshine beside the wall of the cemetery containing the grave of Lawrence of Arabia, reading the long letter which (as with succeeding letters) now found its place naturally in the newspaper's correspondence columns:

From Professor (Emeritus) René Gray

Sir, my mind, doubtless like the minds of many of your regular readers, has been much exercised these past few days following the publication (July 3) of the letter received by the Thames Valley Police. I beg the courtesy of your columns to make one or two observations.

This is not a poem by Alfred Austin, though the words 'A. Austin' appear beneath it. The name 'Austin' does not seem to refer to a make of motor car: 'A'-registration Austins date from 1983–84, and there is no resemblance between this date and those given in brackets. The dates given are not Austin the poet's dates. He was born in 1835, and died in 1913. There is a remote possibility that the last two digits of his birth-date have been transposed for some reason, but the death-date is plainly wrong. Dying in 1913, he was 78 years old at the time of his death. By a strange coincidence the transposition of these digits gives us the '87' which is written here. I conclude that the dates are not all they seem, and most likely constitute the key to the cypher.

The figures do not appear to give geographical co-ordinates. They do not match the format of Ordnance Survey co-ordinates, and they are not co-ordinates of latitude and longitude, since Great Britain lies between the 50th and 60th lines of

---

latitude and between the longitudes 2°E and 10°W. We are left with six digits which somehow must give the clue to the interpretation of the words of the message.

I have not been able to work out the cypher. I have tried the first word, followed by the eighth, followed by the fifth after that (giving either 'Find ... my ... the skylit', or 'Find ... frosted ... skylit ... me'). I have re-transposed the sequences of digits, to no better effect. I have tried lines, first words of lines, last words of lines. I have taken the digits in pairs, i.e. as 18, 53 (or 35) and 87 with the same result. I have alternated the beginnings of the lines with the ends of the lines, and vice versa.

I have simplified the expression '1853–87' by interpreting the hyphen as a minus sign. The answer, '1766', does not produce any happier result. The only sensible word produced is yielded by taking letters in that sequence in the first line, thus giving 'F-i-s-h', but the message does not continue. (A red herring, possibly!)

There are a large number of other combinations and permutations, but no method other than trial and error for seeing whether any make any sense.

The overriding advantage of the mechanical method of deciphering is that the poem itself does not have to make sense; a random sequence of words would fulfil exactly the same purpose of concealing the message. Hence odd words such as 'tiger' need not fall into the category of important words at all: in its place, 'chairman' or 'post-box' would do equally well; these words meet the requirements of the metre, but would not be included in the deciphered message. Likewise, the upper case 'T' in the middle of line 13 is not significant. The fact that the poem does make some kind of sense in places thus merely adds to the bafflement.

If this line of thinking is correct, it does not matter

what the poem says, or what it means. What is needed is the services of a skilled cryptographer.	Yours faithfully, RENÉ GRAY, 137 Victoria Park Road, Leicester

Morse read the letter once only, and decided to wait until his return to the King's Arms (where he had the two earlier cuttings) in order to have a more careful look at the good professor's analysis and suggested methodology. He sounded an engaging sort of fellow, Gray – especially with that bit about the 'chairman' and the 'post-box'.

Back in Dorchester that afternoon, Morse went into the public library and looked up 'Austin' in *The Oxford Companion to English Literature.* He'd heard of Austin the poet – of course he had; but he'd never known anything much about him, and he was certainly unaware that any poem, or even line, produced by the former poet laureate had merited immortality.

From the library Morse walked on to the post office, where he bought a black and white postcard of Dorchester High Street, and stood for an inordinate length of time in the queue there. He didn't know the price of the stamp for a postcard, and didn't wish to waste a first-class stamp if, as he suspected, the official tariff for postcards was a few pence lower. It was, he realized, quite ridiculous to wait so long for such a little saving.

But wait Morse did.

*

Lewis received the card the following morning, the message written in Morse's small, neat, and scholarly hand:

> Mostly I've not been quite
> so miserable since last year's
> holiday, but things are
> looking up here in D.
> Warmest regards to you
> (and to Mrs Lewis) – but
> not to any of our other
> colleagues. Have you been
> following the Swedish lass?
> I reckon I know what the
> poem means.
> Definitely home Sat.
>
> M

This card, with its curmudgeonly message, was delivered to police HQ in Kidlington – since Morse had not quite been able to remember Lewis's Headington address. And by the time it was in Lewis's hands, almost everyone in the building had read it. It might, naturally, have made Lewis a little cross – such contravention of the laws of privacy.

But it didn't. It made him glad.

CHAPTER SEVENTEEN

Extract from a diary dated Friday, 10 July 1992

Please God let me wake from this dream! Please God may she not be dead! Those words – the ones I so recently wrote – for them may I be forgiven! Those terrible words! – when I disavowed my love for my own flesh and blood, for my own children, for my daughter. But how could I be forgiven? The fates decree otherwise and ever have so decreed. The words may be blotted out but they will remain. The paper may be burned in the furnace but the words will persist for evermore. Oh blackness! Oh night of the soul! Throw open the wide door of Hell, Infernal Spirits, for it is I who approach – all hope of virtue, all hope of life abandoned! I have reached the Inferno and there now read that grim pronouncement of despair above its portal.

I am sunk deep in misery and anguish of mind and spirit. At my desk I sit here weeping bitter tears. I shout Forgive me! Forgive me! And then I shout again Forgive me! Everyone forgive me! Had I still belief in God I would seek to pray. But I cannot. And even now – even in the abyss of my despair – I have not told the truth! Let it be known that tomorrow I shall once more be happy – some of tomorrow's hours will bring me happiness again. She is coming. She is coming here. She herself has arranged and organized. She it is who has wished to come! For my sake is this? Is this for my need – my grief's sake? Yet such considerations are of minor consequence. She is coming, tomorrow she is <u>coming</u>. More precious to me is that woman even than the mother who suffers all that pain . . .

(Later.) I am so low I wish I were dead. My selfishness my <u>self</u>-pity is so great that I can have no pity for the others – the others who grieve so greatly. I have just re-read one of Hardy's poems. I used to know it by heart. No longer though and now my left forefinger traces the lines as slowly I copy it out:

> I seem but dead man held on end
> To sink down soon . . . O you could not know
>   That such swift fleeing
>   No soul foreseeing –
> Not even I – would undo me so.

I never really managed to speak to you my daughter. I never told you my darling daughter because I did not know – and now you can never know why and can never understand.

I have reached a decision. This journal shall be discontinued. Always when I look back on what I have written I see nothing of any worth – only self-indulgence – theatricality – over-emotionalism. Just one plea I make. It was never forced or insincere or hypocritical. No, never!

But no more.

CHAPTER EIGHTEEN

A 'strange coincidence' to use a phrase
By which such things are settled now-a-days
(Lord Byron, *Don Juan*)

CLAIRE OSBORNE turned right from the A40 down into Banbury Road, knowing that she would have to drive only three or four hundred yards along it, since she had received a detailed map through the post. She was a little surprised – a lot surprised – when she spotted, on her right, the Cotswold House, a considerably more striking and attractive building than the 'suburban, modern, detached' blurb of *The Good Hotel Guide* had led her to expect. She experienced an unexpected feeling of delight as she parked her Metro MG (what a disaster not taking that to Lyme!) on the rusty-red asphalt in front of the double-fronted guest-house, built of honey-coloured Cotswold stone in the leafy environs of North Oxford.

Flower-baskets in green, red, purple, and white hung all around her as she rang the bell at the front door, on which a white notice announced 'No Vacancies'. But Claire had earlier found a vacancy, and booked it: a vacancy for two.

The door was opened by a tall, slim man, with a shock of prematurely grey hair, black eyebrows, a slightly diffident smile, and a soft Irish brogue.

'Hello.'

'Hello. My name's Mrs Hardinge, and I think you'll find—'

'Already found, Mrs Hardinge. And I'm Jim O'Kane. Now do come in, won't you? And welcome to the Cotswold House.' With which splendid greeting he picked up her case and led her inside, where Claire felt immediately and overwhelmingly impressed.

Briefly O'Kane consulted the bookings register, then selected a key from somewhere, and led the way up a semi-circular staircase.

'No trouble finding us, I trust?'

'No. Your little map was very helpful.'

'Good journey?'

'No problems.'

O'Kane walked across the landing, inserted a key in Room 1, opened the door, ushered his guest inside, followed her with the suitcase, and then, with a courteous, old-world gesture, handed her a single key – almost as if he were presenting a bouquet of flowers to a beautiful girl.

'The key fits your room here *and* the front door, Mrs Hardinge.'

'Fine.'

'And if I could just remind you' – his voice growing somewhat apologetic – 'this is a non-smoking guest-house . . . I *did* mention it when you rang.'

'Yes.' But she was frowning. 'That means – everywhere? Including the bedrooms?'

'Especially the bedrooms,' replied O'Kane, simply if reluctantly.

Claire looked down at the single key. 'My husband's been held up in London—'

'No problem! Well, only *one* problem perhaps. We're always a bit pushed for parking – if there are *two* cars . . .?'

'He'll have his car, yes. But don't worry about that. There seems to be plenty of room in the side-streets.'

O'Kane appeared grateful for her understanding, and asked if she were familiar with Oxford, with the North Oxford area. And Claire said, yes, she was; her husband knew the area well, so there was no trouble there.

Wishing Mrs Hardinge well, Mr O'Kane departed – leaving Claire to look with admiration around the delightfully designed and decorated accommodation. *En suite*, too.

O'Kane was not a judgemental man, and in any case the morality of his guests was of rather less importance to him than their comfort. But already the signs were there: quite apart from the circumstantial evidence of any couple arriving in separate cars, over the years O'Kane had observed that almost every wedded woman arriving first would show an interest in the in-house amenities and the like. Yet Mrs Hardinge(?) had enquired about none of these . . . he would have guessed too (if asked) that she might well pay the bill from her own cheque-book when the couple left – about 50 per cent of such ladies usually did so. In the early days of his business career, such things had worried O'Kane a little. But not so much now. Did it matter? Did it really matter? Any unwed couple could get a *mortgage* these days – let alone a couple of nights' accommodation in a B & B. She was a pleasantly spoken, attractive woman; and as O'Kane walked down the stairs he hoped she'd have a happy time with that Significant Other who would doubtless be arriving soon, ostensibly spending the weekend away from his wife at some Oxford conference.

Oxford was full of conferences . . .

Claire looked around her. The co-ordinated colour scheme of décor and furnishing was a sheer delight – white, champagne, cerise, mahogany – and reproductions of late-Victorian pictures graced the walls. Beside the help-yourself tea and coffee facilities stood a small fridge, in which she saw an ample supply of milk; and two wine glasses – and two champagne glasses. For a while she sat on the floral-printed bedspread; then went over to the window and looked out, over the window-box of busy Lizzies, geraniums, and petunias, down on to the Banbury Road. For several minutes she stood there, not knowing whether she was happy or not – trying to stop the clock, to live in the present, to grasp the moment . . . and to hold it.

Then – her heart was suddenly pounding against her ribs. A man was walking along the pavement towards the roundabout. He wore a pink, short-sleeved shirt, and his forearms were bronzed – as if perhaps he might recently have spent a few days beside the sea. In his left hand he carried a bag bearing the name of the local wineshop, Oddbins; in his right hand he carried a bag with the same legend. He appeared deep in thought as he made his way, fairly slowly, across her vision and proceeded up towards the roundabout.

What an amazing coincidence! – the man might have thought had she pushed open the diamond-leaded window and shouted 'Hi! Remember me? Lyme Regis? Last weekend?' But that would have been to misunderstand matters, for in truth there was no coincidence at all. Claire Osborne had seen to that.

There was a soft knock on her door, and O'Kane asked if she – if either of them – would like a newspaper in the morning: it was part of the service. Claire smiled. She liked the man. She ordered *The Sunday Times.* Then, for a little while after he was gone, she wondered why she felt so sad.

It was not until just before 9 p.m. that Dr Alan Hardinge arrived – explaining; excusing, but as vulnerable, as loving as ever. And – bless him! – he had brought a bottle of Brut Imperial, *and* a bottle of Skye Talisker malt. And almost, *almost* (as she later told herself) had Claire Osborne enjoyed the couple of hours they'd spent together that night between the immaculately laundered sheets of Room 1 in the Cotswold House in North Oxford.

Morse had arrived home at 2.30 p.m. that same day. No one, as far as he knew, was aware that he had returned (except Lewis?); yet Strange had telephoned at 4 p.m. Would Morse be happy to take on the case? Well, whether he would be happy or not, Morse was *going* to take on the case.

'What case?' Morse had asked, disingenuously.

At 5 p.m. he had walked down to Summertown and bought eight pint-cans of newly devised 'draught' bitter, which promised him the taste of a hand-pulled, cask-conditioned drop of ale; and two bottles of his favourite Quercy claret. For Morse – considerably out of condition still – the weight felt a bit too hefty; and outside the Radio Oxford building he halted awhile and looked behind him in the hope of seeing the oblong outline of a red double-decker coming up from the city centre. But there was no bus in sight, so he walked on. As he passed the Cotswold House he saw amongst other things the familiar white sign 'No Vacancies' on the door. He was not surprised. He had heard very well of the place. He wouldn't mind staying there himself.

Especially for the breakfasts.

CHAPTER NINETEEN

I like to have a thing suggested rather than told in full.
When every detail is given, the mind rests satisfied, and
the imagination loses the desire to use its own wings
(Thomas Aldrich, *Leaves from a Notebook*)

STRANGE had been really quite pleased with all the
publicity. Seldom had there been such national interest
in a purely notional murder; and the extraordinary if
possibly unwarranted ingenuity which the public had
already begun to exercise on the originally printed
verses was most gratifying – if not as yet of much
concrete value. There had been two further offerings
in the Letters to the Editor page in the Saturday, 11
July's issue of *The Times*:

From Gillian Richard

Sir, Professor Gray (July 9) seems to me too lightly to dismiss one factor in the Swedish Maiden case. She is certainly, in my view, alive still, but seemingly torn between the wish to live – and the wish to die. She has probably never won any poetry competition in her life, and I greatly doubt whether she is to be found as a result of her description of the natural world. But she is *out* there, in the natural world – possibly living rough; certainly not indoors. I would myself hazard a guess, dismissed by Professor Gray, that she is in a *car* somewhere, and here the poem's attribution (A. Austin 1853–87) can give us the vital clue. What about an A-registration Austin? It would be a 1983 model, yes; and might we not have the registration number, too? I suggest A 185 – then three letters. If we suppose 3=C, 8=H, and 7=G (the third, eighth, and seventh letters of the alphabet), we have A 185 CGH. Perhaps then our young lady is languishing in an ageing Metro? And if so, sir, we must ask one question: who is the owner of that car? Find her!

Yours etc.,
GILLIAN RICHARD,
26 Hayward Road,
Oxford.

From Miss Polly Rayner

Sir, I understand from your report on the disappearance a year ago of a Swedish student that her rucksack was found near the village of Begbroke in Oxfordshire. It may be that I am excessively addicted to your own crossword puzzles but surely we can be justified in spotting a couple of 'clues' here? The '-broke' of the village name is derived from the Anglo-Saxon word 'brok', meaning 'running water' or 'stream'. And since 'beg' is a synonym of 'ask', what else are we to make of the first three words in line 7: 'Ask the stream'? Indeed, this clue is almost immediately confirmed two lines later in the injunction 'ask the sun'. 'The Sun' is how the good citizens of Begbroke refer to their local hostelry, and it is in and around that hostelry where in my view the police should reconcentrate their enquiries.

Yours faithfully,
POLLY RAYNER,
President,
Woodstock Local History Society,
Woodstock,
Oxon.

That was more like it! Strange had earlier that day put the suggested car registration through the HQ's traffic computer. No luck! Yet this was just the sort of zany, imaginative idea that might well unlock the mystery, and stimulate a few more such ideas into the bargain. When he had rung Morse that same Saturday afternoon (he too had read the postcard!) he had not been at all surprised by Morse's apparent – surely only 'apparent'? – lack of interest in taking over the case immediately. Yes, Morse still had a few days' leave remaining – only to the Friday, mind! But, really, this case was absolutely up the old boy's street! Tailor-made for Morse, this case of the Swedish Maiden . . .

Strange decided to leave things alone for a while though – well, until the next day. He had more than enough on his plate for the minute. The previous evening had been a bad one, with the City and County police at full stretch with the (virtual) riots on the Broadmoor Lea estate: car-thefts, joy-riding, ram-raids, stone-throwing . . . With Saturday and Sunday evenings still to come! He felt saddened as he contemplated the incipient breakdown in law and order, contempt for authority – police, church, parents, school . . . Augh! Yet in one awkward, unexplored little corner of his mind, he knew he could *almost* understand something of it all – just a fraction. For as a youth, and a fairly privileged youth at that, he remembered harbouring a secret desire to chuck a full-sized brick through the window of one particularly well-appointed property . . .

But yes – quite definitely, yes! – he would feel so very much happier if Morse could take over the responsibility of the case; take it away from his own, Strange's, shoulders.

Thus it was that Strange had rung Morse that Saturday afternoon.

'*What* case?' Morse had asked.

'You know bloody well—'

'I'm still on furlough, sir. I'm trying to catch up with the housework.'

'Have you been drinking, Morse?'

'Just starting, sir.'

'Mind if I come and join you?'

'Not this afternoon, sir. I've got a wonderful – odd, actually! – got a wonderful Swedish girl in the flat with me just at the moment.'

'Oh!'

'Look,' said Morse slowly, 'if there *is* a breakthrough in the case. If there *does* seem some reason—'

'You been reading the correspondence?'

'I'd sooner miss *The Archers*!'

'Do you think it's all a hoax?'

Strange heard Morse's deep intake of breath: 'No! No, I don't. It's just that we're going to get an awful lot of false leads and false confessions – you know that. We always do. Trouble is, it makes us look such idiots, doesn't it – if we take everything *too* seriously.'

Yes, Strange accepted that what Morse had just said was exactly his own view. 'Morse. Let me give you a ring tomorrow, all right? We've got those bloody yoiks out on Broadmoor Lea to sort out . . .'

'Yes, I've been reading about it while I was away.'

'Enjoy your holiday, in Lyme?'

'Not much.'

'Well, I'd better leave you to your ... your "wonderful Swedish girl", wasn't it?'

'I wish you would.'

After Morse had put down his phone, he switched his CD player on again to the Immolation Scene from the finale of Wagner's *Götterdämmerung*; and soon the pure and limpid voice of the Swedish soprano, Birgit Nilsson, resounded again through the chief inspector's flat.

CHAPTER TWENTY

When I complained of having dined at a splendid table
without hearing one sentence worthy to be remembered,
he [Dr Johnson] said, 'There is seldom any such
conversation'

(James Boswell, *The Life of Samuel Johnson*)

IN THE small hours of Sunday, 12 July, Claire Osborne
still lay awake, wondering yet again about what exactly
it was she wanted from life. It had been all right – it
usually was 'all right'. Alan was reasonably competent,
physically – and so loving. She liked him well enough,
but she could never be in love with him. She had given
him as much of herself as she could; but where, she
asked herself, was the memorability of it all? Where the
abiding joy in yet another of their brief, illicit, slightly
disturbing encounters?

'To hell with this sex lark, Claire!' her best friend in
Salisbury had said. 'Get a man who's interesting, that's
what I say. Like Johnson! Now, he was interesting!'

'*Doctor* Johnson? He was a great fat slob, always
dribbling his soup down his waistcoat, and he was
smelly, and never changed his underpants!'

'Never?'

'You know what I mean.'

'But everybody wanted to hear him *talk*, didn't they? That's what I'm saying.'

'Yeah. I know what you mean.'

'Yeah!'

And the two women had laughed together – if with little conviction.

Alan Hardinge had earlier said little about the terrible accident: a few stonily spoken details about the funeral; about the little service they were going to hold at the school; about the unexpected helpfulness of the police and the authorities and support groups and neighbours and relatives. But Claire had not questioned him about any aspect of his own grief. She would, she knew, be trespassing upon a territory that was not, and never could be, hers . . .

It was 3.30 a.m. before she fell into a fitful slumber.

At the breakfast table the following morning she explained briefly that her husband had been called away and that there would be just her: coffee and toast, please – nothing more. A dozen or so newspapers, room-numbered in the top-right corner, lay in a staggered pile on a table just inside the breakfast room – *The Sunday Times* not amongst them.

Jim O'Kane seldom paid too much attention to the front page of the 'Sundays'; but ten minutes before Claire had put in an appearance, he'd spotted the photograph. Surely he'd seen that young girl before! He took *The Sunday Times* through to the kitchen where, under the various grills, his wife was watching the progress of bacon, eggs, tomatoes, mushrooms, and sausages. He pointed to the black and white photograph on the front page:

'Recognize her?'

Anne O'Kane stared at the photograph for a few seconds, quizzically turning her head one way, then the other, seeking to assess any potential likeness to anyone she'd ever met. 'Should I?'

'I think *I* do! You remember that young blonde girl who called – about a year ago – when we had a vacancy – one Sunday – and then she called again – later – when we hadn't?'

'Yes, I do remember,' Anne said slowly. 'I *think* I do.' She had been quickly reading the article beneath the photograph, and she now looked up at her husband as she turned over half a dozen rashers of bacon. 'You don't mean . . .?'

But Jim O'Kane *did* mean.

Claire was on her last piece of toast when she found her hostess standing beside her with the newspaper. 'We pinched this for a minute – hope you didn't mind.'

'Course not.'

'It's just that' – Anne pointed to the reproduction – 'well, it looks a bit like a young girl who called here once. A young girl who disappeared about a year ago.'

'Long time, a year is.'

'Yes. But Jim – my husband – he doesn't often forget faces; and I think,' she added quietly, 'I think he's right.'

Claire glanced down at the photograph and the article, betraying (she trusted) not a hint of her excitement. 'You'd better tell them – the police, hadn't you?'

'I suppose we should. It's just that Jim met one of the men from CID recently at a charity do, and this fellow said one of the biggest problems with murders is all the bogus confessions and hoax calls you always get.'

'But if you *do* recognize her—'

'Not one hundred per cent. Not really. What I do remember is that this girl I'm thinking of called and asked if we'd got a room and then when she knew what it would cost she just sort of . . . Well, I think she couldn't afford it. Then she called back later, this same girl . . .'

'And you were full?'

Anne O'Kane nodded sadly, and Claire finished a last mouthful of toast. 'Not always easy to know what to do for the best.'

'No.'

'But if your husband knows this CID man he could always just, you know, mention it unofficially, couldn't he?'

'Ye-es. Wouldn't do any harm. You're right. And he only lives just up the road. In one of the bachelor flats.'

'What's his name? Lord Peter Wimsey?'

'Morse. Chief Inspector Morse.'

Claire looked down at her empty plate, and folded her white linen table napkin.

'More toast?' asked Anne O'Kane.

Claire shook her head, her flawlessly painted lips showing neither interest nor surprise.

CHAPTER TWENTY-ONE

It is only the first bottle that is expensive

(French proverb)

CLAIRE OSBORNE had discovered what she wanted that same morning. However, it was not until the following morning, 13 July (Sunday spent with Alan Hardinge), that she acted upon her piece of research. It had been terribly easy – just a quick look through the two-inch-thick phone-book for Oxford and District which lay beside the pay-phone: several Morses, but only one 'Morse, E.' – and the phone number, to boot! Leys Close, she learned from the Oxford street-map posted on the wall just inside the foyer, looked hardly more than two hundred yards away. She could have asked the O'Kanes, of course . . . but it was a little more exciting not to.

It was another fine sunny morning; and having packed her suitcase and stowed it in the boot of the Metro, and with permission to leave the car ('Shouldn't be all that long,' she'd explained), she walked slowly up towards the roundabout, soon coming to the sign 'Residents Only: No Public Right of Way', then turning left through a courtyard, before arriving at a row of two-storey, yellow-bricked, newish properties, their woodwork painted a uniform white. The number she sought was the first number she saw.

After knocking gently, she noticed, through the window to her left, the white shelving of a kitchen unit and a large plastic bottle of Persil on the draining board. She noticed, too, that the window directly above her was widely open, and she knew that he must be there even before she saw the vague silhouette behind the frosted glass.

What the hell are you doing here? – is that what she'd expected him to say? But he said nothing as he opened the door, bent down to pick up a red-topped bottle of semi-skimmed Co-op milk, stood to one side, inclined his head slightly to the right, and ushered her inside with an old-world gesture of hospitality. She found herself in a large lounge with two settees facing each other, the one to her left in a light honey-coloured leather, to which Morse pointed, and in which she now sat – a wonderfully soft and comfortable thing! Music was playing – something with a sort of heavyweight sadness about it which she thought she almost recognized. Late nineteenth century? Wagner? Mahler? Very haunting and beautiful. But Morse had pressed a panel in the sophisticated bank of equipment on the shelves just behind the other settee, a smaller one in black leather, in which he seated himself and looked across at her, his blue eyes showing a hint of amusement but nothing of surprise.

'No need to turn it off for me, you know.'

'Of course not. I turned it off for *me*. I can never do two things at the same time.'

Looking at the almost empty glass of red wine which stood on the low coffee table beside him, Claire found herself doubting the strictly literal truth of the statement.

'Wagner, was it?'

Morse's eyes lit up with some interest. 'It does show some Wagnerian harmonic and melodic traits, I agree.'

What a load of crap, the pompous oaf! Blast him. Why didn't he just *tell* her? She pointed to the bottle of Quercy: 'I thought you couldn't cope with two things at once?'

'Ah! But drinking's like breathing, really. You don't have to think about it, do you? And it's good for you – did you know that? There's this new report out saying a regular drop of booze is exceedingly good for the heart.'

'Not quite so good for the liver, though.'

'No.' He smiled at her now, leaning back in the settee, his arms stretched out along the top, wearing the same short-sleeved pink shirt she'd seen him in the previous Saturday. He probably needed a woman around the house.

'I thought you were supposed to wait till the sun had passed the yard-arm, or something like that.'

'That's an odd coincidence!' Morse pointed to *The Times* on the coffee table. 'It was in the crossword this morning: "yard-arm".'

'What is a yard-arm, exactly?'

Morse shook his head. 'I'm not interested in boats or that sort of thing. I prefer the Shakespeare quote – remember? That line about "the prick of noon"?'

'"The bawdy hand of the dial is now upon the prick of noon"?'

'How on earth did you know that?'

'I once played the Nurse in *Romeo and Juliet*.'

'Not the sort of thing for a schoolgirl—'

'University, actually.'

'Oh. I was never on the boards much myself. Just the once really. I had a line "I do arrest thee, Antonio". For some reason it made the audience laugh. Never understood why . . .'

Still clutching her copies of the previous day's *Sunday Times* and the current issue of *The Times*, Claire looked slowly around at the book-lined walls, at the stacks of records everywhere, at the pictures (one or two of them fractionally askew). She especially admired the water-colour just above Morse's head of the Oxford skyline in a bluey-purple wash. She was beginning to enjoy the conversational skirmishing, she admitted that; but there was still something *irritating* about the man. For the first time she looked hard, directly across at him.

'You're acting *now*, aren't you?'

'Pardon?'

'You're pretending you're not surprised to see me.'

'No, I'm not. I saw you sitting outside the Cotswold House yesterday; smoking a cigarette. I was walking down to Cutteslowe for a newspaper.'

'Mind if I smoke now?'

'Please do. I've, er, stopped myself.'

'Since when?'

'Since this morning.'

'Would you like one?'

'Yes, please.'

Claire inhaled deeply, crossed her legs as she sat

down again, and pulled her Jaeger skirt an inch or so below her knees.

'Why didn't you say hello?' she asked.

'I was on the opposite side of the road.'

'Not very pally, was it?'

'Why didn't you say hello to me?'

'I didn't see you.'

'I think you did, though.' His voice was suddenly gentle and she had the feeling that he knew far more about her than he should. 'I think you saw me late Saturday afternoon as well – just after you'd arrived.'

'You *saw* me? You saw me when you walked by with your booze?'

Morse nodded.

Blast him! Blast him! 'I suppose you think you know why I've come here now.'

Morse nodded again. 'It's not because I'm psychic, though. It's just that Jim, Mr O'Kane, he rang me yesterday . . .'

'About this?' She held up the newspapers.

'About the girl possibly calling there, yes. Very interesting, and very valuable, perhaps – I don't know. They're going to make a statement. Not to me though, I'm on holiday. Remember?'

'So it's a bit of a wasted journey. I was going to tell you—'

'Not a wasted journey – don't say that!'

'I – I kept thinking about the girl – all day yesterday . . . well, quite a few times yesterday . . . You know, her calling there and perhaps not having the money and then—'

'How much does a single room cost there now?'

'I'm not sure. And you're acting again! You know perfectly well I booked a *double*, don't you? A double for two nights. You asked O'Kane – you nosey bloody parker!'

For several seconds Morse seemed to look across the room at her with a steady intensity. 'You've got beautifully elegant legs,' he said simply; but she sensed that her answer may have caused him a minor hurt. And suddenly, irrationally, she wanted him to come across the room to her, and take her hand. But he didn't.

'Coffee?' he asked briskly. 'I've only got instant, I'm afraid.'

'Some people prefer instant.'

'Do you?'

'No.'

'I don't suppose I can, er, pour you a glass of wine?'

'What on earth makes you suppose that?'

'Quite good,' she commented, a minute or so later.

'Not bad, is it? You need a lot of it though. No good in small quantities.'

She smiled attractively. 'I see you've finished the crossword.'

'Yes. It's always easy on a Monday, did you know that? They work on the assumption that everybody's a bit bleary-brained on a Monday morning.'

'A lot of people take *The Times* just for the crossword.'

'Yep.'

'And the Letters, of course.'

Morse watched her carefully. 'And the Letters,' he repeated slowly.

Claire unfolded her own copy of *The Times*, 13 July, and read aloud from a front-page article:

CLUES TO MISSING STUDENT

Both *The Times* offices and the Thames Valley Police are each still receiving about a dozen letters a day (as well as many phone calls) in response to the request for information concerning the disappearance a year ago of Karin Eriksson, the Swedish student who is thought to be the subject of the anonymous verses received by the police and printed in these columns (July 3). Chief Superintendent Strange of Thames Valley CID himself believes that the ingenious suggestions received in one of the latest communications (see Letters, page 15) are the most interesting and potentially the most significant hitherto received.

'You must have read that?'

'Yes. The trouble is, just like Mr and Mrs O'Kane said, you can't follow up everything. Not even a tenth of the things that come in. Fortunately a lot of 'em are such crack-pot...' He picked up his own copy and turned to page 15, and sat looking (again) at the 'ingenious suggestions'.

'Clever – clever analysis,' he remarked.

'Obviously a very clever fellow – the one who wrote that.'

'Pardon?' said Morse.

113

'The fellow who wrote that letter.'

Morse read the name aloud: 'Mr Lionel Regis? Don't know him myself.'

'Perhaps nobody does.'

'Pardon?'

'See the address?'

Morse looked down again, and shook his head. 'Don't know Salisbury very well myself.'

'It's *my* address!'

'Really? So – are you saying *you* wrote this?'

'Stop it!' she almost shrieked. '*You* wrote it! You saw my address in the visitors' book at Lyme Regis, and you needed an address for this letter, otherwise your – your "ingenious suggestions" wouldn't be accepted. Am I right?'

Morse said nothing.

'You *did* write it, didn't you? *Please* tell me!'

'Yes.'

'Why? Why go to all this silly palaver?'

'I just – well, I just picked someone from the top of my mind, that's all. And you – you were there, Claire. Right at the top.'

He'd spoken simply, and his eyes lifted from her legs to her face; and all the frustration, all the infuriation, suddenly drained away from her, and the tautness in her shoulders was wonderfully relaxed as she leaned back against the soft contours of the settee.

For a long time neither of them spoke. Then Claire sat forward, emptied her glass, and got to her feet.

'Have you got to go?' asked Morse quietly.

'Fairly soon.'

'I've got another bottle.'

'Only if you promise to be nice to me.'

'If I tell you what lovely legs you've got again?'

'*And* if you put the record on again.'

'CD actually. *Bruckner Eight.*'

'Is that what it was? Not all that far off, was I?'

'Very close, really,' said Morse. Then virtually to himself: for a minute or two, very close indeed.

It was halfway through the accord movement and three-quarters of the way through the second bottle that the front doorbell rang.

'I can't see you for the minute, I'm afraid, sir.'

Strange sniffed, his small eyes suspicious.

'Really? I'm a little bit surprised about that, Morse. In fact I'm surprised you can't see *two* of me!'

CHAPTER TWENTY-TWO

In a Definition-and-Letter-Mixture puzzle, each clue consists of a sentence which contains a definition of the answer and a mixture of the letters

(Don Manley, *Chambers Crossword Manual*)

THERE WERE just the two of them in Strange's office the following morning, Tuesday, 14 July.

It had surprised Strange not a little to hear of Morse's quite unequivocal refusal to postpone a few days of his furlough and return immediately to HQ to take official charge of the case; especially in view of the latest letter – surely the break they'd all been hoping for. On the other hand there were more things in life than a blonde damozel who might or might not have been murdered a year ago. This bloody 'joy'(huh!)-riding, for a start – now hitting the national news and the newspaper headlines. It all served, though, to put things into perspective a bit – like the letter he himself had received in the post ('Strictly Personal') that very morning:

To Chief Superintendent Strange,
Kidlington Police HQ

Dear Sir,
It is naturally proper that our excellent whodunnit writers should pretend that the average criminal in the UK can

boast the capacity for quite exceptional ingenuity in the commission of crime. But those of us who (like you) have given our lives to the detection of such crime should at this present juncture be reminding everyone that the vast majority of criminals are not (fortunately!) blessed with the sort of alpha-plus mentality that is commonly assumed. Obviously if any criminal is brought to book as a result of the correspondence etc. being conducted in sections of the national press, we shall all be most grateful. But I am myself most doubtful about such an outcome, and indeed in a wider sense I am very much concerned about the precedent involved. We have all heard of trial by TV, and we now seem to be heading for investigation by correspondence column. This is patently absurd. As I read things, the present business is pretty certainly a hoax in any case, with its perpetrator enjoying himself (or I suppose herself?) most hugely as various correspondents vie with one another in scaling ever steeper and steeper peaks of interpretive ingenuity. If the thing is *not* a hoax, I must urge that all investigation into the matter be communicated *in the first instance* to the appropriate police personnel, and most certainly not to radio, TV, or newspapers, so that the case may be solved through the official channels of criminal investigation.

Yours sincerely,
Peter Armitage
(former Assistant Commissioner, New Scotland Yard)
PS I need hardly add, I feel sure, that this letter is not for publication in any way.

But this must almost certainly have been written before its author had seen the latest communiqué from the most intrepid mountaineer so far: the writer of the quite extraordinary letter which had appeared in the correspondence columns of *The Times* the previous morning.

Strange now turned to Lewis. 'You realize it's the break, don't you?'

Lewis, like every other police officer at HQ, had read the letter; and, yes, he too thought it was the break. How else? But he couldn't understand why Strange had asked him – *him* – along that morning. He was very tired anyway, and should by rights have been a-bed. On both Saturday and Sunday nights, like most officers in the local forces, his time had been spent until almost dawn behind a riot-shield, facing volleys of bricks and insults from gangs of yobbos clapping the skidding-skills of youths in stolen cars – amongst whom (had Lewis known it) was a seventeen-year-old schoolboy who was later to provide the key to the Swedish Maiden mystery.

'Lewis! You're listening, aren't you?'

'Sorry, sir?'

'You do *remember* Morse belly-aching about transferring the search from Blenheim to Wytham?'

'Yes, sir. But he wasn't on the case more than a day or so.'

'I know that,' snapped Strange. 'But he must have had some *reason*, surely?'

'I've never quite been able to follow some of his reasons.'

'Do you know how much some of these bloody searches cost?'

'No, sir.'

Nor perhaps did Strange himself, for he immediately changed tack: 'Do you think Morse was right?'

'I dunno, sir. I mean, I think he's a great man, but he sometimes gets things awfully wrong, doesn't he?'

'And he more often gets things bloody *right*!' said Strange with vehemence.

It was an odd reversal of rôles, and Lewis hastened to put the record straight. 'I think myself, sir, that—'

'I don't give a *sod* what you think, Sergeant! If I want to search Wytham Woods I'll bloody well search 'em till a year next Friday if I – if *I* – think it's worth the candle. All right?'

Lewis nodded wordlessly across the table, watching the rising, florid exasperation in the Super's face.

'I'm not sure where I come into all this—' he began.

'Well, I'll tell you! There's only one thing you can do and I can't, Sergeant, and that's to get the morose old bugger back to work here – smartish. I'm under all sorts of bloody pressure . . .'

'But he's on holiday, sir.'

'I *know* he's on bloody holiday. I saw him yesterday, drinking shampers and listening to Schubert – with some tart or other.'

'Sure it was *champagne*, sir?'

But quietly now, rather movingly, Strange was making his plea: 'Christ knows why, Lewis, but he'll always put himself out a bit for you. Did you realize that?'

He rang from Morse's own (empty) office.

'Me, sir. Lewis.'

'I'm on holiday.'

'Super's just had a word with me—'

'Friday – that's what I told him.'

'You've seen the letter about Wytham, sir?'

'Unlike you and your philistine cronies, Lewis, my daily reading includes the royal circulars in *The Times*, the editorials—'

'What do I tell the Super, sir? He wants us – you and me – to take over straightaway.'

'Tell him I'll be in touch – tomorrow.'

'Tell him you'll ring, you mean?'

'No. Tell him I'll be back on duty tomorrow morning. Tell him I'll be in my office any time after seven a.m.'

'He won't be awake then, sir.'

'Don't be too hard on him, Lewis. He's getting old – and I think he's got high blood pressure.'

As he put down the phone, with supreme contentment, Lewis knew that Strange had been right – about Morse and himself; realized that in the case of the Swedish Maiden, the pair of them were in business again – w.e.f. the following morning.

In his office, Strange picked up the cutting from *The Times* and read the letter yet again. Quite extraordinary!

From Mr Lionel Regis

Sir, Like most of your other correspondents I must assume that the 'Swedish Maiden' verses were composed by the person responsible for the murder of that unfortunate young lady. It is of course possible they were

---

sent as a hoax, but such is not my view. In my opinion it is far more probable that the writer is exasperated by the inability of the police to come anywhere near the discovery of a *body*, let alone the arrest of a murderer. The verses, as I read them, are a cry from the murderer – not the victim – a cry for some discovery, some absolution, some relief from sleepless, haunted nights.

But I would not have written to you, sir, merely to air such vague and dubious generalities. I write because I am a setter of crossword puzzles, and when I first studied the verses I had just completed a puzzle in which the answer to every clue was indicated by a definition of the word to be entered, and also by a sequenced *anagram* of the same word. It was with considerable interest therefore – and a good measure of incredulity – that I gradually spotted the fact that the word WYTHAM crops up, in anagrammatized form, in each of the five stanzas. Thus: THAW MY (stanza 1); [stre]AM WHY T[ell'st] (stanza 2); WHAT MY (stanza 3); [s]AW THYM[e] (stanza 4); and [no]W THY MA[iden] (stanza 5).

The occurrence of *five* such instances is surely way beyond the bounds of coincidence. (I have consulted my mathematical friends on this matter.) 'Whytham', I learn (I am not an Oxford man), is the name of some woods situated to the west of Oxford. If the verse tells us anything then, it is surely that the body sought is to be found in Wytham Woods, and it is my humble suggestion that any further searches undertaken should be conducted in that quarter.

Yours,
LIONEL REGIS,
16 Cathedral Mews,
Salisbury.

Like Lewis, Strange remembered exactly what Morse had said on his postcard: 'I reckon *I* know what the poem means!', and he pushed the newspaper aside, and looked out across the car park. 'Lionel Regis, my arse!' he said quietly to himself.

CHAPTER TWENTY-THREE

On another occasion he was considering how best to
welcome the postman, for he brought news from a world
outside ourselves. I and he agreed to stand behind the
front door at the time of his arrival and to ask him
certain questions. On that day, however, the postman
did not come

(Peter Champkin,
The Sleeping Life of Aspern Williams)

WEDNESDAY, 15 July, was never going to be a particularly memorable day. No fire-faced prophet was to bring
news of the Message or the name of the One True God.
Just a fairly ordinary transitional sort of day in which
events appeared discrete and only semi-sequential;
when some of the protagonists in the Swedish Maiden
case were moved to their new positions on the chess-
board, but before the game was yet begun.

At a slightly frosty meeting held in the Assistant
Chief Constable's office at 10.30 a.m., the Swedish
Maiden case was reviewed in considerable detail by the
ACC himself, Chief Superintendent Strange, and
Detective Chief Inspectors Johnson and Morse. General
agreement was reached (only one dissident voice) that
perhaps there was little now to be gained from any
prolongation of the extensive and expensive search-

programme on the Blenheim Palace Estate. The decision was reported too, emanating from 'higher authority', that Morse was now i/c and that Johnson would therefore be enabled to take his midsummer furlough as scheduled. Such official verbiage would fool no one, of course – but it was possibly better than nothing at all.

Amongst the items reviewed was yet another letter, printed that morning in *The Times*:

From Mr John C. Chavasse

Sir, The Wood (singular not plural please) at Wytham is a place most familiar to me and I suspect to almost all generatations of young men who have taken their degrees at Oxford University. Well do I remember the summer weekends in the late 40s when together with many of my fellow undergraduates I cycled up through Lower Wolvercote to Wytham.

In lines 14 and 15 of the (now notorious!) verses, we find 'A creature white' (*sic*) 'Trapped in a gin' (*sic*),

'Panting like a hunted deer' (*sic*). Now if this is *not* a cryptic reference to a gin-and-whatnot in that splendid old hostelry in Wytham, the White Hart – then I'm a Dutchman, sir! But I am convinced (as an English-man) that such a reference can only serve to corrobor-ate the brilliant analysis of the verses made by Mr Lionel Regis (Letters, July 13).

Yours faithfully,
JOHN C. CHAVASSE,
21 Hayward Road,
Bishop Auckland.

Around the table, 'Mr Lionel Regis' looked slightly sheepish; but not for long, and now it was all an open secret anyway. He realized that there would be little he could do for a day or so – except to re-read all the material that had accumulated from the earlier enquiries; to sit tight; to get Lewis cracking on the admin; and perhaps to try to think a bit more clearly about his own oddly irrational conviction that the young student's body *would* be found – and found in Wytham Wood(s). There *was* that little bit of new evidence, too – the call from the O'Kanes. For if their memories served them to any degree aright, then Karin Eriksson had at some point gone *down* the Banbury Road from the roundabout; it was the testimony of the man who had been waiting for a bus there that Sunday noon-time which should have been given credence – not that of the man who had driven along Sunderland Avenue.

Such and similar thoughts Morse shared with Sergeant Lewis in the early afternoon. Already arrangements were well in hand for the availability of about twenty further members of various local forces to supplement the thirty due to be switched immediately from Blenheim. One annoying little hold-up, though. The head forester at Wytham, Mr David Michaels, was unfortunately away that day at a National Trust conference in Durham. But he was expected home later that night, his wife said, and would almost certainly be available the following morning.

Things *were* moving, that afternoon. But slowly. And Morse was feeling restless and impatient. He returned home at 4 p.m., and began typing a list of gramophone records . . .

Before leaving him the previous Monday, a quarter

of an hour after Strange's inopportune interruption, Claire Osborne had asked him to send her his eight Desert Island Discs and the versions he possessed of the Mozart *Requiem*. It was high time she started to improve her mind a bit, she'd said; and if Morse would promise to try to help her . . .? So Morse had promised, and reiterated his promise as he'd kissed her briefly, sweetly, fully on the lips, at her departure.

'You do know my address, I think?' she'd shouted from the gate.

Morse was still not *quite* sure of numbers seven and eight as he sat and slowly typed his list that afternoon.

A quarter of an hour or so before Morse had begun his labour of love, Philip Daley swaggered loutishly out of his class-room in the Cherwell School, just along the Marston Ferry Road in North Oxford. Only two more days to go! Roll on! School would be finishing on the 17th and he couldn't wait to get shot of it. Shot of it for good and all! His dad (his dad's own words) didn't give a fuckin' toss, though his mum (as he knew very well) would have been glad if he could have settled down to schoolwork and stayed on in the sixth form and maybe landed up with a decent job and all that bullshit. But other thoughts were uppermost in his bitterly discontented mind as he walked up the Banbury Road that afternoon. At lunch-time he'd asked one of the girls from his class, the one with the blouseful, whether she'd go with him to the end-of-term disco; and she'd said he must be bloody jokin' and anyway she'd already got a feller, 'adn't she? Soddin' cunt! As he walked up to the shops he crashed his fist against some ancient wooden fencing there: fuck it, fuck it, *fuck* it! Just wait till Friday, though. He'd show the fuckin' lot of 'em.

It was at 7.15 p.m., twelve hours after reaching HQ earlier that day, that Lewis sat down at his home in Headington to his beloved eggs and chips.

Blast him! thought Claire, as she turned first to one side and then the other in her bed that night. She could not understand at all why he was monopolizing her thoughts – but he was. And blast that other copper – that fat slob of a man who'd stood there talking to him on the doorstep for almost a quarter of an hour. She'd have had to leave very soon anyway, she realized that. But it had meant there had been no time to develop that little passage of intimacy between them ... and now, and again, and again, he was passing through her mind. Bloody nuisance, it all was! Only temporary, she trusted – this inability to sleep, this inability to thrust him from her thoughts. She just hoped she'd get a letter from him in the next *post*, that's all. He said he'd write; he'd promised; and she'd been looking out eagerly for the postman.

On that day, however, the postman did not come.

CHAPTER TWENTY-FOUR

The Grantor leaves the guardianship of the Woodlands to the kindly sympathy of the University ... The University will take all reasonable steps to preserve and maintain the woodlands and will use them for the instruction of suitable students and will provide facilities for research

(Extract from the deed under which Wytham Wood was acquired by the University of Oxford on 4 August 1942 as a gift from Col. ffennell)

MANY Oxonians know 'Wytham' as the village on the way to the wood. But Morse knew the spot as the village, situated on the edge of the wood, which housed the White Hart Inn; and he pointed lovingly to the hostelry the next morning as Lewis drove the pair of them to their meeting with the head forester.

'Did you know,' asked Morse (consulting his leaflet) 'that in the parish of Wytham, a large part of it covered with woods, the ground rises from the banks of the Thames – or "Isis" – to a height of 539 feet at Wytham Hill, the central point of the ancient parish?'

'No, sir,' replied Lewis, turning right just after the pub into a stretch of progressively narrowing roadway that was very soon marked by the sign 'Private Property: University of Oxford'.

'You don't sound very interested—'

'Look!' shouted Lewis. 'See *that?*'

'No!' In his youth Morse had almost invariably been the boy in the group who missed out; whilst his school-mates were perpetually spotting birds' eggs, the blue flash of kingfishers, or gingery foxes momentarily motionless at the edge of cornfields, the young Morse had seldom seen anything; the old Morse had seen nothing now.

'What exactly *was* the cause of all the excitement, Lewis?'

'Deer, sir. Roe deer, I think. Two of them, just behind—'

'Are they different from normal deer?'

'I don't reckon you're going to be too much help in this neck of the woods, sir.'

Morse made no comment on such a nicely turned phrase, as Lewis drove half a mile or so further, with an area of fairly dense woodland on his left, until he reached a semi-circular parking lot, also on his left. 'Cars must be left at one of the two car parks shown on the plan', the map said; and in any case a locked barrier across the road effectively blocked further progress to motor vehicles. Lewis pulled the police car in beside an ancient, rusting Ford.

'Good to see some people care, sir,' ventured Lewis, pointing to an RSPB sticker on one side window and a larger 'Save the Whale' plea on the other.

'Probably here for a snog under the sycamores,' Morse replied cheerfully.

A low, stone-built cottage stood thirty yards or so

back on the further side of the track. 'That must be where Mr Michaels lives, sir. Nice view – looking right across there to Eynsham.'

'C'mon,' said Morse.

It was just past the barrier, which they negotiated via a kissing-gate, set in its V-shaped frame, that the two detectives came, on their left, to a large clearing, some 100 yards square, with fir-saplings planted around the fenced perimeter, in which was set a whole complex of sheds and barns, built in horizontally slatted wood, with piles of spruce- and fir-logs stacked nearby, and with several tractors and pieces of tree-felling machinery standing beside or beneath the open-fronted barns.

From the furthest shed a figure walked down the slope to greet them – a man of about fifty or so, blue-eyed, closely bearded, and little short of six foot – introducing himself as David Michaels, the head forester. They shook hands with the man, Morse being careful to keep slightly behind Lewis as a black and white dog, bounding energetically after his master, sought to introduce himself too.

In the forester's hut, Michaels briefly described the lay-out of the woods (plural!), referring repeatedly to the four Ordnance Survey maps on the inner wall, themselves pinned together in a large oblong to give a synoptic view of the whole area under the forester's charge. There was a University Committee, the policemen learnt, administering Wytham Woods, to whom he (Michaels) was personally responsible, with a University Land Agent acting as Executive Officer; and it was to the latter that the police would need to apply formally.

Permits to walk in the woods (this in answer to Lewis) were issued, on request, to any resident teachers or administrators in the University, and of course to any other citizen, Town or Gown, who was able to provide adequate cause, and no criminal impediment, for wishing to visit the area.

Morse himself became more interested when Michaels moved closer to the maps and expanded on the woods' main attractions, his right forefinger tracing its way through what (to Morse) was a wonderfully attractive-sounding catalogue: Duck Pond; The Follies; Bowling Alley; Cowleaze Copse; Froghole Cottage; Hatchett Lane; Marley Wood; Pasticks; Singing Way; Sparrow Lane ... almost like the music of the woods and birds themselves.

But as he watched and listened, Morse's heart was sinking slightly lower. The woodlands were vast; and Michaels himself, now in his fifteenth year there, admitted that there were several areas where he had never – probably *would* never – set foot; parts known only to the badgers and the foxes and the deer and the families of woodpeckers. Yet somehow the mention of the woodpeckers appeared to restore Morse's confidence, and he gratefully accepted the forester's offer of a guided tour.

Lewis sat on the floor in the back of the rugged, powerful, ineffably uncomfortable and bouncy Land-rover, with Bobbie, the only dog allowed in the woods. Morse sat in the front with Michaels, who spent the next ninety minutes driving across the tracks and rides and narrow paths which linked the names of his earlier litany.

For a while Morse toyed with the idea of bringing in the military perhaps – a couple of thousand men from local units, under the command of some finicky brigadier sitting in Caesar's tent and ticking off the square yards one by one. Then he put his thought into words:

'You know I'm beginning to think it'd take an army a couple of months to cover all this.'

'Oh, I don't know,' replied Michaels. Surprisingly? 'No?'

Patiently the forester explained how during the summer months there were dozens of devotees who regularly checked the numbers of eggs and weights of fledglings in the hundreds of bird-boxes there; who laid nocturnal wait to observe the doings of the badgers; who clipped tags and bugging devices to fox-cubs; and so many others who throughout the year monitored the ecological pattern that Nature had imposed on Wytham Woods. Then there were the members of the public who were forever wandering around with their birdwatchers' guides and their binoculars, or looking for woodland orchids, or just enjoying the peace and beauty of it all . . .

Morse was nodding automatically through much of the recital, and he fully took the point that Michaels was making; he'd guessed as much anyway, but things were clearer in his mind now.

'You mean there's a good deal of ground we can probably forget . . .'

'That's it. And a good deal you can't.'

'So we need to establish some priorities,' Lewis chirped up from the rear.

'That was the, er, general conclusion that Mr Michaels and myself had just reached, Lewis.'

'Eighteen months ago, all this was, you say?' asked Michaels.

'Twelve, actually.'

'So if . . . if she'd been . . . just *left* there, you know, without trying to hide her or anything . . .?'

'Oh yes, there probably wouldn't be all that much of her still around – you'll know that better than most. But it's more often "found in a shallow grave", isn't it? That's the jargon. Not surprising though that murderers should want to cover up their crimes: they often dig a bit and put twigs and leaves and things over . . . over the top. But you need a spade for that. In the summer you'd need a *sharp* spade – and plenty of time, and a bit of daylight, and a bit of nerve . . . They tell me it takes a couple of sextons about eight hours to dig a decent grave.'

Perhaps it was the crudity and cruelty of the scene just conjured up which cast a gloom upon them now – and they spoke no more of the murder for the rest of the bumpy journey. Just about birds. Morse asked about woodpeckers, and Michaels knew a great deal about woodpeckers: the green, the great-spotted, the lesser-spotted – all had their habitats within the woods and all were of especial interest to birdwatchers.

'You interested in woodpeckers, Inspector?'

'Splendid birds,' muttered Morse vaguely.

*

Back in the hut, Morse explained the limitation of his likely resources and the obvious need therefore for some selective approach. 'What I'd really like to know is this – please don't feel offended, Mr Michaels. But if *you* wanted to hide a body in these woods, which places would come to mind first?'

So Michaels told them; and Lewis made his notes, feeling a little uneasy about his spelling of some of the names which Morse had earlier found so memorable.

When twenty minutes later the trio walked down towards the police car, they heard a sharp crack of a gun.

'One of the farmers,' explained Michaels. 'Taking a pot at some pigeons, like as not.'

'I didn't see any guns in your office,' commented Lewis.

'Oh, I couldn't keep 'em *there*! Against the law, that is, Sergeant.'

'But I suppose you must have one – in your job, sir?'

'Oh yeah! Couldn't do without. In a steel cabinet in there' – Michaels pointed to the low cottage – 'well and truly locked away, believe me! In fact, I'm off to do a bit of shooting now.'

'Off to preserve and maintain some of the local species, Mr Michaels?'

But the degree of sarcasm behind Morse's question was clearly ill-appreciated by the bearded woodsman, who replied with a decided coolness: 'Sometimes – quite often – it's essential to keep some sort of stability within *any* eco-system, and if you like I'll tell you a few things about the multiplication-factor of one or two of our randier species of deer. If I had my way, Inspector, I'd issue 'em all with free condoms from that white machine in the gents at the White Hart. But they wouldn't take much notice of me, would they?' For a few seconds Michaels' eyes glinted with the repressed anger of a professional man being told his job by some ignorant amateur.

Morse jumped in quickly. 'Sorry! I really am. It's just that as I get older I can't really think of killing things. Few years ago I'd have trodden on a spider without a thought, but these days – I don't know why – I almost feel guilty about swatting a daddy-long-legs.'

'You wouldn't find *me* killing a daddy-long-legs!' said Michaels, his eyes still hard as they stared unblinkingly back at Morse's. Blue versus blue; and for a few seconds Morse wondered what exactly Michaels *would* kill . . . and would be killing now.

CHAPTER TWENTY-FIVE

For wheresoever the carcase is, there will the eagles be
gathered together

(St Matthew, ch. 24, v. 28)

REGIS'S (Morse's) cracking of the Swedish Maiden
verses had sparked off a whole series of letters about
the Great Wood at Wytham. But only one of these
letters was to be published by *The Times* that week – the
latest in a correspondence which was gripping the
interest of that daily's readers:

From Stephen Wallhead, RA

Sir, It was with interest that I read what must surely be the final analysis of the Swedish Maiden affir. I had not myself, of course, come within a mile of the extraordinarily subtle interpretation (Letters, July 13) in which Wytham Woods are suggested – surely *more* than suggested – as the likeliest resting-place of that unfortunate girl. My letter can make only one small addendum; but I trust an interesting one, since the injunction 'Find the Woodman's daughter' (1. 6 of the verses) may now possibly be of some vital significance.

An oil-on-canvas painting, *The Woodman's Daughter*, was worked on by John Everett Millais in 1850–1. It depicts the young son of a squire offering a handful of strawberries to the young daughter of a woodman.

Millais (as always) was meticulous about his work, and the whole picture is minutely accurate in its research: for example, we know from the artist Arthur Hughes that the strawberries in the boy's hand were bought at Covent Garden in March 1851!

The background to this picture shows a woodland area with a clear perspective and a distinctive alignment of trees, and in my view it is at least a possibility that even allowing for decades of cutting-down and replantation the original site could be established. But there is the point, sir! From the diary of one of the artist's friends, Mrs Joanna Matthews, RA, we learn as follows: 'Millais is hard at work painting the background of his picture from nature in *Wytham Wood*' (my italics). Could not such a background point the place where the body is to be found? And may we not further infer that our murderer has not only an intimate knowledge of the woods themselves but also of the Pre-Raphaelite painters?

Yours faithfully,
STEPHEN WALLHEAD,
Wymondham Cottage,
Helpston, Lincs.

Early on the morning of Friday, 17 July, this letter had been seen by Strange, Morse, Lewis, and most of the personnel on duty at Thames Valley HQ. But not by everyone.

'Just tell me exactly what the 'ell we're supposed to be looking for!' Constable Jimmy Watt complained to his colleague, Constable Sid Berridge, as the two of them halted for a while, side by side, in the riding between Marley Wood on their right and Pasticks on their left.

Seventeen of them, there were, working reasonably scientifically through this particular stretch. Watt had been seconded only that day, taken (quite willingly) off traffic duties, while Berridge had already spent the earlier part of his week in Blenheim. And, in truth, their present duties were unwelcome to neither of them, for the temperature was already warm that morning, the sky an almost cloudless Cambridge blue.

'We're looking for a condom, Jimmy – preferably one with a handful of fingerprints on it—'

'Wha'? Bloody year ago?'

'—so's Morse'll be able to discover which 'and he pulled it on with.'

'We used to call 'em "french letters" in my day,' said Watt, with a hint of nostalgia in his voice.

'Yeah. Things change, though.'

'Yeah! Some of us missed out a bit, don't you reckon? The way some of these young 'uns . . .'

'Yeah.'

'Who'd you wanna go in *there* with, though?' Watt pointed to his left, to the dense patch of forestation nearby.

Berridge rose to the challenge: 'Brigitte Bardot? Liz Taylor? Joan Collins? Madonna? Me next-door neighbour's wife—'

'In *there*, though?'

Berridge decided to scale down his previous decision: 'Perhaps not . . . Perhaps only the woman next-door.'

*

It had been an hour earlier, at 8.30 a.m., that a member of the Wytham Trust had addressed their party, and explained why Pasticks could be a reasonably safe each-way bet for a site where a body may have lain undisturbed for a longish time. Why? Well, most people would think that the cutting-down of trees and the selling of the wood to wholesale dealers was invariably going to be a profitable undertaking. Not so! The expense of hiring men to saw down trees, to trim the fallen timber, then to transport and treat it, and finally to sell it to furniture dealers, or fencing designers, or the rest – such expense would always be considerable. And the Trust had long since agreed that it could do little better than see the whole business of thinning the woods, etc., as, well, as tit-for-tat: *they* would pay nothing for the cutting-back of the various copses and spinneys; and in turn the wood-cutters and carters would receive the proceeds from the tens of thousands of assorted tree-trunks that were annually removed from Wytham Woods. But occasionally there was a bit of a hiccup in the system – when, for example, a few of the areas of re-forestation were not quite ready for such biennial decimation; when the thinning of a particular area ought, for whatever reason, to be delayed for a couple of years.

Such a situation had in fact arisen the year before in the very latest plantation (1958–62) – a mixed hard-wood affair of Norwegian spruce, oak, beech, red cedar – in the area called Pasticks. And that wouldn't be a bad place to leave a body! The trees there allowed in very little light; and in the middle of it all were three or four old spinneys that had existed even before the Enclosure Acts. Dense places. Double-dense.

For Berridge and Watt the task certainly looked uninviting. From any point some two or three yards within the wood it seemed almost as if a curtain had been drawn in front of them, cutting them off from any further investigation, with the leafless horizontal and perpendicular branches of the trees there forming a sort of blurring criss-cross mesh of brown across their vision.

It was a good many hours later, at 3.55 p.m., that the deeply and progressively more pessimistic pair of constables heard a shout of triumph from some-where to their left. A body had been found; and very soon each wing of the search-party had enfolded the scene like the wings of a mother-bird protecting her young.

The foxes had already been there – often enough by the look of it – and the badgers, and the birds of the air ... for the bones of what appeared to be a single human being had been dragged apart there – in some cases seemingly removed – from their familiar configu-ration. Yet not so far removed as to render the pristine pattern unrecognizable. A femur still lay in its approxi-mately normal relationship to its pelvis; a few ribs still in roughly parallel formation above it; a shoulder bone in a vaguely formal relationship with the vertebrae; and the vertebrae themselves about two or three feet separated from a comparatively small and badly savaged skull; not far from which was a faded, tasselled neck-scarf, still boasting its original colours – the twin proud colours of the Swedish national flag.

CHAPTER TWENTY-SIX

Science is spectrum analysis: art is photosynthesis
(Karl Kraus, *Half Truths One and a Half Truths*)

WORD quickly spread and the verdict in all quarters was the same: here he was – only a couple of days into the investigation, only one day into the search, and eureka! Clever bugger, Morse! A bit lucky, perhaps. Could have been another week before they'd found her if they'd started at the other, the western, side of the woods.

'Touch nothing!', 'Keep your distance!' had been the orders of the day; and it had been around an unmolested, untrodden area of four or five square yards of woodland, carpeted with a thick, darkish-brown pile, that a rather irregular cordon had been drawn.

Morse had arrived on the scene within twenty minutes, and now stood there silently, not venturing beyond the waist-high red and white tape, his eyes recording the evidence before him. He saw the dislocated pattern of the bones; the scattered, residual clothes; and especially he saw the tasselled scarf beside the horridly damaged head. It reminded him of something from a DIY manual, in which various arrows point from the outer-lying parts towards a putative centre, giving instruction for the assemblage of the purchase: 'Bring this part into *there*; attach this part to *that*; connect *here*; it will fit, all of it, if only you take your time, read the instructions carefully, and know that you are going wrong if more than gentle force is required for the final assembly.' Occasionally Morse moved his weight slightly on the packed twigs and spindles beneath his feet; but still he said nothing. And the others standing there were silent too, like awkward mourners at a funeral.

Lewis, busily negotiating that afternoon with the University authorities, would not be with him. But neither of them, neither Morse nor Lewis, would be of much use at this stage. It was Max who was going to be the important personage, and Max had already been informed, was already on his way; Max who ten minutes later made his lumbering progress across the crackling bracken, and stood wheezing heavily beside Morse.

Silently, just as Morse had done earlier, the hump-backed surgeon surveyed the sorry sight which lay at the foot of an evergreen of some sort, the lower branches leafless, brittle, dead. If any attempt had been made to conceal the body, it was not now apparent; and disturbingly (as others had already noticed) a few of the major bones, including the whole of the lower left arm, had been carried away somewhere – to some den or earth or sets. From the look of it the clothes were slightly better preserved than the body: several strips of stained white, and substantial remnants of what looked like blue jeans, perhaps; and some yellowish, straw-coloured hair still gruesomely attached to the skull.

But Morse hadn't kept his eyes long on the skull . . .

'This what you've been looking for, Morse?'

'Yes. I think that's her.'

'Her?'

'I'm certain it's a "her",' said Morse with finality.

'Do you know the last words my old mother said? She'd been baking earlier in the day – the day she died. Then she was taken to her bed, but she still wanted to see how the fruit cake was doing. And it was flat. The bloody thing forgot to *rise*, Morse! And she said, "You know, life's full of uncertainties". Then she closed her eyes – and died.'

'It's the girl,' repeated Morse simply.

Max made no further comment, staring guardedly on as Morse nodded to the scenes-of-crime officer and the police photographer, both of whom had been standing waiting for some while. If there was anything of any import there that Morse should have seen, he was not aware of it; but he still felt nervous about the patch of ground, and instructed both to keep as far as possible from the grisly finds.

After a few minutes of photographic flashing, Max stepped rather gingerly into the area, hooked a pair of ancient spectacles around his large ears, looked down at the scattered skeleton, and picked up a bone.

'Femur, Morse. *Femur, femoris*, neuter. The thigh bone.'

'So?'

Max placed the bone down carefully and turned to

Morse. 'Look, old friend, I don't very often ask you for any forensic guidance, but just for once give me a little advice, will you? What the hell am I supposed to do with this bloody lot?'

Morse shook his head. 'I'm not sure.' But suddenly his eyes glowed as if some inner current had been activated. 'I knew she'd be here, Max,' he said slowly. 'Somehow I *knew* it! And I'm going to find out who murdered our Swedish Maiden. And I want you to help me, Max! Help me paint a picture of what went on in this place.'

The almost Messianic fierceness with which Morse had enunciated these words would have affected most people. But not Max.

'You're the artist, dear boy: I'm just a humble scientist.'

'How long will you be?'

'Looking at the bones, you mean?'

'And the clothes . . . and the underclothes.'

'Ah, yes! I remember. You've always had an interest in underclothes.' He consulted his watch. 'Opening time at six? I'll see you in the upstairs bar at the White Hart—'

'No. I've got a meeting back at HQ at half-past six.'

'Really? I thought *you* were in charge of this case, Morse.'

There were the four of them again: the ACC, Strange, Johnson, and Morse; and for the latter, naturally, congratulations were generous. For Johnson, however, there were very mixed fedings: Morse had come up with the girl's body in a couple of days, whilst he had come up with nothing in a twelve-month. That was the simple truth of the matter. It was good for the *case*, of course; but not much good for his own morale or his rating amongst his colleagues, or for his wife ... or indeed for his newly acquired mother-in-law. But when, an hour later, the meeting broke up, he shook Morse's hand and wished him well, and almost meant it.

After the ACC and Johnson had left, Strange in turn wished Morse continued success, observing that now Morse had come up with a body, all that remained for him was to come up with a murderer, so that he, Strange, would be able to get a nice little report and send it to the DPP. No problems! Then they'd kick the smart-alec defence lawyers up the arse, and stick the bugger who did it in the nick for the rest of his natural. Put a rope round his bloody neck, too, if Strange had *his* way.

'Just as well we didn't hang the Birmingham Six,' said Morse quietly.

Chapter Twenty-Seven

It was a maxim with Foxey – our revered father,
gentlemen – 'Always suspect everybody'
                    (Charles Dickens, *The Old Curiosity Shop*)

On the following morning, Saturday, 18 July, Morse appeared, as Lewis saw things, somewhat distanced, somewhat reserved. It was customary for the chief to start, if not always to continue, any case with a surfeit of confidence and exuberance, and doubtless that would soon be the way of things again; just not for the moment.

'Not really all *that* much to go on there, sir.' Lewis nodded to the two red box-files on the table.

'I've done my homework too, you know.'

'Where do we start?'

'Difficult. We ought really to wait till we hear from Max before we do too much.'

'All this DNA stuff, you mean?'

'DNA? He doesn't know what it *stands* for!'

'When's the report due?'

'Today some time, he said.'

'What's that mean?'

'Tonight?' Morse shrugged. But he suddenly sat forward in the black leather chair, appeared to sharpen up, took out his silver Parker pen, and began making a few minimal notes as he spoke:

'There are several people we've got to see pretty soon.'

'Who are you thinking of, sir?'

'Of whom am I thinking? Well, number one, there's the fellow who found the rucksack – Daley. We'll go through his statement with a nit-comb. I never did like the sound of him.'

'You never met him, did you?'

'Number two. There's the YWCA woman who spoke with Karin before she left for Oxford. She sounds nice.'

'But you never—'

'I spoke to her on the phone, Lewis, if you must know. She sounds nice – that's all I said. You don't *mind*, do you?'

Lewis smiled to himself. It was good to be back in harness.

'Number three,' resumed Morse. 'We must have a long session with that Wytham fellow – the Lone Ranger, or whatever he's called.'

'Head forester, sir.'

'Exactly.'

'Did you like *him*?'

Morse turned over the palm of his right hand, and considered his inky fingers. 'He virtually told us where she was, didn't he? Told us where *he* would hide a body if he had to . . .'

'Not likely to have told us if he'd put it there *himself* though, surely? Self-incrimination, that!'

Morse said nothing.

'The witnesses who said they saw her, sir – any good going back over them?'

'Doubt it, but ... Anyway, let's put 'em down, number four. And number five, the parents—'

'Just the mother, sir.'

'—in Uppsala—'

'Stockholm, now.'

'Yes. We shall have to see her again.'

'We shall have to *tell* her first, surely.'

'If it is Karin, you mean?'

'You don't really have much doubt, do you, sir?'

'No!'

'I suppose you'll be going there yourself? To Stockholm, I mean.'

Morse looked up, apparently with some surprise. 'Or you, Lewis. Or *you*!'

'Very kind of you, sir.'

'Not kind at all. Just that I'm scared stiff of flying – you know that.' But the voice was a little sad again.

'You all right?' Lewis asked quietly.

'Shall be soon – don't worry! Now, I just wonder whether Mr George Daley's still working on the Blenheim Estate.'

'Saturday, though. More likely to be off today.'

'Yes ... And his son – Philip, was it? – the lad who had a short-term birthday present of a camera, Karin Eriksson's camera. He was still at school last year.'

'Probably still is.'

'No – not precisely so, Lewis. The state schools in Oxfordshire broke up yesterday, the seventeenth.'

'How'd you know that?'

'I rang up and found out. That's how.'

'You've been having a fair old time on the phone!' said Lewis happily, as he got to his feet – and went for the car.

As he drove out along the A44 to Begbroke, Lewis's eyes drifted briefly if incuriously to his left as Morse opened an envelope, took out a single handwritten sheet of A4, and read it; not (in fact) for the first, or even the fourth, time:

Dear Chief Inspector,

V m t f y l and for your interesting choice of records.

It would make a good debate in the Oxford Union – 'This house believes that openness in matters of infidelity is preferrable to deception.' But let me tell you what you want to know. I was married in '76, divorced in '82, remarried in '84, separated in '88. One child, a daughter now aged 20. Work that out, clever-clogs! As you know I consort fairly regularly with a married man from Oxford, and at less frequent intervals with others. So there! And now – Christ! – *you* come along and I hate you for it because you're monopolizing my thoughts just when I'd told myself I was beyond all that nonsense.

I write for two reasons. First to say I reckon I've got some idea how that young girl who monopolizes *your* thoughts may have come by a bit of cash. (Same way I did!) Second to say you're an arrogant sod! You write to me as if you think I'm an ignorant little schoolgirl. Well let me tell you you're not the only sensitive little flower in the whole bloody universe. You quote these poets as if you think you're connected on some direct personal line with them all. Well you're wrong. There's hundreds of extensions, just like in the office I used to work. So there!

Please write again.

Dare I send you a little of my love? C.

Morse hadn't noticed the misspelling before; and as he put the letter away he promised himself not to mention it . . . when he wrote back.

'I'm still not quite sure why we're interviewing Mr Daley, sir.'

'He's hiding something, that's why.'

'But you can't say *that*—'

'Look, Lewis, if he's *not* hiding something, there's not much reason for us interviewing him, is there?'

Lewis, not unaccustomedly, was bewildered by such zany logic; and he let it go.

Anyway, Morse was suddenly sounding surprisingly cheerful.

CHAPTER TWENTY-EIGHT

Be it ever so humble there's no place like home for sending one slowly crackers

(Diogenes Small, *Obiter Dicta*)

GEORGE DALEY, on overtime, was planting out flowers in the Blenheim Garden Centre when he looked up and saw the two men, the shorter of them flashing a warrant card briefly in front of his face. He knew what it was all about, of course. *The Oxford Mail* had been taking a keen interest in the resurrected case; and it would be only a matter of time, Daley had known, before the police would be round again.

'Mr Daley? Chief Inspector Morse. And this is Sergeant Lewis.'

Daley nodded, prodded his splayed fingers round a marigold, and got to his feet. He was a man in his mid-forties, of slim build, wearing a shabby khaki-green pork-pie hat. This he pushed back slightly, revealing a red line on his sweaty forehead.

'It's that thing I found, I suppose?'

'Those things – yes,' said Morse carefully.

'I can only tell you the same as I told 'em at the time. I made a statement and I signed it. Nothin' else as I can do.'

Morse took a folded sheet of A4 from his inside

pocket, opened it out, and handed it to Daley. 'I'd just like you to read this through and make sure it's – well, you know, see if there's anything else you can add.'

'I've told you. There's nothin' else.' Daley rubbed a hand across an unshaven cheek with the sound of sandpaper on wood.

'I'd just like you to read it through *again*,' said Morse simply. 'That's all.'

'I shall need me specs. They're in the shed—'

'Don't worry now! Better if you give yourself a bit of time. No rush. As I say, all I want you to do is to make sure everything's there just as you said it, nothing's been missed out. It's often the little things, you know, that make all the difference.'

'If there was anythin' else I'd've told the other inspector, wouldn't I?'

Was it Lewis's imagination, or was there a momentary glint of anxiety in the gardener's pale eyes?

'Are you in this evening, Mr Daley?' asked Morse.

'Wha' – Saturday? I usually go over the pub for a jar or two at the weekends but—'

'If I called at your house about – what, seven?'

George Daley stood motionless, his eyes narrowed and unblinking as he watched the two detectives walk away through the archway and into the visitors' car park. Then his eyes fell on the photocopied statement once more. There was just that one thing that worried him, yes. It was that bloody boy of his who'd fucked it all up. More trouble than they were worth, kids. Especially *him*! Becomin' a real troublemaker he was, gettin' in all hours – like last night. Three bloody thirty a.m. With his mates, he'd said – after the end-of-term knees-up. He'd got a key all right, of course, but his mother could never sleep till he was in. Silly bitch!

'Where to, sir?' queried Lewis.

'I reckon we'll just call round to see Mrs Daley.'

'What do you make of Mr?'

'Little bit nervous.'

'Most people get a bit nervous with the police.'

'Good cause, some of 'em,' said Morse.

Lewis had earlier telephoned Margaret Daley about her husband's whereabouts, and the woman who opened the door of number 2 Blenheim Villas showed no surprise. She appeared, on first impressions, a decided cut or two above her horticultural spouse: neatly dressed, pleasantly spoken, well groomed – her light-brown hair professionally streaked with strands of blonde and grey.

Morse apologized for disturbing her, looked around him at the newly decorated, neatly furnished, through-lounge; offered a few 'nice-little-place-you-have-here' type compliments; and explained why they'd called and would be calling again – one of them, certainly – at seven o'clock that evening.

'It was you, Mrs Daley, wasn't it, who got your husband to hand the rucksack in?'

'Yes – but he'd have done it himself anyway. Later on. I know he would.'

The shelves around the living area were lined with china ornaments of all shapes and sizes; and Morse walked over to the shelf above the electric fire, and carefully picked up the figure of a small dog, examining it briefly before replacing it on its former station.

'King Charles?'

Margaret Daley nodded. 'Cavalier King Charles. We had one – till last February. Mycroft. Lovely little dog – lovely face! We all had a good cry when the vet had to put him down. Not a very healthy breed, I'm afraid.'

'People living next to us have one of those,' ventured Lewis. 'Always at the vet. Got a medical history long as your arm.'

'Thank you, Lewis. I'm sure Mrs Daley isn't over-anxious to be reminded of a family bereavement—'

'Oh, it's all right! I quite like talking about him, really. We all – Philip and George – we all loved him. In fact he was about the only thing that'd get Philip out of bed sometimes.'

But Morse's attention appeared to have drifted far from dogs as he gazed through the french windows at the far end of the room, his eyes seemingly focused at some point towards the back of the garden – a garden just over the width of the house and stretching back about fifty feet to a wire fence at the bottom, separating the property from the open fields beyond. As with the patch of garden in the front, likewise here: George Daley, it had to be assumed, reckoned he did quite enough gardening in the course of earning his daily bread at Blenheim, and carried little if anything of his horticultural expertise into the rather neglected stretch of lawn which provided the immediate view from the rear of number 2.

'I don't believe it!' said Morse. 'Isn't that *Asphodelina lutea?*'

Mrs Daley walked over to the window.

'There!' pointed Morse. 'Those yellow things, just across the fence.'

'Buttercups!' said Lewis.

'You've, er, not got a pair of binoculars handy, Mrs Daley?'

'No – I – we haven't, I'm afraid.'

'Mind if we have a look?' asked Morse. 'Always contradicting me, my sergeant is!'

The three of them walked out through the kitchen door, past the (open) out-house door, and on to the back lawn where the daisies and dandelions and broad-leaf plantain had been allowed a generous freedom of movement. Morse himself stepped up to the fence, looking down at the ground around him; then, curso-rily, at the yellow flowers he had spotted earlier, and which he now agreed to be nothing rarer than butter-cups. Mrs Daley smiled vaguely at Lewis; but Lewis was now listening to Morse's apparently aimless chatter with far greater interest.

'No compost heap?'

'No. George isn't much bothered with the garden here, as you can see. Says he's got enough, you know . . .' She pointed vaguely towards Blenheim, and led the way back in.

'How do you get rid of your rubbish then?'

'Sometimes we go down to the waste disposal with it. Or you can buy those special bags from the council. We *used* to burn it, but a couple of years ago we upset the neighbours – you know, bits all over the washing and—'

'Probably against the bye-laws, too,' added Lewis; and for once Morse appeared to appreciate the addendum.

It was Lewis too, as they were leaving, who spotted the rifle amid the umbrellas, the walking sticks, and the warped squash racket, in a stand just behind the front door.

'Does your husband do a bit of shooting?'

'Oh *that*! George occasionally . . . yes . . .'

Gently, for a second time, Lewis reminded her of the law's demands: 'Ought to be under lock and key, that. Perhaps you'd remind your husband, Mrs Daley.'

Margaret Daley watched them through the front window as they walked away to their car. Just a bit of a stiff-shirt, the sergeant had been, about their legal responsibilities. Whereas the inspector – well, he'd seemed much nicer with his interest in dogs and flowers and the decoration in the lounge – *her* decoration. Yet during the last few minutes she'd begun to suspect her judgement a little, and she had the feeling that it would probably be Morse who would be returning that evening. Not that there was anything to worry about, really. Well, just the one thing, perhaps.

*

157

In spite of that day being Saturday – and the first of the holidays – Mrs Julie Ireson, careers mistress at the Cherwell School, Oxford, had been quite willing to meet Lewis just after lunch; and Lewis was anxious to get the meeting over as soon as possible, for he was desperately tired and had been only too glad to accept Morse's strict directive for a long rest – certainly for the remainder of the day, and perhaps for the next day, Sunday, too – unless there occurred any dramatic development.

She was waiting in the deserted car park when Lewis arrived, and immediately took him up to her first-floor study, its walls and shelves festooned with literature on nursing, secretarial courses, apprenticeship schemes, industrial training, FEs, polys, universities ... For Lewis (whose only career advice had been his father's dictum that he could do worse than to keep his mouth mostly shut and his bowels always open), a school-based advice centre for pupils leaving school was an interesting novelty.

A buff-coloured folder containing the achievements of Philip Daley was on the table ready for him. Non-achievements rather. He was now just seventeen years old, and had officially abandoned any potential advancement into further education w.e.f. 7 July – the previous day. The school was prepared to be not overpessimistic about some minor success in the five GCSE subjects in which, the previous term, he had tried (though apparently not overhard) to satisfy his examiners: English; Technical Drawing; Geography; General Science; and Communication Studies. Over the years, however, the reports from his teachers, even in nonacademic subjects, had exhibited a marked lack of enthusiasm about his attitude and progress. Yet until fairly recently he appeared not to have posed any great problem to the school community: limited, clearly, in intellectual prowess; limited too in most technical and vocational skills; in general about average.

Current educational philosophy (Lewis learned) encouraged a measure of self-evaluation, and amongst other documents in the folder was a sheet on which eighteen months previously, in his own handwriting, Philip had filled in a questionnaire about his six main 'Leisure Interests/Pastimes', in order of preference. The list read thus:

1. Football
2. Pop music
3. Photography
4. Pets
5. Motorbikes
6. TV

'He can spell OK,' commented Lewis.

'Difficult to misspell "pets", Sergeant.'

'Yes. But – well, "photography' ...

'Probably had to look it up in the dictionary.'

'You didn't like him?' said Lewis slowly.

'No, I'm afraid I didn't. I'm glad he's gone, if you must know.' She was younger than Lewis had expected: perhaps more vulnerable too?

'Any particular reason?'

'Just general, really.'

'Well, thanks very much, Mrs Ireson. If I could take the folder?'

'Any particular reason you want to know about him?'

'No. Just general, really,' echoed Lewis.

He slept from 6.30 that evening through until almost ten the following morning. When he finally awoke, he learned there had been a telephone message the previous evening from Morse: on no account was he to come in to HQ that Sunday; it would be a good idea, though, to make sure his passport was in order.

Well, well!

CHAPTER TWENTY-NINE

Every roof is agreeable to the eye, until it is lifted; then we find tragedy and moaning women, and hard-eyed husbands

(Ralph Waldo Emerson, *Experience*)

IT WAS two minutes to seven by the Jaguar's fascia clock when Morse pulled up in the slip-road outside number 2 Blenheim Villas. He was fairly confident of his ground now, especially after reading through the folder that Lewis had left. Certain, of course, about the electric fire in the Daleys' main lounge; almost certain about the conversion of the old coal-house into a utility room, in which, as they'd walked out to the garden, he'd glimpsed the arrangement of washing-machine and tumble-drier on newly laid red tiles; not *quite* so certain about the treeless back garden though, for Morse was ridiculously proud about never having been a boy scout, and his knowledge of camp-fires and cocoa-barbecues, he had to admit, was almost nil.

For once he felt relieved to be on his own as he knocked at the front door. The police as a whole were going through a tough time in public esteem: alle-gations of corrupt officers, planted evidence, improper procedures – such allegations had inevitably created suspicion and some hostility. And – yes, Morse knew it

– he himself was on occasion tempted to overstep the procedural boundaries a little – as shortly he would be doing again. It was a bit like a darts player standing a few inches in front of the oche as he threw for the treble-twenty. And Lewis would not have brooked this; and would have told him so.

In the lounge, in a less than convivial atmosphere, the Daleys sat side by side on the settee; and Morse, from the armchair opposite, got down to business.

'You've managed to go through the statement again, Mr Daley?'

'You don't mind the wife being here?'

'I'd prefer it, really,' said Morse innocently.

'Like I said, there's nothin' as I can add.'

'Fine.' Morse reached across and took the now rather grimy photocopy and looked through it slowly himself before lifting his eyes to George Daley.

'Let me be honest with you, sir. It's this camera business that's worrying me.'

'Wha' abou' i'?' (If the dietitian sometimes had paid overnice attention to her dental consonants, Daley himself almost invariably ignored them.)

Morse moved obliquely into the attack: 'You interested in photography yourself?'

'Me? Not much, no.'

'You, Mrs Daley?'

She shook her head.

'Your son Philip is though?'

'Yeah, well, he's got fairly interested in it recently,

hasn't he, luv?' Daley turned to his wife, who nodded vaguely, her eyes on Morse continuously.

'Bit more than "recently", perhaps?' Morse suggested. 'He put it down on his list of hobbies at school last year – early last year – a few months before you found the camera.'

'Yeah, well, like I said, we was going to get him one anyway, for his birthday. Wasn't we, luv?' Again, apart from a scarce-discernible nod, Margaret Daley appeared reluctant verbally to confirm such an innocent statement.

'But you've never had a camera yourself, you say.'

'Correck!'

'How did you know the film in the camera was finished then?'

'Well, you know, it's the numbers, innit? It tells you, like, when you've got to the finish.'

'When it reads "ten", you mean?'

'Somethin' like that.'

'What if there are twelve exposures on the reel?'

'Dunno.' Daley appeared not to be at all flustered by the slightly more aggressive tone of the question. 'It was probably Philip as said so.' Again he turned to his wife. 'Was his ten or twelve, luv? D'you remember?'

Morse pounced on the answer: 'So he had a camera *before?*'

'Yeah, well, just an el cheapo thing we bought him—'

'From Spain.' (Mrs Daley had broken her duck.)

'Would you know how to get the film *out* of a camera, Mr Daley?'

'Well, not unless, you know—'

'But it says here' – Morse looked down at the statement again – 'it says here that you burnt the film.'

'Yeah, well, that's right, isn't it, luv? We shoulda kept it, I know. Still, as I said – well, we all do things a bit wrong sometimes, don't we? And we said we was sorry about everything, didn't we, luv?'

Morse was beginning to realize that the last three words, with their appropriate variants, were a rhetorical refrain only, and were not intended to elicit any specific response.

'Where did you burn it?' asked Morse quietly.

'Dunno. Don't remember. Just chucked it on the fire, I suppose.' Daley gestured vaguely with his right hand.

'*That's* electric,' said Morse, pointing to the fireplace.

'And we got a grate for a coal-fire next door. All right?' Daley's voice was at last beginning to show signs of some exasperation.

'Did you have a fire that day?'

'How the 'ell am I supposed to remember *that*?'

'Do *you* remember, Mrs Daley?'

She shook her head. 'More than a year ago, isn't it? Could you remember that far back?'

'I've not had a coal-fire in my flat for fifteen years, Mrs Daley. So I could remember, yes.'

'Well, I'm sorry,' she said quietly, 'I can't.'

'Did you know that the temperature in Oxfordshire that day was seventy-four degrees Fahrenheit?' (Morse thought he'd got it vaguely correct.)

'Wha'! At ten o'clock at night?' Clearly Daley was losing his composure, and Morse took full advantage.

'Where do you *keep* your coal? Your coal-house has been converted to a utility-room – your wife showed—'

'If it wasn't here – all right, it wasn't *here*. Musta been in the garden, mustn't it?'

'What do you burn in the garden?'

'What do I burn? What do I *burn*? I burn bloody twigs and leaves and—'

'You haven't got any trees. And even if you had, July's a bit early for leaves.'

'Oh, for Christ's sake! Look—'

'No!' Suddenly Morse's voice was harsh and authoritative. '*You* look, Mr Daley. If you do burn your rubbish out there in the garden, come and show me where!' All pretence was now dropped as Morse continued: 'And if you make up any more lies about *that*, I'll bring a forensic team in and have 'em cart half your lawn away!'

They sat silently, the Daleys, neither looking at the other.

'Was it you who got the film developed, Mr Daley? Or was it your son?' Morse's voice was quiet once more.

'It was Philip,' said Margaret Daley, finally, now assuming control. 'He was friendly with this boy at school whose father was a photographer and had a dark-room an' all that, and they developed 'em there, I think.' Her voice sounded to Morse as if it had suddenly lost its veneer of comparative refinement, and he began to wonder which of the couple was potentially the bigger liar.

'You must tell me what those photographs were.' Morse made an effort to conceal the urgency of his request, but his voice betrayed the fear that all might well be lost.

'He never kept 'em as far as I know—' began Daley.

But his wife interrupted him: 'There were only six or seven out of the twelve that came out. There was some photos of birds – one was a pinkish sort of bird with a black tail—'

'Jay!' said Daley.

'—and there was two of a man, youngish man – probably her boyfriend. But the others, as I say . . . you know, they just didn't . . . come out.'

'I must have them,' said Morse simply, inexorably almost.

'He's chucked 'em out, surely,' observed Daley. 'What the 'ell would he keep 'em for?'

'I must have them,' repeated Morse.

'Christ! Don't you understand? I never even *saw* 'em!'

'Where is your son?'

Husband and wife looked at each other, and husband spoke: 'Gone into Oxford, I should think – Sa'day night . . .'

'Take me to his room, will you?'

'We bloody *won't*!' growled Daley. 'If you wanna look round 'ere, Inspector, you just bring a search-warrant, OK?'

'I don't need one. You've got a rifle behind the front door, Mr Daley, and it's odds-on you've got a box of cartridges somewhere lying around. All I need to do to take your floorboards up if necessary is to quote to you – just *quote*, mind – Statutory Instrument 1991 No. 1531.

Do you understand? The pair of you? That's *my* only legal obligation.'

But Morse had no further need for inaccurate improvisations regarding the recently enacted legislation on explosives. Margaret Daley rose to her feet and made to leave the lounge.

'You won't search Philip's room with *my* permission, Inspector. But if he has kept them photos I reckon I just might know . . .'

Morse heard her on the stairs, his heart knocking against his ribs: Please! Please! Please!

No word passed between the two men seated opposite each other as they heard the creak of floorboards in the upstairs rooms. Nor was much said when Margaret Daley returned some minutes later holding seven coloured prints which she handed to Morse – wordlessly!

'Thank you. No others?'

She shook her head.

After Morse was gone, Margaret Daley went into the kitchen where she turned on the kettle and spooned some instant Nescafé into a mug.

'I suppose you're out boozing,' she said tonelessly, as her husband came in.

'Why the 'ell didn't you tell *me* about them photos?'

'Shut up!' She spat out the two words viciously and turned towards him.

'Where the 'ell did you find 'em, you—'

'Shut up! And listen, will you? If you must know, I've

been looking in his room, George Daley, because if we don't soon get to know what's goin' on and do something about it he'll be in bloody jail or something, that's why! See? There were twelve photos, five of the girl—'

'You stupid bitch!'

'Listen!' she shrieked. 'I never gave him *them*! I've hidden 'em; and now I'm gonna get rid of 'em; and I'm not gonna show 'em to you! You don't give a sod about anything these days, anyway!'

Daley walked tight-lipped to the door. 'Stop moaning, you miserable cunt!'

His wife had taken a large pair of kitchen scissors from a drawer. 'Don't you ever talk to me like that again, George Daley!' Her voice was trembling with fury.

A few minutes after hearing the front door slam behind him, she went upstairs to their bedroom and took the five photographs out of her underwear drawer. All of them were of Karin Eriksson, nakedly or semi-nakedly lying in lewdly provocative postures. She could only guess how often her son had ogled these and similar photographs which he kept in a box at the back of his wardrobe, and which she had discovered when spring-cleaning his room the previous April. She took the five photographs to the loo, where standing over the pan she sliced strip after strip from the face, the shoulders, the breasts, the thighs, and the legs of the beautiful Karin Eriksson, intermittently flushing the celluloid slivers down into the Begbroke sewers.

CHAPTER THIRTY

A man's bed is his resting-place, but a woman's is often
her rack

(James Thurber, *Further Fables for Our Time*)

THE AMBULANCE, its blue light flashing, its siren
wailing, finally pulled into the Casualty Bay of the John
Radcliffe 2 Hospital at 9.15 p.m. The grey face of the
man hurriedly carried through the automatic doors on
a stretcher – the forehead clammy with sweat, the
breathing shallow and laboured – had told its immediate story to the red-belted senior nurse, who straightaway rang through to the medical houseman on duty,
before joining one of her colleagues in taking off the
man's clothes and fastening a hospital gown around his
overweight frame. A series of hurried readings – of
electrocardiograph, blood pressure, chest X-ray – soon
confirmed the fairly obvious: a massive coronary throm-
bosis, so very nearly an immediately fatal one.

Two porters pushed the trolley swiftly along the
corridors to the Coronary Care Unit, where they lifted
the heavy man on to a bed; around which curtains were
quickly drawn, and five leads connected to the man's
chest and linked to monitors, which now gave continuous details of heart rhythm, blood pressure, and pulse
rate, on the screen beside the bed. A very pretty, slightly

169

plump young nurse looked on as the houseman administered a morphine injection.

'Much hope?' she queried quietly a minute or two later, as the two of them stood at the central desk, where the VDU monitors from each of the small ward's six beds were banked.

'You never know, but . . .'

'Quite a well-known man, isn't he?'

'Taught me as a student. Well, I went to his lectures. Blood – that was his speciality, really; and he was a world authority on VD! Police get him in all the time, too – PMs, that sort of thing.'

The nurse looked at the monitor: the readings seemed significantly steadier now, and she found herself earnestly willing the old boy to survive.

'Give him some Frusemide, Nurse – as much as you like. I'm worried about all that fluid on his lungs.'

The houseman watched the monitor for another few minutes, then went over to the bed again, where the nurse had just placed a jug of water and a glass on the bedside locker.

After the houseman had left, Nurse Shelick remained beside the sick man's bed and looked down at him with that passionate intensity she invariably felt for her patients. Although still in her twenties, she was really one of that old-fashioned school who believed that whatever the advantages of hyper-technology, the virtues of simple human *nursing* were almost as indispensable. She laid the palm of her right hand across the wet, cold brow, and for the next few minutes wiped his face gently with a warm, damp flannel – suddenly aware that his eyes had opened and were looking up at her.

'Nurse?'

'I can hear you – yes?'

'Will you ... will you ... get in touch ... with someone for me?'

'Of course! Of course!' She bent her right ear towards the purple lips, but without quite making out what he was saying.

'Pardon?'

'Morse!'

'I'm sorry. Please say it again. I'm not quite sure—'

'Morse!'

'I still ... I'm sorry ... please.'

But the eyes of the man who lay upon the bed had closed again, and there was no answer to her gently repeated queries.

The time was 11.15 p.m.

The head forester's beautiful young wife was also in bed at this time. She too lay supine; and still lay supine, wakeful and waiting, until finally at 11.35 p.m. she heard the front door being opened, then locked, then bolted.

In spite of four pints of Burton ale and two whiskies at the White Hart, David Michaels knew that he was very sober; far *too* sober – for there was something sadly amiss when a man couldn't get drunk, he knew that. After cleaning his teeth, he went into the bedroom, shed his clothes swiftly, and slid under the lightweight duvet. She always slept naked, and after their marriage he had followed her example – often finding himself erotically aroused not so much by the fact or the sight of her nakedness as by the very thought of it. And now as he moved in beside her in the darkened room, he knew that she was suddenly and wonderfully necessary once more. He turned his body towards her and his right hand reached gently across her and fondled her breast. But with her own right hand she grasped his wrist, and with surprising strength moved it from her.

'No. Not tonight.'

'Is there something wrong?'

'I just don't want you tonight – can't you understand?'

'I think I understand all right.' Michaels' voice was dull and he turned to lie on his back.

'Why did you have to tell them?' she asked fiercely.

'Because I know the bloody place better than anyone else, that's why!'

'But don't you realize—?'

'I had to tell them something. God! Don't you see that? I didn't *know*, did I?'

She sat up in bed and leaned towards him, her right hand on the pillow beside his head. 'But they'll think *you* did it, David.'

'Don't be so stupid! I wouldn't be giving them information if it was *me*. Can't you see that? I'm the very *last* person they're going to suspect. But if I hadn't agreed to help . . .'

She said nothing more; and he wondered for a while whether it would be sensible to go down and make a couple of cups of piping-hot coffee for them, and then perhaps turn on the bedside lamp and look upon his lovely bride. But there was no need. Seemingly Cathy Michaels had accepted the logic of his words, and her mind was more at ease; for she now lay down again and turned towards him, and soon he felt the silky caress of her inner thigh against him.

CHAPTER THIRTY-ONE

> The background reveals the true being of the man or
> thing. If I do not possess the background, I make the
> man transparent, the thing transparent
>
> (Juan Jiménez, *Selected Writings*)

IT WAS rather like trying to see the answer to a tricky
crossword clue, Morse decided, as at 11 o'clock that
same night he sat in his North Oxford lounge, topping
up his earlier libations with a few fingers of Glenfiddich,
and looking yet again at the photographs that Margaret
Daley had given him. The closer he got to the clue –
the closer he got to the photograph – the less in fact he
saw. It was necessary to stand away, to see things in
perspective, to look *synoptically* at the problem.

As he had just considered the photographs, it was
the man himself, pictured in two of them, who had
monopolized his interest: a small- to medium-sized
man, in his late twenties perhaps, with longish fair hair;
a man wearing a white T-shirt and faded-blue denims,
with a sunburnt complexion and the suggestion of a
day's growth of stubble around his jowls. But the detail
was not of sufficient definition or fidelity for him to be
wholly sure, as if the cameraman himself – or almost
certainly the camera*woman* – had scarcely the experience needed to cope with the problems of the bright

sunlight that so obviously pervaded the garden in which the snaps had been taken. But although Morse knew little (well, nothing) about photography, he was beginning to suspect that there might be slightly more competence in the arrangement of the 'subject' in relation to the 'background' than he'd originally supposed.

The man had been photographed at an oblique angle across the garden, with a house clearly shown to the left of the figure: a three-storey, rosy-bricked house, with a french window on the ground floor, slightly ajar, with another window immediately above it, and one above that, all painted white, and with a black drain-pipe reaching down to ground level; and to the figure's right a smallish tree of some sort with large curly leaves, unidentifiable to Morse who knew little (well, nothing) of such things. But there was even more to learn. Clearly the photographer had been kneeling down, or sitting down, to take the shots, for the man's head showed some way above the line of the garden wall, which rose clearly behind the, shrubs and foliage. Even more to learn though! – Morse decided, as he studied the background yet again. The roof-line of the house stretched away in a slightly convex curve (as it appeared) above the man's head, and then was cut off in the middle of the top of the photograph; but not before suggesting that the house could be one of a terrace, perhaps?

It was amazing, Morse told himself, how much he'd managed to miss when first he'd considered the photographs; and with the strange conviction that there would certainly be a final solution to the mystery if only he looked at it long enough, he stared and stared until he thought he could see two houses instead of one, although whether this was an advance in insight or in inebriation, he couldn't be sure. So what, though? So what if it *were* part of a terrace? The number of three-storeyed, red-bricked terraces in the UK was myriad; and just in Oxford alone it must be . . . Morse shook his head and shook his thoughts. No. It was going to be almost impossible to locate the house and the garden; so the only thing left was the young man's face, really.

Or was it . . .?

Suddenly an exciting thought occurred to him. A straight line could be seen as a curve, so he'd been supposing, either because the camera had looked at it in a particular way, or because in a larger view the line began to bend in a sort of rounded perspective. But such explanations were surely far less probable than the utterly obvious fact that was staring him, literally *staring* him, in the face; the fact that the roof-line of the terraced houses which formed the backdrop here might *look* as if it was curving in a convex fashion for one supremely simple and wholly adequate reason: it *was* curving!

Could it be . . .? Could it be . . .? Did Morse, even now, think he *knew* where it was? He felt the old familiar tingle across his shoulders, and the hairs at the nape of his neck were suddenly erect. He rose from his arm-chair and went over to his bookshelves, whence he extracted the thick Penguin *Oxfordshire*, in the 'Build-ings of England' series; and his right hand shook slightly as he traced 'Park Town' in the index – page 320. On which page he read:

> Laid out in 1853–5. This was North Oxford's first development, built on land originally intended for a workhouse. The trust created for its developments promised elegant villas and [Morse's eyes snatched at the next word] terraces. What it became is this: two crescents [the blood tingled again] N and S of an elliptical central garden, with stone frontages in late-classical style, and bricked at the rear [!] with attractive french windows [!] leading on to small walled [!] gardens.

Phew!
Ye gods!
Bloody hell!
If he were so disposed (Morse knew) he could go and identify the house at that very moment! It *must* be in Crescent S – the sunshine would rule out Crescent N; and with that tree with its big, furry, splayed (beautiful!) leaves; and the drain-pipe, and the windows, and the wall, and the grass . . .

As he sat down again in the black leather settee, Morse's face was betraying a high degree of self-gratification – when the phone rang. It was now a quarter to midnight, and the voice was a woman's – husky, slightly timid, north-country.

*

She identified herself as Dr Laura Hobson, one of the new girls in the path labs; one of Max's protegées. She had been working late with Max – on Morse's bones – when just before 9 p.m. she'd found him lying there on the floor of the lab. Heart attack – severe heart attack. He'd been unconscious most of the time since they'd got him to hospital . . . but the sister had rung her (Dr Hobson) and the possibility was that he (Max) had been trying to ask for him (Morse) – if he (Morse) knew what she (Dr Hobson) was trying to say . . .

Oh dear!

'Which ward's he in?'

'Coronary Care Unit—'

'Yes! But *where*?'

'The JR2. But it's no good trying to see him now. Sister says—'

'You want to bloody *bet*?' snapped Morse.

'Please! There's something else, Inspector. He'd been working on the bones all day and—'

'Bugger the bones!'

'But—'

'Look. I'm most grateful to you, Dr, er . . .'

'Hobson.'

'. . . but please forgive me if I hang up. You see,' suddenly Morse's voice was more controlled, more gentle, 'Max and I – well, we . . . let's say we don't either of us have too many friends and . . . I want to see the old sod again if he's going to die.'

But Morse had already put down the phone, and Dr Hobson heard nothing of the last five words. She too felt very sad. She had known Max for only six weeks.

Yet there was something basically kindly about the man; and only a week before she'd had a mildly erotic dream about that ugly, brusque, and arrogant pathologist.

At least for the present, however, the pathologist appeared to have rallied quite remarkably, for he was talking to Nurse Shelick rationally, albeit slowly and quietly, when he learned of his visitor; and threatened to strike the houseman off the medical register unless Morse (for such it was) were admitted forthwith.

But one patient newly admitted to the JR2 had not rallied that night. Marion Bridewell, an eight-year-old little West Indian girl, had been knocked down by a stolen car on the Broadmoor Lea estate at seven o'clock that evening. She had been terribly badly injured.

She died just after midnight.

CHAPTER THIRTY-TWO

And Apollo gave Sarpedon dead to be borne by swift companions, to Death and Sleep, twin brethren, who bore him through the air to Lycia, that broad and pleasant land

(Homer, *Iliad*, xvi)

'HOW ARE you, old friend?' asked Morse with spurious cheerfulness.

'Dying.'

'You once told me that we're all moving towards death – at the standard rate of twenty-four hours *per diem*.'

'I was always accurate, Morse. Not very imaginative, agreed; but always accurate.'

'You've still not told me how—'

'Somebody said . . . somebody said, "Nothing matters very much . . . and in the end nothing really matters at all".'

'Lord Balfour.'

'You always were a knowledgeable sod.'

'Dr Hobson rang—'

'Ah! The fair Laura. Don't know how men ever keep their hands off her.'

'Perhaps they don't.'

'I was thinking of her just now . . . Still have any erotic daydreams yourself, Morse?'

'Most of the time.'

'Be nice – be nice if she was thinking of me . . .'

'You never know.'

Max smiled his awkward, melancholy smile, but his face looked tired and ashen-grey. 'You're right. Life's full of uncertainties. Have I ever told you that before?'

'Many a time.'

'I've always . . . I've always been interested in death, you know. Sort of hobby of mine, really. Even when I was a lad . . .'

'I know. Look, Max, they said they'd only let me in to see you if—'

'No knickers – you know that?'

'Pardon? Pardon, Max?'

'The bones, Morse!'

'What about the bones?'

'Do you believe in God?'

'Huh! Most of the *bishops* don't believe in God.'

'And you used to accuse *me* of never answering questions!'

Morse hesitated. Then he looked down at his old friend and answered him: 'No.'

Paradoxically perhaps, the police surgeon appeared comforted by the sincerity of the firm monosyllable; but his thoughts were now stuttering their way around a discontinuous circuit.

'You *surprised*, Morse?'

'Pardon?'

'You *were*, weren't you? Admit it!'

'Surprised?'

'The bones! Not a *woman*'s bones, were they?'

Morse felt his heart pounding insistently somewhere – everywhere – in his body; felt the blood sinking down from his shoulders, past his heart, past his loins. *Not a woman's bones* – is that what Max had just said?

It had taken the hump-backed surgeon some considerable time to say his say; and feeling a tap on his shoulder, Morse turned to find Nurse Shelick standing behind him. 'Please!' her lips mouthed, as she looked anxiously down at the tired and intermittently closing eyes.

But before he left Morse leaned forward and whispered in the dying man's ear: 'I'll bring us a bottle of malt in the morning, Max, and we'll have a wee drop together, my old friend. So keep a hold on things – please keep a hold on things! . . . Just for me!'

It would have been a joy for Morse had he seen the transient gleam in Max's eyes. But the surgeon's face had turned away from him, towards the recently painted, pale-green wall of the CCU. And he seemed to be asleep.

Maximilian Theodore Siegfried de Bryn (his middle names a surprise even to his few friends) surrendered to an almost totally welcome weariness two hours after Chief Inspector Morse had left; and finally loosed his grip on the hooks just after three o'clock that morning. He had bequeathed his mortal remains to the Medical Research Foundation at the JR2. He had earnestly wished it so. And it would be done.

Many had known Max, even if few had understood

his strange ways. And many were to feel a fleeting sadness at his death. But he had (as we have seen) a few friends only. And there was only one man who had wept silently when the call had been received in his office in Thames Valley Police HQ at Kidlington at 9 a.m. on Sunday, 19 July 1992.

CHAPTER THIRTY-THREE

What is a committee? A group of the unwilling,
picked from the unfit, to do the unnecessary
  (Richard Harkness, *New York Herald Tribune*, 15 June 1960)

SUNDAY is not a good day on which to do business. Or
to expect others to be at work – or even to be out of
bed. But Dr Laura Hobson was out of bed fairly early
that morning, and awaiting Morse at the (deserted)
William Dunn School of Pathology building at 9.30
a.m.

'Hello.'

'Hello.'

'You're Inspector Morse?'

'Chief Inspector Morse.'

'Sorry!'

'And you're Dr Hobson?'

'I am she.'

Morse smiled wanly. 'I applaud your grammar, my
dear.'

'I am not your "dear". You must forgive me for being
so blunt: but I'm no one's "luv" or "dear" or "darling"
or "sweetheart". I've got a name. If I'm at work I prefer
to be called Dr Hobson; and if I let my hair down over
a drink I have a Christian name: Laura. That's my little
speech, Chief Inspector! You're not the only one who's

heard it.' She was smiling sufficiently as she spoke though, showing small, very white teeth – a woman in her early thirties, fair-complexioned, with a pair of disproportionately large spectacles on her pretty nose; a smallish woman, about 5 foot 4 inches. But it was her voice which interested Morse: the broad north-country vowels in "luv" and "blunt"; the pleasing nairm she had – and perhaps the not unpleasant prospect of meeting her sometime orver a drink with her hair doon . . .

They sat on a pair of high stools in a room that reminded Morse of his hated physics lab at school, and she told him of the simple yet quite extraordinary findings. The report on which Max had been working, though incomplete, was incontestable: the bones discovered in Wytham Woods were those of an adult male, Caucasian, about 5 foot 6 inches in height, slimly built, brachycephalic, fair-haired . . .

But Morse's mind had already leaped many furlongs ahead of the field. He'd been sure that the bones had been those of Karin Eriksson. All right, he'd been wrong. But now he *knew* whose bones they were – for the face of the man in the photograph was staring back at him, unmistakably. He asked only for a photocopy of Dr Hobson's brief, preliminary report, and rose to go.

The pair of them walked to the locked outer door in silence, for the death of Max was heavy on her mind too.

'You knew him well, didn't you?'

Morse nodded.

'I feel so sad,' she said simply.

Morse nodded again. '"The cart is shaken all to pieces, and the rugged road is at its end."'

She watched him, the slightly balding grey-haired man, as he stood for a few seconds beside his Jaguar. He held the photocopied report in his left hand, and raised it a few inches in farewell. She relocked the door, and walked thoughtfully back to the lab.

Morse wondered about driving up to the JR2, but decided against it. There was little time anyway. An urgent meeting of senior police officers had been summoned for 11 a.m. at the HQ building, and in any case there was nothing he could do. He drove along Parks Road, past Keble College, and then turned right into the Banbury Road. He had a few minutes to spare, and he took the second right turn now, and drove on slowly into Park Town, driving clockwise along the North Crescent, and along the South Crescent ... There would be little chance of doing much that day though, and in any case it would be better to postpone things for twenty-four hours or so.

Senior personnel from both the City and the County Forces were meeting at a time of considerable public disquiet – and criticism. Hitherto the impression had been abroad that known ringleaders were joy-riding and shop-ramming almost with impunity; and that the police were doing little to check the teenage tearaways who were terrifying many sections of the community on the Broadmoor Lea estate. There was little justification for such a view, since the police were continually finding themselves hamstrung by the refusal of the local inhabitants to come out and name names and co-operate in seeking to clean up their crime-ridden neighbourhood. But the death of Marion Bridewell had changed all that.

During this Sunday, 19 July, major decisions were taken, and their immediate implementation planned: a string of arrests would be made in a co-ordinated swoop the following morning, with special sittings of magistrates' courts scheduled for the following two evenings; council workmen would be sent in during the next few days to erect bollards and to construct sleeping-policeman humps across selected streets; police presence on the estate during the next week would be doubled; and a liaison committee of police officers, local head-teachers, social workers, and church ministers would be constituted forthwith.

It was a long and sometimes ill-humoured meeting; and Morse himself contributed little of any importance to the deliberations, for in truth his mind was distanced, and only once had his interest been fully engaged. It had been Strange's inveterate cynicism about committees which had occasioned the little contretemps:

'Give us a week or two at this rate,' he growled, 'and we'll have a standing committee, a steering committee, an *ad hoc* committee – every committee you can put a name to. What we should be doing is hitting 'em where it hurts. *Fining* 'em; fining their dads; docking it off their dads' wages. That's what I reckon!'

The Chief Constable had agreed quietly. 'Splendid idea – and the new legislation, I think, is going to be a big help to us. But there's just one snag, isn't there? You see, a good many of these young lads haven't *got* any fathers, Superintendent.'

Strange had looked disconcerted then.

And Morse had smiled his second smile of the day.

CHAPTER THIRTY-FOUR

The newly arrived resident in North Oxford is likely to
find that although his next-door neighbour has a first-
class degree from some prestigious university this man is
not quite so clever as his wife

(*Country Living*, January 1992)

MORSE was on his own when finally, in mid-morning
the following day, he drove down to Park Town, this
time again slowly circling the two crescents on either
side of the elliptical central garden, well stocked with
trees and flowering shrubs. There were plenty of parking spaces, and after his second circuit he pulled in the
Jaguar along the south side and walked past the fronts
of the dozen Italianate properties which comprised the
attractive stone-faced terrace. At the eastern end he
turned down an alley-way, and then into the lane, about
three yards wide, which ran behind the properties. To
his right the continuous brick wall which protected the
small back gardens was only about five feet in height,
and he realized that it would not even be necessary to
enter any of the gardens to find the one he was looking
for. It was all childishly easy – no Holmesian intellect
needed here; indeed a brief Watsonian reconnoitre
would have established the spot almost immediately.
Thus it was that after only a couple of minutes Morse

found himself leaning over the curved coping-stones of the western-most property, and finding the details on his photographs so easily matchable here: the configuration of the black drain-pipes, the horizontal TV aerial, and then, crucially, the tree upon whose lower bough a child's red swing was now affixed. At the left of the garden, as Morse observed it, was a wooden garden seat, its slats disintegrating; and he felt thrillingly certain that it was from this seat, in this very garden, that someone – and most probably Karin Eriksson herself – had taken the two photographs of the fairheaded, bracycephalic, slimly built . . . what else had Dr Hobson said? He couldn't remember. And it didn't matter. Not at all.

He walked to the imposing front door of the end property, designated 'Seckham Villa' by a small plaque on the right-hand wall of the porch; and below it, three bells: second floor Dr S. Levi; first floor Ms Jennifer Coombs; ground floor Dr Alasdair McBryde. An area clearly where D.Phils and Ph.Ds proliferated. He rang the bottom bell.

The door was opened by a tallish, heavily bearded man in his mid-thirties, who studied Morse's authorization cautiously before answering any questions. He was over from Ostrylia (he said) with his wife, to pursue some research project in micro-biology; they had been in the flat since the previous August, and would be returning home in two weeks' time; he'd learned of the property from a friend in Mansfield College who had been keeping an eye open for suitable accommodation the previous summer.

The previous August . . .

Was this to be Morse's lucky day?

'Did you know the people – did you *meet* the people who were here before you?'

'Fried not,' said the Australian.

'Can I – have a quick look inside?'

Rather unenthusiastically, as it seemed, McBryde led the way into the lounge, where Morse looked around the rather splendid, high-ceilinged room, and tried to attune his senses to the vaguest vibrations. Without success. It was only when he looked out through the french window at the sunlit patch of lawn that he felt a frisson of excitement: a dark-haired little girl in a pink dress was swinging idly to and fro beneath the tree, her white ankle-socked feet just reaching the ground.

'Your daughter, sir?'

'Yeah. You got any kids yourself, Inspector?'

Morse shook his head. 'Just one more thing, sir. Have you got your book, you know, your rent-book or whatever handy? It's important I get in touch with the, er, people who were here just before you last year . . .'

McBryde stepped over to an escritoire beside the french window and found his Property Payment book, the legend 'Finders Keepers' on the cover.

'I'm not in arrears,' said McBryde with the suggestion of his first smile.

'So I see. And I'm not a bailiff, sir,' said Morse, handing back the book.

The two men walked back towards the entrance, and McBryde knocked very gently on the door to his right, and put his ear to the panel.

'Darling? Darling?'

But there was no reply.

At the front door Morse asked his last question.

'Finders Keepers – that's the Banbury Road office, is it?'

'Yeah. You off there now?'

'I think I'll drop in straightaway, yes.'

'Is your car parked here?'

Morse pointed to the Jaguar.

'Well, I should leave it here, if I were you. Only five minutes' walk, if that – and you'll never park in North Parade.'

Morse nodded. Good idea. And the Rose and Crown was just along in North Parade.

Before leaving Park Town however, Morse strolled across into the central oval-shaped garden separating the Crescents, where he read the only notice he could find, fixed to the trunk of a cedar tree:

THIS GARDEN, LAID OUT CIRCA 1850, IS MAINTAINED
BY THE RESIDENTS FOR PLEASURE AND PEACE.
PLEASE RESPECT ITS AMENITIES.
NO DOGS, BICYCLES, BALL GAMES, OR TRANSISTORS.

For a few minutes Morse sat on one of the wooden seats, where someone had obviously not respected the amenities, for an oblong plate, doubtless commemorating the name of a former inhabitant, had been recently prised from the back. It was a restful spot though, and Morse now walked slowly round its periphery, his mind half on Max's death, half on the photographs taken in the back garden of the ground-floor flat at Seckham Villa. As he turned at the western edge of the garden, he realized that this same Seckham Villa was immediately across the road from him, with the maroon Jaguar parked just to the left of it. And as once again he admired the attractive frontages there, he suspected perhaps that a heavily bearded face had suddenly pulled itself back behind the rather dingy curtains in the front room of Seckham Villa, where Mrs Something McBryde lay suffering from goodness knows what. Was her husband slightly more inquisitive than he'd appeared to be? Or was it the Jaguar – which often attracted some interested glances?

Thoughtfully Morse walked out of Park Town, then left into the Banbury Road. Finders Keepers was very close. So was North Parade. So was the Rose and Crown.

CHAPTER THIRTY-FIVE

Doing business without advertising is like winking at a girl in the dark. You know what you are doing, but nobody else does

(Stewart Henderson Britt, *New York Herald Tribune*, 30 October 1956)

AFTER two pints of cask-conditioned ale in the Rose and Crown, Morse walked the short distance to Finders Keepers, where he was soon ushered through the outer office, past two young ladies busy with their VDUs, and into the inner sanctum of Mr Martin Buckby, the dark, smartly suited manager of Property Letting Services. It was fairly close to lunch-time, but the manager would be only too glad to help – of course he would.

Yes, his department was responsible for letting a good many of the Park Town properties, most of which had been converted from single homes into two, sometimes three, flats and were more often than not let out to graduates, occasionally to students. Naturally the accommodation varied, but some of the flats, especially those on the ground floor – or first floor, as some of them called it – were roomy, stylish, and well maintained. The letting year usually divided itself into two main periods: October to June, covering the academic year at Oxford University; and then June/July to the

end of September, when very frequently various overseas tenants were interested in short-term leases.
Advertisements for the availability of such accommodation were regularly placed in *The Oxford Times*; and
occasionally in *Property Weekly*. But only advertised once,
for the flats were almost invariably snapped up straightaway. Such adverts gave a brief description of the
property available, and the price asked: about £200–
£250 a week for a short-term let (at current rates) and
slightly less, proportionately, for a long-term let. Business, in the first instance, was usually conducted by
phone, often through agents; and someone – either the
client himself or a representative of an agency – would
go along to view the property ('Very important, Inspector!') before the paperwork was completed, either
there in the firm's offices or, increasingly now, directly
by fax interchange with countries overseas. A deposit
would be lodged, a tenancy agreement signed, reference given – that was how it worked. There was no
guarantee of bona fides, of course, and basically one had
to rely on gut-reaction; but the firm experienced very
few problems, really. When the client was due to move
in, a representative would go along to open the property, hand over keys, explain the workings of gas,
electricity, stop-cocks, central heating, fuses, thermo-
stats, everything, and to give the client a full inventory
of the property's effects – this inventory to be checked
and returned within seven days so that there could be
no subsequent arguments about the complement of
fish-knives or feather pillows. The system worked well.
The only example of odd behaviour over the previous

year, for example, had been the overnight disappearance of a South American gentleman who had taken his key with him – and absolutely nothing else. And since, as with all short-term lets, the whole of the rental was paid in advance, as well as an extra deposit of £500, no harm had been done there – apart from the need to change the lock on the front door and to get a further clutch of keys cut.

'Did you report that to the police, sir?'

'No. Should I have done?'

Morse shrugged.

He had a good grasp now of the letting procedure; yet his mind was always happier (he explained) with specific illustrations than with generalities; and if it were proper for him to ask, for example, what Dr McBryde was paying for the ground-floor flat at Seckham Villa . . .?

Buckby found a green folder in the filing cabinet behind him and quickly looked through it. 'Thirteen hundred pounds per month.'

'Phew! Bit steep, isn't it?'

'It's the going rate – and it's a lovely flat, isn't it? One of the best in the whole crescent.' Buckby picked out a sheet from the folder and read the specification aloud.

But Morse was paying scant attention to him. After all, that was the manager's job, wasn't it? To make the most of what Morse had seen with his own eyes as a pretty limited bit of Lebensraum, especially for a married couple with one infant – at least one infant.

'Didn't you just say that the maximum for a short-term let was two hundred and fifty pounds a week?'

Buckby grinned. 'Not for *that* place – well, you've seen it. And what makes you think it's a *short*-term let, Inspector?'

The blood was tingling at the back of Morse's neck, and subliminally some of the specifications that Buckby had recited were beginning to register in his brain. He reached over and picked up the sheet.

> Hall, living room, separate dining room, well-fitted kitchen, two bedrooms, studio/study, bathroom, full gas CH, small walled garden

Two bedrooms . . . and a sick wife sleeping in one of them . . . studio . . . and a little girl sitting on a swing . . . God! Morse shook his head in disbelief at his own idiocy.

'I really came to ask you, sir, if you had any record of who was living in that property last July. But I think – I *think* – you're going to tell me that it was Dr Alasdair McBryde; that he hasn't got a wife; that the people upstairs have got a little dark-haired daughter; that the fellow probably hails from Malta—'

'Gibraltar, actually.'

'You've got some spare keys, sir?' asked Morse, almost despairingly.

In front of Seckham Villa the Jaguar sat undisturbed; but inside there were to be no further sightings of Dr

McBryde. Yet the little girl still sat on the swing, gently stroking her dolly's hair, and Morse unlocked the french window and walked over the grass towards her.

'What's your name?'

'My name's Lucy and my dolly's name's Amanda.'

'Do you live here, Lucy?'

'Yes. Mummy and Daddy live up there.' Her bright eyes lifted to the top rear window.

'Pretty dolly,' said Morse.

'Would you like to hold her?'

'I would, yes – but I've got a lot of things to do just for the moment.'

Inside his brain he could hear a voice shouting, 'Help, Lewis!' and he turned back into the house and wondered where on earth to start.

CHAPTER THIRTY-SIX

Nine tenths of the appeal of pornography is due to the indecent feelings concerning sex which moralists inculcate in the young; the other tenth is physiological, and will occur in one way or another whatever the state of the law may be

(Bertrand Russell, *Marriage and Morals*)

LEWIS arrived at Seckham Villa at 2.15 that afternoon, bringing with him the early edition of *The Oxford Mail*, in which many column-inches were devoted to the wave of car crime which was hitting Oxfordshire – hitting the national press, too, with increasing regularity. Everyone and everything in turn was blamed: the police, the parents, the teachers, the church, the recession, unemployment, lack of youth facilities, car manufacturers, the weather, the TV, the brewers, left-wing social workers, and right-wing social workers; original sin received several votes, and even the Devil himself got one. Paradoxically the police seemed to be more in the dock than the perpetrators of the increasingly vicious crimes being committed. But at least the operation that morning had been successful, so Lewis reported: the only trouble was that further police activity in Wytham Woods was drastically curtailed – four men only now, one of them standing guard over the area cordoned off in Pasticks.

The temporarily dispirited Morse received the news with little surprise, and briefly brought Lewis up to date with his own ambivalent achievements of the morning: his discovery of the garden where in all probability Karin Eriksson had spent some period of time before she disappeared; and his gullibility in allowing McBryde – fairly certainly now a key figure in the drama – more than sufficient time to effect a hurried escape.

At the far end of the ground-floor entrance passage, fairly steep stairs, turning 180 degrees, led down to the basement area in Seckham Villa, and it was here that the first discovery was made. The basement comprised a large, modernized kitchen at the front; and behind this, through an archway, a large living area furnished with armchairs, a settee, coffee tables, bookshelves, TV, HiFi equipment – and a double-bed of mahogany, stripped down to a mattress of pale blue; and beside the bed, a jointed series of square, wooden boards, four of them, along which, for the length of about ten feet, ran two steel rails – rails where, it was immediately assumed, a cine-camera had recently and probably frequently been moving to and fro.

Morse himself (with Lewis and one of the DCs) spent most of his time that afternoon in this area, once the fingerprint men, the senior scenes-of-crime officer and the photographer had completed their formal tasks. Clear fingerprints on the (unwashed) non-stick saucepan and cutlery found in the kitchen sink would doubtless match the scores of others found throughout the flat, would doubtless be McBryde's, and (as Morse saw things) would doubtless advance the investigation not one whit. No clothing, apart from two dirty pairs of beige socks found in one of the bedrooms; no toiletries left along the bathroom shelves; no videos; no correspondence; no shredded letters in either of the two waste-paper baskets or in the dustbin outside the back door. All in all it seemed fairly clear that the flat had been slimmed down – recently perhaps? – for the eventuality of a speedy get-away. Yet there were items that had *not* been bundled and stuffed into the back of the white van which (as was quickly ascertained) McBryde had used for travelling; and cupboards in both the ground-floor and the basement contained duvets, sheets, pillow-cases, blankets, towels, and table cloths – clearly items listed on the tenant's inventory; and the kitchen pantry was adequately stocked with tins of beans, fruit, salmon, spaghetti, tuna fish, and the like.

Naturally however it was the trackway beside the basement double bed which attracted the most interest, much lifting of eyebrows, and many lascivious asides amongst those investigators whose powers of detection, at least in this instance, were the equal of the chief inspector's. Indeed, it would have required a man of monumental mutton-headedness not to visualize before him the camera and the microphone moving slowly alongside the mattress to record the assorted feats of fornication enacted on that creaking charpoy. For himself Morse tried not to give his imagination too free a rein. Sometimes up at HQ there were a few pornographic videos around, confiscated from late-night raids or illegal trafficking. Often had he wished to view some of the crude, corrupting, seductive things; yet equally often had he made it known to his fellow officers that he at least was quite uninterested in such matters.

In a corner of the kitchen, bundled neatly as if for some subsequent collection by Friends of the Earth, was a heap of old newspapers, mostly the *Daily Mail*, and various weeklies and periodicals, including *Oxford Today*, *Oxcom*, *TV Times*, two RSPB journals, and the previous Christmas offers from the Spastic Society. Morse had glanced very hurriedly through, half hoping perhaps to find the statutory girlie magazine; but apart from spending a minute or so looking at pictures of the black-headed gulls on the Loch of Kinnordy, he found nothing there to hold his interest.

It was Lewis who found them, folded away inside one of the free local newspapers, *The Star*. There were fourteen A4 sheets, stapled together, obviously photo-copied (and photocopied ill) from some glossier and fuller publication. On each sheet several photographs of the same girl were figured (if that be the correct verb) in various stages of undress; and at the bottom of each sheet there appeared a Christian name, followed by details of height, bust, waist, hips, dress- shoe- and glove-measurements, and colour of hair and eyes. In almost every case the bottom left-hand picture was of the model completely naked, and in three or four cases striking some sexually suggestive pose. The names were of the glitzy showgirl variety: Jayne, Kelly, Lindy-Lu, Mandy . . . and most of them appeared (for age was not given) to be in their twenties. But four of the sheets depicted older women, whose names were possibly designed to reflect their comparative maturity: Elaine, Dorothy, Mary, Louisa ... The only other information given (no addresses here) was a (i), (ii), (iii), of priority 'services', and Lewis, not without some little interest himself (and amusement), sampled a few of the services on offer: sporting-shots, escort duties, lingerie, stockings, leather, swim-wear, summer dresses, bras, nude-modelling, hair-styling, gloves. Not much to trouble the law there, surely. Three of the girls though were far more explicit about their specialisms, with Mandy listing (i) home videos, (ii) pornographic movies, (iii) overnight escort duties; and with Lindy-Lu, pictured up to her thighs in leather boots, proclaiming an accomplished proficiency in spanking.

And then, as Morse and Lewis were considering these things, the big discovery was made. One of the two DCs who had been given the job of searching the main lounge above had found, caught up against the top of one of the drawers in the escritoire, a list of names and addresses: a list of clients, surely! Clients who probably received their pornographic material in plain brown envelopes with the flap licked down so very firmly. And there, fourth from the top, was the name that both Morse and Lewis focused on immediately: George Daley, Blenheim Villas, Begbroke, Oxon.

Morse had been delighted with the find – of course he had! And his praise for the DC had been profuse and (in Lewis's view) perhaps a trifle extravagant. Yet now as he sat on the settee, looking again at the unzippings and the unbuttonings of the models, reading through the list of names once more, he appeared to Lewis to be preoccupied and rather sad.

'Everything all right, sir?'

'What? Oh yes! Fine. We're making wonderful progress. Let's keep at it!'

But Morse himself was contributing little towards any further progress; and after desultorily walking around for ten minutes or so, he sat down yet again and picked up the sheet of addresses. He would have to tell Lewis, he decided – not just yet but ... He looked again at the seventeenth name on the list: for he was never likely to forget the name that Kidlington HQ had given him when, from Lyme Regis, he'd phoned in the car registration H 35 LWL:

Dr Alan Hardinge.

He picked up the pictures of the models and looked again through their names and their vital statistics and their special proficiencies. Especially did he look again at one of the maturer models: the one who called herself 'Louise'; the one who'd had all sorts of fun with her names at the Bay Hotel in Lyme Regis; the woman who was photographed here, quite naked and totally desirable.

Claire Osborne.

'Pity we've no address for – well, it must be a modelling agency of some sort, mustn't it?'

'No problem, Lewis. We can just ring up one of these johnnies on the list.'

'Perhaps *they* don't know.'

'I'll give you the address in ten minutes if you really want it.'

'I don't want it for myself, you know.'

'Of course not!'

Picking up his sheets, Morse decided that his presence in Seckham Villa was no longer required; and bidding Lewis to give things another couple of hours or so he returned to HQ; where he tried her telephone number.

She was in.

'Claire?'

'Morse!' (She'd recognized him!)

'You could have told me you worked for an escort agency!'

'Why?'

Morse couldn't think of an answer.

'You thought I was wicked enough but not quite so wicked as that?'

'I suppose so.'

'Why don't you get yourself in your car and come over tonight? I'd be happy if you did . . .'

Morse sighed deeply. 'You told me you had a daughter—'

'So?'

'Do you still keep in touch with the father?'

'The father? Christ, come off it! I couldn't tell you who the father *was*!'

Like the veil of the Temple, Morse's heart was suddenly rent in twain; and after asking her for the name and address of the modelling agency (which she refused to tell him) he rang off.

Ten minutes later, the phone went on Morse's desk, and it was Claire – though how she'd got his number he didn't know. She spoke for only about thirty seconds, ignoring Morse's interruptions.

'Shut up, you silly bugger! You can't see more than two inches in front of your nose, can you? Don't you realize I'd have swapped all the lecherous sods I've ever had for you – and instead of trying to understand all you ask me – Christ! – is who fathered—'

'Look, Claire—'

'No! *You* bloody look! If you can't take what a woman tells you about herself without picking over the past and asking bloody futile questions about why and who he was and—' But her voice broke down completely now.

'Look, please!'

'No! You just fuck off, Morse, and don't you ring me again because I'll probably be screwing somebody and enjoying it such a lot I won't want to be interrupted—'

'Claire!'

But the line was dead.

For the next hour Morse tried her number every five minutes, counting up to thirty double-purrs each time. But there was no answer.

Lewis had discovered nothing new in Seckham Villa, and he rang through to HQ at 6 p.m., as Morse had wished.

'All right. Well, you get off home early, Lewis. And get some sleep. And good luck tomorrow!'

Lewis was due to catch the 7.30 plane to Stockholm the following morning.

CHAPTER THIRTY-SEVEN

To be buried while alive is, beyond question, the most terrifying of those extremes which has ever fallen to the lot of mere mortality

(Edgar Allan Poe, *Tales of Mystery and Imagination*)

THE DEATH of Max was still casting a cloak of gloom round Morse as he sat in his office the following morning. During the previous night his thoughts had been much preoccupied with death, and the mood persisted now. As a boy, he had been moved by those words of the dying Socrates, suggesting that if death were just one long, unbroken, dreamless sleep, then a greater boon could hardly be bestowed upon mankind. But what about the body? The soul might be able to look after itself all right, but what about the physical body? In Morse's favourite episode from *The Iliad*, the brethren and kinsfolk of Sarpedon had buried his body, with mound and pillar, in the rich, wide land of Lycia. Yes! It was fitting to have a gravestone and a name inscribed on it. But there were those stories that were ever frightening – stories about people prematurely interred who had awoken in infinite and palpitating terror with the immovable lid of the coffin only a few inches above them. No! Burning was better than burying, surely ... Morse was wholly ignorant of the immediate procedures effected once the curtains closed over the light-wooded coffins at the crematoria . . . like the curtains closing at the end of *Götterdämmerung*, though minus the clapping, of course. All done and finished quickly, and if somebody wanted to sprinkle your mortal dust over the memorial gardens, well, it might be OK for the roses, too. He wouldn't mind a couple of hymns either: 'The day thou gavest', perhaps. Good tune, that. So long as they didn't have any prayers, or any departures from the Authorized Version of Holy Writ . . . Perhaps Max had got it right, neatly side-stepping the choice of interment or incineration: the clever old sod had left his body to the hospital, and the odds were strongly on one or two of his organs giving them plenty to think about. Huh!

Morse smiled to himself, and suddenly looked up to see Strange standing in the doorway.

'Private joke, Morse?'

'Oh, nothing, sir.'

'C'mon! Life's grim enough.'

'I was just thinking of Max's liver—'

'Not a pretty sight!'

'No.'

'You're taking it a bit hard, aren't you? Max, I mean.'

'A bit, perhaps.'

'You seen the latest?'

Strange pushed a copy of *The Times* across the desk, with a brief paragraph on the front page informing its readers that 'the bones discovered in Wytham Woods are quite certainly not those of the Swedish student whose disappearance occasioned the original verses and their subsequent analysis in this newspaper. (See Letters, page 13)'.

'Anything to help us there?' asked Morse dubiously, opening the paper.

'Scraping the barrel, if you ask me,' said Strange.

Morse looked down at page 13:

From Mr Anthony Beaulah

Sir, like the text of some early Greek, love-lyric, the lines on the Swedish student would appear to have been pondered over in such exhaustive fashion that there is perhaps little left to say. And it may be that the search is already over. Yet there is one significant (surely?) aspect of the verses which has hitherto received scant attention. The collocation of 'the tiger' with 'the burning of the night' (lines 9 and 12) has indeed been commented upon, but in no *specific* context. In my view, sir, one should perhaps interpret the tiger (the cat) as staring back at drivers in the darkness. And the brilliantly simple invention which has long steered the benighted driver through the metaphorical forest of the night? Cat's eyes!

I myself live too far away from Oxford to be able to test such a thesis. But might the police not interpret this as a genuine clue, and look for some stretch of road (in or around Wytham?) where cat's eyes have recently been installed?

Yours
ANTHONY BEAULAH,
Felsted School,
Essex.

'Worth getting Lewis on it?' queried Strange, when Morse had finished reading.

'Not this morning, sir. If you remember he's, er, on

his holidays.' Morse looked at his wrist-watch. 'At this minute he's probably looking out of the window down at Jutland.'

'Why didn't *you* go, Morse? With all these Swedish blondes and that . . .'

'I thought it'd be good experience for him.'

'Mm.'

For a while the two were silent. Then Strange picked up his paper and made to leave.

'You made a will yet, Morse?'

'Not much to leave, really.'

'All those records of yours, surely?'

'Bit out of date, I'm afraid. We're all buying CDs now.'

'Perhaps *they'll* be out of date soon.'

Morse nodded. Strange was not in the habit of saying anything quite so perceptive.

CHAPTER THIRTY-EIGHT

Men are made stronger on realization that the helping
hand they need is at the end of their own right arm
(Sidney J. Phillips, speech, July 1953)

ON THE forty-kilometre bus ride from Arlanda airport
southwards towards Stockholm, Lewis enjoyed what for
him was the fairly uncommon view of a foreign country.
After a while the tracts of large pine and fir woods
changed to smaller coppices and open fields; then farm-
houses, red, with barns that were red too, and a few
yellow, wooden, Dutch-roofed manor houses, just before
the outskirts of Stockholm, with its factories and tidy,
newish buildings – and all so very clean and litter-free.
In wooded surroundings within the city itself, three- and
four-storeyed blocks of flats took over; and finally the
end of the journey, at the Central Station terminal.

Lewis had never studied a foreign language at
school, and his travel abroad had hitherto been
restricted to three weeks in Australia, two weeks in Italy,
and one afternoon in a Calais supermarket. The fact
that he had no difficulty therefore in summoning a taxi
was wholly due to the excellent English of the young
driver, who soon brought Lewis into the suburb of
Bromma – more specifically to an eight-storey block of
white flats in Bergsvägen.

The Stockholm CID had offered to send one of its own men to meet him, but Lewis had not taken advantage of this when he'd arranged the details of his visit the previous morning. Seldom was it that he could assert any independent judgement in an investigation; and here was his chance.

The entrance hall was of polished pink granite, with the long list of tenants' names displayed there:

ANDREASSON	8A
ENGSTRÖM	8B
FASTÉN	7A
OLSSON	7B
KRAFT	6A
ERIKSSON	6B

Sixth floor!

Lewis felt excited at the sight of the name; it was almost as if . . . as if he felt he was going to make some significant discovery.

The door, bearing the name-plate ERIKSSON, was opened by a woman in her mid-forties, of medium height, plumply figured, hazel-eyed, and with short, brownish-blonde hair.

'Mrs Eriksson?'

'Irma Eriksson,' she insisted as he shook her hand, and entered the apartment.

The small hallway was lined with cupboards, with what looked like a home-woven mat on one wall and a large mirror on the other. Through the open door to the right Lewis glimpsed a beautifully fitted kitchen, fresh and gleaming, with a copper kettle and old plates on its walls.

'In here, Mr Lewis.' She pointed smilingly to the left and led the way.

Her English was very good, utterly fluent and idiomatic, with only a hint of a foreign accent, just noticeable perhaps in the slight lengthening of the short 'i' vowels ('Meester Lewis').

The place was all so *clean*; and so particularly clean was the parquet flooring that Lewis wondered whether he should offer to take off his shoes, for she herself stood there in her stockinged feet as she gestured him to a seat on a low, brown-striped settee.

As he later tried to describe the furnishings to Morse, he felt more conscious than anything about the huge amount of stuff that had been packed into this living room: two coffee tables of heavy, dark wood; lots of indoor plants; groups of family portraits and photographs all around; dozens of candle holders; a large TV set; pretty cushions everywhere; vases of flowers; a set of Dala horses; two crucifixes; and (as Lewis learned later) a set of Carl Larsson prints above the bricked fireplace. Yet in spite of all the clutter, the whole room was light and airy, the thin curtains pulled completely back from the south-facing window.

Conversation was easy and, for Lewis, interesting. He learned something of the typical middle-class housing in Swedish cities; learned how and why the Erikssons had moved from Uppsala down to Bergsvägen almost a year ago after ... after Karin had, well, whatever had happened. As Lewis went briefly through the statement she had made a year ago, Irma Eriksson was watching him closely (he could see that), nodding here and there, and at one or two points staring down sadly at a small oriental carpet at her feet. But yes, it was all there; and no, there was nothing she could add. From that day to this she had received no further news of her daughter – none. At first, she admitted, she'd hoped and hoped, and couldn't bring herself to believe that Karin was dead. But gradually she had been forced to such a conclusion; and it was better that way, really – to accept the virtual certainty that Karin had been murdered. She was grateful – how not? – for the recent efforts the English police had made – again! – and she had been following the newspaper correspondence of course, receiving cuttings regularly from an English friend.

'Can I get you coffee? And a leetle Swedish Schnapps, yes?'

When she went out to the kitchen, Lewis could scarcely believe that it had been himself who had answered 'yes' to the first, and 'yes' to the second. So often in his police career he'd prayed for Morse to be on hand to help him; but not now. He stood up and walked slowly round the room, staring long at some of the photographs; and especially at one of them: at three young ladies standing arm in arm, dressed in Swedish national costume.

'Ah! I see you've found my beautiful daughters.'

She had moved in silently, and now stood beside him, still in her stockinged feet, some five or six inches shorter than the six-foot sergeant; and he could smell the sweet summer freshness of her, and he felt an unfamiliar tic in a vein at his right temple.

'Katarina, Karin, Kristina.' She pointed to each in turn. 'All of them better looking than their momma, no?'

Lewis made no direct reply as he still held the framed photograph. So much alike the three of them: each with long, straight gold-blonde hair; each with clear-complexioned, high-cheekboned faces.

'That's Karin – in the middle, you say?' Lewis looked at her again, the one who was looking perhaps just a little more serious than her sisters.

Momma nodded; then, unexpectedly, took the photograph from Lewis's hands and replaced it – with no explanation for her slightly brusque behaviour.

'How can I help you any more?' She sat cross-legged opposite Lewis in an armchair, tossed back her small, squat glass of Schnapps, before sipping the hot, strong coffee.

So Lewis asked her a lot of questions, and was soon to be forming a much clearer picture of the daughter about whom her mother spoke so lovingly now.

Karin had been a reasonably clever girl, if occasionally somewhat idle; she had left her secondary school in Uppsala at the age of eighteen, with good prospects before her; attractive, *very* good at swimming and tennis; and with a series of badges and diplomas from school societies and guides' groups for birdwatching, orienteering, rock-climbing, judo, embroidery, and amateur musicals. It was just after she had left school that Irma's husband, Staffan Eriksson, had moved in with a darkly seductive brunette he had met on a business trip to Norway and, well, that was about it really. She uncrossed her legs and looked over at Lewis with a gentle smile.

'Another Schnapps?'

'Why not?' said Mr Lewis.

Katarina (Irma Eriksson resumed), the eldest daughter (should it be 'elder' now, though?), was married and working with the European Commission in Strasbourg as an interpreter; the youngest (younger) daughter, Kristina – still only eighteen – was in her last year of schooling, studying social sciences. She was living at home, there in the flat, and if Mr Lewis would like to see her . . .? If Mr Lewis were *staying* in Stockholm?

The troublesome tic jerked in Lewis's temple once more, as he turned the conversation back to Karin.

What was Karin *like* – as a person? Well, her mother supposed she would call her 'independent' – yes, above all, independent. The summer before she'd gone to England, she'd spent two months on a kibbutz near Tel Aviv; and the year before that she'd joined a group of enthusiastic environmentalists in the Arctic Circle. But she was never (for the first time Irma Eriksson had seemed to struggle with her English vocabulary) she was never an 'easy' young girl. No! That wasn't the word at all! She was never the sort of girl who went to bed, you know . . .?

'Was she – do you think she was a virgin, Mrs Eriksson?'

'"Irma", please!'

'As far as you know . . . Irma?'

'I'm not sure. Apart from the trouble in Israel, if she had sex with anyone it would be with someone she liked. You know how I mean, don't you?'

'She was fond of birdwatching, you said?' Lewis was losing his way. (Or was he?)

'Oh, yes! Never did she go out on any holiday or walk without taking the binoculars.' (The idiom was breaking down – just a bit.)

There was just the one thing left now which Morse had asked him to confirm: the passport and the work-permit procedures for a young lady like Karin.

No problem. For the first time Lewis thought he saw the underlying grief behind the saddened eyes, as she explained that Sweden did not belong to the EC; that all Swedish nationals needed to apply for work-permits in the UK if they proposed to stay for any length of time; that even for au pair work it was wholly prudent so to do. But Karin had not applied for such a permit; she gave herself only three weeks in the UK; and for this, her Swedish passport, valid for a ten-year period, would have been sufficient.

Lewis was suddenly aware that if there *had* been anything mildly flirtatious in the woman's manner, the situation had now changed.

'You kept Karin's passport, didn't you?' she continued quietly.

Lewis nodded, and his slight frown prompted her quick explanation:

'You see, I suppose we hoped she might – if she were

217

still alive – she might apply for a new passport – if she'd *lost* it. Do you see . . .?'

Lewis nodded again.

'And she hasn't, has she, Mr Lewis? So!' She got up briskly, and put her feet into a pair of black, semi-heeled shoes. 'So!'

'I'm afraid we can't bring you any hopeful news – not really,' said Lewis, himself now rising to his feet.

'It's all right. I knew from the start, really. It's just . . .'

'I know. And thank you. You've been very helpful. Just one more thing – if I could just *borrow* a photo of the three girls . . .?'

As they stood in the hallway, Lewis ventured a genuine compliment:

'You know, I always envy people like you, Mrs – Irma – you know, people who can speak other languages.'

'We start learning English early though. In the fourth grade – ten years of age. Well, I was twelve myself, but my daughters all learn from ten.'

They shook hands, and Lewis walked down to the ground floor, where he stood for several minutes beside a play area surrounded by a low palisade of dark-brown wooden slats – not a potato-crisp packet in sight. It was early afternoon now on a beautiful summer's day, with a cloudless blue sky and a yellow sun – like the colours of the flag on the rucksack found at Begbroke, Oxfordshire.

Standing on her high balcony, Irma Eriksson

watched him go. As soon as he had disappeared into the main thoroughfare, she stepped back into her flat and let herself into the rear bedroom, where the ensuing conversation was held in Swedish:

'Was he intelligent?'

'Not particularly. Very nice though – *very* nice.'

'Did you ask him to bed with you?'

'I might have done if *you* hadn't been here.'

'Do you think he suspected anything?'

'No.'

'But you're glad he's gone?'

Irma Eriksson nodded. 'Shall I get you coffee?'

'Please!'

When her mother had left, the young lady looked at herself in the long wall-mirror in the shaded room, deciding that she was looking tired and dark around the eyes. Yet had Lewis seen her there that afternoon he would have been impressed by her pale and elegant beauty; would have been struck immediately too by a very close likeness to the photograph of the student found in the rucksack at Begbroke, Oxfordshire.

CHAPTER THIRTY-NINE

In a world in which duty and self-discipline have lost out to hedonism and self-satisfaction, there is nothing like closing your eyes and going with the flow. At least in a fantasy, it all ends happily ever after

(Edwina Currie, *The Observer*, 23 February 1992)

ALAN HARDINGE had gained a first in both parts of the Natural Sciences Tripos at Cambridge; had stayed on in that university for a Ph.D.; then done two years' research at Harvard before being elected in 1970 to a fellowship at the 'other place'. A year later he had courted a librarian from the Bodleian, had married her six months later, subsequently siring two offspring, both girls: the one now in her second year at Durham reading Psychology; the other dead – killed nineteen days earlier as she cycled down Cumnor Hill into Oxford.

He had not been wholly surprised to receive the phone call from Chief Inspector Morse that morning of Tuesday, 21 July, and a meeting was arranged for 2 p.m. the same day, in Hardinge's rooms, overlooking the front quad of Lonsdale College.

'What does your wife know about your interests in Seckham Villa?'

'Nothing. Absolutely nothing. So *please* can we keep

Lynne – my wife – out of this? She's still terribly upset and nervy – God knows what . . .'

Dr Hardinge spoke in disjunct bursts, punctuated by the equivalent of verbal dashes. He was a smallish, neat man, with crinkly grey hair, darkly suited still in high summer, when many of his colleagues were walking along the High in T-shirts and trainers.

'I can't promise that, of course—'

'Don't you see? I'd do anything – anything at all – to see that Lynne's not hurt. I know it sounds weak – it *is* weak – it's what we all say – I know – but it's true.' From his hunched shoulders Hardinge's face craned forward like that of an earnest tortoise.

'Know this man?' Morse handed across one of the photographs taken in the garden of Seckham Villa.

Hardinge took a pair of half-lensed spectacles from their case; but appeared not to need them, glancing for only a second or two at the photograph before handing it back.

'James – or Jamie? – Myton. Yes, I know him – knew him – sort of jack-of-all-trades really.'

'How did you get to know him?'

'Look – it'll be better if I tell you – about myself – I think it will.'

Morse listened with interest, and with no moral reproof, as Hardinge stated his apologia for a lifetime of sexual adventurism.

As a boy a series of older women had regularly intruded themselves into his dreams, and he had readily surrendered himself, *almost* without guilt, into the sexual fantasies he found he could so easily conjure up

221

for himself – fantasies in which there were no conse-
quences, no disappointments. In his twenties he would
willingly have preferred – *did* prefer – to watch the
pornographic films and videos that were then so readily
available. Then he'd met Lynne – dear, honest, trusting
Lynne – who would be utterly flabbergasted and so hurt
and ashamed if she even began to suspect a fraction of
the truth. After his marriage, though, his fantasies
persisted; grew even. He was experiencing a yearning
for ever greater variety in his sexual gratification, and
this had gradually resulted in a string of rather sordid
associations: with private film clubs; imported videos
and magazines; live sex-shows; 'hostess' parties – for all
of which he'd become a regular and eager client. The
anticipation of such occasions! The extraordinarily
arousing words that became the open sesame to such
erotic entertainments: 'Is everybody known?'

'And that's what happened regularly at Seckham
Villa?'

'Fairly regularly – seldom more than five or six of us
– usually people we'd met once or twice before.'

Morse watched the middle-aged, dapper deceiver,
leaning forward all the time, with his aquiline cast of
feature, his pale complexion, his slightly pernickety
enunciation. He felt he should have despised the man
a little; but he couldn't do that. If Hardinge were a
bit of a pervert, he was an extraordinarily honest
one; and with his faded, watery eyes he looked rather
tired and rather lost; weak, and not pretending to be
strong.

'You're not a "medical" doctor, sir?' asked Morse when the carnal confessions were complete.

'No. I just wrote a Ph.D. thesis – you know how these things are.'

'On?'

'Promise not to laugh?'

'Try me.'

'"The comparative body-weight of the great tit within the variable habitats of its North European distribution".'

Morse didn't laugh. Birds! So many people in the case seemed interested in birds . . .

'*Original* research, was that?'

'No other kind, as far as I know.'

'And you were *examined* in this?'

'You don't get a doctorate otherwise.'

'But the person who examined you – well, he couldn't know as much as *you*, could he? By definition, surely?'

'*She*, actually. It's the – well, they say it is – the *way* you go about it – your research; the way you observe, record things, categorize them, and then draw some kind of conclusion. Bit like your job, Inspector.'

'All I was thinking, sir, is that it might not have been difficult for you to fabricate a few of the facts . . .'

Hardinge frowned, his head moving forward on his shoulders once more. 'I am *not*, Inspector, fabricating anything about Seckham Villa – if that's what you're getting at.'

'And you first met Claire Osborne there.'

223

'She told you that was her name?'

'"Louisa Hardinge", too.'

Hardinge smiled sadly. 'Her one and only tribute to me! But she loves changing her name – all the time – she doesn't really know who she is ... or what she wants, Inspector. She's a sort of chameleon, I suppose. But you'll probably know that, won't you? I understand you've met her.'

'What *is* her name?'

'Her birth-certificate name? I don't really know.'

Morse shook his head. Was there *anyone* telling him the truth in this case?

'She never went to Seckham Villa herself – as far as I know,' resumed Hardinge. 'I met her through an agency. McBryde – you've spoken to him? – through McBryde. They give you photographs – interests – you know what I mean.'

'Measurements?'

'Measurements.'

'And you fell for her?'

Hardinge nodded. 'Not difficult to do that, is it?'

'You still in love with her?'

'Yes.'

'She with you?'

'No.'

'You'll have to give me the address of the agency.'

'I suppose so.'

'How do you manage to get all the stuff without your wife knowing?'

'Plain envelopes – parcels – here – to my rooms. I get lots of academic material delivered here – no problem.'

'No problem,' repeated Morse quietly, with some distaste in his voice at last, as the authority on the great tits wrote down a brief address.

Hardinge watched from his window as the chief inspector walked along to the Porters' Lodge beside the well-watered, weedless lawn of the front quad. He'd seemed an understanding man, and Hardinge supposed he should be grateful for that. If he'd been a little brighter, perhaps, he would have asked one or two more perceptive questions about Myton, though. Certainly Hardinge knew amongst other things the TV company the lecherous cameraman claimed to have worked for. Yet oddly enough the chief inspector had seemed considerably more interested in Claire Osborne than in the most odious man it had ever been his, Hardinge's, misfortune to encounter.

CHAPTER FORTY

Then the little Hiawatha
Learned of every bird its language,
Learned their names and all their secrets
(Henry Wadsworth Longfellow, *The Song of Hiawatha*)

THAT afternoon PC Pollard was completely 'pissed off' with life as he later reported his state of mind to his Kidlington colleagues. He'd spoken to no one for more than two hours, since the two fellows from the path lab had been along to examine the cordoned off area, to dig several spits out of the brownly carpeted earth where the bones had lain, and to cart them off in transparent polythene bags. Not that they'd said much to him when they had been there just after lunch-time: the sort of men (Pollard had little doubt) with degrees in science and bio-chemistry and all that jazz. He appreciated the need for such people, of course, although he thought the force was getting a bit too full of these smart-alecs from the universities. He appreciated too that it was important to keep people away from the scene of the crime – if it *was* a crime. Exactly who these people were though, he wasn't sure. It was a helluva way from the car park for a couple to carry a groundsheet for a bit of clandestine sex; and they wouldn't go *there*, surely? He'd seen a few birdwatchers as he'd been driven along; but again, not *there*. Too dark and the birds couldn't *fly* in there anyway; it'd be like aeroplanes flying through barrage-balloon cables.

The afternoon was wearing tediously on, and for the umpteenth time Pollard consulted his wrist-watch: 4.25 p.m. A police car was promised up along the Singing Way at 5 p.m.; with further instructions, and hopefully with a relief – unless they'd decided to scrub the whole thing now the ground had been worked over, now the first excitement was over.

4.45 p.m.

4.55 p.m.

Pollard folded away his copy of the *Sun* and picked up the flask they'd given him. He put on his black and white checkered cap, and walked slowly through the woodland riding, wholly unaware that a tiny white-fronted tree-creeper was spiralling up a beech tree to his left; that a little further on a lesser-spotted wood-pecker was suddenly sitting very still on a short oak branch as the crunching steps moved alongside.

Another pair of eyes too was watching the back of the shirt-sleeved constable as he walked further and further away; the eyes of a man who made no move-ment until the woodland around was completely still again, with only the occasional cries of the birds – the thin 'tseet-tseet' of the tree-creeper, and after a while the high 'qui-qui' of the woodpecker – to be heard in that late, still, summer afternoon. For unlike Constable Pollard this man knew much about the woods and about the birds.

The man made his way into the area behind the

cordoned square, and, leaning forward, his eyes constantly fixed to the ground, began to tread slowly, as systematically as the terrain would allow, for about twenty yards or so before turning and retracing his steps along a line four or five feet further into the forest; repeating this process again and again until he had covered an area of roughly fifteen yards square. Once or twice he picked up some object from the densely matted floor, only to throw it aside immediately. Such a pattern of activity he repeated on the left-hand side of the cordoned area – into which he ventured at no point – working his way patiently along, ever watchful, ever alert, and occasionally freezing completely like a statue-waltzer once the music has abruptly stopped. In this fashion he worked for over an hour, like an ox that pulls the ploughshare to the edge of the field, then turns round on itself and plods a parallel furrow, right to left ... left to right. Boustrophedon.

It was just after 6 p.m. when he found it. *Almost* he had missed it – just the top of the black handle showing. His eyes gleamed with the elation of the hunter pouncing on his quarry; but even as he pocketed his find his body froze once more. A rustle ... nearby. Very near. Then, just as suddenly, he felt his shoulder muscles relax. Wonderfully so. The fox stood only three yards in front of him, ears pricked, staring him brazenly in the eye – before turning and padding off into the undergrowth, as if deciding that this intruder, at least, was unlikely to molest its time-honoured solitary territory.

*

The police car was very late ('Traffic!' the driver said) and the four of them – the three at the vehicular access points to the woods, and Pollard himself – couldn't alas be relieved until 7 p.m. Priority was still with the joy-riding kids, and no one seemed to know *who* was in charge of things there anyway: Sergeant Lewis had buggered off for a skiing holiday in Sweden – Christ! – and Chief Inspector bloody Morse was temporarily 'unavailable', probably in a pub. Pity the walkie-talkie wouldn't function a bit better, probably all those bloody trees, eh?

The tree-creeper was gone, and the lesser-spotted woodpecker was gone, as Pollard plodded reluctantly back to his post.

And something else was gone too.

CHAPTER FORTY-ONE

Little by little the agents have taken over the world.
They don't do anything, they don't make anything –
they just stand there and take their cut

> (Jean Giraudoux, *The Madwoman of Chaillot*)

WHETHER the agency was very busy, or whether the phone was out of order, or whether someone just didn't want to speak to him, Morse couldn't know. But it was 4.30 p.m. before he finally got through, and 5 p.m. before, crawling with the other traffic, he finally pulled into the small concreted parking area of the Elite Booking Services in Abingdon Road. The establishment (as it seemed to Morse) should ideally have been a glitzy, marble-and-glass affair, with a seductive and probably topless brunette contemplating her long scarlet fingernails at reception. But things were not so.

The front room of the slightly seedy semi-detached property was so cluttered with file-cases and cardboard boxes that room could be found for only two upright chairs – for the two women proprietors: one, very large, and certainly ill-advised to be wearing a pair of wide, crimson culottes; the other rather small and flat-chested, black-stockinged and minimally skirted. Both were smoking menthol cigarettes; and judging from the high-piled ashtrays around the room, both were continuously smoking menthol cigarettes. Instinctively Morse felt that the latter (if either) would be the boss. But it was the large woman (in her late twenties?) who spoke first:

'This is Selina – my assistant. I'm Michelle – Michelle Thompson. How can I help you?'

The smile, on the rounded dimpled cheeks, seemed warm enough – attractive even – and Morse, reluctantly taking Selina's seat, asked his questions and received his answers.

The agency was the receptor, the collator, and the distributor of 'information', from all quarters of the country, which might be of interest and use to assorted businesses, ranging from TV companies to film producers, clothes designers to fashion organizers, magazine editors to well, all right, purveyors of rather less salubrious products. In its Terms and Conditions contracts, the agency dissociated itself officially, legally, completely, from any liability arising from the *misuse* of its services. When a particular client hired a particular model, such a booking was made with the strict proviso that any abuse of contractual obligation was a matter to be settled between model and client – never model and agency. But such trouble was rare – very rare. McBryde had been a client for about two years: a very *good* client, if full and prompt payment were the criterion – 80 per cent of the negotiated fee to the model; 20 per cent to the agency.

Each spring a Model Year Book was produced; there were always new models, of course, and always new clients – with new, differing interests. But one of the

Terms and Conditions ('Terribly important, Inspector!') was that any information originally divulged *to* the agency concerning individual models, and any information subsequently learned *by* the agency about the activities of either clients or models, would always remain a matter of the strictest confidentiality. Must still remain so now, unless, well ... But at least the inspector could understand that once trust was gone ...

'And that's why you never contacted the police?'

'Exactly,' asserted Ms Thompson.

The link with the YWCA in London was very simple. The woman the police had earlier interviewed, Mrs Audrey Morris, was her sister. On the Friday before Karin had hitch-hiked to Oxford, Audrey had phoned to say that they had a young Swedish student with them who was down to her last few pennies; that the YWCA had given her a ten-pound note from the charity fund; that Audrey had written out the name, address, and telephone number of the Elite agency, and assured Michelle that the young lady was shapely, *very* photogenic, and probably sufficiently worldly-wise to know that a suitable session with a photographer might well work wonders for an impoverished pocket.

'You work on Sundays?'

'Sunday's a good day for sin, Inspector. And we had a client willing and waiting – if she came.'

'And she came?'

'She rang us from a call-box in Wentworth Road in North Oxford and Selina here went up in the Mini to fetch her—'

232

Morse could contain himself no longer. 'Bloody hell! Do you realize how much time and trouble you could have saved us? No wonder we've got so much unsolved crime when—'

'What *crime* exactly are we talking about, Inspector?'

Morse let it go, and asked her to continue.

But that was about it – little more to say. Selina had brought her there, to Abingdon Road: attractive, bronzed, blonde, full-figured, skimpily dressed; with a rucksack – yes, a red rucksack, and with very little else. The client from Seckham Villa had been on the look-out for such and similar offerings. A phone call. A verbal agreement: £100 for a one-hour session – £80 to the girl, £20 to the agency.

'How did she get up to Park Town?'

'Dunno. She said she'd walk up to the centre – only five minutes – and get a bite to eat. Didn't seem to want much help. Independent sort of girl.'

So that was that. At least for the present.

Before he left Morse asked to look through the current Model Year Book, a thick black-covered brochure from which, fairly certainly – or from a previous edition of which – the selected photocopies found at Seckham Villa had been taken. The photographs were all in black and white, but in this edition Morse could find neither Claire nor Louisa amongst the elegant ladies in their semi-buttoned blouses and suspendered stockings. No Karin either among the Ks: just Katie, and Kelly, and Kimberly, and Kylie . . .

'If I can take this?'

'Of course.'

'And I may have to bother you again, I'm afraid – with my sergeant.'

As Morse was leaving the phone rang and Selina made forward as if to take the call. But the senior partner picked up the receiver first, placed her hand over the mouthpiece, and bade her visitor farewell. Thus it was Selina the Silent who accompanied the chief inspector to the door, and who, a little to Morse's surprise, walked out with him to the Jaguar.

'There's something I want you to know,' she said suddenly. 'It's not important, I know, but . . .'

Unlike the Cockney ancestry of her partner's speech, the vowels here were curiously curly: the vowels of Oxfordshire and Gloucestershire.

'I picked her up, you see. She was a lovely girl.'

'Yes?'

'Don't you see? I *wanted* her, Inspector. I asked her if she would see me – afterwards. I've got plenty of money, and she'd got . . . she'd got nothing.' A tear, soon to roll slowly down the thin cheek, had formed in the right eye of Selina, the sleeping, weeping partner of the Agency.

Morse said nothing, trusting that for once his instincts were right.

'She said "no",' continued the woman simply. 'That's what I want you to know really: she wouldn't have done . . . *some* things. She just *wouldn't*. She wasn't for sale – not in the way most of them are.'

Morse laid a hand on a bony shoulder, and smiled at

her understandingly, hoping that he'd assimilated whatever it was she'd wanted to tell him. He thought he had.

As he drove away, Morse could see the mightily dimensioned Michelle still busily engaged with the needs of another client. She was certainly the dominant partner in the business; but he wondered who might be the dominant partner in the bed.

He was not back in Kidlington HQ until a quarter to seven, where he learned that some directive was needed – pretty soon! – about the personnel in Wytham Woods. Was the police team there to be disbanded? On the whole Morse thought it was becoming a waste of time to maintain any further watch. But logic sometimes held less sway in Morse's mind than feeling and impulse, and so he decided that perhaps he *would* continue with it after all.

He drove out of the HQ car park and turned on the radio; but he'd just missed it – blast! – and he heard the signing-off signature-tune of *The Archers* as he headed towards Oxford, wondering how much else he might have missed that day.

Turning right at the Banbury Road roundabout he continued down to Wolvercote and called in at the Trout, where for more than an hour he sat on the paved terrace between the sandstone walls of the inn and the low parapet overlooking the river: drinking, and thinking – thinking about the strangely tantalizing new facts he was learning about the death of the Swedish Maiden.

Lewis rang at 10.15 p.m. He was back. He'd had a reasonably successful time, he thought. Did Morse want to see him straightaway?

'Not unless you've got some extraordinary revelation to report.'

'I wouldn't go quite so far as that.'

'Leave it till the morning, then,' decided Morse.

Not that any decision Morse made that night was to be of very much relevance, since the routines of virtually every department at police HQ were to be suspended over the next three or four days. Trouble had broken out again at Broadmoor Lea, where half the inhabitants were complaining bitterly of under-policing and the other half protesting violently about police over-reaction; council workmen there were being intimidated; copy-cat criminality was being reported from neighbouring Bucks and Berks; another high-level two-day conference had been called for Thursday and Friday; the Home Secretary had stepped in to demand a full report; and the investigation of a possible crime committed perhaps a year earlier in either Blenheim Park or Wytham Woods or where-bloody-ever (as the ACC had put the case the following morning) was not going to be the number-one priority in a community where the enforcement of Law and Order was now in real jeopardy.

CHAPTER FORTY-TWO

To some small extent these Greek philosophers made use of observation, but only spasmodically until the time of Aristotle. Their legacy lies elsewhere: in their astonishing powers of deductive and inductive reasoning

(W. K. C. Guthrie, *The Greek Philosophers*)

LEWIS'S report from Sweden had been far more interesting, far more potentially suggestive, than Morse could have hoped. The flesh was being put on the bones, as it were – though no longer those particular bones which had been discovered in Pasticks. The thoughts of others too appeared to be shifting away from any guesswork concerning the likeliest spot in which to dig for the Swedish Maiden, and towards the possible identity of the murderer who had dug the hole in the first place – his (surely a 'he'?) interests, his traits, his psychological identikit, as it were. Especially the thoughts behind the latest letter to *The Times*, which Morse read with considerable interest on the morning of Friday, 24 July.

From the Reverend David M. Sturdy	deeply impressed by the ingenuity expended by your correspondents on the now
Sir, like so many of your regular readers I have been	notorious Swedish Maiden verses. All of us had hoped

that such ingenuity would eventually reap its reward – especially the wholly brilliant analysis (July 13) resulting in the 'Wytham hypothesis'. It was therefore with much disappointment that we read (Tuesday, July 21) the findings of the police pathologist in Oxford.

I cannot myself hope to match the deductive logic of former correspondents. But is it not profitable to take a leaf out of Aristotle's book, and to look now for some *inductive* hypothesis? Instead of asking what the original author intended as clues, we should perhaps be asking an entirely different question, viz., what do the verses tell us about the person who wrote them, especially if such a person were trying to conceal almost as much as he was willing to reveal.

Two things may strike the reader immediately. First, the archaisms so prevalent in the verses ('tell'st', 'know'st', 'Wither', 'thy', 'thee', etc.) which strongly suggest that the author is wholly steeped in the language of Holy Writ. Second, the regular resort to hymnological vocabulary: 'The day thou gavest, Lord, is ended' (l. II); 'As pants the hart for cooling streams' (l. 15); 'When I survey the wondrous cross' (l. 17) – all of which seem to corroborate the view that the author is a man *regularly* conditioned by such linguistic influences.

May I be allowed therefore to put two and two together and make, not a murderer, but a minister of God's church? May I go even further? And suggest a minister in the Church of Rome, where the confessional is a commonplace, and where in rare circumstances a priest may be faced with a grievous dilemma – the circumstances, say, when a sinner confesses to an appalling crime, and when the priest may be tempted to compromise the sacred principle of confidentiality and to warn society about a self-confessed psychopath, especially so if the psychopath himself has expressed a wish for such a course of action to be pursued.

Might it not be worthwhile then for the Thames Valley CID to conduct some discreet enquiries among the RC clergy within, say, a ten-mile radius of Carfax?

Yours truly,
DAVID M. STURDY
St Andrew's Vicarage,
Norwich.

This letter was also read by Inspector Harold Johnson on holiday with his wife on the Lleyn Peninsula in North Wales. The small village store was not in the habit of stocking *The Times*, but he had picked up a copy on a shopping trip to Pwllheli that morning, and felt puzzled by the reference to 'the findings of the police pathologist in Oxford'. Not just puzzled, either; a whole lot *pleased*, if he were honest with himself. It wasn't very specific, but it must surely mean that the girl still hadn't been found. They'd found some *other* poor sod. Huh! That must have shot bloody Morse in the foot. Shot him up the arse if Strange had his finger on the trigger. He was reading the letter again quickly as his wife was arranging the supermarket carrier bags in the boot of the Maestro.

'What are you smiling at, darling?' she asked.

On Broadmoor Lea, the erection of bollards and concrete blocks, the construction of humps across the streets, and the simpler expedient of digging several holes to the depth of several feet – these activities had put a virtual stop to any possibility of further joy-riding.

All a bit makeshift, but all quite effective. There was revulsion too at the young girl's death. And more public co-operation. The police were winning. Or so it appeared. Marion Bridewell had been knocked down by a car (a shiny new BMW stolen from High Wycombe) with four youths inside. The car itself had been abandoned on the neighbouring Blackbird Leys estate, but a good many of the local inhabitants knew who one or two of them were; and some few bystanders, and some few indeed who had earlier applauded the teenagers' skills, were now semi-willing to testify to names and incidents. Earlier that week fourteen youths and two men in their early twenties had been arrested on the estate, and charged with a variety of motoring offences; six of them were still sitting in the cells. There would very soon be four more of them – the BMW four; and looking at things from the point of view of both the City and the County Constabularies, it was fairly certain that normal police duties could be resumed almost immediately.

The following day, Saturday 25 July, Philip Daley had caught the bus into Oxford at 11 a.m., and his mother had watched him disappear up to the main road before venturing quietly, fearfully, into his bedroom with the hoover. The red-covered pocket diary she'd given him for Christmas had remained unused in his drawer until earlier that month, when the entries had started. The first had been on Saturday the 4th, the writing cramped and ill-fitted into the narrow daily space:

Another tonight. Wow!!! What a squeeler
what a bute. I never been so exited before.

And then the last, a fortnight later:

Finish Finis End! We never meant it
none of us. The screems sounded just like
the tires but we never meant it.

Margaret Daley looked down again at the date,
Saturday, 18 July. Her heart was sinking again within
her, and in her misery she wished that she were dead.

CHAPTER FORTY-THREE

It is not the criminal things which are hardest to confess,
but those things of which we are ashamed

(Rousseau, *Confessions*)

MRS MARGARET DALEY pulled her white Mini into
the tarmacadamed area ('For Church Purposes Only')
just above St Michael and All Angels at the northern
end of the Woodstock Road in Oxford – a white,
pebble-dashed edifice, with a steeply angled roof sur-
mounted, at the apex of the gable, by a small stone
cross. Although she was not a regular worshipper –
once a month or so, with the occasional Easter or
Whitsun or Christmas service – Margaret's face was not
unfamiliar there, and on the morning of Sunday, 26
July, she exchanged a few semi-smiling greetings; a few
only, however, for the congregation was thin for the
first Holy Mass at 8 a.m.

The car was George's really, but so often he used the
Blenheim Estate van for getting around that it was
almost always possible for her to have the prior call;
and especially so on Sunday mornings. There had been
very few cars on the road as she had driven down the
dual-carriageway to the Pear Tree roundabout – her
mind deeply and agonizingly preoccupied.

It had begun two years earlier, when George had

bought the video; a bit surprising in any case, because he was no great TV addict, preferring a pint in the Sun most evenings to a diet of soaps. But he *had* bought a video machine; and soon he'd bought a few videotapes to go with it – the highlights of great sporting occasions, mostly: England's 1966 victory in the World Cup; Botham's miracles against the Australians; that sort of thing. The machine had been a rather complex affair, and from the outset there had been a taboo on anyone else manipulating it without his lordship's permission and supervision. It was *his* toy. Such possessiveness had irked young Philip a little, but the situation had been satisfactorily resolved when the lad had been presented with a small portable TV of his own on his fifteenth birthday. But in spite of his growing collection of tapes, her husband seldom actually watched them. Or so she'd thought. Gradually, however, she'd begun to realize that he *did* watch them – when she was away from the house; and particularly so on the regular occasions she was out, twice a week: aerobics on Tuesdays; WI on Thursdays. It had been one Tuesday night when she had been feeling unwell and flushed that she had left the class early and returned home to find her husband jumping up from his seat on the floor beside the TV screen, hurriedly flicking the 'Stop' switch on the video, turning over to the ITV channel, and taking out the tape. The next day, when he was at work, she had managed, for the first time, to get the wretched thing working – and had witnessed a few minutes of wholly explicit and (to her) monstrously disgusting pornography. She had said nothing though; had still said nothing.

But other things were fitting into place. About once every three weeks a brown, plain A4 envelope would be found among George's limited mail, containing, as she'd guessed, some sort of magazine of about thirty or forty pages. Often the post would arrive before George left for work; but she had taken the next opportunity of a later delivery partially to steam open the flap on such a communication, and to discover more than sufficient to confirm her suspicions. But again she'd said nothing; had still said nothing; and would still say nothing. For although it was half of her trouble, it was the half of her trouble that she could the better bear . . .

Perhaps things were slightly easier as she followed the Order of Mass that early Sunday morning, glancing the whiles around her at the familiar stations of the cross as she sat in a pew at the rear of the church. She knew next to no Latin herself – only what she had learned as a young girl from the RC services in the Douay Martyrs' Secondary School in Solihull. But especially had she then loved the sound of some of the long words they'd all sung: words like 'immolatum' from the *Ave Verum Corpus* – a serious-minded word, she'd always thought, sort of grand and sad and musical with all those 'm's in it. Although she'd never really known what it meant, she felt disappointed that they'd got rid of most of the Latin and gone for a thin kind of Englishness in the services; felt this disappointment again now as the Celebrant dismissed them:

'The Mass is ended. Go in peace.'

'Thanks be to God,' she'd replied, and waited in her

place – until only one other solitary soul lingered there, still kneeling, head bowed, in one of the side pews.

After a few mild exhortations in the porchway to his departing flock, Father Richards re-entered the church; and as he did so Margaret Daley rose and spoke to him, requesting a confessional hearing at one of the appropriate times: Saturdays, 11–12 a.m.; 5.30–6.15 p.m. Perhaps it was the earnestness of her manner, perhaps the moist film of her incipient tears, perhaps her voice – unhappy, hesitant, and trembling . . . But whichever, it mattered not. Father Richards took her gently by the arm and spoke quietly into her ear.

'If it will help, my child, come now! Let Christ, through His cross and through His resurrection, set you free from all your sins!'

It was not in the normal confessional box at all; but in a small study in the Manse behind the church that Father Richards heard as much as Margaret Daley felt willing to tell him. But even then she lied – lied when she said she had gone into her son's bedroom to collect his dirty washing, lied about her deepest and most secret fears.

Twice, surreptitiously, Father Richards had looked down at his wrist-watch as he listened. But he refrained from interrupting her until she had told him enough, until he thought he understood enough. The burden of her sin was heavy; yet even heavier (he sensed it) was her guilt at prying into the affairs of others; her anguished conviction that it was precisely *because* of her prying, *because* of her snooping, that there had been such terrible secrets to discover. Had she *not* done so ... *the secrets themselves might not have existed.* This was her punishment. Oh God! What could she do?

For a while Father Richards offered no words of consolation; it was important, he knew, for the waters to be drained from the poisoned cistern. But soon – soon he would speak to her. And so it was that he sat and waited and listened until she was dry-eyed again; until her guilt and humiliation and self-pity were for the moment spent. She may have told him a lot or a little, she wasn't sure; but she had told him enough, and now it was time for him to speak.

'You must talk to your son, my child, and you must feel able to forgive him; and you must pray to God for guidance and strength. And this I promise – that I too will pray to God for you.' Momentarily there was a twinkle in the old priest's eyes. 'You know, with the two of us praying for the same thing, He might just listen a little bit harder.'

'Thank you, Father,' she whispered.

The priest placed his hand gently on hers, and closed his eyes as he recited the absolution: 'May God Almighty have mercy on you, forgive your sins, and lead you in the paths of righteousness.'

An 'Amen' was called for, but Margaret Daley had been unable to enunciate a single word, and now walked out of the Manse, and fiddled in her handbag for the car keys. The Mini was the only car remaining on the parking area, but another person was standing there, probably waiting for a lift, it seemed; the person who had been kneeling in the church after everyone else had gone; a person who now turned round and looked into Margaret's face – then looked past her face, unrecognizing, and turned away. The look had lasted but a second, yet in that second Margaret Daley's scalp had thrilled with sudden fear.

CHAPTER FORTY-FOUR

Impressions there may be which are fitted with links and which may catch hold on each other and render some sort of coalescence possible

(John Livingstone Lowes, *The Road to Xanadu*)

ON THE morning of Monday, 27 July, Morse and Lewis were back in business at Kidlington HQ: Lewis (at Morse's insistence) once more going through his Swedish trip in meticulous detail – especially through the furnishings and the photographs on view in Irma Eriksson's living room; and Morse (as always) seeking to convince himself that there was probably some vital clue he'd already missed; or, if not *missed* exactly, some clue whose true significance had hitherto eluded him. Since early that morning he had, as it were, been shaking the atoms laterally in the frying pan, hoping that a few hooks and eyes might link together and forge some new chain of thought; a new *train* of thought ... train *spotting* ... *bird*-spotting ... birds ... yes, birds (like dogs!) had figured all over the place so far, especially the lesser-spotted woodpecker – 'spotted' (that word again!) – yet still the link refused to make itself. He considered once again Karin's list of hope-fully-soon-to-be-identified British birds, and realized that as yet he had made no contact with the woman who lived down near Llandovery ... the home of the red kites ... Llandovery, out into Wales along the A40 ... A40, the third of the possibilities ... the third of the roads that led off from the Woodstock Road roundabout. Inspector Johnson had done his pedestrian best with the road out to Blenheim Park; and he himself, Morse, had done his (equally pedestrian?) best with the road posted down to Wolvercote and Wytham. But what if *both* of them had been wrong? Morse had re-read the statement made by Mrs Dorothy Evans (not an aunt, it appeared, but some second or third cousin, twice or thrice removed) in which she'd affirmed quite simply that Karin Eriksson had never visited her, never even telephoned her at that time; in fact had not seen 'little Karin' since that now largish girl was ten years old. No! The solution to the murder lay there in Oxford, in the environs of Oxford, Morse was convinced of that.

At 10.30 a.m. he decided that he had to speak to David Michaels once more; the man who had pointed the way – almost literally so – to the body found in Pasticks; the man who knew the woodland ridings out at Wytham better than almost any man alive.

From the very roundabout where Karin Eriksson might well have made her fatal decision, Lewis drove down through the twisting road of Lower Wolvercote, past the Trout Inn, and then up the hill towards Wytham village.

'What exactly *is* a handbrake-turn?' Morse had asked suddenly.

'Don't you know – really?'

'Well, of course, I've got a vague idea . . .'

'Just a minute, sir. Wait till we're round this next bend and I'll show you.'

'No! I didn't—'

'Only a joke, sir.'

Lewis laughed at his chief's discomfiture, and even Morse managed to produce a weak smile.

The police car drove up to the T-junction at Wytham village, turned left, then immediately right, past the dovecote in the car park of the White Hart, then right again into the lane that led up into Wytham Woods. On a gate-post to the right was fixed a bold notice, black lettering on an orange background:

WYTHAM AMATEUR
OPERATIC SOCIETY
presents
THE MIKADO
BY
GILBERT & SULLIVAN
Thursday July 30th, Friday
July 31st, & Saturday August 1st
TICKETS £3.50
(Senior Citizens & Children £2.50)

'The wife's very fond of Gilbert and Sullivan. Far better than all your Wagner stuff, that,' ventured Lewis.

'If you say so, Lewis.'

'Full o' tunes – you know what I mean?'

'We don't go in for "tunes" in Wagner – we go in for "continuous melody".'

'If you say so, sir.'

They drove up to the semi-circular clearing at the edge of the Great Wood.

'We did it at school. I wasn't in it myself, but I remember, you know, everybody dressing up in all that oriental clobber.'

'*The Mikado*, you mean? Oh, yes. Well done!'

Morse seemed for a while almost half asleep, as Lewis stopped the car and looked across at the stone cottage where Michaels lived.

'We're in luck, sir.' Lewis wound down his window and pointed to the forester, a rifle under his right arm, its barrel tilted earthwards at 45 degrees, the black and white Bobbie happily sniffling the route ahead of him.

'Start the car up again, Lewis,' said Morse very quietly.

'Pardon?'

'Back to the village!' hissed Morse.

As the car momentarily drew alongside, it was Morse's turn to wind his window down.

'Morning, Mr Michaels. Lovely morning!'

But before the forester could reply, the car had drawn away; and in his rear-view mirror Lewis could see Michaels standing and staring after them, a look of considerable puzzlement on his face.

*

They were almost the first customers in the White Hart, and Morse ordered a pint of Best Bitter for himself.

'Which would you prefer, sir? We've got—'

'Whatever the locals drink.'

'Straight glass or handle?'

'Straight. Optical illusion, I know, but it always looks as if it holds more.'

'Both hold exactly—'

But Morse had turned to Lewis: 'You'd better not have too much. You're driving, remember.'

'Orange juice – that'll be fine, sir.'

'And, er . . .' Morse fiddled in his trouser pockets. 'I don't seem to have any coins on me. I'm sure the landlord doesn't want to change a twenty this early in the day.'

'Plenty of change—' began the landlord, but Morse had turned to the wall with his pint and was studying a medieval map of the old parishes around Wytham . . .

At the time Morse was lifting his first pint, Alasdair McBryde was standing beside reception at the Prince William Hotel in Spring Street, just opposite Paddington railway station. After leaving Oxford – with what a frenetic burst of mental and physical energy! – he had driven the swiftly, chaotically loaded van via the M40 up to London, where he'd parked it in a lock-up garage off the Seven Sisters Road before taking the tube, and a suitcase, to Paddington – to the Prince William. It gave him considerable confidence that he could, if necessary, be standing in front of the departure board of the mainline BR station within one minute of stepping outside this hotel – or if need be by *jumping* outside it, for the sole window of his *en suite* bedroom was no more than six feet above the pavement.

The hotel proprietor was a small, perpetually semi-shaven Italian who spent half his working hours at reception studying the racing columns of the *Sporting Life*. He looked up as McBryde took out his wallet.

'You stay another day, Mr Mac?'

'Mc' had been the only part he could read of the semi-legible scrawl with which his guest had signed the register. And there was no typed name on any cheque to help; no cheque at all – just the two crisp twenty-pound notes he received each day for the following night's B & B, with the repeated injunction (as now) from Mr Mac: 'Give the change to the breakfast girl!' Not a big tip though, for the daily rate was £39.50.

Soon Luigi Bertolese was again reading through the runners in the 2 p.m. at Sandown Park, and looking especially at a horse there named 'Full English', with some moderate form behind him. He looked down too at one of the twenties, and wondered if the Almighty had whispered a tip in his ear.

'So you see, old friend? You *see*?' Morse beamed hugely as he finished his second pint. 'It was all due to *you*. Again!'

Lewis *could* see: for once was able to see perfectly clearly. And this for him was the joy of working with the strange man called Morse; a man who was somehow able to extricate himself from the strait-jacketing circumstances of any crime and to look at that crime from some exterior vantage point. It wasn't fair really! Yet Lewis was very proud to know that he, with all his limitations, could sometimes (as now) be the catalytic factor in the curious chemistry of Morse's mind.

'You having any lunch, sir?'

Morse had been talking for half an hour or so, quietly, earnestly, excitedly. It was now 12.15 p.m.

'No. Today I'll take my calories in liquid form.'

'Well, I think I'll get myself—'

'Here!' Morse took the precious twenty-pound note from his wallet. 'Don't go mad with it! Get yourself a cheese sandwich or something – and another pint for me.' He pushed his glass across the slightly rickety table. 'And get a beer-mat or something and stick it under one of these legs.'

For a few seconds as he stood at the bar Lewis looked back at his chief. Several other customers were now seated around, and one youth looked almost embarrassingly blissful as he gazed into the bespectacled eyes of the rather plain young woman sitting beside him. He looked, Lewis decided, almost as happy as Chief Inspector Morse.

CHAPTER FORTY-FIVE

His addiction to drinking caused me to censure
Aspern Williams for a while, until I saw as true
that wheels must have oil unless they run on nylon
bearings. He could stay still and not want oil, or
move – if he could overcome the resistance
(Peter Champkin, *The Waking Life of Aspern Williams*)

IN HER laboratory, Dr Laura Hobson had now begun
to write her report, after resuming her analysis of the
Wytham bones. Not really 'resuming' though, for the
bones had hardly left her over the weekend. Quite early
on she'd spotted the slight groove on the lower-left rib:
it might have been the sharp incision of a rodent's
tooth, of course; but it looked so distinctive, that thinly
V-shaped mark. It was almost as if someone had deliberately made a notch in the rib – with a knife or similar
instrument. It might be important? But no, that was the
wrong way of looking at things. It *might* be important –
no question mark; and Laura was oddly anxious to
score a few Brownie-points on her first real enquiry. In
any case she'd very much like to ingratiate herself a
little with the strange policeman who had monopolized
her thoughts these last few days. It was odd how you
couldn't shake someone out of your mind, however
hard you tried. And for Laura that weekend Morse

should, she felt, have been reported to the Monopolies'
Commission . . .

Once more she studied the scene-of-crime photographs, and she could identify quite easily the bone
that was engaging her interest now. It had obviously
lain *in situ* – not disseminated as so many of the others;
and she felt fairly certain that the incision which her
patient investigation had revealed was unlikely to have
been caused by the tooth of some wild creature, tearing
away a morsel from the still-fleshed bones. *Could* the
notch have been caused by a knife, she wondered: after
all, she was working, was she not, upon a *murder*? So if
it wasn't the foxes or the badgers or the birds . . . Again
she adjusted the focus of the powerful microscope upon
the top of the rib-bone, but she knew there could never
be any *definite* forensic findings here. The very most she
would suggest in her report was that the marked
incision made slantwise across the top of the bottom-
left rib-bone might possibly have been caused by some
incisor tooth, or more probably some sharp implement
– a knife, say. And if it *were* a knife that had been driven
through the lower chest, it could well be, probably *was*,
the cause of death. The body would have bled a good
deal, with the blood saturating the clothing (if any?)
and then seeping into the soil beneath the body; and
not even the intervening months of winter, not even
the last of the leaves and the accumulating débris from
the growth all round, would ever completely obliterate
such traces. That angle, though, was being pursued in
the University Agricultural Research Station (coinci-
dentally situated out at Wytham) and doubtless she

would be hearing something soon. So what, though? Even if there were clear signs of blood to be found there, at the very most *she* would have a blood group, and *Morse* would be able to assume that the body had been murdered *in situ*. Big deal.

Morse! She'd heard he was a bit of a stickler for spelling and punctuation, and she wanted to make as good an impression as she could. Halfway down the first page of her report she was doubtful about one word, and spying a *Chambers Dictionary* on Max's shelves she quickly looked up the spelling of 'noticeable'.

It was the *Pocket Oxford Dictionary* that was being consulted (over 'proceeding') by another report-writer that afternoon, in the Thames Valley Police HQ. Orthographic irregularities were not an uncommon phenomenon in Lewis's writing; but he was improving all the time, and (like his chief) was feeling very happy with life as he transcribed the full notes he had taken on his Swedish investigation.

At 4 p.m., Mrs Irma Eriksson knocked lightly on the door of her daughter's bedroom, and brought in a tray carrying a boiled egg and two rounds of buttered toast. The flu had been virulent, but the patient was feeling a good deal better now, and very much more relaxed.

As was her mother.

*

At 6.45 p.m. the first – well, the first serious – rehearsal was under way for *The Mikado*. It was quite extraordinary, really, how much local talent there always was; even more extraordinary was how willingly, eagerly almost, this local talent was prepared to devote so much of its time to amateur theatricals, and to submit (in this instance) to the quite ridiculous demands of a producer who thought he knew – and in fact *did* know – most of the secrets of pulling in audiences, of ensuring laudatory reviews in the local press, of guiding the more talented vocalists into the more demanding rôles, and above all of soothing the petty squabbles and jealousies which almost inevitably arise in such a venture.

Three hours, his wife had said – about that; and David Michaels had been waiting outside the village hall since 9.30 p.m. It wasn't all that far from home – back down the lane, past the pub, then right again up the road into the woods – little more than a mile, in fact; but it was now beginning to get really dark, and he was never going to take any chances with his lovely wife. His talented wife, too. She'd only been a member of the chorus-line in the Village Review the previous Christmas; but it had been agreed by all that a bigger part would be wholly warranted in the next production. So she'd been auditioned; and here she was as one of the three little Japanese girls from school. Nice part. Easy to learn.

She finally emerged at 10.10 p.m. and a slightly impatient Michaels drove her immediately along to the White Hart.

'Same as usual?' he asked, as she hitched herself up on to a bar stool.

'Please.'

So Michaels ordered a pint of Best Bitter for himself; and for his wife that mixture of orange juice and lemonade known as 'St Clements' – a mixture designed to keep the world's bell-ringers in a state of perpetual sobriety.

An hour later, as he drove the Land-rover back up to the cottage, Michaels felt beside the gear-lever for his wife's hand, and squeezed it firmly. But she had been very silent thus far; and remained so now, as she tucked the libretto under her arm and got out, locking the passenger door behind her.

'It's going to be all right, is it?' he asked.

'Is *what* going to be all right?'

'What do you think I mean? The Mickadoo!'

'Hope so. You'll enjoy *me*, anyway.'

Michaels locked his own side of the Land-rover. 'I want to enjoy you now!'

She took his hand as they walked to the front porch.

'Not tonight, David. I'm so very tired – please understand.'

Morse too was going home at this time. He was somewhat over-beered, he realized that; yet at least he'd everything to celebrate that day. Or so he told himself as he walked along, his steps just occasionally slightly unbalanced, like those of a diffident funambulist.

*

259

Dr Alan Hardinge decided that Monday evening to stay in college, where earlier he'd given a well-rehearsed lecture on 'Man and his Natural Environment'. His largely American audience had been generously appreciative, and he (like others that evening) had drunk too much – drunk too much wine, had too many liqueurs. When at 11.30 p.m. he had rung his wife to suggest it would be wiser for him to stay in his rooms overnight, she had raised not the slightest objection.

Neither Michaels, nor Morse, nor Hardinge, was destined to experience the long unbroken sleep that Socrates had spoken of, for each of the three, though for different reasons, had much upon his mind.

CHAPTER FORTY-SIX

A fool sees not the same tree that a wise man sees
(William Blake, *The Marriage of Heaven and Hell*)

WEDNESDAY, the 29th July, was promising to be a busy day; and so it proved.

Inspector Johnson had returned from his holiday the day before, and was now au fait with most of the latest developments in the Swedish Maiden case. At 9.30 a.m. he girded his loins – and rang Strange.

'Sir? Johnson here.'

'Well?'

'I've been sorry to read things haven't worked out at Wytham—'

'Yes?'

'It's just that if you'd be prepared to give me the chance of some men in Blenheim again—'

'*No* chance. Don't you realize that while you've been lying bare-arsed on the beaches we've had all these bloody joy-riders—'

'I've read all about it, sir. All I was thinking—'

'Forget it! *Morse* is in charge now, not you. All right, he's probably making a bloody mess of it. But so did *you*! And until I give the say-so, he's staying fully in charge. So if you'll excuse me, I've got a train to catch.'

*

Morse also had a train to catch and left on the ten o'clock for London, where Lewis had arranged for him to meet a representative of the Swedish Embassy (for lunch), and the supervisor of the King's Cross YWCA (for tea).

For Lewis himself, after seeing Morse off at Oxford railway station, there were a great many things still to be done. Preliminary enquiries the previous day had strongly suggested – confirmed really – that Morse's analysis of the case (to which Lewis, and Lewis alone, was hitherto privy) was substantially correct in most respects. Often in the past Morse had similarly been six or so furlongs ahead of the field only later to find himself running on the wrong racecourse. This time, though, it really did look as if the old boy was right; and from Lewis's point of view it was as if he'd dreamed of the winner the night before and was now just going along to the bookmaker's to stick a few quid on a horse that had already passed the winning post.

Fortunately the pressure was temporarily off the troubles at Broadmoor Lea, and it was no difficulty for Lewis to enlist some extra help. Two DCs were assigned to him for the rest of the day; and this pair were soon off to investigate both the City and the County records of car thefts, car break-ins, car vandalism, etc., in the few days immediately following the last sighting of the Swedish Maiden. Carter and Helpston had seemed to Lewis a pretty competent couple; and so, later that Wednesday, it would prove to be the case.

In mid-morning, Lewis rang *The Oxford Mail* and spoke to the editor. He'd like to fax some copy – copy which Morse had earlier drafted – for that evening's edition. All right? No problem, it appeared.

NEW DEVELOPMENTS IN SWEDISH MAIDEN MYSTERY

DETECTIVE Chief Inspector Morse of the Thames Valley CID is confident that recently unearthed evidence has thrown a completely new light on the baffling case of Karin Eriksson, who disappeared in Oxford more than a year ago, and whose rucksack was discovered soon afterwards in a hedgerow-bottom at Begbroke. A body found after a search of Wytham Woods has proved not to be that of the Swedish student, and the chief inspector told our reporter that further searches of the area there have now been called off. Murder enquiries continue, however, and it is understood that the focus of police activity is now once again centred on the Blenheim Estate in Woodstock – the scene of the first phase of intensive enquiries just over a year ago.

The police are also asking anyone to come forward who has any information concerning Dr Alasdair McBryde, until very recently living at Seckham Villa, Park Town, Oxford. Telephone 0865 846000, or your nearest police station.

Later in the day both Chief Superintendent Strange and Chief Inspector Johnson were to read this article: the former with considerable puzzlement, the latter with apparently justifiable exasperation.

And someone else had read the article.

The slim Selina had been more than a little worried ever since Morse had called at the agency. Not worried

263

about any sin of commission; but about one of omission, since she'd been almost certain, when Morse had asked for anything on McBryde, that there *had* been a photograph somewhere. Each Christmas the agency had given a modest little canapé-and-claret do; and later that afternoon in Abingdon Road, and temporarily minus the mighty Michelle, she had decided where, if anywhere, the photograph might be. She looked in the files under 'Parties, Promotions etc.', and there it was: a black and white six- by four-inch photograph of about a dozen of them, party hats perched on their heads, wine glasses held high in their hands – a festive, liberally lubricated crew. And there, in the middle, the bearded McBryde, his arms round two female co-revellers.

Morse had bought a copy of *The Times* in Menzies bookstall at Oxford railway station. In the context of the case as a whole, the two Letters to the Editor which he read just after Didcot (the crossword finished all but one clue) were not of any great importance. Yet the first was, for Morse, the most memorable letter of them all, recalling a couplet he'd long been carrying around in his mental baggage.

From Mr Gordon Potter

Sir, My interest in the Swedish Maiden verses is minimal; my conviction is that the whole business is a time-consuming hoax. Yet it is time that someone added a brief gloss to the admirable letter printed in your columns (July 24). If we are to seek a priest of Roman Catholic persuasions as the instigator of the verses, let me suggest that he will also almost certainly be an admirer of the greatest poet-scholar of our own century. I refer to A. E. Housman. How else do we explain line 3 of the printed verses ('Dry the azured skylit water')? Let me quote Norman Marlow in his critical commentary, *A. E. Housman*, page 145:

'Two of the most beautiful lines in Housman's work are surely these:

And like a skylit water stood
The bluebells in the azured wood.

Here again is a reflection in water, and this time the magic effect is produced by repeating the syllable "like" inside the word "skylit" but inverted as a reflection in water is inverted.'

Yours faithfully
J. GORDON POTTER,
'Arlington',
Leckhampton Road,
Cheltenham,
Glos.

And the second, the sweetest:

From Miss Sally Monroe

Sir, 'Hunt' (l. 18)? 'kiss' (l. 20)? And so far I only know one poem by heart. 'Jenny kissed me when we met', by Leigh Hunt (1784–1859).

Yours faithfully
SALLY MONROE (aged 9 years)
22 Kingfisher Road,
Bicester,
Oxon.

CHAPTER FORTY-SEVEN

Yonder, lightening other loads,
The seasons range the country roads,
But here in London streets I ken
No such helpmates. only men
(A. E. Housman, *A Shropshire Lad*)

MORSE'S day was satisfactory – but little more.

He had arrived a quarter of an hour late, with the diesel limping the last two miles into Paddington at walking-pace, for reasons (Morse suspected) not wholly known even to the engine-driver. But he still arrived in good time at the Swedish Embassy in Montague Place for his meeting with Ingmar Engström, a slim, blond fellow in his forties, who seemed to Morse to exude a sort of antiseptic cleanliness, yet who proved competent and helpful, and willing to instigate immediate enquiries into the matter which Morse (with the greatest care) explained to him.

Lunch was brought into Engström's office, and Morse looked down unenthusiastically at the thin, pale slice of white-pastried quiche, the half jacket potato, and the large separate bowl of undressed salad.

'Very good for the waist-line,' commented the good-humoured Swede. 'And no sugar in *this* either.

Guaranteed genuine!' he added, pouring two glasses of chilled orange juice.

Morse escaped from Montague Place as soon as good manners allowed, professing profuse gratitude but refusing further offers of cottage-cheese, low-fat yoghurt, or fresh fruit, and was quite soon to be heard complimenting the landlord of a Holborn pub on keeping his Ruddles County Bitter in such good nick.

Seldom had tea as a meal, never had tea as a beverage, assumed any great importance in Morse's life. Although relieved therefore not to be faced with the choice of China or Indian, he could well have done without the large plastic cup of weak-looking luke-warm tea which he poured for himself from the communal urn in the virtually deserted canteen of the YWCA premises. For a while they chatted amiably, if aimlessly: Morse discovering that Mrs Audrey Morris had married a Welshman, was still married to the same Welshman, had no children, just the one sister – the one in Oxford – and, well, that was that. She'd been trained as a social worker in the East End, and taken the job of superintendent of the YWCA four years since. She enjoyed the job well enough, but the situation in London was getting desperate. All right, the hostel might be two rungs up from the cardboard-box brigade, but all the old categories were gradually merging now into a sort of communal misery: women whose homes had been repossessed; wives who had been battered; youngish girls who were unemployed or improvident or penniless – or usually all three; birds of passage; and druggies, and potential suicides, and of course quite frequently foreign students who'd miscalculated their monies – students like Miss Karin Eriksson.

Morse went through the main points of the statement she had made the previous summer, but there was, it seemed, nothing further she could add. Like her younger sister she was considerably overweight, with a plump, attractive face in which her smile, as she spoke, appeared guileless and co-operative. So Morse decided he was wasting his time, and sought answers to some other questions: questions about what Karin was *like*, how she behaved, how she'd got on with the others there.

Was it that Morse had expected a litany of seductive charms – the charms of a young lady with full breasts ever bouncing beneath her low-cut blouse, with an almost indecently short skirt tight-fitting over her bottom, and her long, bronzed legs crossed provocatively as she sat sipping a Diet Coke . . . or a Cognac? Only *half* expected though, for his knowledge of Karin Eriksson was slowly growing all the time; was growing now as Mrs Morris rather gently recalled a girl who was always going to catch men's eyes, who was certainly aware of her attraction, and who clearly enjoyed the attention which it always brought. But whether she was the sort of young woman whose legs would swiftly – or even slowly – ease apart upon the application of a little pressure, well, Audrey Morris was much more doubtful. She'd given the impression of being able to keep herself, and others, pretty much under control. Oh yes!

'But she – she might lead men on a bit, perhaps?' asked Morse.

'Yes.'

'But maybe' – Morse was having some difficulty – 'not go much further?'

'Much further than what?'

'What I'm saying is, well, we used to have a word for girls like that – when I was at school, I mean.'

'Yes?'

'Yes.'

'"Prick-teaser"? Is that the word you're looking for?'

'Something like that,' said Morse, smiling in some embarrassment as he stood up and prepared to leave; just as Karin Eriksson must have stood up to take her leave from these very premises, with ten pounds in her purse and the firm resolve (if Mrs Morris could be believed) of hitch-hiking her way not only to Oxford, but very much further out along the A40 – to Llandovery, the home of the red kite.

Audrey Morris saw him out, watching his back as he walked briskly towards the underground station at King's Cross, before returning to her office and phoning her sister in Oxford.

'I've just had your inspector here!'

'No problems, I hope?'

'No! Quite dishy though, isn't he?'

'Is he?'

'Come off it! *You* said he was.'

'Did you give him a glass of that malt?'

'What?'

'You didn't give him a *drink*?'

269

'It's only just gone four now.'

'A-u-d-r-e-y!'

'How was *I* to know?'

'Didn't you smell his *breath*?'

'Wasn't near enough, was I?'

'You didn't manage things at all well, did you, sis!'

'Don't laugh but – I gave him a cup of *tea*.'

In spite of the injunction, the senior partner of Elite Booking Services laughed long and loud at the other end of the line.

Morse arrived back in Oxford at 6.25 p.m., and as he crossed over the bridge from Platform 2 he found himself quietly humming one of the best-known songs from *The Mikado*:

> My object all sublime
> I shall achieve in time
> To let the punishment fit the crime,
> The punishment fit the crime . . .

CHAPTER FORTY-EIGHT

Players, Sir! I look on them as no better than creatures
set upon tables and joint stools to make faces and
produce laughter, like dancing dogs

(Samuel Johnson, *The Life of Samuel Johnson*)

FOR SEVERAL persons either closely or loosely connected with the case being reported in these pages, the
evening of Thursday, 30 July, was of considerable
importance, although few of the persons involved were
aware at the time that the tide of events was now
approaching its flood.

7.25 p.m.

One of the three little maids peered out from one
side of the tatty, ill-running stage-curtain and saw that
the hall was already packed, 112 of them, the maximum
number stipulated by the fire regulations; saw her
husband David – bless him! – there on the back row.
He had insisted on buying himself a ticket for each of
the three performances, and that had made her very
happy. Did he look just a little forlorn though, contributing nothing to the animated hum of conversation all
around? He'd be fine though; and she – *she* felt shining
and excited, as she stepped back from the curtain and
rejoined her fellow performers. All right, there were
only a few square yards 'backstage'; such a little *stage*

too; such an inadequate, amateurish orchestra; such a pathetic apology for lighting and effects. And yet ... and yet the magic was all around, somehow: some competent singers; excellent make-up, especially for the ladies; lovely costumes; super support from the village and the neighbourhood; and a brilliant young pianist, an undergraduate from Keble, who wore a large earring, who could sing the counter-tenor parts from the Handel operas like an angel, and who spent most of his free time on lonely nocturnal vigils watching badgers in the nearby woods.

Yes, for Cathy Michaels the adrenaline was flowing freely, and any worries her husband might be harbouring for her – or she for *him*! – were wholly forgotten as with a few sharp taps of the conductor's baton there fell a hush upon the hall; and with the first few bars of the overture, *The Mikado* had begun. Quickly she looked again in one of the mirrors there at the white-faced, black-haired, pillar-box-red-lipped Japanese lady who was herself; and knew why David found her so attractive. David ... a good deal older than she was, of course, and with a past of which she knew so very little. But she loved him, and would do anything for him.

7.50 p.m.

The four youths, aged twelve, fourteen, seventeen, and seventeen, were still being held in police custody in St Aldate's. Whereas collectively on the East Oxford estates they had, by all accounts, appeared a most intimidating bunch, individually they now looked unre-

markable. Quite quickly after their arrest had the
bravado of this particular quartet disintegrated, and as
Sergeant Joseph Rawlinson now looked again at one of
the seventeen-year-olds, he saw only a nervous, surly,
not particularly articulate lad. Gone was the bluster and
aggression displayed in the back of the police car when
they had picked him up from home – and now they
were taking him back.

'These things all you had on you, son?'

'S'pose so, yeah.'

Rawlinson picked them up carefully, one by one,
and handed them across. 'Fiver, £1, £1, 50p, 10p, 5p,
5p, 5p, 2p, 2p, 1p, OK? Comb; Marlboro cigarettes;
disposable lighter; packet of condoms, Featherlite –
only one left; half a packet of Polos; two bus tickets,
one blue Biro. OK?'

The youth stared sullenly, but said nothing.

'And *this*!' Rawlinson picked up a red-covered diary
and flicked quickly through the narrow-ruled pages
before putting it in his own jacket pocket. 'We're going
to keep this, son. Now I want you to sign *there*.' He
handed over a typed sheet and pointed to the bottom
of it.

Ten minutes later Philip Daley was once more in the
back of a police car, this time heading out to his home
in Begbroke, Oxon.

'Makes you wonder, Sarge!' ventured one of the constables as Rawlinson ordered a coffee in the canteen.

'Mm.' Joe Rawlinson was unhappy about committing

himself too strongly on the point: his own lad, aged fifteen, had become so bolshie these last six months that his mum was getting very worried about him.

'Still, with this – what's it? – Aggravated Vehicle-taking Bill. Unlimited fines! Might make 'em think a bit harder.'

'Got sod-all to start with though, some of 'em.'

'You're not going soft, Sarge?'

'Oh no! I think I'm getting harder,' said Rawlinson quietly, as he picked up his coffee, and walked over to an empty table at the far corner of the canteen.

He hadn't recognized the lad. But he'd recognized the *name* immediately – from that time the previous summer when he'd been working under Chief Inspector Johnson out at Blenheim. It could, of course, have just been one of those minor coincidences that were always cropping up in life – had it not been for the diary: a bit disturbing, some of the things written in *that*. In fact he'd almost expected to meet his old chief Johnson out on the estates at the weekend, amid the half-bricks and the broken bottles. But someone had said he was off on holiday – lucky bugger! Still, Rawlinson decided to get in touch if he could; try to ring him up tomorrow.

8.15 p.m.

Anders Fastén, a very junior official at the Swedish Embassy, had at last found what he was looking for. It had been a long search, and he realized that if only the files had been kept in a more systematized fashion he would have saved himself many, many hours. He would mention this fact to his boss; and – who knows? – the next tricky passport query might be answered in minutes. But he was pleased to have found it: it was *important,* he'd been informed. In any case, his boss would be pleased. And he much wanted to please his boss, for she was very beautiful.

9 p.m.

Sergeant Lewis had arrived home from HQ half an hour earlier, had a meal of eggs (two), sausages (six), and chips (legion), and now sat back in his favourite chair, turned on the BBC news, and reviewed his day with considerable satisfaction . . .

Especially, of course, had Morse been delighted with the photograph of Alasdair McBryde; and even more delighted with the fact that, on his own initiative, Lewis had given instructions for police leaflets to be printed, and for adverts to be placed in the following day's *Oxford Mail,* Friday's edition of *The Oxford Times* – and the *Evening Standard.*

'Masterstroke, that is!' Morse had exclaimed. 'What made you think of the *Evening Standard?*'

'You said you were sure he'd gone to London, sir.'

'Ah!'

'Didn't meet him by any chance?' Lewis had asked happily . . .

After the weather forecast – another fine sunny day, with temperatures ranging from 22 degrees Celsius in the south – Lewis put out the regular two milk-tokens, locked and bolted the front door, and decided on an early night. He heard his wife humming some Welsh melody as she washed up the plates and he went through to the kitchen and put his arms round her.

'I'm off to bed – bit weary.'

''appy too, by the sound of you. 'ad a good day?'

'Pretty good.'

'That because bloody Morse beggared off and left you on your own?'

'No! Not really.'

She dried her hands and turned to him. 'You enjoy workin' for 'im, don't you?'

'Sometimes,' agreed her husband. 'It's just that he sort of – *lifts* me a bit, if you know what I mean.'

Mrs Lewis nodded, and draped the dish-cloth over the tap. 'Yes, I do,' she replied.

10.30 p.m.

It was half an hour since Dr Alan Hardinge had decided it was time to walk along to St Giles' and take a taxi out to his home on Cumnor Hill. But still he sat sipping Scotch in the White Horse, the narrow pub separating the two wings of Blackwell's bookshop in the Broad. The second of his two lectures had not been an unqualified success, and he was aware that his subject-matter had been somewhat under-rehearsed, his delivery little more than perfunctory. And only one glass of wine to accompany a mediocre menu!

Still, £100 was £100 . . .

He was finding that however hard he tried, it was

becoming progressively more difficult for him to get drunk. He hadn't read any decent literature for months, yet Kipling had been a hero in his youth and vaguely he recalled some words in one of the short stories: something about knowing the truth of being in hell 'where the liquor no longer takes hold, and the soul of a man is rotten within him'. He knew though that he was becoming increasingly maudlin, and he opened his wallet to look again at the young girl . . . He remembered the agonies of anxiety they had both experienced, he and his wife, the first time she was *really* late back home; and then that terrible night when she had not come back at all; and now the almost unbearable emptiness ahead of him when she would never come home again, never again . . .

He took out too the photograph of Claire Osborne from amongst his membership and credit cards: a small passport photograph, she staring po-faced at the wall of a kiosk somewhere – not a good photograph, but not a bad likeness. He put it away and drained his glass; it was ridiculous going on with the affair really. But how could he help himself? He was in love with the woman, and he was lately re-acquainted with all the symptoms of love; could so easily spot it in *others* too – or rather the lack of it. He knew perfectly well, for example, that his wife was no longer in love with him, but that she would never let him go; knew too that Claire had never been in love with him, and would end their relationship tomorrow if it suited her.

One other thing was worrying him that night – had been worrying him increasingly since the visit of Chief

Inspector Morse. He wouldn't do anything immediately, but he was fairly sure that before long he would be compelled to disclose the truth about what had occurred a year ago . . .

10.30 p.m.

After watching the weather forecast, Claire Osborne turned off the ITN *News at Ten* – another half-hour of death, destruction, disease, and disaster. She was almost getting anaesthetized to it, she felt, as she poured herself a gin and dry Martini, and studied one of the typed sheets that Morse had sent her:

MOZART: Requiem (K626)

Helmuth Rilling (Master Works)
H. von Karajan (Deutsche Grammophon)
Schmidt-Gaden (Pro Arte)
Victor de Sabata (Everest)
Karl Richter (Telefunken)

In two days' time she would have her fortieth birthday and she was going to buy a tape or a record of the *Requiem*. All Morse's versions, he'd said, were records: 'But they're not going to be pressing any more records soon, and some of these are museum-pieces anyway.' Yet for some reason she wanted to buy one of the ones *he'd* got, although she realized it would probably be far more sensible to invest in a CD player. Herbert von Karajan was the only one of the five conductors she'd

heard of, and 'Deutsche Grammophon' looked and
sounded so impressive . . . Yes, she'd try to get that one.
Again she looked down at the sheet, trying to get the
correct spelling of that awkward word 'Deutsche' into
her head, with its tricky 't', 's', 'c', 'h', 'e' sequence.

Ten minutes later she had finished her drink, and
put down the empty glass. She felt very lonely. And
thought of Morse. And poured herself another drink,
this time putting a little more ice in it.

'*God Almighty!*' she whispered to herself.

4.30 a.m.

Morse woke in the soundless dark. From his youth
he had been no stranger to a few semi-erotic daydreams, yet seldom at night did he find himself actually
dreaming of beautiful women. But just now – oddly! –
he dreamed a very vivid dream. It had not been of any
of the beautiful women he'd so far met in the case –
not of Claire Osborne, nor of the curly-headed dietitian, nor of Laura Hobson – but of Margaret Daley, the
woman with those blondish-grey streaks in her hair;
hair which had prompted Lewis to ask his cardinal
question: 'Why do you think people want to make
themselves look older than they are, sir? Seems all the
wrong way round to me.' But Margaret Daley had
appeared quite young in Morse's dream. And there had
been a letter somewhere in that dream: 'I thought of
you so much after you were gone. I think of you still
and ask you to think of me occasionally – perhaps even
come to visit me again. In the hope that I don't upset

you, I send you my love . . .' But there *was* no letter of course; just the words that someone had spoken in his mind. He got up and made himself a cup of instant coffee, noting on the kitchen calendar that the sun would be rising at 05.19. So he went back to bed and lay on his back, his hands behind his head, and waited patiently for the dawn.

CHAPTER FORTY-NINE

An association of men who will not quarrel with one
another is a thing which never yet existed, from the
greatest confederacy of nations down to a town-meeting
or a vestry

(Thomas Jefferson, *Letters*)

DR LAURA HOBSON, one of those who had not been
invited across the threshold of Morse's dreams, entered
his office the following morning just before nine
o'clock, where after being introduced to Sergeant Lewis
she took a seat and said her say.

It didn't, she admitted, boil down to very much
really, and it was all in the report in any case. But her
guess was that the man whose bones were found in
Pasticks was about thirty years of age, of medium height,
had been dead for at least nine or ten months, might
well have been murdered – with a knife-wound to the
heart, and that perhaps delivered by a right-handed
assailant. The traces of blood found beside and beneath
the body were of group O; and although the blood
could have been the result of other injuries, or of other
agencies, well, she thought it rather doubtful. So that
was it. The body had most probably 'exited' (Morse
winced) on the spot where the bones were found; not
likely to have been carried or dragged there after death.

There *were* other tests that could be carried out, but (in Dr Hobson's view at least) there remained little more to be discovered.

Morse had been watching her carefully as she spoke. At their first meeting he'd found her north-country accent (Newcastle, was it? Durham City?) just slightly off-putting; but he was beginning to wonder if after a little while it wasn't just a little *on*-putting. He noticed again, too, the high cheek-bones, and the rather breathless manner of her speaking. Was she *nervous* of him?

Morse was not the only one who looked at the new pathologist with some quiet admiration; and when she handed him the four typed sheets of her report, Lewis asked the question he'd wanted to put for the last ten minutes.

'You from Newcástle?'

'Good to hear it pronounced correctly! Just outside, actually.'

Morse listened none too patiently as the two of them swapped a few local reminiscences before standing up and moving to the door.

'Anyway,' said Lewis, 'good to meet you.' Then, waving the report: 'And thanks for this, luv!'

Suddenly her shoulders tightened, and she sighed audibly. 'Look! I'm not your "luv", Sergeant. You mustn't mind me being so blunt, but I'm no one's "luv" or—'

But suddenly she stopped, as she saw Morse grinning hugely beside the door, and Lewis standing somewhat discomfited beside the desk.

'I'm sorry, it's just that—'

'Please forgive my sergeant, Dr Hobson. He means well – don't you, Lewis?'

Morse watched the slim curves of her legs as she left the office, the colour still risen in her cheeks.

'What was all that about?' began Lewis.

'Bit touchy about what people call her, that's all.'

'Bit like *you*, sir?'

'She's nice, don't you think?' asked Morse, ignoring the gentle gibe.

'To be truthful, sir, I think she's a smasher.'

Somehow this plain statement of fact, made by an honest and honourable man, caught Morse somewhat off his guard. It was as if the simple enunciation of something extremely obvious had made him appreciate, for the first time, its *truth*. And for a few seconds he found himself hoping that Dr Laura Hobson would return to collect something she'd forgotten. But she was a neatly organized young woman, and had forgotten nothing.

Just before Morse and Lewis were leaving for a cup of coffee in the canteen, a call came through from PC Pollard. This rather less-than-dedicated vigilante of Pasticks had been one of four uniformed constables detailed to the compass-point entrances of Blenheim Park; and he was now ringing, with some excitement in his voice, to report that the Wytham Woods Land-rover, driven by David Michaels (whom he'd immediately recognized), had just gone down to the garden centre there. Should he try to see what was happening? Should he – *investigate*?

Morse took the portable phone from Lewis. 'Good man! Yes, try to see what's going on. But don't make it too obvious, all right?'

'How the hell's he going to do that?' asked Lewis when Morse had finished. 'He's in *uniform.*'

'Is he? Oh.' Morse appeared to have no real interest in the matter. 'Make him feel important though, don't you think?'

Chief Inspector Johnson was on his second cup of coffee when Morse and Lewis walked into the canteen. Raising a hand he beckoned Morse over: he'd welcome a brief word, if that was all right? Just the two of them though, just himself and Morse.

Ten minutes later, in Johnson's small office on the second floor, Morse learned of the red diary found the previous day on the person of Philip Daley. But before the two detectives discussed this matter, it was Johnson who'd proffered the olive-branch.

'Look. If there's been a bit of bad feeling – well, let's forget it, shall we? What do you say?'

'No bad feeling on my side,' claimed Morse.

'Well, there was on mine,' said Johnson quietly.

'Yeah! Mine, too,' admitted Morse.

'OK then?'

'OK.'

The two men shook hands firmly, if unsmilingly, and Johnson now stated his case. There'd been a flood of information over the past few days, and one sting was now pretty certain: Daley Junior had been one of the four youths – though not the driver – in the stolen BMW that had killed Marion Bridewell. From all accounts, the back wheels had slewed round in an uncontrollable skid and knocked the poor little lass through a shop window.

'Bit of an odd coincidence, certainly – the boy being involved in both cases,' commented Morse.

'But coincidences never worried you much, did they?'

Morse shrugged. 'I don't reckon he had much to do with the Eriksson case, though.'

'Except he had the camera,' said Johnson slowly.

'Ye-es.' Morse nodded, and frowned. Something was troubling him a little; like a speck of grit in a smoothly oiled mechanism; like a small piece of shell in a soft-boiled egg.

Since the tragedy, Mrs Lynne Hardinge, a slim, well-groomed, grey-haired woman of fifty, had thrown herself with almost frenetic energy into her voluntary activities: Meals on Wheels, Cruse, Help the Aged, Victim Support . . . Everyone was saying what a wonderful woman she was; everyone commented on how well she was coping.

At the time that Morse and Johnson were talking together, she got out of the passenger seat in the eight-windowed Volvo, and taking with her two tin-foiled cartons, main course and sweet, knocked firmly on a door in the Osney Mead estate.

Most of those who received their Meals on Wheels four times a week were grateful and gracious enough. But not quite all.

'It's open!'

'Here we are then, Mrs Gruby.'

'Hope it's not that fish again!'

'Lamb casserole, and lemon pudding.'

'Tuesday's was cold – did you know that?'

'Oh dear!'

The wonderfully well-coping voluntary worker said no more, but her lips moved fiercely as she closed the door behind her. Why didn't you stick it in the fucking oven then, you miserable old bitch? Sometimes she felt she could go quite, *quite* mad. Just recently too she'd felt she could easily *shoot* somebody – certainly that pathetic two-timing husband of hers.

CHAPTER FIFTY

There is but one truly serious philosophical problem, and that is suicide. Judging whether life is or is not worth living amounts to answering the fundamental question of philosophy

(Albert Camus, *The Myth of Sisyphus*)

IT WAS immediately following Morse's almost unprecedentedly alcohol-free lunch (cheese sandwich and coffee) that the crucial break in the case occurred. And it was Lewis's good fortune to convey the tidings to the canteen, where Morse sat reading the *Daily Mirror*.

When earlier in the week Morse had argued that a car would have been required, that a car would have been essential, that a car would have to be disposed of – when earlier Morse had argued these points, the firing plugs in Lewis's practical mind had sputtered into life: cars lost, cars stolen, cars vandalized, cars burned, cars abandoned, cars found on the streets, cars towed away – Lewis had straightway gauged the possibilities; and drawing a vaguely twenty-mile radius round Oxford, after consultation with the Traffic Unit, he had been able to set in motion a programme of fairly simple checks, with attention focused on the few days following the very last sighting of Karin Eriksson.

The key evidence would have been difficult to *miss*,

really, once the dates were specified, since Lt. Col. Basil Villiers, MC, had rung the police on no less than twelve occasions during the period concerned, complaining that the car found abandoned and vandalized, and thereafter further vandalized and finally fired, was a blot on the beautiful landscape – a disgrace, an eyesore, and an ugliness; that he (the aforesaid Colonel) had not fought against despotism, dictatorship, totalitarianism, and tyranny to be fobbed off with petty excuses concerning insurance, liability, obligation, and availability of personnel. But it had only been after considerable difficulty (number plates now gone, though registration markings still on the windows) that the owner of the vehicle had been traced, and the offending 'eyesore' towed away from the neighbourhood of the Colonel's bungalow to some vehicular Valhalla – with a coloured photograph the only memento now of what once had been a newborn, sleek, and shining offspring of some Japanese assembly line.

The keying-in of the registration number now (as presumably a year earlier?) had produced, within a few seconds, the name and address of the owner: James Myton, of 24 Hickson Drive, Ealing; or rather *formerly* of 24 Hickson Drive, Ealing, since immediate enquiries at this address had confirmed only that James Myton had not lived there for more than a year. Swansea DVLC had sent three letters to the said address, but without reply. LMJ 594E was a lapsed registration, though still not deleted, it appeared, from the official records kept in South Wales.

As for Myton himself, his name had appeared on

Scotland Yard's missing-persons list for the second half of 1991. But in that year over 30,000 persons were registered as 'missing' in London alone; and a recent report, wholly backed by Sir Peter Imbert himself, suggested that the index was becoming so inaccurate that it should be restarted from scratch, with a completely fresh re-check on each of the legion names listed. As Morse saw things though, it was going to take considerably more than a 're-check' to revive any hopes of the missing Mr James Myton ever being found alive again.

By mid-afternoon there was firm corroboration from Ealing that the body found in Pasticks was that of James William Myton, who as a boy had first been taken 'into care' by the local authority; later looked after by an ageing couple (now deceased) in Brighton; and thereafter supervised for a time by HM Borstal Service on the Isle of Wight. But the young man had always shown a bit of practical talent; and in 1989, aged twenty-six, he had emerged into the outside world with a reputation for adequate competence in carpentry, interior design, and photography. For eighteen months he had worked in the TV studios at Bristol. A physical description from a woman living two doors away from him in Ealing suggested 'a weakish sort of mouth in which the lower teeth were set small and evenly spaced, like the crenellations of a young boy's toy fort'.

'She should have been a novelist!' said Morse.

'She *is* a novelist,' said Lewis.

At all events Myton was not now to be found; and unlikely to be found. Frequently in the past he had been a man of no permanent address; but in the present Morse was sure that he was a permanent dweller in the abode of the dead – as the lady novelist might have phrased it in one of her purplier passages.

Yet things were going very well on the whole – going very much as Morse had predicted. And for the rest of the afternoon the case developed quietly: no surprises; no set-backs. At 5.45 p.m. Morse called it a day and drove down to his flat in North Oxford.

For about two hours that afternoon, as on every week-day afternoon, the grossly overweight wife of Luigi Bertolese sat at the receipt of custom in the Prince William Hotel, whilst her husband conducted his daily dealings with Mr Ladbroke, Turf Accountant. The early edition of the *Evening Standard* lay beside her, and she fixed her pair of half-lenses on to her small nose as she began reading through. At such times she might have reminded some of her paying guests of an owl seated quietly on a branch after a substantial meal – half dopey as the eyelids slowly descended, and then more than commonly wise as they rose . . . as they rose again *now* when number 8 came in, after his lunch. And after his drink – by the smell of him.

The photograph was on the front page, bottom left: just a smallish photograph and taken when he'd had a beard, the beard he'd shaved off the day after his arrival at the hotel. Although Maria Bertolese's English was fairly poor, she could easily follow the copy beneath:

'The police are anxious to interview this man, Alasdair McBryde ...'

She gave him the room-key, handed over two twenty-pound notes, and nodded briefly to the newspaper.

'I doan wanna no trouble for Luigi. His heart is not good – is bad.'

The man nodded, put one of the twenties in his wallet, and gave her back the other: 'For the breakfast girl, please.'

When Luigi Bertolese returned from the betting shop at four o'clock, number 8, cum luggage, had disappeared.

At the ticket office in the mainline Paddington termi-nus, McBryde asked for a single to Oxford. The 16.20, calling at Reading, Didcot Parkway, and Oxford, was already standing at Platform 9; but there was ten minutes to spare, and from a British Telecom booth just outside the Menzies bookshop there he rang a number (direct line) in Lonsdale College, Oxford.

Dr Alan Hardinge put the phone down slowly. A fluke he'd been in his rooms really. But he supposed McBryde would have caught up with him somewhere, sometime; there would have been a morning or an afternoon or an evening when there had to come a rendering of accounts, a payment of the bill, *eine Rechnung*, as the Germans said. He'd agreed to meet the man of course. What option had he? And he *would* see him; and they would have a distanced drink together, and talk of many things: of what was to be done, and what was not to be done.

And then?

Oh God! What then?

He put his head in his hands and jerked despairingly at the roots of his thick hair. It was the *cumulative* nature of all these bloody things that was so terrible. Several times over the last few days he'd thought of ending it all. But, strangely perhaps, it had not been any fear concerning death itself that had deterred him; rather his own inability to cope with the *practical* aspects of any suicide. He was one of those people against whom all machinery, all gadgetry, would ever wage perpetual war, and never in his life had he managed to come to terms with wires and switches and fuses and screws. There was that way of ending things in the garage, for example – with closed doors and exhaust fumes; but Hardinge suspected he'd cock that up completely. Yet he'd have to do something, for life was becoming intolerable: the failure of his marriage; his rejection by the only woman he'd really grown to love; the futility of academic preferment; his pathetic addiction to pornography; the death of his daughter; and now, just a few minutes ago, the reminder of perhaps the most terrible thing of all . . .

The second performance of *The Mikado*, as Morse recalled, was scheduled, like the first, for 7.30 p.m. Still plenty of time to get ready and go, really. But that evening too he decided against it.

The first night had been all right, yes – but all a bit nervy, a bit 'collywobbly', as the other girls had said. They'd be in really good form that second night, though. David had said she'd been fine the first night – *fine*! But she'd be better now; she'd show him!

With five minutes to go, she peeped round the curtain again and scanned the packed audience. David's ticket for each of the three nights had been on the back row, and she could see one empty seat there now, next to the narrow gangway. But she could see no David. He must, she thought, be standing just outside the hall, talking to somebody before the show began. But seat K5 was destined to remain unoccupied that evening until, during the last forty minutes, one of the programme-sellers decided she might as well give her aching feet a welcome rest.

CHAPTER FIFTY-ONE

He that is down needs fear no fall,
He that is low, no pride
(John Bunyan, *The Pilgrim's Progress*)

WHETHER Morse had been expecting something of
the kind, Lewis wasn't at all sure. But certain it was that
the Chief Inspector appeared less than surprised when
the telephone call came through from Dr Alan Hardinge the following morning. Could he see Morse,
please? It wasn't desperately urgent – but well, yes it
was desperately urgent really, at least for him.

Morse was apparently perfectly content for Lewis to
interject one or two obvious questions, just to keep
things flowing – the meanwhile himself listening carefully, though with a hint of cynicism around his lips.
Perhaps, as Lewis saw things, it had been the preliminary niceties that had soured his chief a little:

> MORSE: I was very sorry to learn of your daughter's
> accident, Dr Hardinge. Must have been a – a terrible—
> HARDINGE: How would you know? You've no children of
> your own.

MORSE: How did you know that?
HARDINGE: I thought we had a mutual friend, Inspector.

No, it hadn't been a very happy start, though it had finished far more amicably. Hardinge had readily agreed to have his statement recorded on tape; and the admirably qualified WPC Wright was later to make a very crisp and clean transcription, pleasingly free from the multi-Tipp-Exed alterations that usually characterized Lewis's struggles with the typewriter:

On Sunday, 7 July 1991, I joined four other men
in Seckham Villa, Park Town, Oxford. I am more
embarrassed than ashamed about the shared
interest that brought us together. Those present
were: Alasdair McBryde, George Daley, David
Michaels, James Myton, and myself. McBryde
informed us that we might be in for an
interesting afternoon since a young Swedish
student would be coming to sit for what was
euphemistically termed a photographic session.
We learned she was a beautiful girl, and
desperately in need of money. If we wished to
watch, that would be an extra £50: £100 in toto.
I agreed. So did Daley. So did Michaels. I myself
had arrived first. Daley and Michaels arrived
together a little later, and I had the impression
that the one had probably picked the other up. I
knew next to nothing about these two men except
that they were both in the same line of business –
forestry, that sort of thing. I had met each of

them two or three times before, I had never met them together before.

The fifth man was Myton, whom I'd known earlier, I'm ashamed to say, as the editor of a series of sex magazines whose particular slants ranged from bestiality to paedophilia. He was a smallish, slimly built man, with a weasel-like look about him – sharp nose and fierce little eyes. He often boasted about his time with the ITV Zodiac Production team; and however he may have exaggerated, one thing was perfectly clear: whatever he filmed for videotapes, whatever he photographed for 'stills', Myton had the magical touch of the born artist.

The first part of the afternoon I can remember only vaguely. The room in which we were seated, the basement room, had a largish, erectile screen, and we were there (all except Myton) watching some imported hard-porn Danish videos when we were aware that the eagerly awaited Swedish star had arrived. The doorbell had been rung; McBryde had left us; and soon we were to hear voices just above us, in the garden outside – the voices of Myton and the young woman I now know to have been Karin Eriksson. I remember at that point feeling very excited. But things didn't work out. It soon transpired that the girl had misunderstood the nature of her engagement; that she was happy enough to do a series of nude stills – but only behind a closed door, with a camera, and with one cameraman. No argument.

It was about half an hour later that we heard
the awful commotion in the room immediately
above us, and we followed McBryde up the stairs.
The young woman (we never knew her name until
days later) lay on the bed. She lay motionless
there, with blood all over the white sheets –
vividly red blood, fresh blood. Yet it was not
her blood – but Myton's! He sat there crumpled up
on the floor, clutching his left side and gasping
desperately, his eyes widely dilated with pain –
and fear. But for the moment it was the naked girl
who compelled our attention. There were horridly
bright-red marks around her throat, and her
mouth seemed oddly swollen, with a trickle of
blood slowly seeping down her cheek. Yes, her
cheek. For it was the angle of her head that was
so startling – craned back, as though she were
trying so hard to peer over her forehead to the
headboard of the bed behind her. Then, not
immediately perhaps but so very soon, we knew
that she was dead.

If ever my heart sank in fear and froze in panic
– it was then! Often in the past I had been in some
sex cinema somewhere, and wondered what would
happen if there were a sudden fire and the exits
were blocked with panic-stricken men. The same
sort of thoughts engulfed me now: and then,
behind me – terrifying noises! – I heard a sound
like a kitchen sink clearing itself, and I turned
to see the vomit of dark-red blood suddenly
spurting from Myton's mouth and spilling in a

great gush over the carpet. Six or seven times
his body heaved in mighty spasms – before he too,
like the girl on the bed, lay still.

Of the sequence of events which had led up to
this double tragedy, it is impossible to be
certain. I can't know what the others there
thought; I don't really know what I thought. I
suppose I envisaged Myton filming her as she took
up her various poses; then lusting after her and
trying to assault her there. But she'd fought him
off, with some partial success. More than
partial success.

What was clear to us all was that she'd stabbed
him with a knife, the sort of multi-purpose knife
scouts and guides carry around with them, for she
still clutched the knife even then in her right
hand as if she'd thought he might make for her
again. How she came to have such a weapon beside
her – as I say, she was completely naked – I can't
explain.

My next clear recollection is of sitting with
the other three in the downstairs room drinking
neat whisky and wondering what on earth to do,
trying to devise some plan! Something! Anything!
All of us – certainly three of us – had the same
dread fear in mind, I'm sure of it: of being
exposed to society, to our friends, families,
children, everyone – exposed for what we really
were – cheap, dirty-minded perverts. Scandal,
shame, ruin – never had I known such panic and
despair.

I now come to the most difficult part of my
statement, and I can't vouch for the precise
motives of all of us, or indeed for some specific
details. But the main points of that day are
fairly clear to me still – albeit they seem in
retrospect to have taken place in a sort of blur
of unreality. Let me put it simply. We decided to
cover up the whole ghastly tragedy. It must seem
almost incredible that we took such enormous
trouble to cover ourselves, yet that is what we
did. McBryde told us that the only others who
knew of the Swedish girl's visit were the model
agency, and he said he would see to it that there
was no trouble from that quarter. That left – how
terrible it all now sounds! – two bodies, two
dead bodies. There could be no thought of their
being disposed of before the hours of darkness,
and so it was agreed that the four of us should
reassemble at Seckham Villa at 9.45 p.m.

For the last few months Myton had been living
out of suitcases – out of two large, battered
looking brown suitcases. And in fact had been
staying with McBryde, on and off, for several of
the previous weeks. But McBryde was still
cursing himself for letting the two of them,
Myton and the girl, go out into the back garden,
since if any of the neighbours had seen Karin
Eriksson they would quite certainly have
remembered her clearly. His fears on this score
however seem to have been groundless. As far as
Myton's suitcases and personal effects were

concerned, McBryde himself would be putting them into the back of his van and carting them off to the Redbridge Waste Reception Centre early the following morning. Myton's car was a much bigger headache but the enormous rise in the number of car-related crimes in Oxford that year suggested a reasonably simple solution. It was decided that I should drive the Honda out to the edge of Otmoor at 10.45 p.m. that same night, kick in all the panels, smash all the windows, and take a hammer to the engine. And this was done. McBryde had followed me in his van – and indeed assisted me in my vandalism before driving me back to Oxford.

That was my rôle. But there was the other huge problem – the disposal of two bodies, also the ditching somewhere of the girl's rucksack. Why we didn't decide to dump the rucksack with Myton's suitcases, I just don't know. And what a tragic mistake that proved! The bodies were eventually loaded into the back of McBryde's van which drove off under the darkness of that night – this is what I understand – first to Wytham, where after Michaels had unlocked the gate leading to the woods the two foresters had transferred Myton's body to the Land-rover, and then driven out to dispose of the body in the heart of the woods somewhere – I never knew where.

Then the same men drove out to Blenheim where Daley, naturally, had easy access to any part of the Great Park, and where Karin Eriksson's body, wrapped in a blanket and weighed down with stones, was pushed into the lake there – again I never knew where.

Looking back, the whole thing seems so very crude and cruel. But some people act strangely when they are under stress – and we were all under tremendous stress that terrible day. Whether the others involved will be willing to corroborate this sequence of events, I don't know. What is to be believed is that this statement has been made of my own free will with no coercion or promptings, and that it is true.

The statement was dated 1.viii.1992, and signed by Dr Alan Hardinge, Fellow of Lonsdale College, Oxford, in the presence of Detective Chief Inspector Morse, Detective Sergeant Lewis, and WPC Wright – no solicitor being present, at Dr Hardinge's request.

Whilst Hardinge was still only some halfway through his statement, George Daley, eager as ever to take advantage of overtime, was boxing some petunias in the walled garden at Blenheim Garden Centre. He had not heard the footsteps; but he felt the touch of a hand on his shoulder, and jerked nervously.

'Christ! You got 'ere quick.'

'You said it was urgent.'

'It *is* bloody urgent.'

'What is?'

'Now look—!'

'No, *you* look! The police'll have that statement some time this morning – probably got it already. And we've agreed – you've agreed – remember that!'

Daley took off the ever-present hat, and wiped the back of his right wrist across his sweaty forehead.

'Not any longer I haven't bloody agreed, mate. Look at this!' Daley took a letter from his pocket. 'Came in the post this morning, dinnit? That's why I rang. See what I could get done for? Me! Just for that fuckin' twerp o' mine. No, mate! What we agreed's no good no longer. We double it – or else no deal. Four, that's what I want. Not two. Four!'

'*Four*? Where the hell do you reckon that's coming from?'

'Your problem, innit?'

'If I could find it,' said the other slowly, 'how do I know you're not going—'

'You don't. Trust, innit? I shan't ask nothin' more never though – not if we make it four.'

'I can't get anything, you know that – not till the bank opens Monday.'

There was a silence between them.

'You won't regret it, mate,' said Daley finally.

'*You* will, though, if you ever come this sort of thing again.'

'Don't you threaten me!'

'I'm not just threatening you, Daley – I'll bloody *kill* you if you try it on again.' There was a menace and a power now in his quiet voice, and he turned to go. 'Better if you come to me – fewer people about.'

'Don't mind.'
'About ten – no good any earlier. In my office, OK?'
'Make it *outside* your office.'
The other shrugged. 'Makes no difference to me.'

CHAPTER FIFTY-TWO

Everything comes if a man will only wait
(Benjamin Disraeli, *Tancred*)

AN HOUR after Hardinge had left – had been allowed to leave – Lewis came back into Morse's office with three photocopies of the document.

Morse picked up one set of the sheets and looked fairly cursorily, it appeared, at the transcript of Hardinge's statement. 'What did you make of things?'

'One or two things a bit odd, sir.'

'Only one or two?'

'Well, there's two things, really. I mean, there's this fellow Daley, isn't there? He's at Park Town that afternoon and that night he shoves the girl's body into the lake at Blenheim.'

'Yes?'

'Well, then he leaves the girl's rucksack in a hedge-bottom at Begbroke. I mean—'

'I wish you'd stop saying "I mean", Lewis.'

'Well, you'd think he'd have left it miles away, wouldn't you? He could easily have dumped it out at Burford or Bicester or somewhere. I me—'

'Why not put it in the blanket? With the body?'

'Well, yes. Anywhere – except where he left it.'

'I think you're right.'

'Why don't we ask him then?'

'All in good time, Lewis! You just said *two* things, didn't you?'

'Ah, well. It's the same sort of thing, really. They decided to put Myton's body in Wytham Woods, agreed? And they *did* put it there, because we've found it. What I can't understand is why Michaels told you where it *was*. I mean – Sorry, sir!'

'But he didn't, did he? He didn't exactly give us a six-figure grid-reference.'

'He told you about Pasticks, though.'

'Among other places, yes.' For a while Morse looked out across the tarmac yard, unseeing it seemed, though nodding gravely. 'Ye-es! Very good, Lewis! You've put your finger – two fingers – on the parts of that statement that would worry anyone; anyone even *half* as intelligent as you are.'

Lewis was unsure whether this was exactly the compliment that Morse had intended; but the master was beginning his own analysis:

'You see – ask yourself this. Why did Daley have to dump the rucksack, and then find it *himself*? As you rightly say, why so close to the place they'd just dumped her body? What's the reason? What *could* be the reason? Any reason? Then, again just as you say, why was Michaels prepared to be so helpful to us? Crackers, isn't it – if he didn't want anyone to find the body? So why? Why give us *any* chance of finding it? Why not give us a duff list of utterly improbable sites? God! Wytham's as big as . . .' (Morse had difficulty with the simile) 'as the pond out at Blenheim.'

'"Lake", sir – about two hundred acres of it. Take a bit of dragging, that.'

'Take a *lot* of dragging.'

'Forget it, then?'

'Yes, forget it! I think so. As I told you yesterday, Lewis . . .'

'You still think you were right about that?'

'Oh, yes! No doubt about it. All we've got to do is to sit back and wait. We're going to have people come to *us*, Lewis. We're losing nothing. You can take it from me there'll be no more casualties in this case unless . . . unless it's that silly young sod, Philip Daley.'

'We might as well take a bit of a breather then, sir.'

'Why not? Just one thing you can do on your way home, though. Look in at Lonsdale, will you? See who was on duty at the Porters' Lodge last night, and try to find out if our friend Hardinge had any visitors in his rooms. And if so, how many, and who they were.'

For the moment, however, Lewis seemed reluctant to leave.

'You sure you don't want me to go and pick up Daley and Michaels?'

'I just told you. They'll be coming to *us*. One of 'em will, anyway, unless I'm very much mistaken.'

'Which you seldom are.'

'Which I seldom am.'

'You don't want to tell me which one?'

'Why *shouldn't* I want to tell you which one?'

'Well?'

'All right. I'll bet you a fiver to a cracked piss-pot that the Head Warden, the Lone Ranger, or whatever his name is, will call here – in person or on the phone – before you sit watching the six o'clock news on the telly.'

'Earlier than that, sir – on a Saturday – the TV news.'

'Oh, and before you go, leave these on Johnson's desk, will you? He won't be in till Monday, I shouldn't think, but I promised to keep him fully informed.' He handed over the third set of photocopied pages, and Lewis rose to depart.

'Do you want me to ring you if I find anything?'

'If it's interesting, yes,' said Morse, with apparent indifference.

Earlier that day, Lewis thought he'd had a pretty clear idea of what the case was all about; or what Morse had told him the case was all about. But now on leaving Kidlington HQ his mind was far more confused, as if whatever else had been the purpose of Hardinge's statement it had certainly muddled the waters of *his*, Lewis's, mind, though apparently not that of his chief's.

As it happened (had he remembered it) Morse would have lost any bet that might have been made, for no one, either in person or on the telephone, was to call on him that afternoon. In fact he did nothing after Lewis left. At one point he almost decided to attend the last night of *The Mikado* at Wytham. But he hadn't got a ticket, and it would probably be a sell-out; and in any case he'd bought a CD of Mozart's *Requiem*.

*

Cathy saw him there that final evening, ten minutes before the curtain was scheduled to rise: the bearded, thick-set, independent soul she'd been so happy to marry in spite of the difference in their ages. He was talking quite animatedly to an attractive woman on the row in front of him, doubtless flirting with her just a little, with that dry, easy, confidential tone he could so easily assume. Yet Cathy felt not the slightest spasm of jealousy – for she knew that it was she who meant almost everything to him.

She let the drape fall back across her line of vision, and went back to the ladies' dressing room where, over her left shoulder, she surveyed herself in the full-length mirror. The simple, short black dresses, with their white collars and red belts, and the suspender-held black stockings, had proved one of the greatest attractions of the show; and each of the three perhaps not-so-little maids, if truth were known, was enjoying the slightly titillating exhibitionism of it all. Cathy had omitted to ask David if he really approved; or if he might be just a teeny bit jealous. She hoped he *was*, of course; but, no, he needn't be. Oh no, he needn't ever be.

Like most amateur and indeed professional productions, *The Mikado* had been put together in disparate bits, with almost all chronological sequencing impossible until the dress rehearsal. Thus it was that David Michaels, though attending a good many practices during the previous month, had little idea of what, perhaps rather grandly, was sometimes called the opera's 'plot'.

Nor had his understanding been much forwarded as a result of the first night's performance, for his mind was dwelling then on more important matters. And now, on this final night, his mind was even further distanced, while he watched the on-stage action as if through some semi-opaque gauze; while he listened to the squeaky orchestra as if his ears were stuffed with cotton wool . . .

He recalled that phone call the previous evening, after which he'd driven down to Oxford, had luckily found a parking place just beside Blackwell's bookshop in the Broad, and then walked through Radcliffe Square and across the cobbles into Lonsdale College, where he'd followed his instructions, walked straight past the Porters' Lodge as if on some high behest, and then into Hardinge's rooms in the front quad, where McBryde had already arrived, and where Daley was to appear within minutes.

Over a year it had been since they'd last met – a year in which virtually nothing had occurred; a year during which the police files had been kept open (he assumed); but a year in which he and the others, the quartet of them, would have assumed with ever-growing relief and confidence that no one would, or ever could, now discover the truth about that hot and distant sunny day.

It was that bloody letter in the paper that had stirred it all up again – as well as that man Morse. What a shock it had been when they'd found the body – since he, Michaels, had no idea whatsoever it had been *there* at all. Bad luck, certainly. What a slice of *good* luck though that he'd found the antler-handled knife, because no one was ever going to find *that* again, lying deep as it was in the lake at Blenheim Park. Yes, the last vestige of evidence was at last obliterated, and the situation was beginning to right itself again; or rather *had* been so beginning . . . until he'd taken the second phone call, early that very morning; the call from that cesspit of a specimen out at Begbroke. But Daley could wait for a while; Daley would play along with them for a little longer yet. The one thing Michaels was quite unable to understand was why *Morse* was waiting. And that made him very uneasy. Perhaps everybody was waiting . . .

Suddenly he was conscious of the applause all around him, as the curtain moved jerkily across to mark the end of Act 1 of *The Mikado*.

CHAPTER FIFTY-THREE

As we passed through the entrance archway, Randolph
said with pardonable pride, 'This is the finest view in
England'
(Lady Randolph Churchill, on her first visit to Blenheim)

ON MONDAY, 3 August, Chief Inspector Harold Johnson had spent much of the morning with his City
colleagues in St Aldate's, and it was not until just gone
11 a.m. that he was in his own office back at Kidlington
HQ – where he immediately read the transcript of
Hardinge's evidence. Then re-read it. It was all new to
him, except the bits about the rucksack, of course.
Naturally he had to admit that since Morse had been
on the case the whole complexion of things had
changed dramatically: clues, cars, corpses – why hadn't
he found any of them? Odd really, though: Morse's
obsession had been with Wytham; and his, Johnson's,
with Blenheim. And according to the statement Hardinge had made, *both* of them had been right all along.
He rang through on the internal extension to Morse's
office, but learned that he had just left, with Lewis –
destination undisclosed.

Blenheim! He found the glossy brochure on Blenheim Palace still on his shelves, and he turned to the
map of the House and Grounds. There it was – the

lake! The River Glyme flowed into the estate from the east, first into the Queen Pool, then under Vanbrugh's Grand Bridge into the lake beyond: some two hundred odd acres in extent, so they'd told him, when first he'd mooted the suggestion of dragging the waters. Too vast an undertaking, though; still was. The Queen Pool was fairly shallow, certainly, and there had been a very thorough search of the ground at its periphery. But nothing had been found, and Johnson had always suspected (rightly, it seemed!) that if Karin Eriksson's body had been disposed of in any stretch of Blenheim there, it had to be in the far deeper, far more extensive waters of the lake; had to be well weighted down too, so the locals had told him, since otherwise it would pretty certainly have surfaced soon after immersion, and floated down to the Grand Cascade, at the southern end of the lake, where the waters resume their narrow flow within the banks of the Glyme.

Johnson flicked through the brochure's lavish illustrations and promised himself he would soon take his new wife to visit the splendid house and grounds built by Queen Anne and her grateful parliament for the mighty Duke. What was that mnemonic they'd learned at school? BROM – yes, that was it: Blenheim, Ramilles, Oudenarde, Malplaquet – that musical quartet of victories. Then, quite suddenly, he had the urge to go and look again at that wonderful sight which bursts upon the visitor after passing through the Triumphal Gate.

He drove out to Woodstock, past the Bear and the church on his left, then across a quadrangle and up to the gate where a keeper sat in his box, and where Johnson (to his delight) was recognized.

'You going through, sir?'

Johnson nodded. 'I thought we had one of our lads at each of the gates?'

'Right. You did, sir. But you took 'em off.'

'When was that?'

'Saturday. The fellow who was on duty here just said he wouldn't be back – that's all I know. Reckon as he thought the case was finished, like.'

'Really?'

Johnson drove on through, and there it was again, bringing back so many memories: in the middle distance the towers and finials of the Palace itself; and there, immediately to his right, the lake with the Grand Bridge and Capability Brown's beechwood landscape beyond it. Breathtaking!

Johnson accepted the fact that he was a man of somewhat limited sensitivity; yet he thought he was a competent police officer, and he was far from happy about the statement he'd just read. If this Hardinge fellow could be believed, the evidence Daley had given a year earlier had been decidedly uneconomical with the truth; and that, to Johnson, was irksome – very irksome. At the time, he'd spent a good while with Daley, going over that wretched rucksack business; and he wanted to have another word with Daley. Now!

He drove down past the Palace to the garden centre; but no one there had seen Daley that morning. He might be out at the mill, perhaps? So Johnson drove out of the estate, through Eagle Lodge, and out on to the A4095, where he turned right through Bladon and Long Hanborough, then right again and in towards the western boundary of the estate, parking beside the piles of newly cut stakes in the yard of the Blenheim Estate Saw-Mill. Only once had he been there when earlier he'd been the big white chief, and he was suddenly aware that it would have been considerably quicker for him to have driven across the park instead of round the villages. Not that it much mattered, though.

No one recognized him here. But he soon learned that Daley's van wasn't there; hadn't been there since Friday afternoon in fact, when he'd been looking after some new plantation, by the lake, and when he'd called at the saw-mill for some stakes for supporting saplings. One of the workers suggested that Daley would prob- ably have taken the van home with him for the weekend – certainly so if he'd been working overtime that weekend; and the odds were that Daley was back planting trees that morning.

Johnson thanked the man and drove to the edge of the estate, only just along the road really; then right along a lane that proclaimed 'No Thoroughfare', till he reached Combe Lodge where, Johnson had been told, the gate would probably be locked. But, well, he *was* a policeman, he'd said.

Johnson read the notice on the tall, wooden, green-painted gate:

ACCESS FOR KEYHOLDERS ONLY.

ALL OTHER VEHICLES MUST USE THE GATE IN WOODSTOCK.

DO NOT DISTURB THE RESIDENTS IN THE LODGE.

But there was no need for him to disturb the (single) resident, since a tractor-cum-trailer was just being admitted, and in its wake the police car was waved through without challenge. A little lax perhaps, as Johnson wondered. Immediately in front of him the road divided sharply; and as a lone, overweight lady, jogging at roughly walking pace, took the fork to the right, Johnson took the fork to the left, past tall oak trees towards the northern tip of the lake. Very soon, some two or three hundred yards ahead on his left, he saw the clump of trees, and immediately realized his luck – for a Blenheim Estate van stood there, pulled in beside an old, felt-roofed hut, its wooden slats green with mildew. He drew in alongside and got out of the car to look through a small side-window of glass.

Nothing. Well, virtually nothing: only a wooden shelf on which rested two unopened bags of food for the pheasants. Walking round to the front of the hut, he tried the top and bottom of the stable-type door: both locked. Then, as he stepped further round, something caught the right-hand edge of his vision, and he looked down at the ground just beyond and behind the hut – his mouth suddenly opening in horror, his body held momentarily in the freezing grip of fear.

CHAPTER FIFTY-FOUR

Michael Stich (W. Germany) beat Boris Becker
(W. Germany) 6–4, 7–6, 6–4
(Result of the Men's Singles Championship at
Wimbledon, 1991)

AT THE time that Chief Inspector Johnson had set out
for Woodstock, Lewis was driving, at slightly above the
national speed limit, along the A40 to Cheltenham. It
appeared to have been a late, impulsive decision on
Morse's part:

'You realize, Lewis, that the only person we've not
bothered about in this case so far is auntie whatever-
her-name-is from Llandovery.'

'Not an "auntie" exactly, sir. You know, it's like when
little girls sometimes call women their aunties—'

'No. I don't know, Lewis.'

'Well, it seems Karin called her Auntie Dot or Doss
– this Mrs Evans. "Dorothy", I seem to remember her
Christian name was.'

'You've profited from your weekend's rest, Lewis!'

'Don't you think we ought to get Daley and Michaels
in first though, sir? I mean, if they're prepared to back
up what Dr Hardinge says—'

'No! If I'm right about this case – which I am! – we'll
be in a far better position to deal with those two

gentlemen once we've seen the Lady of Llandovery. Remember that sign at the Woodstock Road round-about? Left to Wytham; right to Woodstock; straight over for the A40 to West Wales, right? So we can be there in . . .? How far is it?'

'Hundred and thirty? Hundred and forty miles? But don't you think we should give her a ring just in case—'

'Get the car out, Lewis. The way you drive we'll be there in three hours.'

'Try for two and a half, if you say so,' replied Lewis with a radiant smile.

It had been after Cheltenham, after Gloucester and Ross-on-Wye, after Monmouth and the stretch of beau-tiful countryside between Brecon and Llandovery, that Morse had come to life again. Never, in Lewis's experi-ence, had he been any sort of conversationalist in a car; but that day's silence had broken all records. And when finally he did speak, Lewis was once again conscious of the unsuspected processes of Morse's mind. For the great man, almost always so ignorant of routes and directions and distances, suddenly jerked up in his passenger seat:

'The right turn in a couple of miles, Lewis – the A483 towards Builth Wells.'

'You don't want to stop for a quick pint, sir?'

'I most certainly *do.* But if you don't mind, we'll skip it, all right?'

'I still think it would've been sensible to ring her, sir.

You know, she might be off for a fortnight in Tenerife or something.'

Morse sighed deeply. 'Aren't you enjoying the journey?' Then, after a pause: 'I rang her yesterday afternoon, anyway. She'll be there, Lewis. She'll be there.'

Lewis remained silent, and it was Morse who resumed the conversation:

'That statement – that statement Hardinge made. They obviously got together the four of them – Hardinge, Daley, Michaels, and McBryde – got together and cooked up a story between them. Your porter couldn't give us any names, you say; but he was pretty sure there were at least three, probably four, of 'em in Hardinge's rooms on Friday night. And if they all stick to saying the same – well, we shall have little option but to believe them.'

'Not that *you* will, sir.'

'Certainly not. *Some* of it might be true, though; some of it might be absolutely crucial. And the best way of finding that out is seeing Auntie Gladys here.'

'Dorothy.'

'You see, there was only *one* really important clue in this case: the fact that the Swedish girl's rucksack was found so quickly – *had* to be found – left beside the road-side – *sure* to be found.'

'I think I'm beginning to see that,' said Lewis, unseeing, as he turned left now at Llanwrtyd Wells, and headed out across the Cambrian Hills.

But not for long. After only a couple of miles, on the left, they came to a granite-built guest-house, 'B & B: Birdwatchers Welcome'. Perhaps it was destined to do a fairly decent trade. Was *certainly* so destined, if there were any birdwatchers around, since there was not another house to be espied anywhere in the deeply wooded landscape.

Mrs Evans, a smallish, dark, sprightly woman in her late forties, showed them into the 'parlour'; and was soon telling them something of herself. She and her husband had lived in East Anglia for the first fifteen years of their (childless) marriage; it was there that she'd met Karin for the first time eight or nine years ago. She, Mrs Evans, was no blood relation at all, but had become friendly with the Eriksson family when they had stayed in the guest-house in Aldeburgh. The family had stayed the next year too, though minus Daddy that time; and thereafter the two women had corresponded off and on fairly regularly: birthday cards, Christmas cards, holiday postcards, and so on. And to the three young Eriksson girls she had become 'Auntie Doss'. When Karin had decided to come to England in 1991, Mrs Evans had known about it; and not having seen the girl for six years or so, had suggested to her mother that if Karin was going to get over towards Wales at all there would always be a welcome for her – and a bed. *And* some wonderful birdwatching, since the beautiful red kites were becoming an increasingly common sight there. What *sort* of girl was Karin? Of course, she'd only been thirteen or fourteen when she'd seen her last but, well – lovely, really. Lovely girl. Attractive – very *proper*, though.

As the conversation between them developed, Lewis found himself looking idly round the room: armchairs, horse-hair settee, mahogany furniture, a coffee table piled high with country magazines, and on the wall above the fireplace a large map of Dyffed and the Cambrian Mountains. It seemed to him a rather bleak and sunless room, and he thought that had she reached this far, the young Karin Eriksson would not have felt too happy there . . .

Morse had now got the good lady talking more rapidly and easily, her voice rising and falling in her native Welsh lilt; talking about why they'd moved back to Wales, how the recession was hitting them, how they advertised for guests – in which magazines and newspapers. On and on. And in the middle of it:

'Oh! Would you both like a cup of tea?'

'Very kind – but no,' said Morse, even as Lewis's lips were framing a grateful 'yes'.

'Tell me more about Karin,' continued Morse. '"Proper" you said. Do you mean "prim and proper" – that sort of thing? You know, a bit prudish; a bit . . . straightlaced?'

'Nor, I dorn't mean *that*. As I say it's five or six years back, isn't it? But she was . . . well, her mother said she'd always got plenty of boyfriends, like, but she knew, well . . . she knew where to draw the line – let's put it like that.'

'She didn't keep a packet of condoms under her pillow?'

'I dorn't think so.' Mrs Evans seemed far from shocked by the blunt enquiry.

'Was she a virgin, do you think?'

'Things change, dorn't they? Not *many* gels these days who ought to walk up the aisle in white, if you ask me.'

Morse nodded slowly as if assimilating the woman's wisdom, before switching direction again. What was Karin like at school – had Mrs Evans ever learned that? Had she been in the – what was it? – Flikscouten, the Swedish Girl Guides? Interested in sport, was she? Skiing, skating, tennis, basketball?

Mrs Evans was visibly more relaxed again as she replied: 'She was always good at sport, yes. Irma – Mrs Eriksson – she used to write and tell me when her daughters had won things; you know, cups and medals, certificates and all that.'

'What was Karin best at, would you say?'

'Dorn't know really. As I say it's a few years since—'

'I do realize that, Mrs Evans. It's just that you've been so helpful so far – and if you could just cast your mind back and try – try to remember.'

'Well, morst games, as I say, but—'

'Skiing?'

'I dorn't think so.'

'Tennis?'

'Oh, she loved tennis. Yes, I think tennis was her favourite game, really.'

'Amazing, aren't they – these Swedes! They've only got about seven million people there, is that right? But they tell me about four or five in the world's top-twenty come from Sweden.'

Lewis blinked. Neither tennis nor any other sport,

he knew, was of the slightest interest to Morse who didn't know the difference between side-lines and touch-lines. Yet he understood exactly the trap that Morse was digging; the trap that Mrs Evans tumbled into straightaway.

'Edberg!' she said. 'Stefan Edberg. He's her great hero.'

'She must have been very disappointed about Wimbledon last year, I should think, then?'

'She was, yes. She told me she—'

Suddenly Mrs Evans's left hand shot up to her mouth, and for many seconds she sat immobile in her chair as if she'd caught a glimpse of the Gorgon.

'Don't worry,' said Morse quietly. 'Sergeant Lewis will take it all down. Don't talk too fast for him, though: he failed his forty words per minute shorthand test, didn't you, Sergeant?'

Lewis was wholly prepared. 'Don't worry about what he says, Mrs Evans. You can talk just how you like. It's not as if' – turning to Morse – 'she's done much wrong, is it, sir?'

'Not very much,' said Morse gently; 'not very much at all, have you, Mrs Evans?'

'How on earth did you guess *that* one?' asked Lewis an hour later as the car accelerated down the A483 to Llandovery.

'She'd've slipped up sooner or later. Just a matter of time.'

'But all that tennis stuff. You don't follow tennis.'

'In my youth, I'll have you know, I had quite a reliable backhand.'

'But how did you—'

'Prayer and fasting, Lewis. Prayer and fasting.'

Lewis gave it up. 'Talking of fasting, sir, aren't you getting a bit peckish?'

'Yes, I am. Hungry *and* thirsty. So perhaps if we can find one of those open-all-day places . . .'

But they got little further. The car-telephone rang and Morse himself picked it up. Lewis could make out none of the words at the other end of the line – just Morse's syncopated rôle:

'*What?*'

'You *sure?*'

'Bloody 'ell!'

'*Who?*'

'*Bloody* 'ell!'

'Yes.'

'Yes!'

'Two and a half hours, I should think.'

'No! Leave things exactly as they are.'

Morse put down the phone and stared ahead of him like some despondent zombie.

'Something to do with the case?' ventured an apprehensively hesitant Lewis.

'They've found a body.'

'Who?'

'George Daley. Shot. Shot through the heart.'

'Where?'

'Blenheim. Blenheim Park.'

'Whew! That's where Johnson—'

'It was Johnson who found him.'

Suddenly Lewis felt the need for a pint of beer almost as much as Morse; but as the car sped nearer and nearer to Oxford, Morse himself said nothing more at all.

CHAPTER FIFTY-FIVE

Thanatophobia (n): a morbid dread of death, or (sometimes) of the sight of death: a poignant sense of human mortality, almost universal except amongst those living on Olympus

(Small's English Dictionary)

DR LAURA HOBSON knelt again beside the body, this time her bright hazel eyes looking up at a different chief inspector: not at Johnson – but at Morse.

'You reckon he was killed instantly?' asked the latter.

She nodded. 'I'm no expert on ballistics but it was possibly one of those seven-millimetre bullets – the sort that expand on contact.'

'The sort they kill deer with,' added Morse quietly.

'It's' – she fingered the corpse – 'er, sometimes difficult to find the entry-hole. Not in this case, though. Look!'

She pointed a slim finger to a small, blood-encrusted hole, of little more than the diameter of a pencil, just below the left shoulder blade of the man who lay prone on the ground between them. 'But you'll see there's never much of a problem with the *exit* hole.' Gently she eased the body over and away from her, pushing it on to its right side, and pointing to a larger hole that had

325

been blasted just below the heart, a hole almost the size of a mandarin orange.

This time, however, Morse was not looking. He was used to death of course; but accident, and terrible injury, and the sight of much blood – such things he could never stomach. So he turned his eyes away, and for a few moments stood staring around him in that quiet woodland glade, where so very recently someone had shot George Daley in the back, and no doubt watched him fall and lie quite still beneath the giant oak tree there. And the owners of seven-millimetre rifles? Morse knew two of them: David Michaels and George Daley. And whatever else might be in doubt, George Daley would have found it utterly impossible to have shot himself with the rifle that was his.

'Any ideas how long?' asked Morse.

Dr Hobson smiled. 'That's the very first question you always asked Max.'

'He told you?'

'Yes.'

'Well, he never told me the answer – never told me how long, I mean.'

'Shall I tell you?'

'Please do!' Morse smiled back at her, and for a moment or two he found her very attractive.

'Ten, twelve hours. No longer than twelve, I don't think. I'll plump for ten.'

Morse, oblivious of the time for most of the day, now looked at his wrist-watch: 8.25 p.m. That would put the murder at about 10 a.m., say? 10.30 a.m.? Yes . . . that sort of time would figure reasonably well if Morse's thinking was correct. Perhaps he *wasn't* right, though! He'd been so bloody certain in his own mind that the case was drawing gently if sombrely towards a conclusion: no more murder, no more deaths. Huh! That's exactly what he'd told Lewis, wasn't it? Just wait! – that's what he'd said. Things'll work out if only we're prepared to wait. Why, only that day he'd waited, before driving off to Wales, without the slightest premonition of impending tragedy.

And he'd been wrong.

There would be greater tragedies in life, of course, than the murder of the mean and unattractive Daley. No one was going to miss the man dramatically much ... except of course for Mrs Daley, Margaret Daley – of whom for some reason Morse had so recently dreamed. But perhaps even she might not miss him all that much, as time gradually cured her heart of any residual tenderness. After a decent burial. After a few months. After a few years.

Yet there was always the possibility that Morse was wrong again.

Lewis was suddenly at his side, bending down and picking up the khaki-green pork-pie hat Daley invariably wore on freezing winter mornings and sweltering summer days alike.

'There's not *much* shooting here, it seems, sir – not like Wytham – not at this time of year, anyway. Some of the tenants have got shot-gun rights – for a bit of pigeon-shooting, or rabbits, and pheasants a bit later on. Not much, though. That's why Mr Williams, the keeper there' – Lewis pointed back in the direction of

Combe Lodge – 'says he *thinks* he may remember a bit of a pop some time this morning. He can't pin it down much closer than that.'

'Bloody marvellous!' said Morse.

'He says there were quite a lot he let through the gate – there's always quite a lot on Mondays. He *thinks* he remembers Daley going through, some time in the morning, but there's always quite a few estate vans.'

'He thinks a lot, your keeper, doesn't he?'

'And one or two joggers, he says.'

'*Literally* one or two?'

'Dunno.'

'Promise me you'll never take up jogging, Lewis!'

'Can we move him?' asked Dr Hobson.

'As far as I'm concerned,' said Morse.

'Anything else, Inspector?'

'Yes. I'd like to ask you along to the Bear and have a few quiet drinks together – a few *noisy* drinks, if you'd prefer it. But we shall have to go and look round Daley's house, I'm afraid. Shan't we, Lewis?'

Behind the spectacles her eyes twinkled with humour and potential interest: 'Anuther tame, mebby?'

She left.

'Anuther tame, please, Dr Hobson!' said Chief Inspector Morse, but to himself.

CHAPTER FIFTY-SIX

The west yet glimmers with some streaks of day:
Now spurs the lated traveller apace
To gain the timely inn

(Shakespeare, *Macbeth*)

THE HOUSE in which the Daleys had lived for the past
eighteen years was deserted. Margaret Daley, so the
neighbours said, had been away since the previous
Thursday, visiting her sister in Beaconsfield; whilst the
boy, Philip, had scarcely been seen since being brought
back home by the St Aldate's police. But no forcible
entry was needed, for the immediate neighbour held a
spare front-door key, and a preliminary search of the
murdered man's house was begun at 9.15 p.m.

Two important pieces of evidence were found
immediately, both on the red formica-topped kitchen
table. The first was a letter from the Oxford Magistrates'
Court dated 31 July – most probably received on
Saturday, 1 August? – informing Mr G. Daley of the
charges to be preferred against his son, Philip, and of
the various legal liabilities which he, the father, would
now incur under the new Aggravated Vehicle Theft
Act. The letter went on to specify the provisions of legal
aid, and to request Daley senior's attendance at the
Oxford Crown Court on the following Thursday when

the hearing of his son's case would be held. The second piece of evidence was half a page of writing from a temporarily departed son (as it appeared) to a now permanently departed father, conveying only the simple message that he was 'off to try and sort something out': a curiously flat, impersonal note, except for the one *post-scriptum* plea: 'Tell Mum she needn't wurry'.

A copy of *The Oxford Mail* for Friday, 31 July, lay on top of the microwave, and a preoccupied Morse scanned its front page briefly:

JOY-RIDERS GET NEW WARNING

THE DRIVER and co-passenger of a stolen car which had rammed a newsagent's shop on the Broadmoor Lea estate were both jailed for six months and each fined £1,500 at Oxford Crown Court yesterday. Sentencing father-of-three Paul Curtis, 25, and John Terence Bowden, 19, Judge Geoffrey Stephens warned:

'Those who drive recklessly and dangerously and criminally around estates in Oxford can now normally expect custodial sentences – and not short ones. Heavier fines too will be imposed as everything in our power is done to end this spate of criminal vandalism.'

(continued: page 3)

But Morse read no further, now wandering rather aimlessly around the ground-floor rooms. In the lounge, Lewis pointed to the row of black video-cassettes.

'I should think we know what's on some of *them*, sir.'

Morse nodded. 'Yes. I'd pinch one or two for the

night if I had a video.' But his voice lacked any enthusiasm.

'Upstairs, sir? The boy's room . . .?'

'No. I think we've done enough for one night. And I'd like a warrant really for the boy's room. I think Mrs Daley would appreciate that.'

'But we don't really need—'

'C'mon, Lewis! We'll leave a couple of PCs here overnight.' Morse had reached another of his impulsive decisions, and Lewis made no further comment. As they left the house, both detectives noticed again – for it was the first thing they'd noticed as they'd entered – that the seven-millimetre rifle which had earlier stood on its butt by the entrance had now disappeared.

'I reckon it's about time we had a quick word with Michaels,' said Morse as in the thickening light they got into the car.

Lewis refrained from any recrimination. So easily could he have said he'd regularly been advocating exactly such a procedure that day, but he didn't.

At 10.30 p.m., with only half an hour's drinking time remaining, the police car drove up to the White Hart, where Morse's face beamed happily: 'My lucky night. Look!' But Lewis had already spotted the forester's Land-rover parked outside the front of the pub.

David Michaels, seated on a stool in the downstairs bar, with Bobbie curled up happily at his feet, was just finishing a pint of beer as Lewis put a hand on his shoulder.

'Could we have a word with you, sir?'

Michaels turned on his stool and eyed them both without apparent surprise. 'Only if you join me in a drink, all right?'

'Very kind of you,' said Morse. 'The Best Bitter in decent shape?'

'Excellent.'

'Pint for me then, and, er – orange juice is it for you, Sergeant?'

'What do you want a word about?' asked Michaels.

The three of them moved over to the far corner of the flagstoned bar, with Bobbie padding along behind.

'Just one thing, really,' replied Morse. 'You've heard about Daley's murder?'

'Yes.'

'Well ... I want to take a look in your rifle-cabinet, that's all.'

'When we've finished the drinks?'

'No! Er, I'd like Sergeant Lewis to go up and—'

'Fine! I'd better just give Cathy a ring, though. She'll have the place bolted.'

Morse saw little objection, it seemed, and he and Lewis listened as Michaels used the phone by the side of the bar-counter and quickly told his wife that the police would be coming up – please let them in – they wanted to look in the rifle-cabinet – she knew where the key was – let them take what they wanted – he'd be home in half an hour – see her soon – nothing to worry about – ciao!

'Am I a suspect?' asked Michaels with a wan smile, after Lewis had left.

'Yes,' said Morse simply, draining his beer. 'Another?'

'Why not? I'd better make the most of things.'

'And I want you to come up to Kidlington HQ in the morning. About – about ten o'clock, if that's all right.'

'I'm not dreaming, am I?' asked Michaels, as Morse picked up the two empty glasses.

'I'm afraid not,' said Morse. 'And, er, I think it'll be better if we send a car for you, Mr Michaels . . .'

A very clean and shining Mrs Michaels, smelling of shampoo and bath-salts, a crimson bath-robe round her body, a white towel round her head, let Sergeant Lewis in immediately, handed him the cabinet key, and stood aside as very carefully he lifted the rifle from its stand – one finger on the end of the barrel and one finger under the butt – and placed it in a transparent plastic container. On the shelf above the stand were two gunsmiths' catalogues; but no sign whatever of any cartridges.

Holding the rifle now by the middle of the barrel, Lewis thanked Mrs Michaels, and left – hearing the rattle of the chain and the thud of the bolts behind him as the head forester's wife awaited the return of her husband. For a while he wondered what she must be thinking at that moment. Puzzlement, perhaps? Or panic? It had been difficult to gauge anything from the eyes behind those black-rimmed spectacles. Not much of a communicator at all, in fact, for Lewis suddenly realized that whilst he was there she had spoken not a single word.

It was completely dark now, and the sergeant found himself feeling slightly nervous as he flicked the headlights to full beam along the silent lane.

Chapter Fifty-Seven

FALSTAFF: We have heard the chimes at midnight,
Master Shallow.
SHALLOW: That we have, that we have, that we have; in
faith, Sir John, we have

(Shakespeare, *Henry IV, Part 2*)

OF THE four men who had agreed to concoct (as Morse now believed) a joint statement about the murder of Karin Eriksson, only McBryde had ranged free in the city of Oxford that night. At 6.30 p.m. he had called in at the Eagle and Child, carrying his few overnight possessions in a canvas hold-all, eaten a cheese sandwich, drunk two pints of splendidly conditioned Burton Ale, and begun thinking about a bed for the night. At 7.45 p.m. he had caught a number 20 Kidlington bus outside St Giles' Church and gone up the Banbury Road as far as Squitchey Lane, where he tried the Cotswold House (recommended to him by Hardinge) but found the oblong, white notice fixed across the front door's leaded glass: NO VACANCIES. Just across the way however was the Casa Villa, and here one double room was still available (the last); which McBryde took, considering as many men had done before him that the purchase of an extra two square yards of bed space was something of a waste – and something of a sadness.

At about the time that McBryde was unpacking his pyjamas and sticking his toothbrush into one of the two glasses in his *en suite* bathroom, Philip Daley stood up and counted the coins.

He had caught the coach from Gloucester Green at 2.30 p.m. Good value, the coach – only £4 return for adults. Disappointing though to learn that a single fare was virtually the same price as a return, and sickening that the driver refused to accept his only marginally dishonest assertion that he was still at school. At 6.30 p.m. he had been seated against the wall of an office building next to the Bonnington Hotel in Southampton Row, with a grey and orange scarf arranged in front of him to receive the coins of a stream (as he trusted) of compassionate passers-by; and with a notice, black Biro on cardboard, beside him: UNEMPLOYED HOMELESS HUNGRY. One of the Oxford boys had told him that COLD AND HUNGRY was best, but the early summer evening was balmy and warm, and anyway it didn't matter much, not that first night. He had £45 in his pocket, and certainly had no intention of letting himself get too hungry. It was just that he wanted to see how things would work out – that was all.

Not very well, though, seemed the answer to that experiment: for he was stiff and even (yes!) a little cold; and the coins amounted to only 83p. He must look too well dressed still, too well fed, too little in need. At nine o'clock he walked down to a pub in Holborn and ordered a pint of beer and two packets of crisps: £2.70. Bloody robbery! Nor were things made easier when a shaven-headed youth with multi-tattooed arms and multi-ringed ears moved in beside him, and asked him if he was the prick who'd been staking out his pitch in the Row; because if so he'd be well advised to fuck off smartish – if he knew what was best for him.

Cathy Michaels repeatedly bent forwards, sideways, backwards, as the heat from the dryer penetrated her thick, raven-black hair, specially cut for *The Mikado* in a horizontal bob, the original blonde just beginning to show again, even if only a few millimetres or so at the roots. For a moment she felt sure she'd heard the Land-rover just outside, and she turned off the dryer. False alarm, though. Usually she experienced little or no nervousness when left alone in the cottage, even at night; and never when Bobbie was with her. But Bobbie was not with her: he was down at the pub with his master . . . and with the policemen. Suddenly she felt fear almost palpably creeping across her skin, like some soft-footed, menacing insect.

Midnight was chiming, and Morse was pouring himself a nightcap from the green, triangular-columned bottle of Glenfiddich – when the phone went: Dr Hobson. She had agreed to ring him if she discovered anything further before the end of that long, long day. Not that there *was* anything startlingly new, and she realized it could easily wait till morning. But no, it couldn't wait till morning, Morse had insisted.

The bullet that had killed Daley had fairly certainly been fired from a seven-millimetre or a .243 rifle, or something very similar; the bullet had entered the back about 2 inches below the left scapula, had exited (no wince this time from Morse) about 1 inch above the heart, and (this certain now) had been instantly fatal. Time? Between 10 a.m. and 11 a.m. – with just a little leeway either side? – 9.30 a.m. and 11.30 a.m., say? Most probably Daley had been shot from a distance of about 50–80 yards: ballistics might just amend this last finding, but she doubted it.

He'd seemed pleased, and she knew she wanted to please him. There was some music playing in the background, but she failed to recognize it.

'You're not in bed yet?' she ventured.

'Soon shall be.'

'What are you doing?'

'Drinking Scotch.'

'And listening to music.'

'Yes, that too.'

'You're a very civilized copper, aren't you?'

'Only half the time.'

'Well, I'd better gor.'

'Yes.'

'Goodnate, then.'

'Goodnight, and thank you,' said Morse quietly.

*

After putting down the phone Laura Hobson sat perfectly still and wondered what was happening to her. Why, he was twenty-five years older than she was!

At least.

Blast him!

She acknowledged to herself the ludicrous truth of the matter, but she could barely bring herself to smile.

CHAPTER FIFTY-EIGHT

He who asks the questions cannot avoid the answers

(Cameroonian proverb)

THERE WAS little evidence of strain or undue appre-
hension on David Michaels' face the following morning
when he was shown into Interview Room 2, where
Sergeant Lewis was already seated at a trestle table, a
tape recorder at his right elbow. He was being held for
questioning (Lewis informed him) about two matters:
first, about the statement made to the police by Dr Alan
Hardinge, a copy of which was now handed to him;
second, about the murder of George Daley.

Lewis pointed to the tape recorder. 'Just to make
sure we don't misrepresent anything, Mr Michaels.
We've been getting a bit of stick recently, haven't we,
about the way some interviews have been conducted?'

Michaels shrugged indifferently.

'And you're aware of your legal rights? Should you
want to be legally represented—'

But Michaels shook his head; and began reading
Hardinge's statement . . .

He had little legal knowledge, but had assumed in
this instance that he could be guilty only of some small-
scale conspiracy to pervert the strict course of truth –
certainly not of justice. It was the criminal 'intention',

the *mens rea*, that really mattered (so he'd read), and no one could ever maintain that his own intention had been criminal that afternoon a year ago . . .

'Well?' asked Lewis when Michaels put the last sheet down.

'That's about the size of it, yes.'

'You're quite happy to corroborate it?'

'Why not? One or two little things I wouldn't have remembered but – yes, I'll sign it.'

'We're not asking for a signature. We'll have to ask you to make your *own* statement.'

'Can't I just copy this one out?'

Lewis grinned weakly, but shook his head. He thought he liked Michaels. 'Now, last time you pretended – *pretended* – you'd not got the faintest idea where any body might be found, right?'

'Yes,' lied Michaels.

'And then, this time round, you *still* pretended you didn't really know?'

'Yes,' lied Michaels.

'So why did you nudge Chief Inspector Morse in the right direction?'

'Double bluff, wasn't it? If I was vague enough, and they *found* it, well, no one was going to think I'd had anything to do with the murder.'

'Who told you it was *murder*?'

'The chap standing there on guard in Pasticks: big chap, in a dark blue uniform and checked cap – policeman, I think he was.'

The constable standing wide-legged across the door of the interview room took advantage of the fact that Lewis had his back towards him, and smiled serenely.

'Why didn't you dump the rucksack in the lake as well?' continued Lewis.

For the first time Michaels hesitated: 'Should've done, I agree.'

'Was it because Daley had his eye on the camera – and the binoculars?'

'Well, one thing's for sure: *he* won't be able to tell you, will he?'

'You don't sound as if you liked him much.'

'He was a filthy, mean-minded little swine!'

'But you didn't know him very well, surely?'

'No. I hardly knew him at all.'

'What about last Friday night?'

'What *about* last Friday night?'

Lewis let it go. 'You'd never met him previously – at your little rendezvous in Park Town?'

'No! I'd only just joined,' lied Michaels. 'Look, Sergeant, I'm not proud of that. But haven't you ever wanted to watch a sex film?'

'I've seen plenty. We pick up quite a few of 'em here and there. But I'd rather have a plate of egg and chips, myself. What about you, Constable Watson?' asked Lewis, turning in his chair.

'Me?' said the man by the door. 'I'd much rather watch a sex film.'

'You wouldn't want your wife to know, though?'

'No, Sarge.'

'Nor would you, would you, Mr Michaels?'

'No. I wouldn't want her to know about anything like that,' said Michaels quietly.

'I wonder if Mrs Daley knew – about her husband, I mean?'

'I dunno. As I say, I knew nothing about the man, really.'

'Last night you knew he'd been murdered.'

'A lot of people knew.'

'And a lot of people *didn't* know.'

Michaels remained silent.

'He was killed with a seven-millimetre gun, like as not.'

'Rifle, you mean.'

'Sorry. I'm not an expert on guns and things – not like you, Mr Michaels.'

'And that's why you took my rifle last night?'

'We'd've taken *anyone*'s rifle. That's our job, isn't it?'

'Every forester's got a rifle that sort of calibre – very effective they are too.'

'So where were you between, say, ten o'clock and eleven o'clock yesterday morning?'

'Not much of a problem there. About ten – no – just *after* ten it must have been – I was with a couple of fellows from the RSPB. We – they – were checking on the nesting boxes along the Singing Way. You know, keeping records on first or second broods, weighing 'em, taking samples of droppings – that sort of thing. They do it all the time.'

'You were helping them?'

'Carrying the bloody ladder most of the time.'

'What about *after* that?'

'Well, we all nipped down to the White Hart – about twelve, quarter-past? – and had a couple of pints. Warm work, it was! Hot day, too!'

'You've got the addresses of these fellows?'

'Not on me, no. I can get 'em for you easy enough.'

'And the barman there at the pub? He knows you?'

'Rather too well, Sergeant!'

Lewis looked at his wrist-watch, feeling puzzled and, yes, a little bit lost.

'Can I go now?' asked Michaels.

'Not yet, sir, no. As I say we need some sort of statement from you about what happened last July . . . then we shall just have to get this little lot typed up' – Lewis nodded to the tape recorder – 'then we shall have to get you to read it and sign it . . . and, er, I should think we're not going to get through all that till . . .' Again Lewis looked at his watch, still wondering exactly where things stood. Then, turning round: 'We'd better see Mr Michaels has some lunch with us, Watson. What's on the menu today?'

'Always mince on Tuesdays, Sarge.'

'Most people'd prefer a sex film,' said Michaels, almost cheerfully.

Lewis rose to his feet, nodded to Watson, and made to leave. 'One other thing, sir. I can't let you go before the chief inspector gets back, I'm afraid. He said he particularly wanted to see you again.'

'And where's he supposed to be this morning?'

'To tell you the truth, I'm not at all sure.'

*

As he walked back to his office, Lewis reflected on what he had just learned. Morse had been correct on virtually everything so far – right up until this last point. For now surely Morse must be dramatically wrong in his belief that Michaels had murdered Daley? In due course they would have to check up on his alibi; but it was wholly inconceivable that a pair of dedicated ornithologists had conspired with a barman from the local pub in seeking to pervert the course of natural justice. Surely so!

At 12.30 p.m., Dr Hobson rang through from South Parks Road to say that, whilst she was an amateur in the byways of ballistics, she would be astounded if Michaels' gun had been fired at any time within the previous few weeks.

'"Rifle",' muttered Lewis, *sotto voce.*

'Is he, er, there?' the pathologist had asked tentatively.

'Back this afternoon some time.'

'Oh.'

It was beginning to look as if everyone wanted to see Morse.

Especially Lewis.

CHAPTER FIFTY-NINE

This is the reason why mothers are more devoted to their children than fathers: it is that they suffer more in giving them birth and are more certain that they are their own

(Aristotle, *Nicomachean Ethics*)

THE NOON-DAY sun shone on the pale-cinnamon stone of the colleges, and the spires of Oxford looked down on a scene of apparent tranquillity as the marked police car drove down Headington Hill towards the Plain, then over Magdalen Bridge and into the High. In the back sat Morse, sombre, and now silent, for he had talked sufficiently to the rather faded woman in her mid-forties who sat beside him, her eyes red from recent weeping, her mouth still tremulous, but her small chin firm and somehow courageous in the face of the terrible events she had only learned about two hours before – when the front doorbell had rung in her sister's council house in Beaconsfield. Yet the news that her husband had been murdered and that her only son had run away from home had left her not so much devastated as dumbfounded, as though a separate layer of emotions and reactions had formed itself between what she knew to be herself, and the external reality of what had occurred.

It had helped a bit too – talking with the chief inspector, who seemed to understand a good deal of what she was suffering. Not that she'd bared her soul *too* much to him about the increasing repugnance she'd felt for the man she'd married; the man who had slowly yet inevitably revealed over the years of their lives together the shallow, devious, occasionally cruel, nature of his character. There had been Philip, though; and for so long the little lad had compensated in manifold ways for the declining love and respect she was feeling for her husband. In nursery school, in primary school, even at the beginning of secondary school, certainly until he was about twelve, Philip had almost always turned to her, his mother; confided in her; had (so preciously!) hugged her when he was grateful or happy. She had been very proud that she was the loved and favoured parent.

Whether it was of deliberate, vindictive intent or not, she couldn't honestly say, but soon after Philip had started at secondary school, George had begun to assert his influence over the boy and in some ways to steal his affection away from her; and this by the simple expedient of encouraging in him the idea of growing up, of becoming 'a man', and doing mannish things. At weekends he would take the boy fishing; often he would return from the Royal Sun in the evening bringing a few cans of light ale with him, regularly offering one to his young son. Then the air-gun! For Philip's thirteenth birthday George had bought him an air-gun; and very soon afterwards Philip had shot a sparrow at the bottom of the garden as it was pecking at some bird-seed she

347

herself had thrown down. What a terrible evening that had been between them, husband and wife, when she had accused him of turning their son into a philistine! Progressively too there had been the coarsening of Philip's speech, and of his attitudes; the brittle laughter between father and son about jokes to which she was never privy; reports from school which grew worse and worse; and the friendship with some of the odious classmates he occasionally brought home to listen to pop music in the locked bedroom.

Then, over a year ago, that almighty row between father and son about the rucksack, which had resulted in an atmosphere of twisted bitterness. Exactly what had happened then, she was still uncertain; but she knew that her husband had lied about the time and place he had found the rucksack. How? Because neither George nor Philip had taken the dog for its walk along the dual-carriageway that morning: *she* had. Philip had gone off to Oxford very early to join a coach party the school had organized; and, on waking, her husband had been so crippled with lumbago that he couldn't even make it to the loo, let alone any lay-by on the dual-carriageway. But she knew George *had* found the rucksack, somewhere – or that someone had given it to him – on that very Sunday when the Swedish girl had gone missing; that Sunday when George had been out all afternoon; and then out again later in the evening, drinking heavily, as she recalled. It must have been that Sunday evening too when Philip had found the rucksack, probably at the back of the garage where, as she knew, he'd been looking for his climbing boots for the school trip to the Peak District – and where, as she suspected, he'd found the camera and the binoculars. Oh yes! She was on very firm ground there – because *she too had found them*, in Philip's room. Only later did she learn that Philip had removed the spool of film from the camera and almost certainly developed it himself at school, where there was a flourishing photographic society (of which Philip was a member) with dark-room facilities readily available.

A good deal of this information Morse had known already, she sensed that. But appearances were that she'd held his attention as tearfully and fitfully she'd covered most of the ground again. He'd not asked her how she knew about the photographs; yet he surely must have guessed. But he would never know about those other photographs, the pornographic ones, the ones of the Swedish girl whom she had recognized from the passport picture printed, albeit so badly, in *The Oxford Times*. No! She would tell Morse nothing about that. Nor about the joy-riding – and her mental turmoil when first she'd read those words in Philip's diary; words which conjured up for her the confused images of squealing tyres and the anguished shrieks of a small girl lying in a pool of her own blood . . . No, it would belittle her son even further if she spoke of things like that, and she would never do it. Wherever he was and whatever he'd done, *Philip would always be her son*.

As the car turned left at Carfax, down towards St Aldate's police station, she saw a dozen or more headjerking pigeons pecking at the pavement; and then fluttering with sudden loud clapping of wings up to the tower above them. Taking flight. Free! And Margaret Daley, her head now throbbing wildly, wondered if she would ever herself feel free again . . .

'Milk and sugar?'

Margaret Daley had been miles away, but she'd heard his words, and now looked up into the chief inspector's face, his eyes piercingly blue, but kindly, and almost vulnerable themselves, she thought.

'No sugar. Just milk, please.'

Morse laid his hand lightly on her shoulder. 'You're a brave woman,' he said quietly.

Suddenly the flood-gates were totally swept away, and she turned from him and wept quite uncontrollably.

'You heard what the lady said,' snarled Morse, as the constable at the door watched the two of them, hesitantly. 'No bloody sugar!'

CHAPTER SIXTY

Music and women I cannot but give way to, whatever my business is

(Samuel Pepys, *Diary*)

JUST AFTER lunch-time Morse was back in his office at HQ listening to the tape of Michaels' interview.

'What do you think, sir?'

'I suppose some of it's true,' admitted Morse.

'About not killing Daley, you mean?'

'I don't see how he could have done it – no time was there?'

'Who did kill him, do you think?'

'Well, there are three things missing from his house, aren't there? Daley himself, the rifle – and the boy.'

'The son? Philip? You think *he* killed him? Killed his father? Like Oedipus?'

'The things I've taught you, Lewis, since you've been my sergeant!'

'Did he love his mum as well?'

'Very much so, I think. Anyway you'll be interested in hearing what she's got to say.'

'But – but you can't just walk into Blenheim Park with a rifle on your shoulder—'

'His mum says he used to go fishing there; says his dad bought him all the gear.'

'Ah. See what you mean. Those long canvas things, you know – for your rods and things.'

'Something like that. Ten minutes on a bike—'

'Has he *got* a bike?'

'Dunno.'

'But *why*? Why do you think—?'

'Must have been that letter, I suppose – from the Crown Court . . .'

'And his dad refused to help?'

'Probably. Told his son to clear off, like as not; told him to bugger off and leave his parents out of it. Anyway, I've got a feeling the lad's not going to last long in the big city. The Met'll bring him in soon, you see.'

'You said it was *Michaels*, though. You said you were pretty sure it must have been Michaels.'

'Did I?'

'Yes, you did! But you didn't seem *too* surprised when you just heard the tape?'

'Didn't I?'

Lewis let it go. 'Where do we go from here, then?'

'Nowhere, for a bit. I've got a meeting with Strange first. Three o'clock.'

'What about Michaels? Let him go?'

'Why should we do that?'

'Well, like you say – he just couldn't have done it in the time. Impossible! Even with a helicopter.'

'So?'

Suddenly Lewis was feeling more than a little irritated. 'So what do I tell him?'

'You tell him,' said Morse slowly, 'that we're keeping him here overnight – for further questioning.'

'On what charge? We just can't—'

'I don't think he'll argue too loudly,' said Morse.

Just before Morse was to knock on Chief Superintendent Strange's door that Tuesday afternoon, two men were preparing to leave the Trout Inn at Wolvercote. Most of the customers who had spent their lunch-time out of doors, seated on the paved terrace alongside the river there, were now gone; it was almost closing time.

'You promise to write it down?'

'I promise,' replied Alasdair McBryde.

'Where are you going now?'

'Back to London.'

'Can I give you a lift to the station?'

'I'd be glad of that.'

The two walked up the shallow steps and out across the narrow road to the car park: PATRONS ONLY. NO PARKING FOR FISHERMEN.

'What about you, Alan?' asked McBryde, as Hardinge drove the Sierra left towards Wolvercote.

'I don't know. And I don't really care.'

'Don't say that!' McBryde laid his right hand lightly on the driver's arm. But Hardinge dismissed the gesture with his own right hand as if he were flicking a fly from his sleeve, and the journey down to Oxford station was made in embarrassed silence.

Back in Radcliffe Square, Hardinge parked on double yellow lines in Catte Street, and went straight up to his rooms in Lonsdale. He knew her number off by heart. Of course he did.

'Claire? It's me, Alan.'

'I know it's you. Nothing wrong with my ears.'

'I was just wondering . . . just hoping . . .'

'No! And we're not going to go over all *that* again.'

'You mean you're not even going to *see* me again?'

'That's it!'

'Not *ever*?' His throat was suddenly very dry.

'You know, for a university don, you don't pick some things up very quickly, do you?'

For a while Hardinge said nothing. He could hear music playing in the background; he knew the piece well.

'If you'd told me you enjoyed Mozart—'

'Look – for the last time! – it's finished. Please accept that! *Finished*!'

'Have you got someone else?'

'What?' He heard her bitter laughter. 'My life's been full of "someone elses". You always knew that.'

'But what if I divorced—'

'For Christ's *sake*! Won't you *ever* understand? It's *over*!'

The line was dead, and Hardinge found himself looking down at the receiver as if someone had given him a frozen fillet of fish for which for the moment he could find no convenient receptacle.

Claire Osborne sat by the phone for several minutes after she had rung off, the wonderful trombone passage from the *Tuba Mirum Spargens Sonum* registering only vaguely in her mind. Had she been too cruel to Alan? But sometimes it was necessary to be cruel to be kind – wasn't that what they said? Or was that just a meaningless cliché like the rest of them? 'Someone else?' Alan had asked.

Huh!

The poorly typed letter (no salutation, no subscription) she had received with the cassette that morning was lying on the coffee table, and already she'd read it twenty-odd times:

I enjoyed so much our foreshortened time together, you and the music. One day of the great lost days, one face of all the faces (Ernest Dowson – not me!). A memento herewith. The *Recordare* is my favourite bit – if I'm pushed to a choice. 'Recordare' by the way is the 2nd person singular of the present imperative of the verb 'recordor': it means 'Remember!'

CHAPTER SIXTY-ONE

A reasonable probability is the only certainty
(Edgar Watson Howe, *County Town Sayings*)

'YOU'RE *sure* about all this, Morse?' Strange's voice was sharp, with an edge of scepticism to it.

'Completely sure.'

'You said that about Michaels.'

'No! I only said I was ninety per cent sure on that.'

'OK.' Strange shrugged his shoulders, tilted his head, and opened his palms in a gesture of acquiescence. 'There are just one or two little things—'

But the phone went on Strange's desk: 'Ah! Ah! Yes! Want to speak to him?'

He handed the phone over to Morse: Dr Hobson. Quite certainly, she said, Michaels' rifle hadn't been fired for weeks. That was all.

Strange had heard the pathologist, just. 'Looks as if you're right about *that*, anyway. We'll give the Met a call. Certain to have scarpered to the capital, don't you reckon, the lad?'

'Ninety per cent sure, sir – and we've already given the Met his description.'

'Oh!'

Morse rose to go, but Strange was not quite finished: 'What first put you on to it?'

For a few moments Morse paused dubiously. 'Several things, I suppose. For example, I once heard someone claim that all three types of British woodpeckers could be found in Wytham Woods. I think I heard it in a pub. Or perhaps I just read it on a beer mat.'

'Useful things, pubs!'

'Then' – Morse ignored the sarcasm – 'I thought if Johnson had opted for Blenheim, it'd pretty certainly turn out to be Wytham.'

'That's grossly unfair.'

'I agree.' Morse got up and walked to the door. 'You know, it's a bit surprising no one ever noticed her accent, isn't it? She must *have* a bit of an accent. I bet you I'll notice it!'

'You're a lucky bugger to hear as well as you do. The wife says I'm getting deafer all the time.'

'Get a hearing aid, sir. They probably wouldn't let you stay in the force, and they'd have to give you a few years' enhancement on the pension.'

'You *think* so? Really?'

'Ninety per cent sure,' said Morse, closing the door behind him and walking thoughtfully back through the maze of corridors to his office.

He'd omitted to acquaint Strange with the biggest clue of all, but it would have taken a little while to explain and it was all a bit nebulous – especially for a man of such matter-of-fact hardheadedness as Strange. But it *had* formed, for him, Morse, the focal point of all the mystery. The normal murderer (if such a person may be posited) would seek to cover up all traces of his victim. And if his victim were someone like Karin

Eriksson, he would burn the clothes, chuck her jewellery and trinkets into the canal, dispose of the body – sink it in some bottomless ocean or cut it up in little bits and take it to the nearest waste-disposal site; even pack it up in those black plastic bags for the dustmen to cart off, since in Morse's experience the only things they *wouldn't* take were bags containing garden waste. So! So if our murderer wanted to rid the earth of every trace of his victim, why, *why*, had he been so anxious for the rucksack and associated possessions to be found? All right, it hadn't worked out all that well, with accidental factors, as almost always, playing their part. But the rucksack *was* found, very soon; the police *were* informed, very soon; the hunt for Karin's murderer *was* under way, very soon. Now if a young Swedish student goes missing *sans everything*, then there is always *less* than certitude that she is dead: thousands of young persons from all parts of Europe, all parts of the world, disappear regularly; get listed as 'missing persons'. But if a young girl goes missing, and at the same time her possessions are discovered in a hedgerow somewhere nearby, then the implications are all too painfully obvious, the conclusions all too readily drawn: the conclusions that Johnson and almost every other policeman in the Thames Valley had drawn a year ago.

Though not Morse.

Perhaps he could, on reflexion, have explained his thinking to Strange without too much difficulty? After all, the key question could be posed very simply, really: why was the murderer so anxious for the police to pursue a murder enquiry? To that strange question

Morse now knew the answer; of that he was quite sure. Well, ninety-nine per cent sure: because the police would be looking for a body, *not for someone who was still alive.*

Ten minutes later, Lewis was ready for him, and together the two detectives drove out to Wytham Woods once more.

CHAPTER SIXTY-TWO

The one charm of marriage is that it makes a life of
deception absolutely necessary for both parties
(Oscar Wilde, *The Picture of Dorian Gray*)

THERE WERE four of them in the living room of the
low-ceilinged cottage: Morse and Lewis seated side by
side on the leather settee, Mrs Michaels opposite them
in an armchair, and the small attractive figure of the
uniformed WPC Wright standing by the door.

'Why haven't you brought David?' asked Mrs
Michaels.

'Isn't he still making a statement, Sergeant?' Morse's
eyebrows rose quizzically as if the matter were of minor
import.

'What are you here for then?' She lifted her eyes
and cocked her head slightly to Morse as if she were
owed some immediate and convincing explanation.

'We're here about your marriage. There's something
slightly, ah, irregular about it.'

'Really? You'll have to check that up with the Registry
Office, not me.'

'Register Office, Mrs Michaels. It's important to be
accurate about things. So let *me* be accurate. David
Michaels discovered that the District Office for anyone
living in Wytham was at Abingdon, and he went there

and answered all the usual questions about when and where you wanted to marry, how old you both were, where you were both born, whether either of you had been married before, whether you were related. And that was that. Two days later you were married.'

'So?'

'Well, everything is really based on *trust* in things like that. If you want to, you can tell a pack of lies. There's one Registrar in Oxford who married the same fellow three times in the same year – one in Reading who managed to marry a couple of sailors!'

Morse looked across at her as if expecting a dutiful smile, but Mrs Michaels sat perfectly still, her mouth tight, her hair framing the clear-skinned features in a semi-circle of the darkest black, the blonde roots so very recently re-dyed.

'Take any reasonably fluent liar – even a fairly clumsy liar,' continued Morse, 'and he'll get away with murder – if you see what I mean, Mrs Michaels. For example, some proof of age is required for anyone under twenty-three, did you know that? But if your fiancé says you're twenty-*four*? Well, he'll almost certainly get away with it. And if you've been married before? Well, if you say you *haven't*, it's going to be virtually impossible to prove, then and there, that you have. Oh yes! It's easy to get married by licence if you're willing to abuse the system.'

'You are saying that I – that we, David and I – we abused the system?'

'You know most English people would have settled for "me and David", Mrs Michaels.' (WPC Wright was aware of that nuance of stress on the word 'English'.)

'I asked you—'

But Morse interrupted her brusquely: 'There was only one thing that couldn't be fiddled in your case: date of birth. You see, some documentation is statutory in that respect – *if the person concerned is a foreign national.*'

A silence now hung over the small room; a palpably tense silence, during which a strange, indefinable look flitted across Mrs Michaels' features as she crossed one leg over the other and clasped her hands round her left knee.

'What's that got to do with me?' she asked.

'You're a foreign national,' said Morse simply, looking across unblinkingly at the lovely girl seated opposite him.

'Do you realize how absurd all this is, Inspector?'

'Did you have to show your passport to the Registrar at Abingdon?'

'There was no *need* for that: I'm *not* a foreign national!'

'No?'

'*No!* My name is – *was* Catharine Adams. I was born in Uppingham, in Rutland – what *used* to be Rutland; I'm twenty-four years old—'

'Can *I* see your passport?' asked Morse quietly.

'As a matter of fact you can't. It's in the post to Swansea – it needs renewing. We are going – me and David! – to Italy in September.' (Lewis could pick up the hint of the accent now, in that word 'Eetaly'.)

'Don't worry! We've already got a copy, you see. The Swedish Embassy sent us one.'

For several moments she looked down at the carpet, the one expensive item in the rather mundane living room in which she'd spent so many hours of her days: a small, rectangular oriental carpet, woven perhaps in some obscure tent in Turkestan. Then, rising, she took a few steps over to a desk, took out her passport, and handed it to Morse.

But Morse knew it all anyway; had already studied the details carefully: the headings, printed in both Swedish and English; the details required, handwritten in Swedish. Underneath the photograph, he read again:

```
Surname        ........................................
Christian  name(s)  ............................
Height  in  cms  (without  shoes)  ..................
Sex        ................................................
Date  of  birth  ....................................
Place  of  birth  ....................................
Civic  Reg.  No.  ....................................
Date  issued  ....................................
How  long  valid  ................................
Signature  ........................................
Remarks  ........................................
```

Katarina Adams (it appeared), height 168 cms in her stockinged feet, of the female sex, had been born on the 29 September 1968, in Uppsala, Sweden.

'Clever touch that, Uppingham for Úppsala,' commented Morse.

'Uppsála – if we must be accurate, Inspector.'

'"Adams" was your married name – your first

married name. And when your husband was killed in a car crash, you kept it. Why not? So . . .'

'So, what else do you want from me?' she asked quietly.

'Just tell me the truth, please! We shall get there in the end, you know.'

She took a deep breath, and spoke quickly and briefly. 'When my sister Karin was murdered, I was in Spain – in Barcelona, as it happened. I got here as soon as I could – my mother had rung me from Sweden. But I could do nothing, I soon realized that. I met David. We fell in love. We were married. I was frightened about work permits and visas and that sort of thing, and David said it would be better if I lied – if *he* lied – about my earlier marriage. Easier and quicker. So? For a start I only went out of the house here a very few times. I wore glasses and I had my hair cut fairly short and dyed black. That's why they asked me to sing in the opera, yes? I looked like the part before they started the auditions.'

Lewis glanced briefly sideways, and thought he saw a look of slight puzzlement on Morse's face.

'Didn't the Registrar *tell* you – tell your husband – that it was all above board anyway?'

'No, I'm sure he didn't. You see we said nothing about this . . . you know. Can't you understand? It was all very strange – all very unsettling and sort of, sort of nervy, somehow. David understood, though—'

'Did you enjoy your holiday in Spain?'

'Very much. Why—?'

'Which airport did you fly from to England?'

'Barcelona.'

'Lots of muggings, they tell me, at Barcelona airport.'

'What's that got to do—?'

'Ever lost *your* handbag? You know, with your keys and passport and credit cards?'

'No. I'm glad to say I haven't.'

'What would you *do* if you lost your passport, say?'

She shrugged. 'I don't know. I'd apply to the Swedish Embassy, I suppose. They'd probably give me a temporary document . . . or something . . .'

'But do you think it would be possible to *fiddle* things, Mrs Michaels? Like it's possible to fiddle a marriage licence?'

'I wish you'd tell me exactly what you're getting at.'

'All right. Let me ask you a simple question. Would it be possible for anyone to apply for someone *else's* passport?'

'Almost impossible, surely? There are all sorts of checks in Sweden: Civic Registration Number – that's what we use in Sweden instead of a birth certificate – details of all the information on the passport that would have to be checked – photograph? No! I don't think it would.'

'I agree with you, I think. *Almost* impossible – though not quite; not for a very clever woman.'

'But I'm *not* a very clever woman, Inspector.'

'No! Again I agree with you.' (Lewis wondered if he'd spotted the slightest trace of disappointment in her eyes.) 'But let's agree it is impossible, right. There is another way, though, a very much easier way of acquiring a passport. A childishly easy way. Someone *gives* you one, Mrs Michaels. Someone *sends* you one through the post.'

'You are leaving me many miles behind, Inspector.'

'No, I'm not,' replied Morse, with a quiet factuality that brooked no argument. 'No one – *no one* – lost any passport at Barcelona, or anywhere else. But you and your elder sister are very much alike, aren't you? My sergeant here brought me a photograph of the three of you from Stockholm. You're all blonde and blue-eyed and high-cheekboned and long-legged and everything else people here expect from the Nordic type. Even your younger sister – the shortest of the three of you – she looks very much like Karin too, at least from her photograph.'

Forcibly she interrupted him: 'Listen! Just *one* moment, please! Have *you* ever felt completely confused – like I feel now?'

'Oh, yes! Quite frequently, believe me. But not now. Not now, Mrs Michaels. And you're not confused either. Because that passport there isn't yours. It belongs to your sister Katarina – Katarina Adams. Your sister who still lives in Uppsála. Your sister who told the Swedish authorities that she'd had her passport stolen, and then applied for another. Simple! You see, your name isn't Katarina Adams at all, is it, Mrs Michaels? It's *Karin Eriksson.*'

Her shoulders suddenly sagged, as if she felt that, in spite of any innocent protestations she might make, she was not going to be believed by anyone; as if on that score at least she would perhaps be well advised to leave her case to the testimony of others.

But Morse was pressing home his advantage; and WPC Wright (though not Lewis) found his further questioning embarrassing and tasteless.

'You've got beautiful legs – would you agree?'

'What?' Instinctively she sought to pull the hem of her knee-length skirt an inch or two lower over her elegant legs; but with little effect.

'You know,' continued Morse, 'when I was talking just now about the Nordic type, I was thinking of the films we used to see of all those sexy Swedish starlets. I used to go to the pictures a lot in those days—'

'Do you want me to do a streep-tease for you?'

'You see, my sergeant here and me – and I – we've got quite a big advantage really, because we've had a chance to study your passport – if it *is* yours—'

She was almost at the end of her tether. 'What *is* it?' she shrieked. 'Please! Please *tell* me! What are you *accusing* me of? All of you?'

Resignedly Morse gestured with his right hand to Lewis; and Lewis, in a flat and melancholy voice, intoned the charge:

'Mrs Karin Michaels – Miss Karin Eriksson – I have to inform you that you are under police arrest on suspicion of murdering one James Myton, on the afternoon of Sunday, July seventh, 1991. It is my duty to warn you that anything you may now say in the presence of the three police officers here may be used in evidence in any future proceedings.'

Morse got up, and now stood above her.

'There's no need for you to say anything, not for the time being.'

'You mean you are accusing me – *me* – of being Karin, my sister? The sister who was *murdered*?'

'You're still denying it?' queried Morse quietly.

'Of course! Of *course*, I am!'

'You can prove it, you know. The Swedish authorities tell us they don't use that "Remarks" section very much at all on the passport – only really if there's some obvious distinguishing mark that can help in establishing identity. On the passport though – the one you say is yours – that section's filled in, in Swedish. And it says, so they tell me, "Pronounced diagonal scar, inner thigh above left knee-cap, eight and a half centimetres in length, result of motoring accident".'

'Yes?' She looked up at the chief inspector as if she almost willed him, dared him, *wanted* him, to prove his accusation.

'So if you *do* have a scar there, it won't necessarily prove *who* you are, will it? But if you haven't . . . if you *haven't*, then you're not now, and never were, the woman described on that passport.'

Karin Eriksson, the murderer of James Myton, now sat completely still for many agonizing seconds. Then slowly, tantalizingly, as if she were some upper-class artiste in a strip-tease parlour, centimetre by centimetre her left hand lifted the hem of the beige velvet skirt above her left knee to reveal the naked flesh upon her inner thigh.

Did she rejoice in the gaze of the two detectives

there? Had she secretly always thrilled to the admiration of the young boys in her high school class at Uppsala – of the tutors on her course? Even perhaps, for a short while, to the lust of the crude and ratty-faced Myton, who had sought to rape her out in Wytham Woods, and whom she had then so deliberately murdered?

And as Morse looked down at the smooth and unscarred flesh above her knee, he found himself wondering for a little while whether he too, like Myton, might not at some point on a hot and sultry summer afternoon have found this girl so very beautiful and necessary.

Lewis drove carefully down the road that led along the edge of the woods towards Wytham village. Beside him was WPC Wright; and in the back sat Karin Eriksson and Chief Inspector Morse.

Almost always, at such a stage in any case, Morse felt himself saddened – with the thrill of the chase now over, with the guilty left to face the appropriate retribution. Often had he pondered on the eternal problem of justice; and he knew as did most men of civilized values that the function of law was to provide that framework of order within which men and women could be protected as they went about their legitimate business. Yes, the criminal must be punished for his misdeeds, for that was the law. And Morse was an upholder of the law. Yet he debated now again, as he felt the body of Karin Eriksson close beside him, that fine distinction between the law and justice. Justice was one of those big words that was so often spelled with a capital 'J'; but really it was so much harder to define than Law. Karin would have to face the law; and he turned to look at her – to look at those beautiful blue eyes of hers, moistened now with the quiet film of tears. For a few seconds, at that moment, there seemed almost a bond between them – between Morse and the young woman who had murdered James Myton.

Suddenly, unexpectedly, she whispered something in his right ear.

'Did you ever have sex with a girl in the back of a car?'

'Not in the back,' whispered Morse. 'In the front, of course. Often!'

'Are you telling me the truth?'

'No,' said Morse.

He was conscious of a brimming reservoir of tears somewhere behind his own eyes as the police car came up to the main road and turned left, down past Wytham towards the police HQ. And for a second or two he thought he felt Karin's left leg pressing gently against him, and so very much he hoped that this was so.

CHAPTER SIXTY-THREE

> All that's left to happen
> Is some deaths (my own included).
> Their order, and their manner,
> Remain to be learnt
> (Philip Larkin, *Collected Poems*)

THE STATEMENT made by Karin Eriksson added little to Lewis's knowledge of the case. Unprecedentedly, Morse had kept him informed, in key respects, from fairly early on of his suspicions surrounding the Swedish Maiden and, eventually, of his virtual certainties. There were one or two significant discrepancies – particularly concerning the amount of money Karin had with her on her arrival in Oxford, and concerning the number of voyeurs who witnessed her photographic session in Seckham Villa. But from the combined statements of Karin herself and of her (wholly legitimate) husband David, it was a straightforward matter to stitch together the sequence of events that occurred on Sunday, 7 July 1991.

Out on the M40 Karin had almost immediately been picked up by a van en route for the Rover Car Plant at Cowley, in Oxford. Dropped off at the Headington roundabout, she had been picked up, again almost immediately, by a BMW and dropped at the Banbury Road roundabout on the Northern Ring Road. Walking a few hundred yards down the Banbury Road (buses on Sunday seemed infrequent) she had noticed the Cotswold House, and on impulse felt how wonderful it would be to spend at least one night in such attractive-looking B & B accommodation. She had knocked and enquired the rates; had been told that there was one single room vacancy; but on learning the tariff had decided to find something a little cheaper, a little later. From a phone-box in Wentworth Road, just opposite the Cotswold House, she had phoned the model agency, and fairly soon been collected and driven down to Abingdon Road, where a telephone arrangement was made with McBryde for Karin to present herself at Seckham Villa, at about 2 p.m., for an hour or so's photographic session – the fee suggested, £80–£120, causing her eyebrows to lift in pleasurable surprise. She had declined further help from the agency, and walked up to St Giles', where she had a ham sandwich and half a glass of lager in the Eagle and Child.

At Seckham Villa she had been admitted by McBryde, and soon introduced to Myton. No hard pornography! – she'd immediately made her position clear on that; but, yes, she was willing to pose for a series of nude and semi-nude studies. And for an extra £20 she'd agreed that two other men there could sit in the 'studio' and watch her. Myton, she learned, was a freelance cinematographer in the sex-video world, and almost straightaway she had felt his eyes stripping off her skimpy summer clothing. But he'd seemed all right. Whilst he was preparing his paraphernalia of tripods, umbrellas, backcloths, reflectors, light-meters, and the rest, she had wandered out briefly into the back garden; and when he had come out a little while later she had found him amusing and good fun. He was a smallish, slim man, with a day's growth of darkish beard, but with much lighter-coloured hair, worn quite long with an absurd short pony-tail held in an elastic band. She had teased him a little about this, and indeed asked him to stand by the wall there while *she* could take a couple of snaps. Soon though McBryde had hurriedly ushered them inside, where she was introduced, perfunctorily, to a man in a lightweight summer-suit, and another man in grey slacks and sports jacket, incongruously (as she remembered on that hot day) holding a green pork-pie hat.

Then the 'session'. She had, she confessed, experienced some flush of excitement as the two silent men (McBryde had only come in later) ogled her as she stripped and posed and donned the see-through lingerie provided, and lay there on the bed in gaping gowns and skimpy negligées. Myton had punctuated her posturings with crude encouragements as gradually she'd felt herself relaxing: 'Christ, that's marvellous! Yeah! Ye-eah! Just hold it there, baby! Keep that hand under your tits and sort of, yes, sort of push 'em at me!' Such manner of talk had excited her and, if she were honest with herself, she'd felt a sort of orgasm of sexual vanity.

Afterwards, when she and Myton were alone, she had asked him to take one or two snaps of her with her

own camera – just as a reminder really – and he'd
readily done so. He'd still not so much as touched her
physically, not yet; but he'd asked her where she was
going and said he had his car outside if she wanted a
lift anywhere. Before leaving McBryde had given her
£100, all in ten-pound notes, which she had placed in
her money-wallet; and then Myton had driven her back
up to the top of the Banbury Road. She told him that
she was thinking of going to the charity pop concert at
Blenheim the next evening, 8 July, and then – suddenly
– as they were passing the Cotswold House she asked
him to stop: she *would* stay there now. But a white
notice – NO VACANCIES – was across the door, and the
lady of the house confirmed sadly that the remaining
room had just been taken. As she was getting back into
the car, she thought she saw a sparrow-hawk flying over
towards the huge trees behind her, and she stopped
and sought to focus her binoculars upon it. Fatal
moment! Myton asked her if she was interested in
birdwatching; and she had shown him her list of hoped-
for spottings. Well, *he* knew exactly where she could see
the woodpecker – probably see *all* the woodpeckers. In
Wytham! He was interested himself in birds: was a
member of the RSPB (this later proving untrue) and
had a permit for walking in Wytham Woods (also
proving to be untrue).

That was the beginning of all her woe.

Setting off from the semi-circular parking area just
before the Great Wood, they had walked diagonally
across a field and then along some leafy woodland
pathway into a thickly forested area, where she remem-

bered the brittle crackling of dead twigs and branches beneath her feet; and then Myton's hands upon her body. At first perhaps she might have been prepared for some limited petting; but very soon he had grown rough and insistent, and told her that he needed her – urgently. Would *have* her! He'd stripped off her thin blouse and pulled her to the floor; but she was herself strong and determined in fighting him off. The pocket of the rucksack in which she kept her binoculars – and her knife – was still open; and she managed to struggle away from him and open the blade of the knife – and plunge it into him . . . It had entered his flesh so easily, like pushing a knife through soft cheese, she said; but a fountain of blood had spurted across the top of her semi-naked body. Unlike the blood though, *he* lay still, utterly still – his eyes wide open and glaring up at her.

She hurled the knife into the trees, picked up her scarlet rucksack, and dressed only in a blood-bespattered skirt she fled the spot in panic – emerging finally into a clearing where, panting and jabbering and whimpering, she ran and ran – she could have no idea how long, how far – before collapsing, and remembering nothing more until she looked up to see a dog, a black and white Welsh Border Collie, and a thick-set, bearded man behind the dog, his face anxious and kindly, looking down at her. A Land-rover was parked a few yards away.

In his cottage David Michaels at first had found it scarcely possible to believe the young woman's extraordinary account of what had occurred. It all seemed like some terrible *nightmare*, she'd pleaded: of a frenetic struggle and of a sudden death, if death it were; or of a man lying in the *agony* of death somewhere out there, somewhere in the woods. Indeed were it not for the blood all over her body, it *must* have been a nightmare surely! The mention of the word 'police' had driven her to hysterical tears; and clearly distressing too was the thought of the *car*, the car that from his cottage window Michaels could see even then across the lane. But *he* would deal with things, he'd promised her that – not knowing what he promised. He learned from her of Seckham Villa, and he made his decision. He got her to bath herself, to swallow half a dozen Disprin; and very soon, so suddenly, so miraculously almost, she had fallen deeply asleep, quite naked between the white sheets of his own double bed. And he realized at that moment that he was just as bad as the rest of them, for he lusted after her, just as other men had lusted after her that afternoon.

At Seckham Villa, Michaels had met the three of them – still there: McBryde, Daley, and Hardinge; and he had begun then to appreciate the complexity of the situation in which they all – including Michaels himself – now found themselves. A plan was conceived. And later executed. Just one detail that was new. Karin's intended visit to the pop concert at Blenheim could be used to their ready advantage, since the discovery of the rucksack and other personal possessions somewhere *near* Blenheim, the day *after* the concert, would throw everyone on to the wrong scent, and would promote dark suspicions of a young lady missing, presumed dead somewhere, doubtless murdered by some drug-crazed, sex-hyped youth whom she'd met at the jamboree. Fear of exposure and financial ruin was more than sufficient motivation for McBryde; fear of exposure and scandal more than sufficient for Hardinge; and a cheque (neither Karin nor David Michaels knew for how much) sufficient to ensure the co-operation of the mercenary Daley.

That night, back in the cottage on the edge of the woods, Karin had become terrifyingly distraught; he had slept with her, for she wished it so; she had sought throughout that night the reassurance of his embrace, and of his love; and gladly, gloriously, he had met her needs.

It had been *her* plan, *her* plea, to go to Wales – away, away somewhere, away anywhere; and the next morning, setting out from Wytham just after 6 o'clock, he had driven there, leaving her in the hands of a kindly woman who must fairly soon (surely, he'd felt) have been in possession of most of the facts herself. The only thing from her rucksack she had taken was £60 – leaving the rest inside her money-wallet: it seemed to them all a convincing detail. From Wales, she had phoned David frequently – sometimes several times each evening. She it was, Karin, who had phoned her mother, together with whom, and with her sisters, the next phase of the plan was conceived: the simple substitution of Katarina's passport, sent to Karin in a plain brown envelope from Barcelona.

Finally, there had been the return to Oxford – and to David Michaels, the man she was learning increasingly to love, and whose solicitude for her, in turn, seemed now to know no bounds. With her hair cut and dyed black, with a pair of black-framed spectacles, she had lived in the cottage in an idyllic state of happiness with David and Bobbie – until a gradual integration into life again: a drink at the village pub, badminton at the village hall, membership of the local operatic society. And marriage! Strange, really, that she could live so happily so near the murder. Yet she could. The nightmare had passed. It was as if a partition existed, a sort of mesh between her and the whole of her life before she'd met David – a mesh like the network of twigs and branches in the spot where the blood had spurted over her.

For the first six months or so David had daily expected to discover the body, especially so as the trees grew bare in that late autumn; or expected others to discover it, as they roamed the ridings and observed the birds, badgers, foxes, squirrels, deer ... But no. And when Morse had asked him where he himself might think of hiding a body, it had never occurred to him that Karin could have run so far, so very far from Pasticks out along by the Singing Way.

Just one more thing. Uncommonly for Swedish people, the Eriksson family were all Roman Catholic (something Lewis had suspected when he had seen the two crucifixes but, sadly, something he hadn't mentioned to Morse) and Karin had discovered the little church in the Woodstock Road. She had passed her driving test earlier that year, and was in the habit of going to Mass on Sunday mornings when David didn't require the Land-rover; and sometimes, when he did, waiting for him to pick her up after the service. Twice a month or so. Then to confession, about which she hadn't told her husband quite everything – certainly holding back from him her slowly formulating fear that her lack of contrition at having killed Myton was almost a greater sin than the killing itself had been; her fear that she might kill again, kill wildly and regardlessly if anyone came to threaten her own and David's happiness. Yet at the same time, an oddly contradictory wish was gradually growing too: the wish that someone would discover the truth of what she'd done; even that some-one would *divulge* that truth . . .

But Father Richards could never do that, he'd said, as he'd comforted her, and prayed with her, and forgiven her in the name of the Almighty Father.

CHAPTER SIXTY-FOUR

The lips frequently parted with a murmur of words.
She seemed to belong rightly to a madrigal
(Thomas Hardy, *The Return of the Native*)

ON THE evening of the day following these events, Wednesday 5 August, Morse, Lewis, and Dr Laura Hobson had enjoyed a little celebration in Morse's office; and at 8.30 p.m. a sober Lewis had driven the other two down to Morse's flat in North Oxford.

'You won't want another drink?' Morse had asked of Lewis, as if the question were introduced by *num*, the Latin interrogative particle expecting the answer 'no'.

'What elegant equipment!' enthused Laura Hobson as she admired Morse's new CD player.

Ten minutes later the pair of them were sitting together, drinking in a diet of Glenfiddich and the finale of *Götterdämmerung*.

'Nothing quite like it in the whole history of music,' announced Morse magisterially, after Brünnhilde had ridden into the flames and the waves of the Rhine had finally rippled into silence.

'You think so?'

'Don't *you*?'

'I prefer Elizabethan madrigals, really.'

For a few moments Morse said nothing, saddened by her lack of sensitivity, it seemed.

'Oh.'

'I *loved* it. Don't be silly!' she said. 'But I've got to be on my way.'

'Can I walk you home?'

'I live too far away. I'm in a temporary flat – in Jericho.'

'I'll drive you home, then.'

'You've had far too much to drink.'

'You can stay here, if you like? I've got a spare pair of pyjamas.'

'I don't usually *wear* pyjamas.'

'No?'

'How many bedrooms do you have?'

'Two.'

'And bedroom number two is free?'

'Just like bedroom number one.'

'No secret passage between them?'

'I could get the builders in.'

She smiled happily, and rose to her feet. 'If there ever *is* going to be anything between us, Chief Inspector, it'll have to be when we're borth a bit more sorber. Better that way. I think *you'd* prefer it that way too, if you're honest.' She laid a hand on his shoulder. 'C'mon. Ring for a taxi.'

Ten minutes later she kissed him lightly on the lips, her own lips dry and soft and slightly opened.

Then she was gone.

*

An hour later Morse lay awake on his back. It was still hot in the bedroom and he had only a light cotton sheet over him. Many varied thoughts were crowding in upon his mind, his eyes ever darting around in the darkness. First it had been the lovely woman who had been there with him that evening; then the case of the Swedish Maiden, with only those last few lines of the complex equation to be completed now; then his failure thus far to locate the bullet that had killed George Daley – this last problem gradually assuming a dominance in his brain . . .

The bullet had been fired from about sixty or so yards – that seemed a firm assumption. So . . . So why hadn't it been found? And why could no one in Blenheim be far more definite about *hearing* it being fired: shooting in Blenheim was not the common occurrence it was in other areas . . . in Wytham, for example. The rifle itself concerned him to a lesser extent: after all, it was far easier to get rid of a rifle than to get rid of a bullet that could have landed up anywhere . . . Morse got out of bed and went to find the Blenheim Park brochure – just as Johnson had done so recently before him. The place where Daley's body had been found could be only – what? – four hundred yards or so from that narrow north-westerly tip of the lake, shaped like the head of one of those cormorants he'd seen in Lyme Regis not all that long ago . . . Yes! He would double the men on the search – on *both* searches, rather. There could be little doubt that Philip Daley must have dumped his father's rifle there somewhere – in the lake itself, like as not. And once they'd found either of them, either the rifle or the bullet—

The phone rang, and Morse grabbed at it.

'That was quick, sir.'

'What do *you* want?'

'The Met, sir. They rang HQ, and Sergeant Dixon thought he ought to let me know—'

'Let *you* know, Lewis? Who the hell's in charge of this bloody case? Just wait till I see Dixon!'

'They thought you'd be asleep, sir.'

'Well, I wasn't, was I?'

'And, well—'

'Well, what?'

'Doesn't matter, sir.'

'It bloody *does* matter! They thought I was in bed with a woman! That's what they thought.'

'I don't know,' admitted the honest and honourable Lewis.

'Or pretty much the worse for booze!'

'Perhaps they thought both,' said Lewis simply.

'Well?'

'Young Philip Daley, sir. Just over an hour ago. Threw himself under a westbound train on the Central Line, it seems – train coming into Marble Arch from Bond Street – driver had no chance, just as he came out of the tunnel.'

Morse said nothing.

'Police knew a bit about the boy. He'd been picked up for shoplifting from a wine store in the Edgware Road and taken in; but the manager decided not to prosecute – he got away with a right dressing-down—'

'That's not *all* you've got to tell me, is it?' said Morse quietly.

'No, sir. You've guessed, I suppose. That was Monday morning, half an hour after the store opened.'

'You're telling me he couldn't have shot his dad, is that it?'

'Not even if he'd been the one to hire that helicopter, sir.'

'Does Mrs Daley know?'

'Not yet.'

'Leave her, Lewis. Leave her. Let her sleep.'

An hour later Morse still lay awake, though now his mind was far more relaxed. It had been like puzzling over a crossword clue and finding a possible answer, but being dissatisfied with that answer, lacking as it did any satisfying inevitability; and then being given an erratum slip, telling him that the *clue* had been wrong in the first place; then being given the *correct* clue; and then . . .

Oh yes!

All along he'd been aware of his dissatisfaction with the *motivation* of Philip Daley for the death of his father. It *could* have happened that way, of course – far odder things in life occurred than that. But the sequence of sudden hatred and carefully plotted murder rang far from true; and Morse considered once more the original facts: the scene of George Daley's murder, beside the little coppice in Blenheim Park, still cordoned off, with nothing but the corpse removed, and even now some weary PC standing guard, or sitting guard ... Odd really, that! Morse had asked for an almost unprecedentedly large number of men in this case; what's more he'd given them all a quite specific task. Yet no one had come up with anything.

And suddenly he knew why!

He jerked up in the bed, as though crudely galvanized, and considered the erratum slip, smiling now serenely to himself. It could be. It *had* to be! And the new answer to the clue was shining and wholly fitting; an answer that 'filled the eye', as the judges said of the champion dogs at Crufts.

It was 2.40 a.m., and Morse knew that he would have to do something if he were ever to get to sleep. So he made himself a rare cup of Ovaltine, and sat for a while at the kitchen table: impatient, as ever, yet content. What exactly made him remember Heisenberg's Uncertainty Principle, he was by no means sure. Physics had long been a closed science to him, ever since at school he had once tried, without success, to take some readings from an incomprehensible piece of equipment called the Wheatstone Bridge. But Heisenberg was a splendid name and Morse looked him up in his encyclopaedia: 'There is always an uncertainty in the values obtained if simultaneous observation is made of *position* ...' Morse nodded to himself. *Time* too, as doubtless old Heisenberg had known.

Morse was soon asleep.

When he awoke, at 7 a.m., he thought he might

perhaps have dreamed of a choir of beautiful women singing Elizabethan madrigals. But it was all a bit vague in his mind; about as vague as exactly what, as a principle, 'Werner Karl Heisenberg (1901–76)' had had in mind.

CHAPTER SIXTY-FIVE

How strange are the tricks of memory, which, often hazy as a dream about the most important events, religiously preserve the merest trifles

(Sir Richard Burton, *Sind Revisited*)

'YOU APPRECIATE therefore, Lewis' – the two of them stood on the scene of Daley's murder the following morning – 'the paramount importance of leaving everything exactly as it was here.'

'But we've had everybody trampling all over the place.'

Morse beamed. 'Ah, but we've got this, haven't we?' He patted the roof of the Blenheim Estate van affectionately.

'Unless one of the lads's been sitting in there having a smoke.'

'If he has, I'll sever his scrotum!'

'By the way, did you have a word with Dixon this morning?'

'Dixon? What the 'ell's Dixon got to do with anything?'

'Nothing,' murmured Lewis, as he turned away to have a final word with the two men standing by the recovery truck.

'Without getting inside at all, you say?' asked the elder of the two.

387

'That's what the chief inspector wants, yes.'

'We can't do it without *touching* the bloody thing though, can we, Charlie?'

Morse himself was standing beside the van, deep in thought, it seemed. Then he walked slowly round it, peering with apparently earnest attention at the ground. But the soil was rock-hard there, after weeks of cloudless weather, and after a little while he lost interest and walked back to the police car.

'That's enough here, Lewis. Let's get over to the lodge: it's time we had another word with Mr Williams.'

As before, Williams' evidence, in specific terms, was perhaps unsatisfactory; but, in general outline, it did serve to establish a working framework for the murder – the only one really the police had. Certainly the crucial point – that Daley had driven through Combe Lodge Gate on the morning of his murder – could be pretty confidently re-affirmed. There had been a good deal of to-ing and fro-ing of two blue tractors, with their trailers, that morning, each of them making three trips from the saw-mill down to the area near the Grand Bridge to load up with recently felled timber. Williams had checked up (he said) with the drivers, and the ferrying had not begun until about 9.45 a.m., or a little later perhaps; and if there was one thing he could feel reasonably confident about it was the fact that Daley had come through the gate at the same time as one of the tractors – because although the gate was opened quite frequently that morning, it had not been *specifically* opened (Williams was *almost* sure) for the estate van. He did remember the van though – quite definite he was about that. He hadn't known Daley well; spoken to him a few times of course, and Daley had often come through the lodge, to and from the saw-mill. Usually, between those working at Blenheim, there would be a hand raised in acknowledgement or greeting. And there was another thing: Daley almost always wore his hat, even in the summer; and, yes, Daley had been wearing his hat that Monday morning.

Morse had pressed him on the point. 'You're *sure* about that?'

Williams breathed out noisily. He felt he was sure, yes. But it was a frightening business, this being questioned and giving evidence, and he was now far less sure than he had been about one or two of the things he'd said earlier. That shot he thought he'd heard, for example: he was less and less sure now that he'd heard it at *all.* So it was better, fairer too, to play it a bit more on the cautious side . . . that's what he thought.

'Well, I think so. Trouble is really about the time. You see, it might have been a bit *later,* I think.'

But Morse appeared no longer interested in the time – or in the shot, for that matter.

'Mr Williams! I'm sorry to keep on about this but it's very important. I know that Mr Daley always wore his hat around the park, and I believe you when you say you *saw* his hat. But let's put it another way: are you sure it was *Mr Daley* who was wearing the hat on Monday morning?'

'You mean,' said Williams slowly, 'you mean it mightn't have been him – driving the van?'

'Exactly.'

Oh dear! Williams didn't know . . . hadn't even

considered ... Two women joggers appeared at the lodge, twisted through the kissing-gate and continued their way into the park itself, their breasts bouncing, their legs (as viewed from the rear) betraying the slightly splay-footed run of the fairer sex. Morse followed them briefly with his eyes, and asked his last question:

'Did you notice any jogger coming *this* way, *out* of the park, on Monday morning? About, let's say, half-past ten? Eleven?'

Williams pondered the question. While everything else seemed to be getting more and more muddled in his mind, the chief inspector had just sparked off a fairly vivid recollection. He thought he *had* noticed someone, yes – a woman. There were always lots of joggers at weekends, but not many in the week; not many at all; and certainly not in the middle of the morning. He thought he *could* remember the woman though; could almost see her now, with the nipples of her breasts erect and pushing through the thin material of her T-shirt. Was that Monday *morning*, though? The simple truth was that he just couldn't be certain and again he was unwilling to commit himself too positively.

'I may have done, yes.'

'Thank you very much, sir.'

What exactly he was being thanked for, Mr Williams was not quite clear, and he was aware that he must have appeared a less-than-satisfactory witness. Yet the chief inspector had looked mightily pleased with himself as he'd left; and he'd said 'very much', hadn't he? It was all a bit beyond the gate-keeper of Combe Lodge in Blenheim Park.

CHAPTER SIXTY-SIX

As when that divelish yron engin, wrought
In deepest hell, and framd by furies skill,
With windy nitre and quick sulphur fraught,
And ramd with bollett rowed, ordaind to kill,
Conceiveth fyre

(Edmund Spenser, *The Faerie Queene*)

THE SEMI-CIRCULAR area where birdwatchers and the occasional loving couple were wont to park was packed with police cars and vans when, half an hour after leaving Blenheim, Lewis drove through the perimeter gate ('The woods are closed to Permit Holders until 10.00 a.m. every day except Sunday') and into the compound, on his left, marked off with its horizontal four-barred, black-creosoted fencing. Here, under the direction of Chief Inspector Johnson, some fifty or so policemen – some uniformed, some not – were systematically conducting their search.

'No luck yet?' asked Morse.

'Give us a chance!' said Johnson. 'Lot of ground to cover, isn't there?'

The large wooden sheds, the stacks of logs and fencing-posts, the occasional clump of trees, the rank growth of untended bushes – all precluded any wholly scientific search-pattern. But there was plenty of time;

there were plenty of men; they would find it, Johnson was confident of that.

Morse led the way up the curving track towards the furthest point from the compound entrance, towards the hut where David Michaels had his office, right up against the recently erected deer-fence. To the left of this track was a line of forty or so fir trees, about thirty feet high; and to the right, the hut itself, the main door standing padlocked now. On the wooden sides of this extensive hut, at the top, were six large bird-boxes, numbered 9–14; and at the bottom there grew rank clumps of nettles. Morse looked back down the sloping track; retraced his steps, counting as he went; then stopped at a smaller open-sided shed in which stood a large red tractor with a timber-lifting device fixed to it. For a minute or two he stood beside the tractor, behind the shed wall, and then, as if he were a young boy with an imaginary rifle, lifted both his arms, curled his right index-finger round an imaginary trigger, closed his left eye, and slowly turned the rifle in an arc from right to left, as if some imaginary vehicle were being driven past – the rifle finally remaining stationary as the vehicle's imaginary driver dismounted, in front of the head forester's hut.

'You reckon?' asked Lewis quietly.

Morse nodded.

'That means we probably ought to be concentrating the search up there, sir.' Lewis pointed back towards Michaels' office.

'Give him a chance! He's not so bright as you,' whispered Morse.

'About fifty, fifty-five yards. I paced it too, sir.'

Again Morse nodded, and the two of them rejoined Johnson.

'Know much about rifles?' asked Morse.

'Enough.'

'Could you use a silencer on a seven-millimetre?'

'"Sound-moderator" – that's the word these days. No, not much good. It'd suppress the noise of the explosion, but it couldn't stop the noise of the bullet going through the sound-barrier. And incidentally, Morse, it might be a .243 – don't forget that!'

'Oh!'

'You were thinking it might be around here, weren't you?' Johnson kicked aside a few nettles along the bottom of the shed, and looked at Morse shrewdly, if a little sadly.

Morse shrugged. 'I'd be guessing, of course.'

Johnson looked down at the flattened nettles. 'You never did have much faith in me, did you?'

Morse didn't know what to say, and as Johnson walked away, he too looked down at the flattened nettles.

'You're quite wrong, you know, sir. He's a whole lot brighter than me, is Johnson.'

But again Morse made no reply, and the pair of them walked down to the low, stone-built cottage where until very lately Michaels and his Swedish wife had lived so happily together.

Just as they were entering, they heard a shot from fairly far off. But they paid little attention to it. As Michaels had informed them, no one was ever going to be too disturbed about hearing a gun-shot in Wytham: game-keepers shooting squirrels or rabbits, perhaps; farmworkers taking a pot at the pestilential pigeons.

Inside the cottage, just beside the main entrance, stood the steel security cabinet from which Michaels' rifle had been taken for forensic examination. But there was no longer any legal requirement for the cabinet to be locked, and it now stood open – and empty. Lewis bent down and looked carefully at the groove in which the rifle had stood, noting the scratches where the butt had rested; and beside it a second groove – with equally tell-tale signs.

'I'm sure you're right,' said Lewis.

'If you remember,' said Morse, 'he told us *himself*, Michaels did. When you told him you'd seen no rifles in the hut he said . . . he said "Oh, I couldn't keep 'em *there*" – those were his exact words, I think.'

'You're still certain he did it, sir?'

'Yes.'

'What about that "Uncertainty Principle" you were on about this morning?'

'What about it?' asked Morse. Infuriatingly.

'Forget it.'

'What's the time?'

'Nearly twelve.'

'Ah, the prick of noon!'

'Pardon?'

'Forget it.'

'We can walk down if you like, sir. A nice little ten-minute walk – do us good. We can work up a thirst.'

'Nonsense!'

'Don't you enjoy walking – occasionally?'
'Occasionally, yes.'
'So?'
'So drive me down to the White Hart, Lewis! What's the problem?'

CHAPTER SIXTY-SEVEN

Scire volunt secreta domus, atque inde timeri
(They watch for household secrets hour by hour
And feed therefrom their appetite for power)
(Juvenal, *Satire III*)

'WHAT PUT you on it this time?' asked Lewis as they sat opposite each other in the small upstairs bar, Morse with a pint of real ale, Lewis himself with a much-iced orangeade.

'I think it wasn't so much finding Daley like he was – out at Blenheim. It was the photographs they took of him there. I don't think it hit me at the time; but when I looked at the photographs I got the idea somehow that he'd just been dumped there – that he hadn't been shot there at all.'

'You mean you just – well, sort of had a *feeling* about it?'

'No. I don't mean that. You may think I work that way, Lewis, but I don't. I don't believe in some unaccountable intuition that just happens occasionally to turn out right. There's got to be *something* there, however vague. And here we had the hat, didn't we? The hat Daley wore wherever he was, whatever the weather. Same bloody hat! He never took it *off*, Lewis!'

'Probably took it off in bed?'

'We don't even know that, do we?' Morse drained his beer. 'Plenty of time for another.'

Lewis nodded. 'Plenty of time! Your round though, sir. I'll have another orange. Lovely. Lots of ice, please!'

'You see,' resumed Morse, a couple of minutes later, 'he was almost certainly wearing his hat when he was shot, and I very much doubt myself that it would have fallen *off*. I'd seen the tight sweat-mark round his forehead when we met him earlier. And even if it *had* fallen off – when he dropped dead – I just had the feeling . . .'

Lewis lifted his eyebrows.

'. . . it wouldn't have fallen *far*.'

'So?'

'So, I reckon it was put down there deliberately, just beside his head – *after* he was shot. Remember where it was? Three or four feet *away* from his head. So the conclusion's firm and satisfactory, as I see it. He was wearing his hat when he was shot, and like as not it stayed on his head. Then when he was moved, and finally dumped, it had come off; and it was placed there beside him.'

'What a palaver!'

Morse nodded. 'But they had to do it. They had to establish an alibi—'

'For David Michaels, you mean?'

'Yes. It was Michaels who shot Daley – I've no doubts on that score. There was the agreement Hardinge told us about, wasn't there, the agreement the four of them made – a statement by the way that contains quite as much truth as falsehood, Lewis. Then something comes along and buggers it all up. Daley got a letter spelling out his financial responsibilities for his boy, and Daley knew that he was the one who had a hold over – well, over *all* the others, really. But particularly over David Michaels! I reckon Daley probably rang him and said he couldn't afford to stick by the agreement; said he was sorry – but he needed more money. And if he didn't get more money pretty soon . . .'

'Blackmail!'

'Exactly. And there may well have been a bit more of *that* than we think.'

'Quite a hold over Michaels, though, when you think of it: knowing he was married to . . . a murderess.'

'Quite a hold. So Michaels agrees – *pretends* he agrees – to go along with it. They'll meet at Wytham earlyish on Monday – quarter to ten, say. No one around much at that time. No birdwatchers allowed in the woods till ten – remember the notice?'

'The RSPB people were there.'

'They turned out to be a blessing in disguise, though.'

'Take it a bit slower, please!'

'Right. Let's just go back a minute. The rendezvous's settled. Daley drives up to Wytham. Michaels has said he'll have some money ready – in notes, no doubt – just after the bank's opened. He's ready. He waits for Daley to drive up to his office. He waits for a clear view of him as he gets out of his estate van. I don't know *exactly* where he was waiting, of course; what I *do* know is that someone as experienced as Michaels, with a telescopic sight, could hit *this*' – Morse picked up his empty glass

– 'no problem! – from a hundred, let alone from fifty yards.'

But any further reconstruction of Daley's murder was temporarily curtailed, since Johnson had walked in, and now sat down beside them.

'What'll you have?' asked Morse. 'Lewis here is in the chair.'

'Nothing for me, thank you, er, Lewis. Look! There's this call for you from forensics about the van. I told 'em I wasn't *quite* sure where you were—'

'What'd they say?'

'They found prints all over the shop – mostly Daley's, of course. But like you said, they found other prints – on the tail-board, on the steering wheel.'

'And I was right about them?'

Johnson nodded. 'Yes. They're Karin Eriksson's.'

At lunch-time that same day, Alasdair McBryde came out of the tube station at Manor House and walked briskly down the Seven Sisters Road – finally turning into one of the parking-and-garage areas of a high-rise block of flats that flanks the Bethune Road. He had spotted the unmarked car immediately: the two men seated in the front, one of them reading the *Sun*. It was quite customary for him to spot danger a mile or so off; and he did so now. Number 14 was the garage he was interested in; but softly whistling the Prelude to Act Three of *Lohengrin*, he walked boldly into the nearest open garage (number 9), picked up a half-filled can of Mobiloil, before nonchalantly retracing his steps to the main road; where, still clutching the dirty can, he walked quietly and confidently away in the direction of Stamford Hill.

'False alarm!' said the policeman with the *Sun*, as he resumed his reading of various illicit liaisons among the glitterati.

At 3.25 p.m., no more than four or five yards from the spot where Chief Inspector Johnson had earlier stood, there amongst the nettles and the cow-parsley and other less readily recognizable plants and weeds, Constable Roy Wilks made his discovery: a .243 bullet – the bullet (surely!) for which the party had been searching. Never, in his life hitherto, had Wilks been the focus of such attention; and never again (as he duly recognized) would he be likely to experience such felicitous congratulations.

Most particularly from Morse.

CHAPTER SIXTY-EIGHT

The Light of Lights
Looks always on the motive, not the deed,
The Shadow of Shadows on the deed alone
              (W. B. Yeats, *The Countess Cathleen*)

'JUST simply, Morse! Just simply! I don't want to know what a clever sod you are. Just a straightforward – brief! – account. If you can manage it.'

Following the final discoveries, new statements had been taken from both David Michaels and Karin Eriksson; and now, the following morning, as he sat in Strange's office, Morse was able to confirm in nearly every respect the pattern of events he'd outlined to Lewis in the White Hart.

Daley had been to the office in Wytham Woods on more than one occasion before, and a meeting had been arranged for 9.45 a.m. on Monday, 3 August. At that time there would, with any luck, be virtually no one around; but only if no one *was* around, would the deed take place. And the deed *did* take place. When Daley got out of the van, Michaels shot him dead with his .243 rifle – the latter buried later out on the Singing Way. To Michaels himself the report had sounded terrifyingly loud; but following it a strangely eerie silence had reasserted itself, and no one had come rushing into the compound there demanding explanation, seeking causes. Nothing. A newly still, clear morning in early August. And a body – which Michaels had swiftly wrapped in black plastic sheeting and lifted into the back of Daley's own van. Only two or three minutes after the murder, this same van was being driven out through Wolvercote, over to the A44 towards Woodstock, left at Bladon, and then into Long Hanborough – and finally up to Combe Lodge, on the western side of the Blenheim Estate. The keys to the lodge gate would doubtless have been somewhere on the body, but the van-driver waited a while and was very quickly rewarded when the gate was opened for a tractor and trailer; and when the van driver, pulling Daley's khaki-green hat down over her short, black hair, moved into the trailer's wake, raising a hand in acknowledgement to any anonymous observer as she drove gratefully through. A few hundred yards along she had spotted an ideal location in which to leave a van, and a body, and a hat. Daley had not been a heavy man, and she herself was a strong young woman; yet she had been unable to lift the corpse – just to pull it over the tailboard, whence it fell with a thud to the hard soil. The plastic sheet was messily sticky with blood, and she had taken it with her as she ran off, across the road, to the tip of the lake, where she washed the blood from her hands and wedged the sheet beneath some reeds. Then, following the arranged plan, she'd jogged her way back – though not, she claimed, through Combe Lodge, as Morse had suggested (and Williams could have sworn) – but down by the western side of the lake, across the small bridge that spans the River Glyme below the Grand Cascade, and out of the park via Eagle Lodge.

'Helluva long way, whichever route she took,' mumbled Strange.

'Some people are fitter than others, sir.'

'Not thinking of *yourself*, are you?'

'No!'

'Bit lucky, though – the fellow at the lodge remembering the van going through.'

'With all respect, sir, I don't think that's true. In fact, it led us all to believe that Daley was alive until after ten o'clock – when David Michaels was miles away with his RSPB pals round the bird-boxes. But Michaels could *never* have done it himself – not by himself – that morning. There was no way at all that *he* could have got out to Blenheim and somehow – somehow – got back to Wytham.'

'But his wife could. That's what you're saying.'

'His wife did.'

'She was a brave girl.'

'She *is* a brave girl, sir.'

'You know, if they'd only have played it straight up and down the wicket from the start – either of them – they'd probably have got away with justifiable homicide, self-defence, take your pick.'

'Perhaps.'

'You don't sound very convinced.'

'I think she's a rather more complex woman than that. Perhaps ... perhaps she couldn't quite persuade herself that killing Myton had been purely in self-defence.'

'You mean – you mean she might have enjoyed it?'

'I didn't say that, sir.'

Strange shook his head. 'I see what you're getting at, though. Prepared – wasn't she? – to drive Daley's body out to Blenheim and . . .'

'She's a complex woman, as I say, sir. I'm not sure I understand her at all really.'

'Perhaps she's a bit of a mystery even to herself.'

Morse got up to leave. 'Same thing in most cases, isn't it? We never really understand people's motives. In all these things it's as if there's a manifestation – but there's always a bit of a mystery too.'

'Now don't you start going all religious on *me*, Morse!'

'No chance of that.'

'I don't suppose anyone'll miss Daley all that much.'

'No. He was a *small* man—'

'Was he? How tall was he?'

'No. I didn't mean small in that sense. But he *was* physically small, yes. Only weighed eight stone, four pounds.'

'How do you know that?'

'They weighed him, sir – *post mortem.*'

CHAPTER SIXTY-NINE

Just as every person has his idiosyncrasies, so has every typewriter

(*Handbook of Office Maintenance*, 9th edition)

THE FOLLOWING day, Friday, 8 August, Morse's attention was early drawn to the correspondence columns of *The Times*.

From Lt. Colonel Reginald Postill

Sir, Over these past years we have all become aware of the increasing influence of trial (and retrial) by TV. We have seen, for example, the collapse of cases brought against the Birmingham Six and the Guildford Four; and doubtless in the years ahead we may confidently anticipate the acquittal of the Towcester Two and the Winchester One.

Are we now to become similarly conditioned to pol-ice enquiries conducted in the nation's quality daily newspapers (including, of course, your own, sir)? I learn that the Thames Valley Police has now been able to prefer charges against persons in the 'Swedish Maiden' case – and this in considerable measure thanks to the original verses published in your correspondence columns. Clearly we should be grateful for such an outcome. But am I alone in being troubled by such a precedent? Am I alone in believing that such affairs,

---

both judicial and investiga-tive, are better left in the hands of those men and women suitably trained in their respective specialisms?	Yours faithfully, REGINALD POSTILL, 6 Baker Lane, Shanklin, Isle of Wight.

Lewis had come into his office as Morse was reading this; and duly read it himself.

'Bit hard that, isn't it? I'd have thought it all helped us quite a bit. I can't myself really see what's wrong with getting a bit of public co-operation and interest.'

'Oh, I agree,' said Morse.

'Perhaps we shouldn't be too much worried about some retired old colonel from the Isle of Wight, sir.'

Morse smiled knowingly across at his old friend. 'What makes you think he's retired?' he asked very quietly.

That same evening, Morse's celebratory mood was undiminished; and he had walked down to Summer-town immediately after *The Archers* and carried back up to his flat four bottles of champagne: not the dearest, it must be admitted – yet not the cheapest either. Strange, Johnson, Lewis – and himself. Four of them. Just for a congratulatory glass or two. Dr Laura Hobson had been invited too (how otherwise?); but she had phoned earlier in the evening to make her apologies – an emergency; sorry, she'd've loved to have been there; but these things couldn't be helped, could they?

Harold Johnson was the first to leave, at 9.15 p.m.

One glass of bubbly, and the plea that the wife would be awaiting him. Yet of all of them it was probably Johnson who was the most grateful soul there that evening: the procedures surrounding the prosecutions of two suspected murderers – David Michaels and Mrs Michaels – would be entrusted now to him, to Johnson and his team, since Morse had announced his intention of resuming immediately his truncated furlough which had begun (so long ago it seemed) in the Bay Hotel at Lyme Regis.

Three glasses of bubbly and ten minutes later, Strange had struggled to his feet and announced his imminent departure.

'Thanks! And enjoy your holiday!'

'If you'll let me.'

'Where are you going this time?'

'I was thinking of Salisbury, sir.'

'Why Salisbury?'

Morse hesitated. 'They've just tarted up the cathedral there, and I thought—'

'You *sure* you're not going religious on me, Morse?'

Two of the champagne bottles were finished, and Morse picked up a third, starting to twist open the wire round its neck.

'No more for me,' said Lewis.

Morse put the bottle back on the sideboard. 'Would you prefer a Newcastle Brown?'

'I think I would, to be honest, sir.'

'C'mon, then!'

Morse led the way through to the cluttered kitchen.

'You trying for *my* job, sir?' Lewis pointed to the ancient portable typewriter that stood at one end of the kitchen table.

'Ah! That! I was just writing a brief line to *The Times*.' He handed Lewis his effort, a messy, ill-typed, xxxx-infested missive.

'Would you like me to re-type it for you, sir? It's a bit . . .'

'Yes, please. I'd be grateful for that.'

So Lewis sat there, at the kitchen table, and retyped the brief letter. That it took him rather longer than it should have done was occasioned by two factors: first, that Lewis himself could boast only semi-competence in the keyboard-skills; second, that he had found himself looking, with increasingly puzzled interest, at the very first line he'd typed. And then at the second. And then at the third . . . Especially did he find himself examining the worn top segment of the lower-case 'e', and the slight curtailment of the cross-bar in the lower-case 't' . . . For the moment, however, he said nothing. Then, when his reasonably clean copy was completed, he wound it from the ancient machine and handed it to Morse.

'Much better! Good man!'

'You remember, sir, that original article in *The Times*? When they said the typewriter could pretty easily be identified if it was ever found? From the "e"s and the "t"s . . .?'

'Yes?'

'You wrote those verses about the girl yourself, didn't you, sir?'

Morse nodded slowly.

'Bloody hell!' Lewis shook his head incredulously.

Morse poured himself a can of beer. 'Champagne's a lovely drink, but it makes you thirsty, doesn't it?'

'Think anyone *else* suspected?' asked Lewis, grinning down at the typewriter.

'Just the one person. Someone from Salisbury.'

'Didn't you say you would be going there, though? To Salisbury?'

'*Might* be, Lewis. Depends.'

Half an hour after Lewis had left, Morse was listening to Lipatti playing the slow movement of the Mozart piano concerto No. 21, when the doorbell rang.

'It's a bit late I know but . . .'

What had been a semi-scowl on Morse's face now suddenly burgeoned into a wholly ecstatic smile.

'Nonsense! It just so happens I've got a couple of bottles of bubbly . . .'

'Will that be enough, do you think?'

'Come in! I'll just turn this off—'

'Please not! I love it. K 467? Right?'

'Where've you parked?'

'I didn't come by car. I thought you'd probably try to get me drunk.'

Morse closed the door behind them. 'I *will* turn it off, if you don't mind. I've never been able to cope with two beautiful things at the same time.'

She followed Morse into the lounge where once more he picked up bottle number three.

'What time will you have to go, my love?'

'Who said anything about going, Chief Inspector?'

Morse put down the bottle and swiftly retraced his steps to the front door, where he turned the key, and shot the bolts, both top and bottom.

EPILOGUE

Life never presents us with anything which may not be looked upon as a fresh starting point, no less than as a termination

(André Gide, *The Counterfeiters*)

THE CORRESPONDENCE columns of *The Times* carried the following letter on Monday, 10 August 1992:

From Detective Chief Inspector E. Morse

Sir, On behalf of the Thames Valley Police, I wish to record the gratitude of myself and of my fellow officers for the co-operation and assistance of *The Times* newspaper. As a direct result of lines of investigation suggested by some of its correspondents about the 'Swedish Maiden' verses, persons now being held in custody will be duly brought to face trial in accordance with the law's demands.

I am, sir,

Yours,
E. MORSE,
Thames Valley Police HQ,
Kidlington,
Oxon.

[This correspondence is now closed. Ed.]

Like the rest of his staff, the editor had been fascinated by the crop of ideas that sprang from the

Swedish Maiden verses; and although the case was now finished he felt he should reply briefly to Morse's letter. In mid-afternoon therefore he dictated a few lines of reciprocal gratitude.

'Do we have a private address for him?' asked his personal secretary.

'No. Just address it to Kidlington HQ – that'll be fine.'

'What about the initial – do we know what that stands for?'

'The "E"?' The editor considered the question for a second or two. 'Er, no. No, I don't think we do.'

Introductory Financial Accounting and Reporting

Barry P. Smith

Open University Press

Open University Press
McGraw-Hill Education
McGraw-Hill House
Shoppenhangers Road
Maidenhead
Berkshire
England
SL6 2QL

email: enquiries@openup.co.uk
world wide web: www.openup.co.uk

and Two Penn Plaza, New York, NY 10121–2289, USA

First published 2010

A catalogue record of this book is available from the British Library

ISBN-13: 978-0-33-524125-5
ISBN-13: 0-33-524125-5

Library of Congress Cataloging-in-Publication Data
CIP data applied for

Typeset by RefineCatch Limited, Bungay, Suffolk
Printed in the UK by Bell & Bain Ltd, Glasgow

Fictitious names of companies, products, people, characters and/or data that
may be used herein (in case studies or in examples) are not intended to represent any real individual, company, product or event.

Mixed Sources
Product group from well-managed
forests and other controlled sources
www.fsc.org Cert no. TT-COC-002769
© 1996 Forest Stewardship Council

FSC

*The **McGraw·Hill** Companies*

Contents

Preface

The purpose of this text is to provide a concise financial accounting revision text. It includes the core components of financial accounting and reporting that (i) are commonly examined on introductory-level undergraduate and professional accounting courses, and (ii) persist as the basis of intermediate and advanced accounting topics.

Accounting students will benefit from this text:

- Each chapter is a concise presentation of a topic. The content is presented in short sections in a straightforward manner and includes illustrative examples.
- Each chapter provides guidance in terms of access to practice questions and further reading. This text is supported by a wealth of online practice material at www.bazwaldo.com.
- The text is exam-oriented in nature. The topics are those that are most commonly examined.
- Students taking advanced accounting courses who require brief revision of the fundamentals can refer to this text as a useful revision resource.

This text will also be of assistance to teachers:

- It is an effective resource for teaching accounting topics at overview level to students who take accountancy as a non-core or elective subject.
- It is an efficient means of revising specific accounting topics.
- Double-entry bookkeeping is included throughout the text but presented separately so that it may be included or omitted according to different teaching approaches.
- www.bazwaldo.com provides a comprehensive resource of questions and solutions for tutorial and examination purposes.

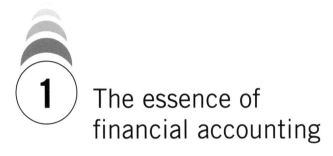

1 The essence of financial accounting

You must be able to explain:

○ The purpose of financial accounting and the qualitative characteristics of financial statements
○ How business transactions affect the accounting equation
○ The mechanics of double-entry bookkeeping

1.1 What is the purpose of financial accounting and reporting?

The primary objective of preparing financial statements is to provide useful information about (i) the performance of an organization during a reporting period and (ii) the status of business at the end of a reporting period.

The contents of financial statements can provide useful information to a number of interested parties, including:

- Existing and potential debt and equity investors.
- Capital market analysts.
- Customers, suppliers, competitors, industry representative bodies.
- Central government (including tax authorities), local government.
- Trades unions, employees.
- Consumer groups, general public.

Different groups can have overlapping information needs. The purpose of financial statements is to satisfy as many of the common needs as is practical to provide. Not all groups necessarily receive all the information that they might wish to receive.

The information that is contained in financial statements should assist user groups in terms of (i) making economic decisions or (ii) assessing the steward-ship of a business. Economic decisions include:

- Whether to buy or sell the shares or debt of a company.
- Whether to engage in business dealings with an organization.
- The basis of salary and wage negotiations between owners, managers and employees of a business.
- Whether to increase or decrease taxation or pursue alleged tax defaulters.

To assess the stewardship of an organization is to hold management accounta-ble for the business resources that are entrusted to them. Financial statements should provide a basis for assessing whether those who are responsible for making good use of the assets of a business have in fact done so.

1.2 What are the 'qualitative characteristics' of financial statements?

The qualitative characteristics of financial statements are the attributes the information should have in order to be considered useful.

High quality information is:

- Relevant – has the potential to influence the decisions of users.
- Reliable – can be depended upon to represent what it is purported to represent.
- Comparable – can be reasonably compared with information from another reporting period or for another business organization.
- Understandable – someone with a reasonable knowledge of business and accounting can understand the significance of the information contained in the financial statements.

It is sometimes necessary to strike a balance between desirable characteris-tics. The information that is most relevant may not be always the most reliable. Relevant information may also take longer to prepare than is desirable as users prefer to receive information on a timely basis. Furthermore, whereas a greater amount of information may make financial statements more comparable, it may also be more difficult to understand them.

1.3 What is the accounting equation?

The accounting equation states that:

Assets = Liabilities + Equity

> **Why is this important?**
> A significant amount of financial accounting is based on this equation.

1.4 Illustrative example of the accounting equation

John Brown decides to set up in business as a buyer and seller of accounting textbooks.

- The business trades under the name EZ-Books.
- John opens a business bank account in the name of EZ-Books and lodges personal savings of £2,500 to that account.
- John negotiates the receipt of a start-up business loan of £5,000 for EZ-Books from his local bank.
- Nothing else happens in the first week.

What are (i) the **resources** and (ii) the **obligations** of EZ-Books at the end of the first week?

(i) The **resources** are the productive means available to carry on the business. At the end of the first week, EZ-Books has **one** resource – the balance in the business bank account. This amounts to £7,500, being a combination of the £2,500 personal savings lodged by John Brown plus the lodgement of the £5,000 business loan received from the bank.

(ii) The **obligations** are financial commitments to external parties. At the end of the first week, EZ-Books has **two** obligations. The first is the obligation to repay the bank loan of £5,000 at some date in the future. The second is the obligation to repay the £2,500 investment made by the owner of the business, John Brown.

If John Brown is the owner of the business, why is his investment of £2,500 treated as an obligation in the financial accounts of EZ-Books?

From an accounting perspective, a business and its owner are regarded as **two independent entities**. This means that John Brown, notwithstanding the fact that he is the owner of EZ-Books, is regarded as an external business party in exactly the same way as the bank providing the loan is an external business party. As such, until the obligations are repaid (if ever), EZ-Books should recognize that John Brown has an ongoing claim on his £2,500 investment just like the bank has a claim on its £5,000 loan.

If 'resources' and 'obligations' are replaced by **assets, liabilities** and **equity**, EZ-Books' accounting equation takes shape as follows:

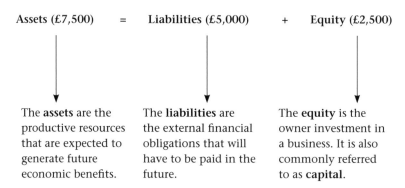

Assets (£7,500)	=	Liabilities (£5,000)	+	Equity (£2,500)

The **assets** are the productive resources that are expected to generate future economic benefits.	The **liabilities** are the external financial obligations that will have to be paid in the future.	The **equity** is the owner investment in a business. It is also commonly referred to as **capital**.

Thus, at the end of the first week, the accounting equation of EZ-Books reveals (i) the assets of the business at that date and (ii) the claims that external parties (including the owner) have on the assets at that same date. The same information is provided in a **statement of financial position**.

1.5 What is a statement of financial position?

> **Why is this important?**
> A statement of financial position is one of the **core** financial statements of **all** business organizations.

A **statement of financial position** is a listing of the assets, liabilities and equity of a business on a given date. It is also commonly referred to as a **balance sheet**.

Every statement of financial position is an expression of the accounting equation because the sum of the assets listed on a statement of financial position is equal to the sum of the liabilities and the equity.

EZ-Books' statement of financial position at the end of the first week is as follows:

	EZ-Books Statement of financial position at the end of the first week
Assets	£
Bank balance	7,500
Liabilities	
Bank loan	5,000
Owner equity	2,500
	7,500

1.6 How do transactions affect the statement of financial position?

During the second week, EZ-Books is involved in four business transactions.

Transaction 1

EZ-Books **purchases** 50 accounting textbooks on credit for £500 on the first day of the second week. Two changes arise:

(i) EZ-Books has acquired an additional asset in the form of **inventory**. Inventory is an asset because EZ-Books expects to benefit in the future by selling the inventory. The inventory is therefore a productive resource that is currently available to EZ-Books.

(ii) EZ-Books has a new liability in the form of a **trade payable**. The trade payable is the party to whom £500 is currently owed. This liability arises because EZ-Books bought the inventory **on credit.**

EZ-Books' statement of financial position after the first transaction is as follows:

		EZ-Books Statement of financial position
Assets	£	Explanatory comments
Inventory	500	The purchased inventory is recorded as an asset.

Bank balance	7,500	No change.
	8,000	Total assets increase by £500.
Liabilities		
Trade payable	500	The obligation to pay for the inventory is a liability.
Bank loan	5,000	No change.
	5,500	The total liabilities increase by £500.
Owner equity	2,500	No change.
	8,000	Total liabilities and equity increase by £500.

Assets (£8,000) still equal liabilities (£5,500) plus owner equity (£2,500) after the transaction is recorded. In other words, the accounting equation returns to equilibrium after the transaction is recorded. This is always the case: the accounting equation, and therefore every statement of financial position, always returns to the equilibrium of 'assets equal liabilities plus equity' after each business transaction is recorded. There are no exceptions.

Transaction 2

EZ-Books **sells** 10 accounting textbooks on credit for £100 on the second day of the second week. An assumption that each textbook is sold for the same price as that at which it was bought is made here for simplification purposes. This assumption is removed in Chapter 3.

    EZ-Books' statement of financial position after the second transaction is as follows:

EZ-Books
Statement of financial position

Assets	**£**	**Explanatory comments**
Inventory	400	The inventory asset decreases because some was sold.
Trade receivable	100	An external party owes EZ-Books because of the sale.
Bank balance	7,500	No change.
	8,000	No change.
Liabilities		
Trade payable	500	No change.
Bank loan	5,000	No change.
	5,500	No change.
Owner equity	2,500	No change.
	8,000	No change.

Note that (i) the accounting equation returns to equilibrium and (ii) the two-fold accounting effect of the second transaction. In the case of the second transaction, two assets were affected: a decrease in the inventory and an increase in a trade receivable. A trade receivable is an asset because it represents a future receipt of cash.

Transaction 3

EZ-Books **sends a cheque** for £300 to the trade payable party on the third day of the second week. The cheque is immediately cashed.

EZ-Books' statement of financial position after the third transaction is as follows:

EZ-Books		
Statement of financial position		
Assets	**£**	**Explanatory comments**
Inventory	400	No change.
Trade receivable	100	No change.
Bank balance	7,200	The bank balance decreases by the amount of the payment.
	7,700	Total assets decrease by £300.
Liabilities		
Trade payable	200	The obligation to the trade payable decreases.
Bank loan	5,000	No change.
	5,200	The total liabilities decrease because of the payment.
Owner equity	2,500	No change.
	7,700	Total liabilities and equity decrease by £300.

In the case of the third transaction, an asset and a liability are affected. As soon as EZ-Books pays some of its obligation to a trade payable, the statement of financial position reflects that fact and shows only the amount still outstanding at the end of the third day. The balance of funds in the bank account is reduced by the amount of the payment.

Transaction 4

John Brown **invests** an additional £1,000 equity in EZ-Books on the fourth day of the second week.

EZ-Books' statement of financial position after the fourth transaction is as follows:

EZ-Books
Statement of financial position

Assets	£	Explanatory comments
Inventory	400	No change.
Trade receivable	100	No change.
Bank balance	8,200	The bank balance increases because of the lodgement.
	8,700	Total assets increase by £1,000.
Liabilities		
Trade payable	200	No change.
Bank loan	5,000	No change.
	5,200	No change.
Owner equity	3,500	The owner investment increases because of the lodgement.
	8,700	Total liabilities and equity increase by £1,000.

The fourth transaction impacts the business bank account asset and the equity account. The additional investment by the owner means that EZ-Books' financial obligation to John Brown has increased by £1,000.

What does recording these four transactions demonstrate?

It is possible to draft a new statement of financial position for EZ-Books after each transaction and, **in every case**, the total assets equal the total liabilities plus the equity. The reason for this is the twofold effect of each transaction on combinations of assets, liabilities and equity, which **always** brings the accounting equation back to equilibrium.

The statement of financial position provides useful information about assets, liabilities and equity but does not provide any details about profits or losses. It was necessary to assume, for the purpose of simplicity, that EZ-Books' inventory was sold for the same price as that at which it was bought. This is not a realistic assumption, particularly if EZ-Books is a profit-oriented organization.

Something more than a statement of financial position is necessary to provide useful information about profits, surpluses, losses or deficits. Chapter 3 (The Income Statement) addresses this matter.

1.7 What is double-entry bookkeeping?

Double-entry bookkeeping is a conventional way of expressing the twofold effect of each transaction on financial statements. EZ-Books' first two weeks of business existence may be recorded using the principles of double-entry bookkeeping. Financial accountants commonly express the twofold effects of transactions in terms of **debits and credits**.

- To make a **debit** entry is to record (i) an **increase** in an asset **or** (ii) a **decrease** in a liability or equity.
- To make a **credit** entry is to record (i) a **decrease** in an asset **or** (ii) an **increase** in a liability or equity.

Recall the first week of EZ-Books. Using double-entry bookkeeping, the initial establishment of the business is recorded as follows:

	Account	dr	cr	Meaning
Debit (dr)	Bank account	2,500		Increase in assets – bank account lodgement
Credit (cr)	Owner equity		2,500	Increase in equity – owner capital investment
dr	Bank account	5,000		Increase in assets – bank account lodgement
cr	Bank loan		5,000	Increase in liabilities – obligation to repay the bank loan

In terms of how the statement of financial position looks, the end result is the same as shown in section 1.5.

EZ-Books' four transactions during the second week may be expressed in terms of debits and credits as follows:

Transaction		Account	dr	cr	Meaning
1	dr	Inventory	500		Increase in assets – inventory purchase
	cr	Trade payable		500	Increase in liabilities – obligation to pay for the inventory
2	dr	Trade receivable	100		Increase in assets – amount receivable as a result of the sale of inventory
	cr	Inventory		100	Decrease in assets – inventory on hand is less than was the case prior to the transaction
3	dr	Trade payable	300		Decrease in liabilities – obligation is part paid so the amount still outstanding is less than was the case prior to the transaction
	cr	Bank account		300	Decrease in assets – a payment reduces that amount in the bank account
4	dr	Bank account	1,000		Increase in assets – lodgement increases the bank balance
	cr	Owner equity		1,000	Increase in equity – new investment of capital by the owner

The resultant statement of financial position is the same as shown in section 1.6.

1.8 Summary and conclusion

The general objective of preparing financial statements is to provide useful information to a range of interested parties. Financial statements are more likely to be useful if they have the characteristics of being relevant, reliable, comparable and understandable.

The accounting equation is fundamental to an understanding of financial accounting. It is reflected in **every** statement of financial position. Regardless of the nature of business transactions, the accounting equation always returns to equilibrium after each and every transaction.

Double-entry bookkeeping is commonly used in financial accounting to communicate the twofold effect of business transactions. Asset increases and liability/equity decreases are expressed as **debit entries**. Asset decreases and liability/equity increases are expressed as **credit entries**.

Chapter 2 considers how the information included in a statement of financial position can be presented in more useful ways.

Test your understanding

1 Which of the following is correct?

	Assets	Liabilities	Equity
	£	£	£
(a)	5,420	9,772	4,352
(b)	11,000	2,800	13,800
(c)	8,625	1,150	7,359
(d)	10,618	1,250	9,368

2 Indicate whether each of the following statements is true or false?

(a) The accounting equation states that, at any point in time, the sum of assets and liabilities of a business is equal to its equity.

(b) A debit entry corresponds to an increase in an asset.

(c) A debit entry corresponds to a decrease in equity.

(d) A credit entry corresponds to an increase in a liability.

(e) A credit entry corresponds to a decrease in an asset.

(f) A debit entry corresponds to an increase in equity.

(g) A credit entry corresponds to a decrease in equity.

(h) The accounting equation returns to equilibrium after every transaction. There are no exceptions to this rule.

(i) An objective of financial reporting is to provide useful information about a business to a wide range of interested external parties.

(j) The qualitative characteristics of financial reporting information include 'relevance' and 'robustness'.

Further practice and reading

1. http://www.bazwaldo.com

   Insert the following code into the website keyword search option to access practice questions relating to this chapter: *2010chapter1*

2. Thomas, A. and Ward, A.M. (2009) *Introduction to Financial Accounting*, 6th edn, McGraw-Hill

   Chapter 3: The nature and objectives of financial accounting

   Chapter 7: The accounting equation and its components

   Chapter 9: Double entry and the general ledger

2 The statement of financial position

You must be able to explain:

○ Why it is useful to distinguish between current and non-current assets and liabilities
○ Why it is useful to include comparative information
○ How other financial statements are related to the statement of financial position

2.1 What is a statement of financial position?

A **statement of financial position** is a listing of the assets, liabilities and equity of a business on a particular date. It can be helpful to think of a statement of financial position as a financial snapshot – it captures the financial status of a business at a particular moment in time.

> A statement of financial position is also commonly referred to as a **balance sheet.**

EZ-Books' statement of financial position (prepared in Chapter 1) at the end of the second business week is as follows:

EZ-Books Statement of financial position at the end of the second week	
ASSETS	**£**
Inventory	400
Trade receivable	100
Bank balance	8,200
Total assets	**8,700**
LIABILITIES	
Trade payable	200
Bank loan	5,000
	5,200
Owner equity	3,500
Total liabilities and equity	**8,700**

EZ-Books' statement of financial position is informative in terms of the nature and amounts of assets, liabilities and equity. However, it could be more useful if it were to distinguish between:

- Current and noncurrent assets and liabilities
- Current and comparative reporting periods

2.2 What are current and noncurrent assets and liabilities?

EZ-Books' statement of financial position presents its assets as 'current assets' and distinguishes between 'current' and 'noncurrent liabilities' as follows:

EZ-Books Statement of financial position at the end of the second week	
ASSETS	**£**
Current assets	
Inventory	400
Trade receivable	100
Bank balance	8,200
	8,700

LIABILITIES	
Current liabilities	
Trade payable	200
Bank loan	1,000
Noncurrent liabilities	
Bank loan	4,000
	5,200
Owner equity	3,500
	8,700

2.2.1 Current and noncurrent assets

Assets should be classified as current on a statement of financial position in any of the following situations:

- The asset is held primarily for the purpose of trading activity and is likely to be sold or consumed within the normal operating cycle of the business. Inventory is a typical example. A business buys inventory in order to sell it 'as is' or to consume it in a manufacturing process.
- The asset is likely to be convertible into cash within twelve months of the date of the statement of financial position. A trade receivable is a typical example. A business would usually expect to collect amounts owed by customers within twelve months.
- The asset is cash or a cash equivalent. Cash in hand and current account bank balances are typical examples.

All other assets should be presented on a statement of financial position as **non-current**. A noncurrent asset is typically expected to be of use to the business for more than one financial year, hence the term 'noncurrent'. Additionally, non-current assets are resources that are acquired for productive use within the business rather than for the purpose of being sold. Typical examples of noncurrent assets include:

- Machinery used in a manufacturing process
- Factory and administration offices occupied by employees
- Office fixtures, fittings and equipment

In each example, the asset is acquired for productive use within the business and there is no explicit intention to sell it. EZ-Books acquires a noncurrent asset in Chapter 4 (Capital and Revenue Expenditure).

2.2.2 Current and noncurrent liabilities

EZ-Books' statement of financial position also separates the current from the noncurrent liabilities. A liability should be classified as current when it is expected to be paid within the normal operating cycle of the business, or no later than twelve months from the date of the statement of financial position. A typical example is a trade payable – it is usual for trade payables to be settled within the normal operating cycle of a business.

Any liability that is not classified as current should be classified as non-current. The presentation of a liability as noncurrent indicates that the amount is not expected to be settled until at least twelve months after the date of the statement of financial position. In EZ-Books' case, one portion of the bank loan (£1,000) will be settled within twelve months and another portion (£4,000) will be settled after twelve months.

Why are the distinctions between current and noncurrent assets and liabilities important?

In addition to merely listing assets in a statement of financial position, presenting them as **current** or **noncurrent** can provide relevant information about the time frame within which at least some are expected to be converted into cash. Similarly, presenting liabilities as current or non-current can provide useful information about when they are due to be settled.

As a result, it becomes possible to identify the productive asset base of the business, the availability of cash, the sources of future operating cash receipts and the time frame within which cash will need to be available to meet financial obligations as they fall due.

2.2.3 Is owner equity split into current and noncurrent components?

No. Financial statements are prepared on the assumption that the owner invest-ment is a long-term commitment. The owner equity is part of what is referred to as the **permanent capital** base. There is no expectation that the investment will be repaid by the business to the owner other than if the business ceases and is wound up.

2.3 What are current and comparative reporting periods?

EZ-Books' statement of financial position could be more useful if it were to include both current and comparative reporting period as follows:

	2nd week £	1st week £
EZ-Books Statement of financial position at the end of the second week		
ASSETS		
Current assets		
Inventory	400	
Trade receivable	100	
Bank balance	8,200	7,500
	8,700	7,500
LIABILITIES		
Current liabilities		
Trade payable	200	
Bank loan	1,000	1,000
Noncurrent liabilities		
Bank loan	4,000	4,000
	5,200	5,000
Owner equity	3,500	2,500
	8,700	7,500

The financial snapshot of assets, liabilities and equity taken at the end of the second week is comparable to the snapshot taken at the end of the first week.

Why is the inclusion of a comparative period important?

While the information provided about a business at a single point in time can be useful, readers of financial statements are also interested in how assets, liabilities and equity have changed over a period of time. As a result, observations about whether or not the financial health of EZ-Books is improving over time become possible. In practice, the statements of financial position of many businesses are published on an annual basis and include comparative figures from the preceding year.

2.4 How are other financial statements related to the statement of financial position?

The statement of financial position is one of a number of financial statements which, when presented together, comprise a complete set of financial statements. The other components of a set of financial statements are a:

- Statement of comprehensive income
- Statement of changes in equity
- Statement of cash flows
- Summary of significant accounting policies and explanatory information

2.4.1 Statement of comprehensive income (Chapters 3 and 9)

A statement of comprehensive income comprises:

- An income statement (Chapter 3)
- Other comprehensive income (Chapter 9)

An income statement presents the detail of the income and expenditure of a business for a period of time. For profit-oriented businesses, it is a calculation of whether the business has made a profit or loss during a reporting period. It complements financial snapshots of assets, liabilities and equity presented in statements of financial position.

Other comprehensive income comprises income and expenses that arise during a reporting period and are attributable to the owner but are not included in the income statement profit calculation.

2.4.2 Statement of changes in equity (Chapter 10)

Any excess of income over expenditure is attributable to the owner of the business and, for this reason, becomes part of owner equity in a period-end statement of financial position. Owner equity increases if income exceeds expenditure because the profit is attributable (owed) to the owner. If a net loss is incurred by the business, the owner equity decreases by the amount of the loss because, ultimately, it is the owner who takes the financial risk associated with investing in a business.

The amount of owner equity presented in statements of financial position can also change for reasons other than profits or other comprehensive income.

In these circumstances, the reasons for changes in owner equity are presented in a statement of changes in equity. The statement of changes in equity is addressed in detail in Chapter 10.

A combination of (i) the statement of comprehensive income and (ii) the statement of changes in equity provides a significant amount of detail about how and why owner equity changes during a reporting period.

2.4.3 Statement of cash flows (Chapter 11)

The purpose of a statement of cash flows is to explain why the cash and cash equivalents (such as bank current accounts and overdrafts) have changed during a reporting period. In the case of EZ-Books, a statement of cash flows would provide an explanation of why the bank balance increased from £7,500 at the end of the first week and £8,200 at the end of the second week. The statement of cash flows is addressed in detail in Chapter 11.

2.4.4 Notes accompanying the financial statements

Accompanying notes provide additional information that is relevant to an understanding of the financial statements. The topic of 'notes', as a component of a complete set of financial statements, is not addressed in this text.

2.5 Summary and conclusion

The primary consideration of this chapter is how to present information in more useful ways. The simple accounting equation introduced in Chapter 1 is expanded to distinguish between current and noncurrent assets and liabilities, and current and comparative reporting periods, and to explain how a statement of financial position is related to the other components of a set of financial statements. Chapter 3 introduces the income statement. The assumption in Chapter 1 of selling inventory for the same price as that at which it was bought is removed for the purpose of calculating and presenting profits and losses in an income statement.

Test your understanding

1 Categorize each of the following as current or noncurrent assets or liabilities:

   (a) Machinery for use in the business
   (b) Trade payables
   (c) Loan receivable within six months
   (d) Loan payable in three years' time
   (e) Inventory
   (f) Cash
   (g) Motor vehicles for use by sales and marketing employees
   (h) Trade receivables
   (i) Bank overdraft

2 The following transactions occur during the first five days of the business existence of Libra:

   Day 1: Owner invests equity capital in Libra amounting to £3,800. The investment is lodged to Libra's bank account.
   Day 2: Libra purchases inventory on credit for £1,650.
   Day 3: Libra sells the entire inventory for £1,650.
   Day 4: Libra makes a bank transfer to the trade payable for £1,250.
   Day 5: Libra receives a cheque from the trade receivable amounting to £1,550. The cheque is lodged.

Required:
Draft Libra's statement of financial position for **each** of the five days.

Further practice and reading

1. http://www.bazwaldo.com

   Insert the following code into the website keyword search option to access practice questions relating to this chapter: *2010chapter2*

2. Thomas, A. and Ward, A.M. (2009) *Introduction to Financial Accounting*, 6th edn, McGraw-Hill

   Chapter 1: Entities and financial reporting statements

   Chapter 14: The final financial statements of sole traders (introductory)

3 The income statement

You must be able to explain:

○ The purpose of the income statement
○ The rationale for and calculation of cost of sales
○ How to account for transactions between a business and its owners

3.1 What is the purpose of the income statement?

The purpose of the income statement is to present the income earned and expenditure incurred by a business during a specified reporting period.

Income usually refers to the revenues earned from the ordinary trading activities of the business. Revenue is generated by selling inventory and providing services.

> An income statement is also commonly referred to as a **profit and loss account**.

Expenditure primarily refers to the costs incurred in the ordinary course of running a business. Examples include the purchase of inventory, wages and salaries, overheads such as light and heat, motor expenses or insurance.

This chapter focuses primarily on transactions involving the sale and purchase of inventory. The logic of cost of sales is explained. The accounting treatment of transactions between the business and the owner is also addressed.

Accounting for other items of expenditure such as overheads, noncurrent assets, and the gains and losses that arise from the disposal of noncurrent assets is addressed in the chapters that follow.

3.2 Illustrative example of accounting for the purchase and sale of inventory

In Chapter 1, it is assumed that the EZ-Books' inventory is sold for the same amount as that at which it is bought. This simplifying assumption is useful in Chapter 1 for the purpose of illustrating the accounting equation, but it is now removed. Profit-oriented businesses sell inventory at prices that are higher than cost and so require a more sophisticated approach to accounting for inventory. The business activities of EZ-Books during its second week are now considered assuming that EZ-Books is a profit-oriented business.

EZ-Books' statement of financial position at the end of the first week is as follows:

EZ-Books Statement of financial position at the end of the first week	
Assets	**£**
Bank balance	7,500
Liabilities	
Bank loan	5,000
Owner equity	2,500
	7,500

During the second week, four transactions occurred. The first two involved the purchase and sale of inventory.

Transaction 1: EZ-Books **purchased** 50 accounting textbooks (inventory) on credit for £500 (a per-book cost of £10).

Transaction 2: EZ-Books **sold** 10 accounting textbooks (inventory) on credit for £200 (a per-book sales value of £20).

Transaction 3: EZ-Books **sends a cheque** for £300 to the trade payable.

Transaction 4: John Brown **invests** an additional £1,000 equity in EZ-Books.

Regarding the second transaction, the selling price per book (£20) is now greater than the purchase price per book (£10). The assumption in Chapter 1 that inventory is sold for the same price as that at which it was bought is therefore discarded.

The accounting objective is to present (i) the income statement for the second week and (ii) the statement of financial position at the end of the second week so that it is informative about the profitability of EZ-Books, and to present a complete list of the assets, liabilities and equity.

EZ-Books' income statement is as follows:

	Income statement for the period ended second week		
	2nd week	1st week	Explanatory comments
	£	£	
Income	200	–	Income is earned during the second week as a result of transaction 1.
Less cost of sales			
Inventory at the beginning of the week (opening inventory)	–	–	No inventory existed until **after** the beginning of the second week.
(plus) Inventory purchases during the week	500	–	Expenditure is incurred **during** the second week as a result of transaction 2.
(minus) Inventory at the end of the week (closing inventory)	(400)	–	Not all inventory that was available for sale during the second week was sold by the end of the second week. The inventory remaining is therefore a resource (asset) that is available for sale during a subsequent period.
Expenditure (cost of sales)	100	–	
Profit earned during the period	100	–	This profit is attributable to the owner of the business and therefore becomes part of owner equity in the *statement of financial position*.

The accounting profit should be calculated by comparing the income earned from selling ten textbooks (£20 per book) with the cost of ten textbooks (£10 per book). The cost of the textbooks sold is more generally referred to as the **cost of goods sold** or **cost of sales**.

The sum of opening inventory and purchases is the cost of inventory that is **available** for sale during the second week. Closing inventory is deducted to remove inventory that was bought but not sold during the second week. The cost of inventory that actually was sold during the second week is all that remains in the income statement.

> The relevance and comparability of a profit calculation is enhanced if the **cost of sales**, rather than cost of purchases or cost of goods available for sale, is deducted from income.

Business transactions that involve the sale and purchase of inventory are, **in the first instance**, recorded in the income statement. Adjustments are made at the end of a reporting period to take account of opening and closing inventories in a cost of sales calculation. The bottom line of the income statement shows a profit of £100. The income statement is consistent with the knowledge that EZ-Books buys textbooks at £10 each and sells them for £20 each.

EZ-Books' statement of financial position is as follows:

	2nd week £	1st week £	Explanatory comments
Statement of financial position at the end of the second week			
Current assets			
Inventory	400		Forty books at £10 each are available for sale at the end of the second week. They are therefore assets at the end of the second week.
Trade receivable	200		An amount is receivable at the end of the second week due to the sale of inventory on credit (transaction 1).
Bank balance	8,200	7,500	The bank balance increases by £1,000 due to owner investment (transaction 4) and decreases by £300 due to part payment of a trade payable (transaction 3).
Total assets	8,800	7,500	

Current liabilities			
Trade payable	200		An amount is payable due to the credit purchase (£500), part of which was paid (£300) (transactions 2 and 3).
Bank loan	1,000	1,000	Current portion of the original bank loan is a current liability.
	1,200	1,000	
Noncurrent liabilities			
Bank loan	4,000	4,000	Noncurrent portion of the bank loan is a noncurrent liability.
Equity			
Owner equity at the beginning of the week	2,500	–	
New equity investment	1,000	2,500	Capital investments made by the owner during the first and second weeks (transaction 4 during second week).
Profit earned during the period	100	–	Profits and losses are attributable to the owner. Details of calculation shown in the *income statement*.
Total liabilities and equity	8,800	7,500	

The inclusion of inventory as a current asset (£400) corresponds to the deduction of closing inventory in the income statement. It represents the inventory that was not sold during the second week of business and is therefore available for sale during the third week.

3.3 What are the bookkeeping entries?

EZ-Books' four transactions during the second week may be expressed in terms of debits and credits. These bookkeeping entries are the basis of the income statement and statement of financial position presented in section 3.2. The adjustment to inventory expenditure to take account of closing inventory is recorded as transaction 5.

Transaction		Account	dr	cr	Meaning
1	dr	Purchases	500		Decrease in equity – purchase of inventory recorded as expenditure
	cr	Trade payable		500	Increase in liabilities – obligation to pay for the inventory purchase
2	dr	Trade receivable	200		Increase in assets – future receipt from a customer
	cr	Sales		200	Increase in equity – income earned
3	dr	Trade payable	300		Decrease in liabilities – payment to supplier decreases the obligation
	cr	Bank account		300	Decrease in assets – payment to supplier decreases the bank balance
4	dr	Bank account	1,000		Increase in assets – lodgement increases the bank balance
	cr	Owner equity		1,000	Increase in equity – additional owner investment
5	dr	Inventory	400		Increase in assets – recognition of the inventory that is still available for sale at the end of the reporting period
	cr	Cost of sales		400	Increase in equity – a reduction in expenditure included in the income statement as a result of removing the expenditure that relates to the closing inventory

Compare the bookkeeping entries above to those presented in section 1.7 of Chapter 1. Transactions involving the sale and purchase of inventory are now presented in an income statement in the first instance, and adjustments made for opening and closing inventories at the end of the reporting period. The reason is to provide information about the profitability of business activities separately from the assets, liabilities and equity that are included in the statement of financial position.

Why is the purchase of inventory a 'debit' entry and why is the sale of inventory a 'credit' entry?

The purchase of inventory increases the available inventory. It is therefore an increase in an asset, which, according to the principles of double-entry bookkeeping, requires a debit accounting entry. Alternatively, the purchase of inventory may be thought of as a decrease in equity due to the fact that business expenditure reduces profit attributable to the owners. A decrease in equity also requires a debit accounting entry.

Correspondingly, a sale of inventory decreases the available inventory. It is a decrease in an asset, which requires a credit accounting entry. Alternatively, the sale of inventory increases profit and therefore the amount of owner equity. An increase in equity also requires a credit entry.

3.4 How are transactions between the business and its owners accounted for?

The fourth transaction during the second week was an investment of £1,000 by the owner. It is reasonable to ask why this £1,000, and indeed the £2,500 that was invested by the owner during the first week, are not accounted for as income in the EZ-Books income statement.

The general rule is: if business owners (John Brown in this example) transact with the business (EZ-Books) **in their capacity as owners**, the transactions are **not** reflected in the income statement. These transactions are recorded instead in the statement of changes in equity. The equity investments made by John Brown during the first two weeks of business are examples of transacting with the business in his capacity as the owner and would therefore be recorded in the EZ-Books statement of changes in equity. Recall from section 2.4 of Chapter 2 that both the income statement and the statement of changes in equity may be required in order to fully explain the changes in owner equity that have taken place during a particular reporting period. The statement of changes in equity is addressed in detail in Chapter 10.

It is possible that the owner may transact with the business in some capacity other than specifically as the owner. For example, John Brown could, for whatever reasons, buy inventory from or sell inventory to EZ-Books. These would be examples of John Brown transacting with EZ-Books as a customer or supplier rather than specifically as the owner. Accordingly, the correct accounting treatment would be to regard John Brown as just another customer or supplier of inventory and to include the transactions in the income statement.

In summary, when there are transactions between the business and the owners of the business, the correct accounting treatment is determined by whether or not the owners are transacting with the business in their capacity as owners.

3.5 What are the three common types of business entity?

Three common types of business entity are (i) sole trader, (ii) partnership and (iii) limited company.

3.5.1 What is a sole trader?

A sole trader is owned and managed by one person. For example, EZ-Books is a sole trader business because it is owned and managed by John Brown. A sole trader business and its owner are, from an accounting perspective, independent entities. From a legal perspective, however, there is no such distinction. The legal implication is that the owner of a sole trader business may be personally liable for losses incurred by the business.

The equity of a sole trader business at any point in time is made up of capital invested by the owner plus profits earned from business activities minus withdrawals made by the owner.

3.5.2 What is a partnership?

A partnership is a business arrangement whereby a number of individuals agree to operate a business in partnership with each other. Profits earned and losses incurred are shared among the partners in accordance with a partnership agreement.

A partnership business is, from an accounting perspective, independent of the partners who run the business. However, from a legal perspective, there is no distinction between individual partners and a partnership business. The legal implication is that partners may be personally liable for partnership business losses.

The equity of a partnership business at any point in time is made up of capital invested by the partners plus profits earned by the partnership business minus withdrawals made by partners.

3.5.3 What is a limited company?

A limited company is a business entity that is owned by shareholders. A share is a unit of ownership in a limited company. Shareholders appoint directors to run the company on a day-to-day basis.

In common with sole trader and partnership business entities, a limited company is, from an accounting perspective, independent of the shareholders. In contrast to sole trader and partnership business entities, however, a limited company is also legally independent of the shareholders. This means that a limited company has a legal existence that is separate from the shareholders who own it. The legal implication is that shareholders of a limited company are not personally liable for losses incurred by the company, hence the term 'limited company'.

The trade-off for limited liability is a more onerous set of financial reporting obligations than is required of sole trader or partnership business entities. The trade-off between limited liability and financial reporting obligations is therefore an important consideration for individuals who intend to set up a new business.

The equity of a limited company at any point in time comprises, at its simplest, issued share capital plus profits minus dividends. An investor in a limited company receives share certificates in return for the capital invested. Share certificates are units of ownership in a limited company. Assuming profits are earned, the profits are attributable to the shareholders and are included as part of company equity, and therefore as an obligation to the shareholders, until such time as they may be distributed as dividends. Losses incurred by a company are also attributable to the shareholders and therefore reduce the shareholders' equity. If a limited company's shareholders' equity is reduced to zero, the shareholders have lost their entire investment but are not personally liable for any further losses.

Is it important to appreciate the existence of several types of business entity?

For the most part, the knowledge required to account for the transactions and events of sole traders, partnerships and companies is the same. The principles covered in this text apply equally to sole traders, partnerships and limited companies so, for the most part, it is not necessary to distinguish between the types of business entity through the text.

Partnership accounting requires some specific considerations if goodwill arises, if new partners are admitted to the partnership, if existing partners retire or if the partnership converts to a limited company. These aspects of partnership accounting are not addressed in this text.

Accounting for the equity of limited liability companies can become somewhat more complicated than noted above owing to the possibility of issuing different types of shares, issuing shares for more than their face value (share premium), and dividends. These matters are considered further in Chapter 10 (Statement of Changes in Equity).

3.6 Summary and conclusion

The income and expenditure of a business is presented in the income statement. Its purpose is to provide information about the profitability of the business. Profits increase owner equity and losses decrease owner equity.

The formula for calculating cost of sales is:

Opening inventory **plus** Purchases **minus** Closing inventory

Cost of sales is a calculation of the cost of the goods that were sold during the reporting period (as opposed to (i) the cost of goods purchased or (ii) the cost of goods available for sale).

When transactions between a business and its owners occur, it is necessary to determine whether or not the owners are transacting with the business in their capacity as owners. If they are, the transactions are not, as a rule, recorded in the income statement.

There are three common types of business entity: sole trader, partnership and limited company. Much of the accounting knowledge required to account for the different types of business entity is common but there are some specifics required for partnerships and limited companies.

Chapter 4 continues the development of financial statements to consider types of expenditure other than inventory expenditure. Capital and revenue types of expenditure affect both the statement of financial position and the income statement.

Test your understanding

1   Alpha's accounting records include the following information for the period ending 31 December 2010:

	£
Inventory 1 January 2010	12,744
Inventory 31 December 2010	15,001
Sales	46,552
Purchases	30,200
Sales returns	1,925
Purchases returns	1,023

Required:
   (i) Calculate the value for cost of sales for the period ending 31 December 2010.
   (ii) Calculate the profit for the period ending 31 December 2010.

2   At the beginning of the week, the assets of a business amounted to £3,400. The assets comprised inventory valued at £200 and a bank balance of £3,200. There were no liabilities. During the week, the following transactions occurred:

1 August: Purchase of inventory on credit £600
2 August: The owner lodges a cheque of £2,500 as an investment of new equity capital in the business
3 August: Sale of inventory on credit £1,100
4 August: Paid £400 of the amount owed to the trade payable
5 August: Received £800 of the amount owed by the trade receivable
7 August: Inventory with a value of £250 was still available at the end of the week

Required:
   (i) Draft the bookkeeping entries required to account for the transactions during the week ending 7 August.
   (ii) Prepare the income statement for the week ending 7 August.
   (iii) Prepare the statement of financial position at 7 August.

Further practice and reading

1. http://www.bazwaldo.com

   Insert the following code into the website keyword search option to access practice questions relating to this chapter: *2010chapter3*

2. Thomas, A. and Ward, A.M. (2009) *Introduction to Financial Accounting*, 6th edn, McGraw-Hill

   Chapter 1: Entities and financial reporting statements

   Chapter 14: The final financial statements of sole traders (introductory)

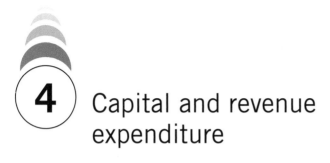

4 Capital and revenue expenditure

You must be able to explain:

○ The difference between capital and revenue expenditure
○ How to account for capital and revenue expenditure
○ How a profit calculation is affected by capital and revenue expenditure

4.1 What is the difference between capital and revenue expenditure?

Although buying inventory in order to sell it for a profit might be the main reason to establish a business, the purchase of inventory is not the only type of expenditure incurred. Machinery, vehicles, office equipment, computer hardware and soft-

> **Capital expenditure** is investment expenditure.
> **Revenue expenditure** is consumption expenditure.

ware, furniture and fittings, stationery, wages and salaries, rent, insurance, light and heat, legal fees, and accountancy fees are just some of the expenditure items necessarily incurred by businesses. Appropriate accounting mechanisms are needed in order to record and present all expenditure in financial statements in as useful a way as possible.

In general, expenditure incurred by a business is classified as one of two types: **capital expenditure** or **revenue expenditure.**

Why is it important to identify expenditure as either capital or revenue expenditure?

It is important because the accounting treatment of capital expenditure differs from the accounting treatment of revenue expenditure.

Expenditure is recorded as capital expenditure if it is expected that the business will benefit from the expenditure not only in the current reporting period but in future reporting periods as well. Common examples of capital expenditure include the acquisition of plant and equipment for use in a factory, motor vehicles for use by a sales and marketing department, or furniture and fittings in administration departments. In each of these examples, the expenditure results in a resource that, in all likelihood, will be productively available to the business for a number of reporting periods. **Capital expenditure is accounted for as an asset and therefore included in statements of financial position.**

If the benefit of expenditure is consumed in the current reporting period, the expenditure is regarded as revenue expenditure. Typical examples of revenue expenditure include light and heat, insurance, and cleaning. In each of these examples, the benefits obtained (whether the light and heat received, the period of insurance cover, or the clean factories and offices) are, subject to possible adjustments considered in Chapter 6, consumed in the current reporting period. **Revenue expenditure is included as expenditure in the income statement in the reporting period in which the expenditure is incurred.**

4.2 Illustrative example of capital and revenue expenditures

EZ-Books' statement of financial position at the end of the second week (and therefore at the beginning of the third week) is as follows:

Statement of financial position at the end of the second week	
	2nd week
	£
Current assets	
Inventory	400
Trade receivable	200
Bank balance	8,200
Total assets	8,800

Current liabilities	
Trade payable	200
Bank loan	1,000
	1,200
Noncurrent liabilities	
Bank loan	4,000
Equity	
Owner equity	3,600
Total equity and liabilities	8,800

Four transactions occurred during the third week of business, as follows:

Transaction 1: EZ-Books **rents an office** for use by the owner. The office is rented on a week-to-week basis. An invoice for the weekly rent, amounting to £75, is received. It is paid by EZ-Books on the last day of the third week.

Transaction 2: EZ-Books **buys furniture** for use in the office. The cost of the furniture is £3,000 and is paid for by cheque before the end of the third week.

Transaction 3: EZ-Books **sells** 20 accounting textbooks for £400. The customer pays for them immediately by cheque. The cheque is lodged before the end of the third week.

Transaction 4: EZ-Books **buys** five accounting textbooks for £50 on credit.

The business expenditure incurred during the third week is a combination of inventory purchases, capital expenditure and revenue expenditure. Income is also generated during the third week as a result of the sale of inventory.

EZ-Books' income statement for the third week is as follows:

Income statement for the period ended third week			
	3rd week	**2nd week**	**Explanatory comments**
	£	£	
Income	400	200	Income earned during the third week (transaction 3) and the second week comparative. See Chapter 3 for the basis of the comparatives.

Less cost of sales

Inventory at the beginning of the week	400	–	Closing inventory at the end of the second week is the opening inventory for the third week.
(plus) Inventory purchases during the week	50	500	Inventory purchases during the third week (transaction 4) and the second week comparative.
(minus) Inventory at the end of the week	(250)	(400)	Forty-five textbooks were available for sale during the third week. Of these, 20 were sold. Closing inventory at the end of the third week therefore comprises 25 textbooks at a cost of £10 per book.
	200	100	
Gross profit	200	100	**Gross profit is the difference between income and the cost of sales.**
Less operating expenses			
Office rent	75	–	Office rent is classified as **revenue expenditure** (transaction 1). It is therefore included in the income statement as a deduction from gross profit to calculate the bottom-line profit for the period.
Profit for the period	125	100	Profit earned during the third week of business and the second week comparative.

The office rent is accounted for as revenue expenditure and included in the income statement because the benefit of the £75 expenditure (the entitlement to use the office) is fully utilized during the third week. There is no benefit to EZ-Books after the end of the third week. If office space is required for the fourth week or subsequently, further expenditure will be incurred at those times.

The gross profit earned during the third week is calculated by comparing the income generated from selling 20 textbooks with the cost of selling that number of textbooks. The cost of selling 20 textbooks is calculated using the cost of sales formula.

Overhead expenditure items are listed below gross profit. The income statement distinguishes between the profit earned solely from the business of buying and selling textbooks (gross profit) and the overall profit of the business after taking all other expenditure into consideration (profit for the period).

EZ-Books' statement of financial position at the end of the third week is as follows:

	Statement of financial position at the end of the third week		
	3rd week	2nd week	Explanatory comments
	£	£	
Noncurrent assets			
Furniture	3,000	–	The expenditure on furniture (transaction 2) is classified as capital expenditure.
Current assets			
Inventory	250	400	Twenty-five textbooks are available for sale at the end of the third week.
Trade receivable	200	200	No change from the second week.
Bank balance	5,525	8,200	The bank account balance decreased due to payments for the office rent (transaction 1) and furniture (transaction 2). The account balance increased due to receipt from sale of inventory (transaction 3). Overall, there is a net decrease.
Total assets	8,975	8,800	
Current liabilities			
Trade payable	250	200	Trade payables increased by the amount of purchase of inventory on credit during the third week (transaction 4).
Bank loan	1,000	1,000	No change from the second week.
	1,250	1,200	
Noncurrent liabilities			
Bank loan	4,000	4,000	No change from the second week.

Equity			
Owner equity	3,725	3,600	The owner equity increased by the amount of the profit earned during the third week (£125).
Total liabilities and equity	8,975	8,800	

The acquisition of the furniture is accounted for as capital expenditure because EZ-Books will benefit from its use for longer than just the third week. It is probable that the furniture will be available for use for several years and, on this basis, can be accounted for as an EZ-Books noncurrent asset.

4.3 What are the bookkeeping entries?

The bookkeeping entries required to account for EZ-Books' four transactions during the third week are as follows:

Transaction		Account	dr	cr	Meaning
1	dr	Office rent	75		Decrease in equity – revenue expenditure on office expense
	cr	Bank account		75	Decrease in assets – bank balance decreases by the amount of the payment
2	dr	Furniture	3,000		Increase in assets – capital expenditure on furniture
	cr	Bank account		3,000	Decrease in assets – bank balance decreases by the amount of the payment
3	dr	Bank	400		Increase in assets – bank balance increases by the amount of the sales receipt
	cr	Sale of inventory		400	Increase in equity – income earned from sale of inventory
4	dr	Purchases	50		Decrease in equity – purchase of inventory is recorded as expenditure

	cr	Trade payable		50	Increase in liabilities – a trade payable obligation arises as a result of the credit purchase
5	dr	Cost of sales	400		Decrease in equity – opening inventory is recorded as expenditure
	cr	Inventory		400	Decrease in assets – opening inventory is removed from the statement of financial position
6	dr	Inventory	250		Increase in assets – closing inventory is recorded on the statement of financial position
	cr	Cost of sales		250	Increase in equity – closing inventory is a deduction in the income statement cost of sales

The revenue expenditure (rent), capital expenditure (furniture) and inventory expenditure in transactions 1, 2 and 4 respectively are all debit entries to begin with but they end up in different parts of the financial statements. Revenue expenditure is included in the income statement and capital expenditure is included in the statement of financial position.

Inventory expenditure is presented, in the first instance, in the income statement (as purchases) but is adjusted at the end of the reporting period for opening and closing inventories on hand. Transaction 5 transfers the inventory on hand at the end of week 2 (£400) from the inventory asset account to the cost of sales calculation. This is because the inventory on hand at the end of week 2 is available for sale in week 3. Transaction 6 similarly adjusts for inventory on hand at the end of week 3: inventory not sold during week 3 is available for sale in subsequent periods and is therefore presented as an asset in the statement of financial position at the end of week 3.

4.4 Accounting issues caused by the distinction between capital and revenue expenditure

4.4.1 Classifying expenditure as capital or revenue expenditure is not always obvious

In most cases, identifying whether expenditure is of a capital or a revenue nature is reasonably straightforward. It is usually easy to determine whether the benefit of the expenditure is consumed in the current accounting period or whether the benefit will extend to future accounting periods. Not all expenditure is so easily classified, however. Consider the following expenditure examples:

- Expenditure incurred to repair furniture.
- Expenditure incurred on an advertising campaign in order to generate new sales.
- Expenditure incurred on staff training in order to increase productivity.

A logical case could be made to account for each of these items as capital expenditure because the benefits to be gained from the repair work, the advertising campaign or the staff training could extend to future accounting periods.

In practice, however, each of these items of expenditure is accounted for as revenue expenditure. The reason is because **it is not enough to hope or vaguely anticipate that the expenditures might generate future benefits in order to treat them as capital expenditure.** Nor is it sufficient, in the case of the furniture repair example, that the furniture is returned merely to a past physical condition without any real enhancement to its productive capacity.

In general, to capitalize expenditure, the expenditure should:

(i)   Result in a new resource or enhance an existing resource, for which there is
(ii) Sufficient certainty that future economic benefits will arise, and
(iii) The future benefits can be quantified with sufficient reliability.

Although an advertising campaign would be expected to generate new sales, it would be difficult to forecast the success of an advertising campaign and to quantify the value of new sales with the level of certainty that is the accounting criterion for capitalizing expenditure. Similarly, while there might be optimistic anticipation of increased staff productivity resulting from staff training, the absence of sufficient certainty regarding any quantifiable benefit would preclude accounting for it as capital expenditure.

4.4.2 How can the profit calculation be accurate if capital expenditure is excluded from the income statement?

The purpose of an income statement is to present the income earned and expenditure incurred by a business during a specified period of time. When expenditure is capitalized, it is presented as an asset on the statement of financial position. It appears, therefore, that capital expenditure (up to this point) does not affect the income statement. However, if the income statement includes only revenue expenditure, it presents only a partial view of the business profitability because some expenditure, namely the capital expenditure, is excluded from the profit calculation. In this circumstance, how is it possible to accurately present the profitability of a business if only the revenue expenditure is included in the income statement?

In brief, depreciation is an accounting mechanism which facilitates the appropriate inclusion of capital expenditure in profit calculations. This is achieved by methodically allocating capital expenditure to the accounting periods during which the business expects to benefit from using the asset. For example, if EZ-Books' owner estimates that the furniture acquired during the third week of business will be of beneficial use for five years, he could allocate the total cost of £3,000 evenly across five years of profit calculations. Each annual income statement would include £600 of expenditure on furniture and would be described in the income statement as 'depreciation'. This topic is addressed in detail in Chapter 5.

4.5 Summary and conclusions

Expenditure is typically classified as either capital or revenue expenditure. The distinction is important because capital expenditure results in the inclusion of an asset on the statement of financial position whereas revenue expenditure is included directly in the income statement as an expense. To include expenditure as capital expenditure, and therefore to increase the assets of a business, communicates a different message from the inclusion of expenditure as revenue expenditure, which reduces profitability.

In most cases, the identification of expenditure as capital or revenue expenditure is a reasonably straightforward exercise. However, there can be circumstances when it is difficult to ascertain with sufficient reliability whether the expenditure will result in future benefits.

Chapter 5 continues the development of financial statements to consider how capital expenditure is allocated to income statements. The allocation mechanism is known as depreciation.

Test your understanding

1 Categorize each of the following as either capital or revenue expenditure:

(a) Acquisition of a new motor vehicle for use in the business.
(b) Repairs to the motor vehicle one year later.
(c) Annual motor insurance for the vehicle.
(d) Replacing the tyres on the motor vehicle five years later.
(e) A parking fine.

2 Categorize each of the following as either capital or revenue expenditure:

(a) Building a new warehouse.
(b) Painting the warehouse two years later.
(c) Building and painting an extension to the warehouse three years later.
(d) Cost of a vending machine for the warehouse canteen.
(e) Warehouse electricity costs.
(f) Rebuilding a warehouse wall that fell down during bad weather.

Further practice and reading

1. http://www.bazwaldo.com

   Insert the following code into the website keyword search option to access practice questions relating to this chapter: *2010chapter4*

2. Thomas, A. and Ward, A.M. (2009) *Introduction to Financial Accounting,* 6th edn, McGraw-Hill

   Chapter 7: The accounting equation and its components

5 Depreciation, disposals and revaluations

You must be able to explain:

- The purpose of depreciation
- How to account for gains and losses on noncurrent asset disposals
- How to account for surpluses and deficits arising from revaluations of noncurrent assets.

5.1 Why are noncurrent assets depreciated?

The **first reason** is to account for the gradual consumption of the benefits of a noncurrent asset. Depreciation is an estimation of the benefits of noncurrent assets that are consumed during a reporting period. As benefits are consumed, the remaining future benefits correspondingly decrease.

> There are **two** primary reasons why noncurrent assets are depreciated.

For example, EZ-Books incurs capital expenditure of £3,000 to acquire furniture. The furniture is included as a noncurrent asset on EZ-Books' statement of financial position because the benefits of the expenditure (being able to work productively) will be gained over a number of reporting periods. As time passes, the furniture becomes increasingly worn or outdated until, sooner or later, it is no longer of productive use. The financial statements of EZ-Books should communicate the gradual consumption of the furniture. The accounting mechanism that achieves this is depreciation.

The **second reason** for depreciation is the inclusion of an appropriate amount of capital expenditure in a periodic income statement. An income statement that completely excludes capital expenditure is misleading because it includes only some of the total expenditure incurred by a business, namely the revenue expenditure. Depreciation is the accounting mechanism that facilitates the inclusion of capital expenditure in income statements.

For example, it is estimated that EZ-Books' furniture, acquired for £3,000, will be of beneficial use for five years. It is estimated that the furniture will have a residual value of £250 at the end of the fifth year. The accounting implications are as follows:

- The £3,000 expenditure is capitalized and recorded as a furniture asset.
- The **depreciable amount** is the difference between the cost of the furniture and its residual value. This amounts to £2,750.
- The £2,750 depreciable amount is allocated to the number of reporting periods it is estimated that EZ-Books will benefit from the furniture. In this example, the number of reporting periods is five.
- An amount of £550 (being £2,750 divided by 5) is included in the income statement each year for five years. The effect of the depreciation is therefore to include a portion of capital expenditure in each year's profit calculation.
- The **carrying value** of the furniture asset in the statement of financial position is reduced by £550 each year for five years.
- At the end of the fifth year, the carrying value of the furniture asset amounts to £250. In theory, this is the amount that will be recovered by selling the furniture rather than continuing to use it.

5.2 Methods of depreciation

> The appropriate method of depreciation depends on the pattern of consumption of an asset's benefits.

There are a number of ways in which a depreciable amount can be allocated to accounting periods. Two common methods are the **straight-line method** and the **reducing balance method**.

5.2.1 What is the straight-line method of depreciation?

The depreciation of furniture in section 5.1 is an example of the straight-line method of depreciation. The depreciable amount is first calculated as the difference between the cost of the asset and the estimated residual value. The depreciable amount is then allocated evenly to the appropriate number of income statements based on the estimated useful life of the asset.

> The straight-line method is appropriate when the benefits of the asset are gained evenly over its useful economic life.

In section 5.1, it is assumed that the benefits of the furniture consumed are approximately the same each year. For this reason, the straight-line method is a reasonable basis for allocating the cost of the asset.

5.2.2 What is the reducing balance method of depreciation?

Computer hardware is an example of an asset for which the reducing balance method of depreciation may be appropriate. If, for example, EZ-Books buys computer hardware at a cost of £3,000 and applies a depreciation percentage of 50% on a reducing balance basis, the income statement and statement of financial position are affected over three years as follows:

Year 1 financial statements
- Income statement includes a depreciation charge of £1,500, being 50% of the original cost of £3,000.
- Statement of financial position includes computer equipment as a non-current asset at a carrying value of £1,500, being the original £3,000 minus the depreciation charge of £1,500.

Year 2 financial statements
- Income statement includes a depreciation charge of £750, being 50% of £1,500.
- Statement of financial position includes computer equipment at a carrying value of £750, being the previous year's carrying value of £1,500 minus the current year's depreciation charge of £750.

Year 3 financial statements
- Income statement includes a depreciation charge of £375, being 50% of £750.
- Statement of financial position includes computer equipment at a carrying value of £375, being the previous year's carrying value of £750 minus the current year's depreciation charge of £375.

> The reducing balance method is appropriate when the pattern of asset consumption is such that a greater proportion of the benefits of the asset are consumed in earlier periods of its useful life.

Applying the reducing balance method means that the periodic amount of depreciation included in income statements declines from one reporting period to the next. In contrast, the straight-line method results in the inclusion of a constant amount of depreciation in each reporting period's income statement.

5.2.3 Bookkeeping entries required to account for depreciation

The bookkeeping entries required to record the initial purchase of computer hardware and the first three years of its depreciation, applying the reducing balance method, are as follows:

Transaction		Account	dr	cr	Meaning
1	dr	Computer hardware	3,000		Increase in assets – computer hardware is acquired
	cr	Bank account		3,000	Decrease in assets – computer hardware is paid for
2	dr	Depreciation of computer hardware	1,500		Decrease in equity – depreciation expense included in year 1 income statement
	cr	Computer hardware accumulated depreciation		1,500	Decrease in assets – carrying value decreases as benefits are consumed
3	dr	Depreciation of computer hardware	750		Decrease in equity – depreciation expense included in year 2 income statement
	cr	Computer hardware accumulated depreciation		750	Decrease in assets – carrying value decreases as benefits are consumed
4	dr	Depreciation of computer hardware	375		Decrease in equity – depreciation expense included in year 3 income statement
	cr	Computer hardware accumulated depreciation		375	Decrease in assets – carrying value decreases as benefits are consumed

The appropriate amount of depreciation is included in the income statement each year and the carrying value of the asset correspondingly declines by the same amount. The bookkeeping entries for only the first three years are included above but equivalent accounting entries would apply to subsequent years.

5.3 Accounting for disposals of noncurrent assets

As a general principle, noncurrent assets are acquired for the purpose of productive use rather than for immediate resale. The benefits of the expenditure are therefore expected to be gained from use rather than from sale. Notwithstanding the general principle, noncurrent assets can be, for a variety of reasons, disposed of. As and when this occurs, it is necessary to account appropriately for the disposal.

> A **gain on disposal** arises when the proceeds exceed the carrying value of the asset.
> A **loss on disposal** arises when the carrying value of the asset exceeds the proceeds received.

Two matters must be considered when a noncurrent asset is disposed of:

(i) The disposed of asset must be removed from the statement of financial position as and from the date of disposal because, from that date, it is no longer a resource that is available to the business.
(ii) The amount of proceeds received may differ from the carrying value of the asset on the statement of financial position at the date of disposal. The difference is the gain or loss on disposal.

5.3.1 Illustrative example of a gain on disposal

EZ-Books disposes of its computer equipment at the beginning of the fourth year. By the date of the disposal, cumulative depreciation of £2,625 over three years reduced the original cost of £3,000 to a carrying value of £375.

Assume that the proceeds of the disposal amount to £400. The amount received in exchange for the asset at the beginning of the fourth year is therefore greater than its carrying value at the date of disposal. A gain on disposal, amounting to £25, has therefore arisen.

How is the disposal accounted for? The required adjustments are as follows:

EZ-Books
Statement of financial position
before and after the disposal of the computer hardware

	Before disposal £	After disposal £	Explanatory comments
Noncurrent asset			
Computer hardware	375		The original cost of the asset, £3,000, is reduced by three years of depreciation. Once the asset is disposed of, it is no longer shown on the statement of financial position.
Current asset			
Bank account		400	The proceeds from the disposal increase the bank account balance.

EZ-Books
Income statement for the
period during which the computer hardware is disposed of

	After disposal £	
Includes:		
Gain on disposal	25	The excess of the proceeds over the carrying value of the asset is included **as a gain** in the income statement.

First, the computer hardware asset decreases by £375 because that asset is no longer available to EZ-Books. Second, the bank asset increases by the £400 proceeds received. Third, a gain on disposal of £25, being the excess of the proceeds over the carrying value of the asset, is included in the income statement as a gain.

Because the proceeds of disposal amount to £400, the amount of benefits actually consumed by EZ-Books after three years of use amounted to £2,600 (the original cost of £3,000 minus the disposal proceeds of £400). Recording the profit on disposal in the income statement effectively adjusts the cumulative depreciation expense that was recorded in three years of income statements to the amount of benefit actually consumed. The amount of computer hardware depreciation recorded in EZ-Books' income statements for the three years of use was £2,625, but this is reduced to £2,600 by the profit on disposal of £25 that is recorded in the fourth-year income statement.

5.3.2 Illustrative example of a loss on disposal

EZ-Books disposes of its computer equipment at the beginning of the fourth year, at which time the carrying value amounts to £375. Assume the proceeds of the disposal amount to £325. The amount received in exchange for the asset at the beginning of the fourth year is therefore less than its carrying value. A loss on disposal, amounting to £50, has therefore arisen.

How is the disposal accounted for in the financial statements? The required accounting adjustments are as follows. The first two adjustments are the same as for a gain on disposal.

<table>
<tr><td colspan="4" align="center">EZ-Books
Statement of financial position
before and after the disposal of the computer hardware</td></tr>
<tr><td></td><td align="center">Before disposal</td><td align="center">After disposal</td><td align="center">Explanatory comments</td></tr>
<tr><td></td><td align="center">£</td><td align="center">£</td><td></td></tr>
<tr><td>*Noncurrent asset*</td><td></td><td></td><td></td></tr>
<tr><td>Computer hardware</td><td align="center">375</td><td></td><td>Once the asset is disposed of, it is no longer shown on the statement of financial position.</td></tr>
<tr><td>*Current asset*</td><td></td><td></td><td></td></tr>
<tr><td>Bank account</td><td></td><td align="center">325</td><td>The proceeds from the disposal increase the bank account balance.</td></tr>
<tr><td colspan="4" align="center">EZ-Books
Income statement
for the period during which the computer hardware is disposed of</td></tr>
<tr><td colspan="4" align="center">After disposal</td></tr>
<tr><td colspan="4" align="center">£</td></tr>
<tr><td>*Includes*:</td><td></td><td></td><td></td></tr>
<tr><td>Loss on disposal</td><td></td><td align="center">50</td><td>The excess of carrying value of the asset over the proceeds is included **as an expense** in the income statement.</td></tr>
</table>

The computer hardware asset decreases by £375 because that asset is no longer available. The bank asset increases by the £325 proceeds received. A loss on disposal of £50, being the excess of the carrying value over the proceeds, is included in the income statement as an expense.

Because the proceeds of disposal amount to £325, the amount of benefits actually consumed by EZ-Books during three years of use amounted to £2,675 (the original cost of £3,000 minus the disposal proceeds of £325). Recording the loss on disposal in the income statement effectively adjusts the cumulative depreciation expense that was recorded in three years of income statements to the amount of benefit actually consumed. The amount of computer hardware depreciation recorded in EZ-Books' income statements for the three years of use was £2,625, but this is increased to £2,675 by the loss on disposal of £50 that is recorded in the fourth-year income statement.

5.3.3 Bookkeeping entries to account for gains and losses on disposals

The bookkeeping entries required to record EZ-Books' disposal of computer hardware and the resultant gain are as follows:

	Account	dr	cr	Meaning
dr	Bank account	400		Increase in assets – proceeds of the disposal increase the bank account balance
cr	Computer hardware		375	Decrease in assets – the asset is removed from the statement of financial position
cr	Gain on disposal of asset		25	Increase in equity – the gain arising on the disposal is included in the income statement as a gain

The bookkeeping entries required to record EZ-Books' disposal of computer hardware and the resultant loss are as follows:

	Account	dr	cr	Meaning
dr	Bank account	325		Increase in assets – disposal proceeds increase the bank account balance
cr	Computer hardware		375	Decrease in assets – the asset is removed from the statement of financial position

cr	Loss on disposal of asset	50	Decrease in equity – the loss on disposal is included in the income statement as an expense

5.4 Accounting for revaluations of noncurrent assets

Depreciation methodically reduces the carrying value of a noncurrent asset. However, not all assets necessarily decrease in value over time. Some noncurrent assets, for example land and buildings, can increase in value notwithstanding their ongoing use. A question that arises is whether and how fluctuations in the market values of noncurrent assets should be reflected in financial statements.

When is revaluation of a noncurrent asset appropriate?

The original cost of a noncurrent asset is called the **historical cost**. Over time, depreciated historical cost may bear little relation to current market values if market values are increasing. In this situation, the amounts at which noncurrent assets are included on a statement of financial position may

> Revaluations of noncurrent assets are appropriate when they enhance the relevance of information in financial statements.

be unhelpful and irrelevant in terms of assessing the asset profile and profitability of a business. The inclusion of noncurrent assets at current market values may provide more useful and up-to-date information.

5.4.1 Illustrative example of a surplus on a noncurrent asset revaluation

EZ-Books acquired a building for £500,000 and depreciated it over 25 years on a straight-line basis. Assume zero residual value. The amount of depreciation included in the income statement on an annual basis is therefore £20,000 (£500,000 allocated over 25 years).

After ten years, the cumulative depreciation is £200,000 (£20,000 each year for ten years). The carrying value of the buildings is £300,000 (£500,000 historical cost minus £200,000 cumulative depreciation).

At the end of the same ten-year period, the market value for similar buildings is £675,000. This means that there is a difference of £375,000 between the market value of the building and its carrying value at the end of the tenth year.

The owner of EZ-Books decides to revalue the building because its inclusion at current market value would enhance the usefulness of the financial statements. The following adjustments are required:

- The building asset increases from £300,000 to £675,000 so that the asset is recorded at its current market value.
- The owner equity correspondingly increases by the £375,000 surplus. The specific component of owner equity that is affected is called the **revaluation reserve**.

The relevant extracts of EZ-Books statement of financial position are as follows:

	EZ-Books		
	Statement of financial position		
	at the end of year 10		
	Before revaluation	**After revaluation**	**Explanatory comments**
	£	£	
Noncurrent asset			
Buildings	300,000	675,000	The asset increases by the amount of the revaluation surplus (£375,000).
Owner equity	300,000	300,000	
Revaluation reserve		375,000	Owner equity increases by the amount of the revaluation surplus. It is specifically recorded in a revaluation reserve. See exception below.
	300,000	675,000	

5.4.2 Illustrative example of a deficit on a noncurrent asset revaluation

At the end of ten years, the market value of EZ-Books' building is £200,000. The market value of the building is therefore £100,000 less than the carrying value of the asset (£300,000). On this basis, a revaluation deficit arises and is accounted for as follows:

- The building asset decreases from £300,000 to £200,000 so that the asset is recorded at current market value.
- The owner equity decreases by £100,000. In the case of a revaluation deficit, the income statement is the component of owner equity that is affected. The revaluation deficit is included as an expense in the income statement.

Extracts from EZ-Books' statement of financial position are as follows:

	EZ-Books Statement of financial position at the end of year 10		
	Before revaluation £	After revaluation £	Explanatory comments
Noncurrent asset			
Buildings	300,000	200,000	The asset decreases by the amount of the revaluation deficit (£100,000).
Owner equity	300,000	300,000	
Loss incurred during the period		(100,000)	Owner equity decreases by the amount of the revaluation deficit. Deficits are included in the income statement. See exception below.
	300,000	200,000	

	EZ-Books Income statement for the period ended year 10	
	Before revaluation £	After revaluation £
Expenses include:		
Deficit arising on revaluation of building		100,000
		Deficits are included in the income statement and reduce owner equity. See exception below.
Loss incurred during the period		(100,000)

5.4.3 Bookkeeping entries to account for revaluation surpluses and deficits

The bookkeeping entry required to give effect to EZ-Books' revaluation surplus is as follows:

	Account	dr	cr	Meaning
dr	Buildings	375,000		Increase in assets – the carrying value of the buildings increases by the surplus
cr	Revaluation reserve		375,000	Increase in equity – a revaluation reserve is included in owner equity

The bookkeeping entry required to give effect to EZ-Books' revaluation deficit is as follows:

	Account	dr	cr	Meaning
dr	Revaluation deficit	100,000		Decrease in equity – the deficit arising from the revaluation exercise is included as an expense in the income statement
cr	Buildings		100,000	Decrease in assets – the carrying value of the buildings decreases by the amount of the deficit

5.4.4 What are the exceptions to how revaluation surpluses and deficits are accounted for?

A revaluation surplus is included in a revaluation reserve **except when** the surplus reverses a deficit previously included in the income statement in relation to the same asset. In this case, the surplus is recorded in the income statement to reverse the previously recorded deficit and, thereafter, recorded as a revaluation reserve.

A revaluation deficit is included in the income statement **except when** the deficit reverses a surplus previously included in a revaluation reserve in relation to the same asset. In this case, the deficit is recorded in the revaluation reserve to reverse the previously recorded surplus and, thereafter, recorded in the income statement.

5.5 Summary and conclusions

Depreciation is an estimate of an asset's benefits that are consumed during a reporting period. Assets are depreciated for two primary reasons: (i) to communicate the consumption of the benefits associated with assets, and (ii) to include an appropriate amount of capital expenditure in a periodic profit calculation.

Two common methods of depreciating assets are the straight-line method and the reducing balance method. The straight-line method is appropriate when the benefits of an asset are consumed evenly over its useful economic life. The amount of depreciation allocated to each reporting period remains constant. The reducing balance method of depreciation is appropriate when a greater proportion of an asset's benefits are consumed in the earlier part of the asset's useful economic life. The amount of depreciation allocated to reporting periods declines over time.

When noncurrent assets are disposed of, gains or losses can arise. A gain arises if the proceeds on disposal exceed the carrying value of the asset at the date of disposal. A loss arises if the carrying value of the asset at the date of disposal exceeds the proceeds received.

The revaluation of a noncurrent asset may enhance the quality of information included in financial statements. Some assets increase in value over time notwithstanding their productive use. As a result, the carrying values may bear little resemblance to current values. In these circumstances, it may be justifiable to revalue assets to a current value.

Test your understanding

1 Caroline acquired the following noncurrent assets for business purposes:

  (a) New furniture at a cost of £4,000
  (b) A motor vehicle at a cost of £24,000

The furniture was purchased on 1 December 2008. It is depreciated at 10% annually on a straight-line basis. Depreciation is charged on a pro rata basis in the year of acquisition.

The motor vehicle was purchased on 1 June 2008. It is depreciated at 25% annually on a reducing balance basis. A full year's depreciation is charged in the year of acquisition.

Required:

  (i) Calculate Caroline's income statement depreciation charge for the year ended 31 October 2010.
  (ii) Calculate the carrying values of the furniture and the motor vehicle for inclusion in Caroline's statement of financial position at 31 October 2010.

2 The accounting records of Ruby include the following amounts at 30 June 2009:

	Office building	Plant and machinery
	£	£
Cost	1,700,000	820,000
Accumulated depreciation	(320,000)	(306,000)
Carrying value	1,380,000	514,000

Up to now, the office building has been depreciated at 2% annually on a straight-line basis. The plant and machinery is depreciated at 25% annually on a straight-line basis. The plant and machinery was all acquired during the 2008 or 2009 financial years.

During the year ended 30 June 2010, the following transactions occur:

  1 July 2009:   The office building is revalued to £2,400,000. The remaining estimated useful life is 40 years.

1 October 2009: New plant is acquired at a cost of £180,000.

1 April 2010: Plant which had cost £240,000, and for which the accumulated depreciation at 30 June 2009 amounted to £180,000, was sold for £75,000.

It is policy to charge a full year's depreciation in the year of acquisition and none in the year of disposal.

Required:
   (i) Draft the bookkeeping entries required to account for the transactions during the 2010 financial year.
   (ii) Calculate Ruby's income statement depreciation charge and gain/loss on disposal for the year ended 30 June 2010.
   (iii) Calculate the carrying values of the noncurrent assets and the revaluation reserve in Ruby's statement of financial position at 30 June 2010.

Further practice and reading

1. http://www.bazwaldo.com

   Insert the following code into the website keyword search option to access practice questions relating to this chapter: *2010chapter5*

2. Thomas, A. and Ward, A.M. (2009) *Introduction to Financial Accounting*, 6th edn, McGraw-Hill

   Chapter 15: Depreciation and noncurrent assets

6 Accruals and prepayments

You must be able to explain:

○ The accruals basis of accounting
○ How to account for an accrual
○ How to account for a prepayment

6.1 What is the accruals basis of accounting?

Under accruals accounting, revenue and gains are initially recorded when they are earned (as opposed to received), and expenses and losses are recorded when they are incurred (as opposed to paid).

The alternative to accruals accounting is a cash basis of accounting. Under cash accounting, transactions and events are recorded only when the cash is received or paid.

> The **accruals basis of accounting** means that business transactions are recorded in financial statements when they occur rather than when the cash is received or paid.

6.1.1 Illustrative example of the difference between accruals accounting and cash accounting

EZ-Books enters into two transactions immediately before the financial period end:

Transaction 1: EZ-Books sells some inventory for £500 **cash**.
Transaction 2: EZ-Books sells all remaining inventory for £1,000 **on credit**.

Extracts from EZ-Books' income statements assuming (i) accruals accounting and (ii) cash accounting are as follows:

EZ-Books Income statement for the period ended 31 December 2010		
	Basis of accounting	
	Accruals	**Cash**
	£	£
Income	1,500	500

The first transaction includes a receipt of cash whereas the second transaction does not. Under the accruals basis of accounting, the income arising from **both** transactions is included in the income statement because £1,500 of income is reliably earned even though £1,000 cash has still to be received in respect of the second transaction.

If the cash basis of accounting is applied, only £500 is recorded as income because only £500 cash has been received by the reporting date. The remaining £1,000 is recorded as income only when the amount is actually received.

Extracts from EZ-Books' statements of financial position assuming (i) accruals accounting and (ii) cash accounting are as follows:

EZ-Books Statement of financial position at 31 December 2010		
	Basis of accounting	
	Accruals	**Cash**
Assets	£	£
Cash	500	500
Inventory		1,000
Trade receivable	1,000	

In both statements of financial position, the cash balance includes only the amount of cash actually received. The 'accruals' statement of financial position includes a trade receivable corresponding to the credit sale. There is no inventory because it has all been sold.

The 'cash' statement of financial position includes inventory of £1,000 because, if the cash has not been received, then the inventory has not been sold by the reporting date.

The accruals basis of accounting is generally agreed to provide the more useful information about the financial performance and position of a business. It is one of the fundamental assumptions that underpin the preparation of financial statements. For this reason, an appreciation of accruals accounting is crucial when preparing financial statements.

The merits of cash accounting are not disregarded, however. Statements of cash flows present the cash inflows and outflows of a business so that the health of a business, in terms of its cash flows, can also be assessed. Statements of cash flows are addressed in detail in Chapter 11.

6.2 How are accruals accounted for?

In most cases, a business is notified of obligations to pay for expenses by receipt of invoices from the suppliers of goods and services. In some circumstances, a supplier invoice may not be on hand for the purpose of updating the financial statements. This occurs most frequently at the end of a reporting period when financial statements are being finalized and supplier invoices in respect of received goods and services have yet to be received.

It is not appropriate to omit an expense from the financial statements for a reporting period merely because the invoice has not been received from a supplier by a certain date. Financial statements should include all expenses incurred during the period for which the financial statements are prepared.

In some cases, an estimate of the amount of the expense may be required. Accounting for an expense in financial statements at the end of a reporting period even though the supplier invoice has yet to be received, and perhaps estimating the relevant amount of the expense, is referred to as an expense accrual.

6.2.1 Illustrative examples of accounting for expense accruals

Assume it is early January and EZ-Books is preparing financial statements for the most recent year ended 31 December. Consider the following:

Issue 1: EZ-Books pays for light and heat on a three-monthly basis. The most recent invoice amounted to £300 for the period ended 31 October. It was received and paid in November. The next invoice will be received at the end of January. **Should EZ-Books make an accrual for light and heat?**

The issue is presented visually as follows:

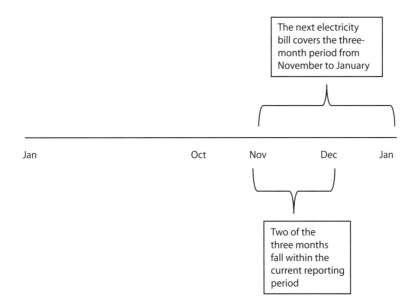

If the reporting period is visualized as a January to December timeline, all of the supplier invoices up to the end of October have been received and included in the financial statements. However, because the next invoice is not received until the end of January, there is no expense included for November and December. An accounting accrual is therefore required in respect of the light and heat expense incurred for these two months.

A reasonable estimate of the amount of the accrual could be based on a review of the expense for the corresponding period in the preceding year or to assume that the amount of the expense for the three months ending 31 January will be about the same as the expense for the three months ended 31 October. On this basis, an accrual of about £200 would be appropriate.

Issue 2: EZ-Books has a number of employees, each of whom is paid on a two-week basis. The next pay date is 5 January. The fortnightly cost of wages is £2,800. **Should EZ-Books make an accrual for wages in the 31 December financial statements?**

The issue is presented visually as follows:

Part of the pay period ending 5 January falls within the reporting period for which the financial statements are prepared. Part of the wages expense should therefore be included in the financial statements for the year ended 31 December. The cost of £2,800 could be reasonably apportioned on the basis of the number of working days that fall into each financial year. If every day of the two weeks is assumed to be a working day, the inclusion of £1,800 for the cost of nine working days as an accrual in the 31 December financial statements would be appropriate.

The bookkeeping entries required to account for the accruals are as follows:

	Account	dr	cr	Meaning
dr	Light and heat	200		Decrease in equity – the income statement includes an accrued expense for November/December light and heat
cr	Accruals		200	Increase in liabilities – a light and heat expense obligation exists at the reporting date
dr	Wages	1,800		Decrease in equity – the income statement includes an expense for the portion of the pay period that falls within the reporting period
cr	Accruals		1,800	Increase in liabilities – a wages expense obligation exists at the reporting date

In both cases the expense is included in the income statement for the period. The obligations that arise from incurring the expenses are included as current liabilities in the statement of financial position at 31 December.

6.3 How are prepayments accounted for?

The possibility also arises that part of the amount of an invoice that is recorded during a reporting period may relate to a subsequent accounting period.

6.3.1 Illustrative example of accounting for expense prepayments

Assume it is early January and EZ-Books is preparing financial statements for the most recent year ended 31 December. EZ-Books obtained public liability insurance as and from the beginning of the previous October. The insurance premium amounted to £400 and the period of insurance runs from 1 October last to next 30 September. EZ-Books received a supplier invoice amounting to £400, recorded it as an expense and paid the supplier.

The issue is presented visually as follows:

Only the period from 1 October to 31 December falls within the current reporting period. Three months of the insurance expense therefore relates to the current reporting period and nine months relates to the subsequent reporting period. Accordingly, £100 of the insurance premium expense relates to the current reporting period and £300 relates to the following reporting period.

An accounting adjustment is required to reduce the initially recorded £400 revenue expense to the £100 expense that applies to the three months of insurance cover that fall within the current reporting period. The remaining £300 is accounted for as an insurance prepayment and is included as an asset in the statement of financial position at 31 December.

The bookkeeping entries required to account for the insurance expense and the prepayment are as follows:

Transaction		Account	dr	cr	Meaning
1	dr	Insurance	400		Decrease in equity – the initial income statement expense is based on receipt of supplier invoice
	cr	Other payable		400	Increase in liabilities – an obligation to pay the insurer arises
2	dr	Other payable	400		Decrease in liabilities – the amount outstanding to the insurer is paid
	cr	Bank account		400	Decrease in assets – payment of the insurance premium reduces the bank balance
3	dr	Prepayment	300		Increase in assets – some of the benefit of insurance cover is receivable in the next reporting period
	cr	Insurance		300	Increase in equity – the income statement expense decreases by the amount of the prepayment

The first two transactions record the insurance expense and its payment without consideration of whether an adjustment might be required at the end of the reporting period. The third transaction is the adjustment required to record that part of the period of insurance cover that should be included as an expense in the subsequent period's income statement. As a result, £100 of insurance premium expense is included in the current period income statement and £300 is included in the income statement of the subsequent period. The prepayment of £300 is included as a current asset in the statement of financial position at 31 December to indicate that the benefit of a payment for insurance is still partially receivable at that date.

6.4 Summary and conclusions

The accruals basis of accounting stipulates that income is included in financial statements at the point at which it is deemed to be earned. Correspondingly, expenses are included at the point at which they are deemed to be incurred. The points at which income is earned or expenses incurred may not necessarily be the same points at which cash is received or paid. Accruals accounting differs from cash accounting in this respect.

Application of the accruals basis of accounting means that only income earned and expenses incurred during a reporting period should be included in the financial statements for that reporting period. This requires consideration of whether the amounts included for income and expenses such as light and heat, wages and insurance are for (i) the full reporting period in question and (ii) no part of any other reporting period. Accrual and prepayment adjustments are made where necessary to achieve this outcome.

Test your understanding

1 The details relating to an electricity account for the year ended 30 June 2010 are as follows:

Opening accrual 1 July 2009	£240

Payments:

1 August 2009 for three months to 31 July 2009	£610
1 November 2009 for three months to 31 October 2009	£720
1 February 2010 for three months to 31 January 2010	£870
1 May 2010 for three months to 30 April 2010	£770
1 August 2010 for three months to 31 July 2010	£840

Required:

(i) Calculate the amount of the electricity accrual at 30 June 2010.

(ii) Calculate the income statement charge for electricity for the year ended 30 June 2010.

2 On 1 January 2010, a business had an insurance prepayment amounting to £12,500 in its financial statements. On 1 August 2010, the annual insurance premium, amounting to £48,000, is paid. The period of insurance cover runs from 1 August 2010 to 31 July 2011.

Required:

(i) Calculate the amount of the insurance prepayment at 31 December 2010.

(ii) Calculate the income statement charge for insurance for the year ended 31 December 2010.

Further practice and reading

1. http://www.bazwaldo.com

   Insert the following code into the website keyword search option to access practice questions relating to this chapter: *2010chapter6*

2. Thomas, A. and Ward, A.M. (2009) *Introduction to Financial Accounting*, 6th edn, McGraw-Hill

   Chapter 17: Accruals and prepayments

7 Irrecoverable debts, estimates and provisions

You must be able to explain:
- How to account for irrecoverable debts
- How to account for allowances for receivables
- The accounting significance of provisions and estimates

7.1 What is an irrecoverable debt?

A trade receivable arises when a sale of goods or services is made on credit. Assuming the income has been earned, the sale is included in the income statement. The trade receivable is included as a current asset on the statement of financial position until the outstanding amount is received from the customer.

If a customer is unable or unwilling to pay the amount owed, the debt is considered to be irrecoverable. The accounting implications are that the sale originally included in the income statement and the trade receivable asset on the statement of financial position should be appropriately cancelled. This process is commonly referred to as 'writing off' the asset.

An irrecoverable debt is also commonly referred to as a **bad debt**.

7.1.1 Illustrative example of an irrecoverable debt

On 2 August, EZ-Books purchased inventory on credit for £300. EZ-Books sold the same inventory on credit to GoBad Limited for £500 on 3 August. On 21 August, GoBad Limited went out of business. It is certain that EZ-Books will not receive any payment from GoBad Limited.

Assume (i) that EZ-Books did not receive payment and that the inventory was never returned. Alternatively, assume (ii) that EZ-Books did not receive payment but the inventory was returned prior to 31 August. EZ-Books' income statement for the month of August is as follows:

	Income statement for the period ended 31 August		
	Assume inventory not returned	Assume inventory returned	Explanatory comments
	£	£	
Income	500	500	In both cases, the income arising from the sale is included in the income statement. The fact that the debt is subsequently irrecoverable does not affect this line.
Less cost of sales			
Inventory at the beginning of the month	–	–	No inventory was on hand at the beginning of August.
(plus) Inventory purchases during the month	300	300	In both cases, the purchase of inventory is included as part of the cost of sales.
(minus) Inventory at the end of the month	–	(300)	If the inventory is not returned, it cannot be included in the closing inventory. If it is returned by the end of the reporting period, it is included in the closing inventory.

Cost of sales	300	–	Calculated in both cases as opening inventory plus purchases minus closing inventory.
Gross profit	200	500	Calculated in both cases as income minus cost of sales.
Irrecoverable debt expense	(500)	(500)	The amount of income that is irrecoverable is included as a deduction from gross profit.
Loss for the month	(300)	–	Calculated in both cases as gross profit minus the irrecoverable debt.

If the inventory is not recovered, then EZ-Books incurs a loss of £300. This amount corresponds to the cost of the inventory to EZ-Books. The £500 sale is recorded as income but effectively cancelled by the irrecoverable debt expense for the same amount.

If the inventory is recovered, then EZ-Books incurs no financial loss. The recovered inventory is available for sale to a new customer. The £500 sale to GoBad Limited is recorded as income but effectively cancelled by the irrecoverable debt expense for the same amount.

The statement of financial position at the end of August is as follows:

	Statement of financial position at 31 August		
	Assume inventory not returned £	Assume inventory returned £	Explanatory comments
Current assets			
Inventory		300	If the inventory is not returned, it cannot be included as an asset. If it is returned by the end of the reporting period, it is included in the assets at 31 August.

Trade receivable			In both cases, when the sale was originally recorded, there was a corresponding trade receivable of £500. However, when the debt is assessed to be irrecoverable, the trade receivable asset is written off.
Total assets	–	300	
Current liabilities			
Trade payable	300	300	Payment to a supplier for the original purchase of the inventory is outstanding until paid.
Equity			
Loss for the month	(300)	–	The loss for the month, as calculated in the income statement, becomes part of the equity of the business.
Total liabilities and equity	–	300	

If the inventory is not recovered, then EZ-Books has no asset. The trade receivable that was originally recorded is cancelled because, if the amount is not recoverable, it is no longer an asset. The trade payable liability is offset by the loss incurred during the month.

If the inventory is recovered, then EZ-Books includes an inventory current asset at 31 August. This is matched by the trade payable liability. No profit or loss is recorded in equity.

The bookkeeping entries required to account for the purchase and sale of inventory and the subsequent irrecoverable debt are as follows:

Transaction		Account	dr	cr	Meaning
1	dr	Purchases of inventory	300		Decrease in equity – inventory purchase is included in the income statement
	cr	Trade payable		300	Increase in liabilities – an obligation to pay for inventory purchased

2	dr	Trade receivable	500		Increase in assets – an amount is receivable from a customer arising from the sale of inventory
	cr	Income		500	Increase in equity – sale of inventory is included in the income statement
3	dr	Irrecoverable debt	500		Decrease in equity – cancellation of the sale for which proceeds are irrecoverable is included in the income statement
	cr	Trade receivable		500	Decrease in assets – cancellation of amount receivable because it is irrecoverable
4	dr	Inventory	300		Increase in assets – if inventory returned, it is included as an asset
	cr	Cost of sales		300	Increase in equity – the income statement is adjusted for inventory purchased but not sold during the reporting period

Transactions 1 and 2 record the purchase and sale of inventory respectively. Transaction 3 records the irrecoverable debt as an expense in the income statement. Transaction 3 effectively cancels the sale in the income statement and the trade receivable on the statement of financial position. If the inventory is recovered, transaction 4 records the closing inventory at 31 August.

7.2 What is an allowance for receivables?

An allowance for receivables is an allowance for the possibility that amounts owed by receivables may not be entirely recoverable.

An allowance for receivables is also commonly referred to as a **bad debt provision**.

At financial reporting period ends, there may be some doubt as to whether some amounts owed by customers will be recovered in the following reporting period. Doubts may be based on knowledge of specific customer circumstances or on past experience that a certain percentage of receivables generally turn out to be irrecoverable. In either case, an allowance for receivables should be included in the financial statements so that the perceived risk associated with receivables at a reporting date is reported.

7.2.1 Illustrative example of an allowance for receivables

> An allowance for receivables is an example of the inclusion of relevant and timely information in financial statements.

EZ-Books' trade receivables at the end of the fifth year of business amounted to £10,000. At that date, the owner identified a receivable amounting to £200 to be irrecoverable and decided to create a general allowance of 5% of receivables. The 5% is based on previous experience of the percentage of receivables that were not recovered.

The calculation of the general allowance for receivables is as follows:

	£
Receivables at the end of the fifth year	10,000
Irrecoverable debt	(200)
	9,800
Allowance for receivables (5%)	490

The amount of the allowance for receivables is calculated **after** any irrecoverable debts have been deducted.

EZ-Books' income statement for the fifth year is as follows:

Income statement for the period ended the fifth year		
	£	**Explanatory comments**
Income	x	
Cost of sales	x	
Gross profit	x	

Irrecoverable debt expense	(690)	Includes the irrecoverable debt of £200 and the allowance for receivables of £490.
Profit for the year	x	The profit is reduced by £690 due to irrecoverable debts and allowances for receivables.

The irrecoverable debt written off and the creation of an allowance for receivables are both described in the income statement as an irrecoverable debt expense.

EZ-Books' statement of financial position at the end of the fifth year is as follows:

	Statement of financial position at end of the fifth year		
	£	£	Explanatory comments
Noncurrent assets		x	
Current assets			
Trade receivable	9,800		The amount presented for receivables is net of the £200 irrecoverable debt.
Less allowance for receivables	(490)		The allowance for receivables is deducted separately. The reason is because the amount of the allowance may still be recovered.
		9,310	The total deduction from the original trade receivable of £10,000 is £690.
Total assets		x	
Liabilities		x	

Equity	x	As the profit is reduced by £690 (see income statement), the equity is correspondingly reduced by the same amount.
Total liabilities and equity	x	

The bookkeeping entries required to account for the irrecoverable debt and the allowance for receivables are as follows:

Transaction		Account	dr	cr	Meaning
1	dr	Irrecoverable debt expense	200		Decrease in equity – the income statement records an expense for the irrecoverable debt
	cr	Trade receivables		200	Increase in assets – trade receivables are reduced by the amount of the irrecoverable debt
2	dr	Irrecoverable debt expense	490		Decrease in equity – the income statement records an expense for the creation of an allowance for receivables
	cr	Allowance for receivables		490	Decrease in assets – the allowance for receivables is a deduction from the trade receivables asset

7.3 Illustrative example of a change in an allowance for receivables

An existing allowance for receivables may be subsequently increased or decreased in response to changes in the assessed risk of default by customers.

Assume EZ-Books' trade receivables at the end of the sixth year amounted to £8,000. There were no irrecoverable debts during the sixth year and the owner wished to maintain the allowance for receivables at 5%.

The allowance for receivables is calculated at the end of the sixth year as 5% of £8,000. The deduction from the £8,000 trade receivables in the statement of financial position at the end of the sixth year should therefore be 5% of £8,000, which amounts to £400.

However, because there is an existing allowance for receivables amounting to £490, it is necessary only to reduce this existing allowance to the amount now required (£400).

EZ-Books' income statement for the sixth year is as follows:

	6th year	5th year	Explanatory comments
Income statement for the period ended the sixth year			
	£	£	
Income	x	x	
Cost of sales	x	x	
Gross profit	x	x	
Irrecoverable debt expense	90	(690)	The fifth year includes the creation of the allowance. The sixth year includes only the change in the allowance.
Profit for the year	x	x	

Only the change in the allowance for receivables is included in the income statement for the current reporting period. In this example, the reduction in the allowance for receivables in the sixth year is included as a gain in the income statement. This is because the expense that was included in the fifth year income statement was, with the benefit of hindsight, too high. The excess fifth-year expense is therefore reversed in the sixth-year income statement.

The statement of financial position at the end of the sixth year is as follows:

	Statement of financial position at end of the sixth year		
	6th year £	5th year £	Explanatory comments
Noncurrent assets	x	x	
Current assets			
Trade receivable	8,000	9,800	Trade receivables are net of irrecoverable debts.
Less allowance for receivables	(400)	(490)	The allowance is reduced at the end of the sixth year to 5% of the trade receivables. The modification of £90 is included in the sixth year income statement as a gain.
	7,600	9,310	
Total assets	x	x	
Liabilities	x	x	
Equity	x	x	
Total liabilities and equity	x	x	

The bookkeeping entries required to account for the decrease in the allowance for receivables is as follows:

Transaction		Account	dr	cr	Meaning
1	dr	Allowance for receivables	90		Increase in asset – a reduction in the amount deducted from trade receivables is the equivalent of an increase in an asset
	cr	Irrecoverable debt expense		90	Increase in equity – the income statement records a decrease in the allowance for receivables. This is a decrease in the risk of irrecoverability, which is the equivalent of a gain

The same accounting logic would apply if there were an increase in the allowance for receivables. An increase in the allowance for receivables results in an additional expense to be included in the income statement. The irrecoverable debt expense would be debited with the amount of the increase and the allowance for receivables would be credited.

7.4 What are the characteristics of provisions and estimates?

7.4.1 What is a provision?

A provision is a liability. The distinguishing feature of a provision is that there is some uncertainty in terms of the exact amount of the liability or the precise timing of its payment. Examples include:

- Provisions for damages arising from the loss of a legal case. The exact amount to be paid may not be known with certainty at the reporting date of the financial statements.
- Provisions for taxation. The amount of taxation to be paid may depend on the resolution of outstanding tax issues. Consequently, the exact amount of taxation to be paid may not be known with certainty at the reporting date of the financial statements.
- Provisions for product warranties. Business managers will, based on experience and knowledge, know whether warranty obligations are likely to arise. But even if the likelihood of claims is known, the exact value of warranty obligations at a reporting date is unlikely to be known.

It is considered useful to include provisions in financial statements, even if they are based on estimates, so that the financial statements are as informative as possible. However, the proviso is that an estimate must be reliable. It is unhelpful to include arbitrary guesses in the financial statements. Provisions are omitted from financial statements if amounts cannot be estimated with a sufficient degree of reliability.

Accounting for provisions is no different from accounting for liabilities about which there is no uncertainty. Provisions are recorded in the liabilities section of a statement of financial position, and the corresponding expenditure that has been incurred is included in the income statement as revenue expenditure or in the statement of financial position as capital expenditure. For example, a provision for taxation would result in the inclusion of a taxation expense in the income statement and the inclusion of a provision for taxation as part of current liabilities in the statement of financial position.

Because uncertainty is an inherent characteristic of provisions, the amounts that are recorded for provisions in financial statements should be regularly reviewed – the uncertainty that previously existed may have been resolved. When uncertainty is no longer present, a provision is no longer required. In such circumstances, the accounting entries that created the provision are reversed.

7.4.2 What are accounting estimates?

Accounting estimates are a normal and common feature of financial accounting and reporting. As long as estimates are reliable, they can enhance the usefulness of financial statements by providing relevant and timely information, even if that information is slightly imperfect. Estimates and estimation techniques apply to assets, liabilities and equity. Liabilities that are based on estimates are specifically referred to as provisions.

> Reliable estimates enhance the relevance and timeliness of financial statements.

In general, estimates may be necessary when the information available for accounting purposes is less than complete. Each of the examples of provisions listed in section 7.4.1 illustrates a situation where the available information is less than perfect. Examples of estimation are also evident in the earlier sections of this chapter – an allowance for receivables, even if based on past experience and knowledge, is still an estimate.

Accruals, prepayments and depreciation also require estimation. Some accruals and prepayments for expenses such as light and heat may necessarily be based on estimates. The useful economic life of a noncurrent asset for the purpose of depreciation is an estimate because how long a noncurrent asset will be of economic use is not usually known with certainty. Furthermore, the choice between straight-line and reducing balance methods of depreciation is an estimate of the pattern of consumption of capital expenditure.

7.5 Summary and conclusions

For a variety of reasons, some trade receivables turn out to be irrecoverable. In such circumstances, the original credit sale and corresponding trade receivables must be cancelled.

Whereas irrecoverable debts are accounted for throughout a financial reporting period, allowances for receivables are considered at financial reporting period end. An allowance for receivables is an estimate of the total trade receivables that are unlikely to be recovered during the subsequent reporting period.

Liabilities about which there is some uncertainty are referred to as provisions. The uncertainty may relate to the exact amount of the liability or the exact timing of its payment. However, notwithstanding the uncertainty, a liability is included in the financial statements and referred to as a provision as long as the amount can be estimated with sufficient reliability.

Accounting for provisions is no different from accounting for liabilities about which there is no uncertainty. However, a provision is required only for as long as uncertainty exists. When uncertainty no longer exists, a provision is no longer required.

In general, estimates are a common feature of the preparation of financial statements. As long as estimates are reliable, they can enhance the usefulness of financial statements by providing relevant and timely information, even though the information may be slightly imperfect.

Test your understanding

1 At 31 December, Jackson's trade receivables amount to £63,200 and the allowance for receivables is £7,115 before considering the following:

  (a) Write off receivables amounting to £9,800 as irrecoverable.
  (b) Make specific allowance for Hugo's £1,050 debt and Omo's £1,250 debt.
  (c) Maintain a general provision, based on past experience, of 4% of the remaining trade receivables.

Required:

  (i) Calculate the irrecoverable debt expense charge to the income statement for the year ended 31 December.
  (ii) Calculate the revised amount for trade receivables.
  (iii) Calculate the revised amount for allowance for receivables.

2 A company commenced the reporting year with trade receivables amounting to £87,000 and an allowance for receivables of £2,750. During the year, two specific receivables amounting to £1,600 were written off as irrecoverable. A debt that had been written off in the previous year amounting to £540 was paid during the current year. At year end, total receivables amounted to £90,000 and the allowance for receivables amounted to £2,100.

Requirement:

Calculate the charge to the income statement for irrecoverable debts.

Further practice and reading

1. http://www.bazwaldo.com

   Insert the following code into the website keyword search option to access practice questions relating to this chapter: *2010chapter7*

2. Thomas, A. and Ward, A.M. (2009) *Introduction to Financial Accounting*, 6th edn, McGraw-Hill

   Chapter 16: Bad debts and provisions for bad debts

   Chapter 30: The final financial statements of limited companies

8) Preparing financial statements from trial balance

8.1 What is the purpose of a trial balance?

A **trial balance** is a list of the account balances in a ledger at the end of a reporting period. The primary purpose of a trial balance is to check that the sum of the debit balances is equal to the sum of the credit balances. A trial balance can also provide a starting point for the preparation of financial statements.

The accounting records of many businesses can be voluminous and, correspondingly, many individual accounts may have a high number of accounting entries. Two accounting matters arise as a result:

(i) The net position regarding individual accounts may not be immediately obvious.
(ii) It may not be certain that the double-entry bookkeeping required to keep the accounting equation in equilibrium has been achieved.

8.1.1 Balancing off ledger accounts

The net position on a ledger account on a particular date is calculated by balancing off the ledger account. Balancing off an account is achieved by:

- Totalling both sides in order to identify the side with the lower total.
- Inserting a balancing figure on the side of the lower total so that the totals on both sides agree with each other.
- Bringing the balancing figure down to the other side as the net position on the account at the balancing-off date.
- The balance on an account is the opening position for the next reporting period.

An example of a ledger account that contains a number of entries made during a reporting period is as follows:

Trade receivables					
1 January	Sales	5,000	4 January	Bank	4,500
3 January	Sales	2,000	13 January	Sales returns	1,000
15 January	Sales	500	28 January	Bank	3,700
21 January	Sales	4,300			

The net position regarding trade receivables at the end of January is not visually obvious, so the account is balanced off as follows:

Trade receivables						Explanatory comments
1 January	Sales	5,000	4 January	Bank	4,500	
3 January	Sales	2,000	13 January	Sales returns	1,000	
15 January	Sales	500	28 January	Bank	3,700	
21 January	Sales	4,300	31 January	Balance c/d	2,600	In the case of this account, a balance is required on the credit side in order to get the sums on both sides to equal each other.
		11,800			11,800	
1 February	Balance b/d	2,600				The balance is brought to the other side. It represents the net position at the end of January and is the starting balance for February.

Asset and expense accounts have debit balances. Income and liability accounts have credit balances.

8.1.2 Confirming that the sum of the debits equals the sum of the credits

It is useful to extract a trial balance from the underlying accounting records to periodically confirm that the total debit entries equal the total credit entries. If the totals are the same as each other, it may be concluded that for every debit entry made to the accounts, there is a corresponding credit entry. It follows that the accounting equation is in equilibrium.

An example of a trial balance in which the sum of the debit balances is equal to the sum of the credit balances is as follows:

	EZ-Books Trial balance at 30 June	
	Debit	Credit
Account	£	£
Bank account	4,500	
Owner equity		9,000
Purchases	4,300	
Motor vehicle	2,100	
Trade payables		1,500
Revenue sales		7,600
Trade receivables	5,500	
Wages and salaries	350	
Insurance premium	650	
Owner drawings	700	
Totals	**18,100**	**18,100**

It may **not** be concluded, however, that the accounts are necessarily 'correct' just because the sum of the debit balances is equal to the sum of the credit balances. For example, debit and credit entries, although equal to each other, may be recorded in the incorrect accounts. Furthermore, a trial balance would not identify that a transaction has been completely omitted from the accounts. A trial balance is therefore helpful in terms of identifying accounting errors **only if** the errors cause the sum of the debit balances not to equal the sum of the credit balances. This occurs for some, but not all, accounting errors.

8.2 Why are adjustments to a trial balance required before the financial statements are prepared?

A number of adjustments to the trial balance are typically required prior to the preparation of financial statements. These adjustments are required for the purpose of including transactions that would usually arise only at the end of a reporting period.

Stocktakes of inventory take place at the ends of reporting periods. Accruals for and prepayments of expenses, allowances for receivables, and provisions are considered at the ends of reporting periods to ensure that income and expenses are included in appropriate reporting periods in a manner that is consistent with the accruals basis of accounting. Other matters such as asset depreciation, asset revaluations, the inclusion of omitted transactions, or the correction of errors may also require attention.

A typical scenario is therefore to extract a trial balance based on the day-to-day activities of a business at which point period end adjustments are incorporated. The combination of the trial balance and period end adjustments is the basis of finalized financial statements.

8.3 Illustrative example of the preparation of financial statements from trial balance

8.3.1 The trial balance

EZ-Books' trial balance at 31 December 2010 is as follows:

	dr	cr
	£	£
Turnover		300,000
Purchases	240,000	
Opening inventory	30,000	
Loan interest	2,500	
Wages and salaries	14,500	

Light and heat	2,000	
Professional fees	3,500	
Motor expenses	500	
Insurance premiums	3,000	
Freehold land	100,000	
Plant and equipment : cost	75,000	
Plant and equipment : accumulated depreciation		15,000
Trade receivables	46,000	
Allowance for receivables		2,000
Bank account	6,000	
Trade payables		33,000
Loan		55,000
Taxation liability		3,400
Owner equity capital investment		50,000
Retained earnings		64,600
	523,000	**523,000**

The following information is also relevant:

1. An inventory stocktake was undertaken on 31 December. The value of the inventory was determined to be £36,000.
2. One piece of equipment, which had originally cost £15,000, was sold during the reporting period for £9,000 cash. The carrying value of the asset at the date of its disposal was £10,000. This transaction has been completely omitted from the accounts.
3. The plant and equipment depreciation policy is 20% per annum on a straight-line basis. It has no residual value. EZ-Books' policy is to charge a full year of depreciation in a period of acquisition of new plant and equipment and none in a period of disposal.
4. The freehold land should be revalued to £150,000 at 31 December.
5. The directors of EZ-Books have assessed that £1,500 of trade receivables are irrecoverable. Furthermore, the allowance for receivables should be increased to £2,500.
6. The trial balance amount for light and heat includes a prepayment of £400 in respect of the next reporting period.

7. Accruals for £200 motor expenses and £500 professional fees are not included in the trial balance.
8. A provision for taxation amounting to £5,000 is not included in the trial balance.
9. The company is involved in an ongoing legal dispute. An estimate of the legal fees incurred to 31 December is £13,000. These legal fees are not recoverable even if the company wins the dispute.
10. The loan liability is not repayable for five years.

The requirement is to prepare EZ-Books' income statement for the period ended 31 December 2010 and a statement of financial position at that date.

8.3.2 Adjustments to the trial balance

Adjustments are required to incorporate the information that accompanies the trial balance.

1. Closing inventory

The closing inventory (£36,000) should be included as a current asset on the statement of financial position and as part of the calculation of cost of sales in the income statement.

2. Disposal of equipment

The gain or loss on disposal is the difference between the proceeds and the carrying value of the asset at the date of disposal. As the carrying value of the asset (£10,000) exceeds the proceeds (£9,000), a loss on disposal of £1,000 arises and must be included in the income statement for the reporting period.

A summary of the disposal calculations is as follows:

	£
Original equipment cost	15,000
Accumulated depreciation at date of disposal	(5,000)
Carrying value at date of disposal	10,000
Proceeds of the disposal	9,000
Loss arising from the disposal	(1,000)

An original cost of £15,000 and a carrying value at date of disposal of £10,000 means that the accumulated depreciation up to the date of disposal must have amounted to £5,000.

As the disposal is completely omitted from the trial balance, the equipment disposed of must be removed from the asset cost account (£15,000) and the asset accumulated depreciation account (£5,000). The proceeds received (£9,000) must be also added to the bank account balance.

3. Depreciation calculation

The calculation of depreciation is as follows:

	£
Cost of plant and equipment	75,000
Cost of equipment disposed of	(15,000)
Cost of equipment subject to depreciation	60,000
Depreciation charge at 20% straight-line	**12,000**

The cost of the equipment disposed of during the reporting period must be deducted from the cost of plant and equipment in the trial balance. The reason is because EZ-Books has a policy of not including depreciation in respect of assets disposed of during the reporting period.

4. Revaluation of land

The revaluation of land increases the carrying value of the land by £50,000. A gain arises from the revaluation exercise as a result of which a revaluation reserve of £50,000 is created.

5. Irrecoverable debts and increase in the allowance for receivables

The amount of trade receivables must be reduced by the amount of irrecoverable debts (£1,500).

The allowance for receivables must increase from £2,000 to £2,500.

The income statement must therefore include an irrecoverable debts expense of £2,000. This amount is the sum of the irrecoverable debts (£1,500) and the increase in allowance for receivables (£500).

6. Prepayment of light and heat

The light and heat expense in the trial balance includes an amount of £400 that relates to a subsequent period. It must be deducted from the light and heat amount included in the trial balance to calculate the expense actually incurred during the current reporting period.

A prepayment of light and heat means that there is a benefit (namely the consumption of light and heat) that will be realized in the next reporting period. At 31 December, this amount is therefore a current asset for EZ-Books.

7. Accruals for motor expenses and professional fees

Adjustments are required for the motor expenses and professional fees incurred during the reporting period but which are not included in the trial balance.

The amounts for motor expenses and professional fees must increase by £200 and £500 respectively in the income statement. Correspondingly, the statement of financial position must include current liabilities in respect of the incurred expenses that are outstanding at 31 December.

8. Provision for taxation

Assuming that the amount of taxation payable in respect of the reporting period is a reliable estimate, the financial statements must include the provision for taxation. The income statement must include a current period taxation expense of £5,000.

The statement of financial position must include a current liability in respect of the total amount of taxation that is reliably estimated to be outstanding at 31 December. The total liability is the sum of the amount included in the trial balance (£3,400) and the provision for the current period expense (£5,000).

9. Provision for legal fees

Legal fees have been incurred during the reporting period but not included in the trial balance. As the fees have been incurred, and the amounts of £13,000 reliably estimated, they must be included in the financial statements as a provision.

The income statement must include a legal fees expense of £13,000.

The statement of financial position must include a current liability in respect of the legal fees for the same amount.

10. Classification of the loan liability

The loan is not repayable by EZ-Books for five years. This means that it should be presented as a noncurrent liability in the statement of financial position.

The adjustments to the trial balance and the resultant finalized amounts for presentation as financial statements are as follows:

	Trial balance		Adjustments		Finalized		Adjustment reference
	dr £	cr £	dr £	cr £	dr £	cr £	
Turnover		300,000				300,000	
Purchases	240,000				240,000		
Opening inventory	30,000				30,000		
Closing inventory : cost of sales				36,000		36,000	1
Closing inventory : asset			36,000		36,000		1
Loan interest	2,500				2,500		
Wages and salaries	14,500				14,500		
Light and heat	2,000			400	1,600		6
Professional fees	3,500		500		4,000		7
Motor expenses	500		200		700		7
Insurance premiums	3,000				3,000		
Disposal of equipment			15,000	14,000	1,000		2
Depreciation of plant and equipment			12,000		12,000		3
Irrecoverable debts			2,000		2,000		5
Legal fees			13,000		13,000		9
Taxation charge			5,000		5,000		8
Freehold land	100,000		50,000		150,000		4
Plant and equipment : cost	75,000			15,000	60,000		2
Plant and equipment : accumulated depreciation		15,000	5,000	12,000		22,000	2, 3
Trade receivables	46,000			1,500	44,500		5
Allowance for receivables		2,000		500		2,500	2, 10
Bank account	6,000		9,000		15,000		6
Prepayments			400		400		
Trade payables		33,000				33,000	
Accruals and provisions				13,700		13,700	7, 9
Loan		55,000				55,000	
Taxation liability		3,400		5,000		8,400	8
Owner equity capital investment		50,000				50,000	
Revaluation reserve				50,000		50,000	4
Retained earnings		64,600				64,600	
	523,000	523,000	148,100	148,100	635,200	635,200	

The original trial balance is adjusted for the inclusion of closing inventory, irrecoverable debts, an increase in the allowance for receivables, provisions for taxation and legal fees, depreciation, accruals and prepayments. The omitted disposal of equipment is now included. The revaluation of land is also included in the finalized figures.

8.3.3 Finalized financial statements

Based on the finalized amounts, EZ-Books' income statement is as follows:

EZ-Books		
Income statement for the period ended 31 December		
	£	£
Turnover		300,000
Cost of sales		
Opening inventory	30,000	
Purchases	240,000	
Closing inventory	(36,000)	
		234,000
Gross profit		66,000
Less administrative and distribution expenses		
Wages and salaries	14,500	
Light and heat	1,600	
Professional fees	4,000	
Motor expenses	700	
Insurance premiums	3,000	
Loss on disposal of equipment	1,000	
Depreciation of plant and equipment	12,000	
Irrecoverable debts	2,000	
Legal fees	13,000	
		51,800
Loan interest		2,500
Profit before taxation		11,700
Taxation		5,000
Profit for the period		**6,700**

EZ-Books' statement of financial position is as follows:

EZ-Books Statement of financial position at 31 December			
ASSETS	£	£	£
Noncurrent assets			
Freehold land			150,000
Plant and equipment : cost		60,000	
Plant and equipment : accumulated depreciation		22,000	
			38,000
			188,000
Current assets			
Inventory		36,000	
Trade receivables	44,500		
Allowance for receivables	(2,500)		
		42,000	
Bank		15,000	
Prepayments		400	
			93,400
TOTAL ASSETS			281,400
Equity and liabilities			
Equity			
£1 ordinary share capital		50,000	
Revaluation reserve		50,000	
Retained earnings		71,300	
			171,300
Noncurrent liabilities			
Loan			55,000
Current liabilities			
Trade payables		33,000	
Taxation		8,400	
Accruals and provisions		13,700	
			55,100
TOTAL EQUITY AND LIABILITIES			281,400

8.4 What are the bookkeeping entries?

The bookkeeping entries required to incorporate the adjustments to the trial balance values in order to produce the finalized amounts are as follows:

Transaction		Account	dr	cr	Meaning
1	dr	Closing inventory	36,000		Increase in assets – closing inventory recorded on the statement of financial position
	cr	Cost of sales		36,000	Increase in equity – closing inventory deducted from opening inventory plus purchases
2	dr	Bank	9,000		Increase in assets – proceeds of disposal are lodged to bank account
	dr	Plant and equipment : accumulated depreciation	5,000		Increase in assets – removal of asset accumulated depreciation
	cr	Plant and equipment : cost		15,000	Decrease in assets – removal of asset cost
	dr	Loss on disposal	1,000		Increase in equity – loss on disposal is included as an expense in the income statement
3	dr	Depreciation	12,000		Increase in equity – depreciation is included as an expense in the income statement
	cr	Plant and equipment : accumulated depreciation		12,000	Decrease in assets – periodic depreciation of an asset increases the accumulated depreciation and decreases the carrying value of the asset
4	dr	Land	50,000		Increase in assets – carrying value of land increases as a result of the revaluation

	cr	Revaluation reserve		50,000	Increase in equity increase – revaluation reserve created as a result of the land revaluation
5	dr	Irrecoverable debts	1,500		Decrease in equity – trade receivable write-off is included as an expense in the income statement
	cr	Trade receivables		1,500	Decrease in assets – irrecoverable debts reduce the trade receivables
	dr	Irrecoverable debts	500		Decrease in equity – an increase in an allowance for receivables is included as an expense in the income statement
	cr	Allowance for receivables		500	Decrease in assets – an increase in the allowance for receivables decreases the net carrying value of the trade receivables
6	dr	Prepayments	400		Increase in assets – a payment in advance. The benefit is to be consumed in the next reporting period
	cr	Light and heat		400	Increase in equity – the expense for light and heat in the income statement is reduced by the amount of the prepayment
7	dr	Motor expenses	200		Decrease in equity – additional expense is included in the income statement
	dr	Professional fees	500		Decrease in equity – additional expense is included in the income statement
	cr	Accruals and provisions		700	Increase in liabilities – expenses incurred during the reporting period are payable at reporting period end

8	dr	Taxation charge	5,000		Decrease in equity – additional expense is included in the income statement
	cr	Taxation liability		5,000	Increase in liabilities – a reliably estimated expense is outstanding at reporting period end
9	dr	Legal fees	13,000		Decrease in equity – additional expense is included in the income statement
	cr	Accruals and provisions		13,000	Increase in liabilities – a reliably estimated expense is outstanding at reporting period end

8.5 Summary and conclusions

A trial balance is a list of the ledger account balances. Its purpose is to periodically confirm the equality of debit and credit bookkeeping entries. Accounting errors that cause the debits not to equal the credits can be identified and resolved at trial balance stage.

A trial balance can also be useful as a basis for the preparation of the period-end financial statements. Period-end adjustments to the trial balance values are commonly required. Common examples are closing inventory, accruals, prepayments, depreciation of noncurrent assets, and allowances for receivables. The correction of accounting errors and the inclusion of transactions previously omitted are also typically addressed at this stage of the preparation of the financial statements. Once the trial balance adjustments are recorded in the accounts, a finalized income statement and statement of financial position may be prepared.

Test your understanding

Ginger's trial balance for the year ended 31 December 2010 is as follows:

	dr £	cr £
Owner equity		225,600
Retained earnings		80,358
Revenue		365,200
Purchases	266,800	
Opening inventory	23,340	
Wages and salaries	46,160	
Rent	13,000	
Motor expenses	3,720	
Insurance	760	
Irrecoverable debts	120	
Allowance for receivables		588
Light and heat	3,074	
Bank overdraft interest	74	
Motor vehicles : cost	24,000	
Motor vehicles : accumulated depreciation		12,240
Fixtures and fittings : cost	28,000	
Fixtures and fittings : accumulated depreciation		16,800
Buildings : cost	100,000	
Buildings : accumulated depreciation		6,000
Land	200,000	
Trade receivables	17,330	
Trade payables		23,004
Bank	3,412	
	729,790	**729,790**

Additional information, none of which is reflected in the trial balance:

1. Inventory at 31 December 2010 is valued at £22,680.
2. Rent prepaid at 31 December 2010 amounts to £1,150.
3. An accrual for light and heat amounting to £475 is required at 31 December 2010.
4. In addition to amounts already written off, further trade receivables amounting to £380 are considered irrecoverable.

5. An allowance for receivables of 4% should be maintained at 31 December 2010.

6. A motor vehicle was disposed of during the year. The vehicle originally cost £8,000 and, at the date of disposal, accumulated depreciation amounted to £5,256. The proceeds received from the sale amounted to £4,500, which was lodged to the bank account. No depreciation is charged on an asset in the year of its disposal.

7. Depreciation is to be charged as follows:
   (i) Buildings : 2% straight-line based on cost.
   (ii) Fixtures and fittings : straight-line method assuming a five-year useful economic life and no residual value.
   (iii) Motor vehicles : 30% annually on a reducing balance basis assuming no residual value.

8. Land should be revalued to £250,000 at 31 December 2010.

Required:
   (i) Prepare Ginger's income statement for the year ended 31 December 2010.
   (ii) Prepare Ginger's statement of financial position at 31 December 2010.

Further practice and reading

1. http://www.bazwaldo.com

   Insert the following code into the website keyword search option to access practice questions relating to this chapter: *2010chapter8*

2. Thomas, A. and Ward, A.M. (2009) *Introduction to Financial Accounting*, 6th edn, McGraw-Hill

   Chapter 10: The balancing of accounts and the trial balance

   Chapter 18: The preparation of final financial statements from the trial balance (advanced)

9 Statement of comprehensive income

You must be able to explain:

○ The nature of comprehensive income
○ The relationship between profit, comprehensive income and owner equity
○ How to calculate and present total comprehensive income

9.1 What is comprehensive income?

There are some types of gains and losses that are not included in an income statement. A surplus on the revaluation of a tangible noncurrent asset is one example. Recall that, assuming it is not reversing a previous deficit on the same asset, a gain on revaluation is included in equity as a revaluation reserve.

Recall also that when owners transact with a business in their capacity as owners, the transactions are not included in the income statement. For example, an owner may invest new equity in the business. This transaction is recorded directly in equity but is not included in the income statement.

Although noncurrent asset revaluation surplus and investments of new owner equity are both gains attributable to a business, neither is included in an income statement. For this reason, the income statement profit calculation may not capture the full extent to which gains have been earned by a business during a reporting period.

How does comprehensive income fit into financial statements that already include an income statement and statement of financial position?

Comprehensive income is an example of presenting information that is relevant to an understanding of the total gains earned during a reporting period.

'Comprehensive income' includes some (but not all) gains and losses that are excluded from an income statement. As such, it is deemed to be a more 'comprehensive' calculation of gains earned by a business during a reporting period.

Total comprehensive income has two components:

(i)   Income statement profit or loss.
(ii) Other comprehensive income.

A noncurrent asset revaluation surplus is one example of 'other comprehensive income'. Other instances of 'other comprehensive income', for example that relate to financial instruments or the translation of the financial statements of foreign operations, are outside the scope of an introductory accounting text.

Are gains and losses that arise from transactions with owners, in their capacity as owners, included in a statement of comprehensive income?

No. Gains and losses that arise from transactions with owners, acting in their capacity as owners, are **not** included in a calculation of comprehensive income. These gains and losses are presented in a statement of changes in equity. The statement of changes in equity is addressed in Chapter 10.

9.2 Illustrative example of a statement of comprehensive income

EZ-Books' statement of financial position at 1 January is as follows:

EZ-Books	
Statement of financial position	
at 1 January	
Noncurrent assets	£
Buildings	50,000

Current assets	
Inventory	10,000
	60,000
Equity	
Owner equity	60,000

During the reporting period ended 31 January, the following events occurred:

Transaction 1: Sold all the inventory on credit for £12,500.
Transaction 2: The owner of EZ-Books invested new equity amounting to £5,000. This amount was lodged to the business bank account.
Transaction 3: The buildings were revalued to £70,000 on 31 January.

EZ-Books' resultant income statement for the reporting period ended 31 January is as follows:

EZ-Books
Income statement
for the period ended 31 January

	£	£	Explanatory comments
Income		12,500	Income arising from sale of inventory.
Less cost of sales			
Opening inventory	10,000		Opening inventory available for sale.
Purchases	–		No purchases during the period.
Less closing inventory	–		No inventory on hand at the end of the period.
		10,000	
Profit for the period		2,500	Profit arising from business activities.

The profit for the period is calculated on the basis of a comparison of the income earned and expenses incurred. Neither the surplus arising from the revaluation of the buildings nor the transaction with the owner is included in the income statement.

EZ-Books' statement of comprehensive income for the reporting period ended 31 January is as follows:

EZ-Books
Statement of comprehensive income
for the period ended 31 January

	£	Explanatory comments
Profit for the period	2,500	Profit as per the income statement.
Other comprehensive income		
Surplus on revaluation of buildings	20,000	Other gain that is included in calculation of comprehensive income.
Total comprehensive income for the period	22,500	

The statement of comprehensive income presents (i) the profit as calculated on the income statement and (ii) other comprehensive income. The 'other comprehensive income' is the revaluation surplus. Comprehensive income for the reporting period therefore amounts to £22,500. The gain arising from the transaction with the owner (in his capacity as owner) is **not** included in the statement of comprehensive income.

Some business organizations may prefer to present an income statement and a statement of comprehensive income as a single financial statement. In this circumstance, the single statement is entitled 'statement of comprehensive income' and includes the same detail as would be included in two separate statements.

EZ-Books' statement of financial position at 31 January is as follows:

EZ-Books
Statement of financial position
at 31 January

Noncurrent assets	£	Explanatory comments
Buildings	70,000	Asset increases to the revalued amount.
Current assets		
Trade receivable	12,500	Asset arises as a result of sale of inventory on credit.
Bank account	5,000	Asset arises as a result of new owner equity investment.
	87,500	
Equity		
Owner equity	65,000	Owner investment increases by £5,000 due to new investment.
Retained earnings	2,500	Profit as per income statement.
Revaluation reserve	20,000	Surplus on revaluation of buildings.
	87,500	

The assets comprise the revalued buildings, a trade receivable in respect of the sale of inventory on credit and a bank balance arising from the equity investment by the owner. There is no inventory on hand at 31 January because it was all sold during January.

Total equity comprises owner's capital investment of £65,000, profit retained within the business of £2,500 and a revaluation surplus of £20,000. There are no liabilities at 31 January.

The total change in equity between 1 January and 31 January amounts to £27,500. Of this amount, £22,500 is attributable to 'comprehensive income' and the other £5,000 is attributable to the transaction with the owner.

9.3 What are the bookkeeping entries?

The bookkeeping entries required to record EZ-Books' January transactions are as follows:

Transaction		Account	dr	cr	Meaning
1	dr	Trade receivable	12,500		Increase in assets – an amount is receivable due to sale of inventory on credit
	cr	Income		12,500	Increase in equity – income earned from sale of inventory is included on the income statement
2	dr	Bank account	5,000		Increase in assets – the owner equity investment is lodged to the bank account
	cr	Owner equity		5,000	Increase in equity – increase is due to new investment by the owner
3	dr	Buildings	20,000		Increase in assets – increase is due to upward revaluation of buildings
	cr	Revaluation reserve/Other comprehensive income		20,000	Increase in equity – a revaluation reserve is part of equity. This amount is also included in a calculation of comprehensive income

| 4 | dr | Cost of sales | 10,000 | | Decrease in equity – the cost of inventory sold is included in the income statement as opening inventory |
| | cr | Inventory | | 10,000 | Decrease in assets – the inventory available for sale at the beginning of the reporting period was sold during the reporting period |

9.4 Summary and conclusions

For a number of reasons, some accounting gains and losses are not included in an income statement calculation of profit or loss. As a result, the calculated income statement profit or loss may not communicate a full appreciation of the extent to which owner equity has changed as a result of the business activities that have occurred during a reporting period.

The statement of comprehensive income extends the income statement profit or loss for a number of additional gains and losses that may arise during a reporting period. A surplus arising on the revaluation of a tangible noncurrent asset is one such example.

Test your understanding

The statement of financial position of Cairo at 30 June 2011 is as follows:

Cairo Statement of financial position at 30 June 2011	
Noncurrent assets	£
Buildings	28,000
Current assets	
Inventory	12,400
	40,400
Equity	
Owner equity	40,400

During the reporting period ended 30 September 2011, the following events occurred:

Transaction 1: Sold the entire inventory for £16,500 cash. The cash receipt was immediately lodged to the business bank account.

Transaction 2: The owner of Cairo invested new equity amounting to £3,000. The amount was lodged to the business bank account.

Transaction 3: Purchased inventory on credit for £7,000. The inventory was still on hand and liability still outstanding at 30 September.

Transaction 4: The buildings were revalued to £50,000 on 30 September.

Transaction 5: Received and paid an insurance invoice amounting to £800.

Required:

Prepare Cairo's statement of comprehensive income (as a single statement) for the three-month period ended 30 September 2011 and the statement of financial position at that date.

Further practice and reading

1. http://www.bazwaldo.com

   Insert the following code into the website keyword search option to access practice questions relating to this chapter: *2010chapter9*

2. Thomas, A. and Ward, A.M. (2009) *Introduction to Financial Accounting*, 6th edn, McGraw-Hill

   Chapter 30: The final financial statements of limited companies

10 Statement of changes in equity

You must be able to explain:

○ The purpose of a statement of changes in equity
○ The items commonly reported in a statement of changes in equity
○ How the statement of changes in equity is related to other financial statements

10.1 Why is it useful to prepare a statement of changes in equity?

The purpose of a statement of changes in equity is to present, in a single statement, all the changes in owner equity that have occurred during a reporting period. Common changes in equity include transactions with owners (acting in their capacity as owners), revaluation of noncurrent tangible assets, income statement profits, and other comprehensive income.

The information in a statement of changes in equity can be linked to the statement of comprehensive income and the statement of financial position.

10.2 Illustrative example of a statement of changes in equity

Bazwaldo Limited was incorporated on 1 January. On that day, 50,000 £1 ordinary shares were issued and paid up. The proceeds of the share issue were used to buy a building for £40,000 on the same day. The statement of financial position of Bazwaldo Limited on 1 January is as follows:

Bazwaldo Limited Statement of financial position at 1 January		
	£	Explanatory comments
Noncurrent asset		
Building	40,000	
Current asset		
Bank balance	10,000	
	50,000	
Equity		
£1 ordinary share capital	50,000	Ordinary share capital is one component of the equity of a limited company.

During the year ended 31 December, the following transactions and events took place:

Transaction 1: An additional 130,000 £1 ordinary shares were issued for £1.50 each. The shares were fully paid up.

Transaction 2: The building was revalued to £60,000. Ignore depreciation of buildings for the purpose of this example.

Transaction 3: A dividend of £10,000 was paid to the shareholders.

A number of other transactions relating to the purchase of inventory, the sale of inventory, and overhead expenses also occurred during the year. As a result, Bazwaldo Limited earned a profit of £45,000.

Bazwaldo Limited's statement of financial position at 31 December is as follows:

Bazwaldo Limited Statement of financial position at 31 December		
		Explanatory comments
Net assets	300,000	'Net assets' is another term for 'assets minus liabilities'.

Equity		
£1 ordinary share capital	180,000	The share capital line includes only the nominal value of the issued shares.
Share premium	65,000	The excess of the share issue proceeds received over the nominal value of the shares is included as a share premium.
Revaluation reserve	20,000	Surplus arising on the revaluation of buildings.
Retained earnings	35,000	Profit minus dividend payment.
	300,000	

The amounts included in Bazwaldo Limited's statement of financial position for share capital and share premium arise as a result of transaction 1. The ordinary share capital increases only by the nominal value of the issued shares. The nominal value is sometimes referred to as its 'par' or 'face' value. When shares are issued for amounts greater than their nominal value, the excess of proceeds received over the nominal value is included as share premium. The share issue price is £1.50 and the nominal value of one share is £1.00. The excess is £0.50 per share, which totals £65,000 for the share premium.

The revaluation reserve arises as a result of the surplus on revaluation of the building (transaction 2). The value of the building on 31 December is deemed to be £60,000, which is £20,000 greater than the carrying amount of £40,000. A revaluation surplus of £20,000 is recorded directly in equity as a revaluation reserve unless it is reversing a previous deficit on the same asset. In this example, the gain is not reversing a previous deficit.

Profits earned by a company during a reporting period are either retained for reinvestment or distributed to the shareholders (who are the owners of the company). A dividend is a distribution of a limited company's profits to its shareholders. Profits that are earned but not distributed to the shareholders are referred to as **retained earnings**. In this example, the retained earnings amount to £35,000, being the profit for the year of £45,000 minus the dividend payment of £10,000 (transaction 3).

Bazwaldo Limited's statement of changes in equity for the year ended 31 December is as follows:

	Ordinary share capital	Share premium	Revaluation reserve	Retained earnings	Total
	£	£	£	£	£
Balance at 1 January	50,000	–	–	–	50,000
Issue of share capital	130,000	65,000	–	–	195,000
Dividends paid	–	–	–	(10,000)	(10,000)
Total comprehensive income	–	–	20,000	45,000	65,000
Balance at 31 December	180,000	65,000	20,000	35,000	300,000

Bazwaldo Limited
Statement of changes in equity for the year ended
31 December

The statement of changes in equity explains how total equity changed from £50,000 on 1 January to £300,000 on 31 December. A share capital issue and a dividend payment are examples of transactions between a business and its owners (acting in their capacity as owners).

The reference to total comprehensive income in the statement of changes in equity provides a useful link to the statement of comprehensive income. In this example, the total comprehensive income comprises £45,000 profit for the year and a £20,000 revaluation surplus. An analysis of the £45,000 profit in terms of income and expenses would be included in an accompanying income statement.

Other items commonly included in statements of changes in equity are transfers between categories of equity and the effects of changes in accounting policies. These matters are outside the scope of this text.

10.3 What are the bookkeeping entries?

The bookkeeping entries required to record the incorporation of Bazwaldo Limited on 1 January are as follows:

Transaction		Account	dr	cr	Meaning
1	dr	Bank balance	50,000		Increase in assets – the proceeds of the share issue are lodged
	cr	£1 ordinary shares		50,000	Increase in equity – owners invest in the ordinary shares of the limited company
2	dr	Buildings	40,000		Increase in assets – a building is acquired
	cr	Bank balance		40,000	Decrease in assets – payment made to acquire the building decreases the bank balance

The first transaction records the initial issuance of ordinary shares at their nominal value. The second transaction records the acquisition of a building at a cost of £40,000.

The bookkeeping entries required to record the transactions that occurred during Bazwaldo Limited's first year are as follows:

Transaction		Account	dr	cr	Meaning
1	dr	Bank balance	195,000		Increase in assets – total proceeds of share issue received and lodged
	cr	£1 ordinary share capital		130,000	Increase in equity – the nominal value of issued shares are recorded
	cr	Share premium		65,000	Increase in equity – the excess of proceeds of share issue over the nominal value of the issued shares are recorded as a share premium
2	dr	Buildings	20,000		Increase in assets – the increased value of the building is recorded
	cr	Revaluation reserve		20,000	Increase in equity – the surplus on revaluation is included in equity as a revaluation reserve

| 3 | dr | Retained earnings | 10,000 | | Decrease in equity – a dividend is a distribution of profit and therefore decreases the equity of a business |
| | cr | Bank balance | | 10,000 | Decrease in assets – the dividend is paid out of bank account |

The first transaction records the full proceeds arising from the issuance of ordinary shares at £1.50 per share. The nominal value of the issued shares is credited to the £1 ordinary share capital account and the excess is credited to the share premium account. The second transaction records buildings revaluation surplus. The third transaction records the dividend payment. The retained earnings decrease by the amount of the dividend distribution.

10.4 Summary and conclusions

A statement of changes in equity is an explanation of the changes in each category of equity that occur during a reporting period. Common categories of equity for a limited company include share capital, share premium, revaluation reserves and retained earnings.

The statement of changes in equity presented in this chapter is for a limited company but the conceptual idea of explaining the changes in components of equity that occur during a reporting period could equally be applied to sole trader and partnership financial statements.

The information in a statement of changes in equity can be linked to the statement of comprehensive income and the statement of financial position.

The next chapter considers cash flows. Up to this point, the accruals basis of accounting has been the basis of financial statements preparation. By definition, the statement of cash flow adopts a cash accounting perspective. Chapter 11 examines how a statement of cash flows is prepared and how it fits with the other financial statements.

Test your understanding

Sparrow's trial balance for the year ended 31 December 2010 is as follows:

	£	£
Revenue		50,000
Purchases	20,000	
Opening inventory	8,000	
Distribution costs	8,000	
Administration expenses	15,550	
Trade receivables	10,000	
Trade payables		20,000
Reorganization costs	2,400	
Cash at bank	8,100	
£0.50 ordinary shares		8,000
10% loan notes		8,000
Noncurrent assets	35,000	
Share premium		3,000
Retained earnings		19,550
Finance costs	400	
Ordinary dividend	1,600	
Tax liability		500
	109,050	**109,050**

Additional information, none of which is reflected in the trial balance:

1. A building with a carrying value of £5,000 must be revalued to £11,000.
2. The balance on the tax liability account represents an overprovision of tax for the previous year. The provision required for the current year is £3,000.
3. Closing inventory is valued at £12,000.
4. Four thousand ordinary shares were issued during the year. The proceeds of the share issue amounted to £8,000.
5. Distribution costs include a prepayment amounting to £575.

Required:
(i) Prepare Sparrow's statement of comprehensive income for the year ended 31 December 2010.
(ii) Prepare Sparrow's statement of changes in equity for the year ended 31 December 2010.
(iii) Prepare Sparrow's statement of financial position as at 31 December 2010.

Further practice and reading

1. http://www.bazwaldo.com

   Insert the following code into the website keyword search option to access practice questions relating to this chapter: *2010chapter10*

2. Thomas, A. and Ward, A.M. (2009) *Introduction to Financial Accounting*, 6th edn, McGraw-Hill

   Chapter 30: The final financial statements of limited companies

Statement of cash flows

11.1 Why is it useful to prepare a statement of cash flows?

A statement of cash flows complements insights gained from a statement of comprehensive income (prepared on an accruals basis) and a statement of financial position.

A statement of cash flows explains (i) where cash has come from during a reporting period and (ii) how it has been spent. In other words, it is an explanation of changes in the cash and bank balances during a reporting period.

While the accruals basis of accounting is one of the fundamental assumptions underlying the preparation of financial statements, information about a business from a cash flow perspective is also valuable. For some, cash flows are easier to appreciate than calculations of profit that include subjective estimates such as depreciation, accruals, prepayments, gains or losses on disposals and irrecoverable debts.

11.2 What are the three main types of cash flow?

Cash flows must be categorized under one of the following headings:

(i)   Operating activities.
(ii) Investing activities.
(iii) Financing activities.

11.2.1 Operating activities

Cash flows from operating activities arise from the principal revenue-generating activities of the business. They typically correspond to the transactions that are included in a calculation of income statement profit or loss.

A calculation of operating cash flows is a valuable indicator of the extent to which a business can generate cash from its own operations without need for external finance. Examples include:

- Cash received from sale of inventory (inflow).
- Cash paid for purchase of inventory (outflow).
- Cash paid for revenue expenses incurred (outflow).
- Tax paid (outflow) and tax refunds (inflow).

The operating cash flows section of a statement of cash flows may also include investment interest received, loan interest paid, dividends received and dividends paid.

11.2.2 Investing activities

Cash flows from investing activities arise from the acquisition and disposal of assets and other investments. A calculation of investing cash flows provides an indication of expenditure on resources that are intended to generate future revenue and cash flows. Examples include:

- Cash paid for purchase of property, plant and equipment (outflow).
- Proceeds received for disposals of property, plant and equipment (inflow).
- Cash paid for equity investments in other companies (outflow).
- Proceeds received for disposals of shares of other companies (inflow).

The investing cash flows section of a statement of cash flows may also include interest received and dividend received if they are not included as operating cash flows.

11.2.3 Financing activities

Cash flows from financing activities are cash receipts from or payments to external providers of finance. Examples include:

- Proceeds received from issuing company shares (inflow).
- Cash receipts of new loans (inflow).
- Cash repayment of loans (outflow).

The financing cash flows section of a statement of cash flows may also include interest paid and dividends paid if they are not included as operating cash flows.

11.3 What are the two methods of preparing a statement of cash flows?

The two methods are (i) the direct method and (ii) the indirect method. The choice of methods affects only the operating activities section of a statement of cash flows. The investing and financing sections are unaffected by the choice of method.

The **direct method** presents cash received from customers and cash paid to both suppliers and employees as the significant classes of operating cash receipts and payments respectively. Using this method, the operating cash flow can be calculated:

(i) Directly by totalling cash receipts and cash payments in the underlying accounting records; or
(ii) By deriving the cash receipts and payments from the financial statements by reconstructing summary ledger accounts for sales, purchases and wages.

The **indirect method** adjusts the income statement profit to derive an operating cash flow amount. The cash flow from operating activities is therefore calculated indirectly using the profit calculation in the income statement as the starting point.

The profit before taxation in the income statement is a common starting point. This figure is typically adjusted for:

(i) Items included in the profit calculation on the accruals basis of accounting but which are not cash flows. Examples include depreciation, gains or losses on disposals of noncurrent assets, irrecoverable debts, and changes in any of accruals, prepayments or provisions during the reporting period.
(ii) Other items included in the profit calculation, which may be cash flows but are not specifically operating cash flows. Examples include loan interest paid or investment income received.

(iii) Changes in inventories, trade receivables and trade payables (collectively referred to as 'working capital') during the reporting period.

11.4 Illustrative example of the preparation of a statement of cash flows

Bazwaldo Limited's statement of comprehensive income for the second year of its existence and its statement of financial position at the end of the second year are as follows:

Bazwaldo Limited Statement of comprehensive income for the year ended 31 December of year 2		
	Year 2	Year 1
	£	£
Revenue	35,997	23,038
Cost of sales	(21,481)	(13,748)
Gross profit	14,516	9,290
Distribution costs	(641)	(410)
Administrative costs	(681)	(436)
Loan interest costs	(495)	(317)
Profit before taxation	12,699	8,127
Taxation	(1,292)	(827)
Profit for the year	11,407	7,300
Other comprehensive income:		
Surplus on property revaluation	3,000	1,920
Total comprehensive income	**14,407**	**9,220**

Bazwaldo Limited Statement of financial position at 31 December of year 2		
ASSETS	Year 2	Year 1
Noncurrent assets	£	£
Property, plant and equipment	13,224	12,554
Current assets		
Inventories	14,332	12,852

Trade receivables	4,356	6,654
Cash and cash equivalents	8,147	194
	26,835	19,700
TOTAL ASSETS	40,059	32,254
EQUITY AND LIABILITIES		
Equity		
Share capital	1,295	1,045
Retained earnings	19,332	10,166
Revaluation reserve	9,000	6,000
	29,627	17,211
Noncurrent liabilities		
Long-term loan	6,000	8,000
Current liabilities		
Trade payables	3,432	5,543
Taxation	1,000	1,500
	4,432	7,043
TOTAL EQUITY AND LIABILITIES	40,059	32,254

Additional information:

1. The depreciation expense for the second year amounted to £2,500. It is included in the calculation of profit before taxation.
2. Property, plant and equipment was disposed of during the second year. At the date of disposal the carrying value of the assets disposed of amounted to £3,750. A gain on disposal of £200 arose and was included in the calculation of the profit before taxation.
3. A dividend was paid during the year.

The requirement is to prepare a statement of cash flows for the year ended 31 December of the second year.

11.4.1 Direct method of preparing a statement of cash flows

Bazwaldo Limited's statement of cash flows is as follows:

Bazwaldo Limited
Statement of cash flows
for the year ended 31 December of year 2 *(Direct method)*

	£	£	Explanatory comments
Cash flows from operating activities			
Cash receipts from customers	38,295		Source: working 1.
Cash paid to suppliers and employees	(24,094)		Source: working 2.
Cash generated from operations		14,201	Subtotal of net cash flow before considering finance costs, dividends and taxation.
Loan interest paid		(495)	Source: working 5. Finance costs could alternatively be included in the financing cash flows section.
Dividend paid		(2,241)	Source: working 6. Dividends paid could alternatively be included in the financing cash flows section.
Taxation paid		(1,792)	Source: working 7.
Net cash from operating activities		9,673	
Cash flows from investing activities			
Payments for purchase of property, plant and equipment	(3,920)		Source: working 8.
Proceeds from disposal of property, plant and equipment	3,950		Source: working 9.
Net cash from investing activities		30	
Cash flows from financing activities			
Proceeds from issue of share capital	250		Source: working 10.
Repayment of long-term borrowings	(2,000)		Source: working 11.
Net cash from financing activities		(1,750)	

Net increase in cash and cash equivalents	7,953	
Cash and equivalents at 31 December year 1	194	Source: statement of financial position.
Cash and equivalents at 31 December year 2	8,147	Source: statement of financial position.

The statement of cash flows explains why the cash and cash equivalents have increased from £194 at the end of year 1 to £8,147 at the end of year 2. In this example, most of the net increase is attributable to the operating activities. The cash inflow from operating activities at £9,673 indicates a healthy operating situation for Bazwaldo Limited.

Regarding the investing activities, payments for the acquisition of new property, plant and equipment was marginally exceeded by proceeds from the disposal of old property, plant and equipment.

In relation to the financing activities, the cash outflow is attributable to repayment of long-term loans. The positive cash flow from operating activities facilitated the repayment of the loans.

The workings that accompany Bazwaldo Limited's statement of cash flows (direct method) are as follows:

Working			Explanatory comments
1	**Cash receipts from customers**		
	Trade receivables at end of year 1	6,654	Source: statement of financial position.
	Revenue generated during year 2	35,997	Source: statement of comprehensive income.
	Cash receipts from customers	(38,295)	In the absence of other information, this must be the cash receipts from customers (to get the correct closing balance).
	Trade receivables at end of year 2	4,356	Source: statement of financial position.
2	**Cash paid to suppliers and employees**		
	Payments to trade payables	25,072	Source: working 3.

	Distribution costs	641	Source: statement of comprehensive income.
	Administrative costs	681	Source: statement of comprehensive income.
	Adjust for depreciation	(2,500)	The income statement expenses include a deprecation charge of £2,500. It is reversed because there is no cash flow associated with depreciation.
	Adjust for profit on disposal	200	The income statement includes a profit on disposal of £200. It is reversed because there is no cash flow associated with a profit on disposal.
		24,094	
3	**Payments to trade payables**		
	Trade payables at end of year 1	5,543	Source: statement of financial position.
	Purchases from trade suppliers during year 2	22,961	Source: working 4.
	Payments to trade payables	(25,072)	In the absence of other information, this must be the cash payments to suppliers (to get the correct closing balance).
	Trade payables at end of year 2	3,432	Source: statement of financial position.
4	**Purchases from trade suppliers**		
	Inventory at end of year 1	12,852	Source: statement of financial position.
	Purchases from trade suppliers during year 2	22,961	In the absence of other information, this must be the purchases from suppliers (to get the correct closing balance).
	Inventory at end of year 2	(14,332)	Source: statement of financial position.
	Cost of sales	21,481	Source: statement of comprehensive income.

5   **Loan interest paid**

Liability at 31 December year 1	–	No opening obligation on the statement of financial position.
Loan interest charge to the income statement	495	Source: statement of comprehensive income.
Loan interest paid	(495)	In the absence of other information, this must be the amount paid (to get the correct closing balance).
Liability at 31 December year 2	–	No closing obligation on the statement of financial position.

6   **Dividend paid**

Retained earnings at 31 December year 1	10,166	Source: statement of financial position.
Profit for the year	11,407	Source: statement of comprehensive income.
Dividends paid	(2,241)	In the absence of other information, this must be the dividend that was paid (to get the correct closing balance).
Retained earnings at 31 December year 2	19,332	Source: statement of financial position.

7   **Taxation paid**

Carrying value at 31 December year 1	1,500	Source: statement of financial position.
Income statement expense for year 2	1,292	Source: statement of comprehensive income.
Taxation paid during year 2	(1,792)	In the absence of other information, this must be the amount paid during the year (to get the correct closing balance).
Carrying value at 31 December year 2	1,000	Source: statement of financial position.

8   **Purchase of property, plant and equipment**

Carrying value at 31 December year 2	12,554	Source: statement of financial position.

	Revaluation	3,000	Source: statement of financial position. The revaluation reserve increased during the year by this amount. It must be due to a revaluation of property, plant and equipment.
	Depreciation expense	(2,500)	Source: additional information. A depreciation charge reduces the carrying value of property, plant and equipment.
	Carrying value of asset disposed of	(3,750)	Source: additional information. If an asset is disposed of, its carrying value is removed from the asset account.
	Additions	3,920	In the absence of other information, this must be the payments for property, plant and equipment additions during the year (to get the correct closing balance).
	Carrying value at 31 December year 2	13,224	Source: statement of financial position.
9	**Proceeds from disposal of property, plant and equipment**		
	Carrying value of asset disposed of	3,750	Source: additional information.
	Gain on disposal	200	Source: additional information.
	Proceeds	3,950	This must be the proceeds received if a gain on disposal of £200 was achieved.
10	**Proceeds from issue of share capital**		
	Carrying value at 31 December year 1	1,045	Source: statement of financial position.
	Proceeds from issue of new share capital	250	In the absence of other information, this must be receipts from a new share issue (to get the correct closing balance).
	Carrying value at 31 December year 2	1,295	Source: statement of financial position.

11	Repayment of long-term borrowings		
	Carrying value at 31 December year 1	8,000	Source: statement of financial position.
	Repayment of borrowings	(2,000)	In the absence of other information, this must be the loan repayments (to get the correct closing balance).
	Carrying value at 31 December year 2	6,000	Source: statement of financial position.

In short, the preparation of a statement of cash flows requires that each line of the statement of financial position is methodically examined for changes that are attributable to cash and non-cash flows. Once the cash flows are identified and adjustments made for the non-cash flows where appropriate, the cash flows are included in the appropriate section of the statement.

11.4.2 Indirect method of preparing a statement of cash flows

Bazwaldo Limited's net cash flows from operating activities, prepared using the indirect method, is as follows:

Bazwaldo Limited			
Statement of cash flows (extract) for			
the year ended 31 December of year 2 (Indirect method)			
	£	£	Explanatory comments
Cash flows from operating activities			
Profit before taxation		12,699	Source: statement of comprehensive income.
Adjustments for:			
Depreciation	2,500		Source: additional information. A depreciation charge is not a cash flow. It is therefore added back to profit for the purpose of deriving a cash flow amount.

Loan interest charge	495	Source: statement of comprehensive income. This amount is included in the calculation of profit as an expense deduction but it is not included in the 'cash generated from operations' subtotal. It is therefore added back.
Gain on disposal of property, plant and equipment	(200)	Source: additional information. This amount is included in the profit calculation as a gain but it is not a cash flow. The gain is therefore reversed for the purpose of deriving a cash flow amount.
Increase in inventories	(1,480)	Source: statement of financial position. See section 11.4.3.
Decrease in trade receivables	2,298	Source: statement of financial position. See section 11.4.3.
Decrease in trade payables	(2,111)	Source: statement of financial position. See section 11.4.3.
	1,502	
Cash generated from operations	14,201	Subtotal of net cash flows before considering finance costs, dividends and taxation.
Loan interest payment	(495)	Source: working 5. Finance costs could alternatively be included in the financing cash flows section.
Dividend paid	(2,241)	Source: working 6. Dividends paid could alternatively be included in the financing cash flows section.
Taxation paid	(1,792)	Source: working 7.
Net cash from operating activities	**9,673**	

Bazwaldo Limited's statement of cash flows, prepared using the indirect method, differs from the direct method only with regard to the cash flows from operating activities. The calculations and presentations of cash flows from investing and financing activities are the same regardless of the method used.

11.4.3 Why are there adjustments for changes in working capital in an indirect method statement of cash flows?

(i) Inventory

Increases and decreases in inventory are included in the cost of sales calculation and are therefore part of the calculation of income statement profit. However, no cash flow occurs as a result of a periodic stocktake or valuation of inventory. Therefore, to the extent that the profit figure is affected by a change in the level of inventory, it must be reversed for cash flow purposes.

Increases in inventory reduce cost of sales and result in a profit that is higher than would be the case if inventory levels remained constant. To reverse the effect of this for cash flow purposes, the increase in inventory is deducted from the profit figure in the statement of cash flows. Correspondingly, a decrease in inventory is added to the profit figure in a statement of cash flows.

(ii) Trade receivables

Illustrative examples of increases and decreases in trade receivables are as follows:

Illustrative increase in trade receivables

Opening balance	100	Receipts from customers	25
Revenue earned	75	Closing balance	150
	175		175

Illustrative decrease in trade receivables

Opening balance	250	Receipts from customers	125
Revenue earned	25	Closing balance	150
	275		275

In each case, the 'revenue earned' is the value that is included in the income statement profit calculation. For cash flow purposes, the 'receipts from customers' is the relevant value. If the indirect method of preparing a statement of cash flows is used, the profit must be adjusted for the difference between 'revenue earned' and 'receipts from customers'. However, the difference between 'revenue earned' and 'receipts from customers' is equal to the difference between the opening and closing balances. Hence, the difference between opening and closing balances may be used because the balances are easily identifiable in the statement of financial position.

An increase in trade receivables means that 'revenue earned' during a reporting period exceeded 'receipts from customers'. Thus, for cash flow purposes, the profit figure must be reduced by the excess of 'revenue earned' over 'receipts from customers'. Correspondingly, a decrease in trade receivables is added to the profit figure in a statement of cash flows.

(iii) Trade payables

Illustrative examples of increases and decreases in trade receivables are as follows:

Illustrative increase in trade payables

Payments to suppliers	50	Opening balance	100
Closing balance	200	Purchases	150
	250		250

Illustrative decrease in trade payables

Payments to suppliers	100	Opening balance	150
Closing balance	75	Purchases	25
	175		175

In each case, the 'purchases' is the value that is included in the income statement profit calculation. For cash flow purposes, the 'payments to suppliers' is the relevant value. If the indirect method of preparing a statement of cash flows is used, the profit must be adjusted for the difference between 'purchases' and 'payments to suppliers'. However, the difference between 'purchases' and 'payments to suppliers' is the same as the difference between the opening and closing balances. Hence, the difference between opening and closing balances may be used.

An increase in trade payables means that 'purchases' during a reporting period exceeded 'payments to suppliers'. Thus, for cash flow purposes, the profit figure must be increased by the excess of 'purchases' over 'payments to suppliers'. Correspondingly, a decrease in trade payables is deducted from the profit figure in a statement of cash flows.

11.5 Summary and conclusions

A statement of cash flows classifies each cash flow as an operating, investing or financing cash flow. When calculating operating cash flows, there are two methods that may be used: the direct method or the indirect method. The calculation and presentation of investing and financing cash flows are not affected by the choice of direct or indirect method of preparation.

The preparation of a statement of cash flows complements (i) the profitability information presented in a statement of comprehensive income, and (ii) information about the assets, liabilities and equity presented in a statement of financial position. Taken together, the three financial statements can provide a useful basis for analysing the performance (statement of comprehensive income and statement of cash flows) and position (statement of financial position) of a business.

The next chapter considers how the financial statements of a business can be methodically interpreted.

Test your understanding

The financial statements of Aqua are as follows:

Statement of comprehensive income for the year ended 30 September 2010	
	£000
Revenue	2,777
Cost of sales	(1,785)
Gross profit	992
Administrative expenses	(221)
Distribution costs	(610)
Profit from operations	161
Income from investments	4
Finance costs	(21)
Profit before tax	144
Income tax	(22)
Profit for the period	122
Other comprehensive income:	
Gain on property revaluation	60
Total comprehensive income	**182**

Statement of financial position as at 30 September 2010	2010 £000	2009 £000
Noncurrent assets	688	510
Current assets		
Inventory	420	464
Trade receivables	290	333
Interest receivable	4	12
Investments	50	
Cash in hand and at bank	82	4
	846	813
TOTAL ASSETS	**1,534**	**1,323**
Equity and liabilities		
£1 ordinary shares	360	300
Share premium	92	92
Revaluation reserve	60	
Retained earnings	7	(85)
	519	307
Noncurrent liabilities		
10% loan notes		50
5% loan notes	329	349
	329	399
Current liabilities		
Bank overdraft		75
Trade payables	550	421
Income tax	100	88
Accruals	36	33
	686	617
TOTAL EQUITY AND LIABILITIES	**1,534**	**1,323**

Additional information:

1. On 1 October 2009, Aqua issued 60,000 £1 ordinary shares at par. The proceeds were used to finance the purchase and cancellation of all its 10% loan notes and some of its 5% loan notes, both at par.
2. The current asset investment is a 30-day government bond.
3. Noncurrent tangible assets include certain properties which were revalued in the year.
4. Noncurrent tangible assets disposed of in the year had a carrying value of £75,000. Cash received on disposal amounted to £98,000.
5. Depreciation charged for the year was £87,000.
6. The accruals balance includes interest payable of £33,000 at 30 September 2009 and £6,000 at 30 September 2010.
7. Interim dividends paid during the year amounted to £30,000.

Required:
   (i) Prepare a statement of cash flows using the **indirect** method for the year ended 30 September 2010.
   (ii) Prepare a statement of cash flows using the **direct** method for the year ended 30 September 2010.
   (iii) Provide an analysis of cash and cash equivalents at 30 September 2010.

Further practice and reading

1. http://www.bazwaldo.com

   Insert the following code into the website keyword search option to access practice questions relating to this chapter: *2010chapter11*

2. Thomas, A. and Ward, A.M. (2009) *Introduction to Financial Accounting*, 6th edn, McGraw-Hill

   Chapter 31: Statement of cash flows

(12) Interpretation of financial statements

You must be able to explain:
- ○ How to interpret common size financial statements
- ○ How to calculate and interpret profitability, activity, liquidity, solvency and investment ratios
- ○ The limitations of ratio analysis and the common mistakes

12.1 What does the interpretation of financial statements involve?

The statements of financial position, comprehensive income, cash flows and changes in equity impart useful information in terms of profits, cash flows, assets, liabilities and equity. But additional insights are available when values are expressed in relative terms and compared over time. For example, it is of some but limited assistance to read that Bazwaldo Limited generated a profit of £100,000 in terms of assessing whether the performance of Bazwaldo Limited is 'successful'. However, to read that the Bazwaldo Limited profit corresponds to 12% of revenue, which is a 35% increase on the comparative period and 23% above the industry norm, reveals much more in terms of the success of Bazwaldo Limited.

The interpretation of financial statements includes expressing accounting values as percentages and ratios and then comparing them to equivalent percentages and ratios for previous reporting periods and/or comparable businesses. A single calculation is of limited use but groups of calculations repeated at periodic intervals can reveal interesting trends, similarities and differences.

12.2 Illustrative example of common size financial statements

An example of common size financial statements is as follows:

<table>
<tr><td colspan="5">Bazwaldo Limited
Statement of comprehensive income for the year ended
31 December of year 2</td></tr>
<tr><td></td><td>Year 2</td><td>Year 2</td><td>Year 1</td><td>Year 1</td></tr>
<tr><td></td><td>£</td><td>%</td><td>£</td><td>%</td></tr>
<tr><td>Revenue</td><td>35,997</td><td>100.0%</td><td>23,038</td><td>100.0%</td></tr>
<tr><td>Cost of sales</td><td>(21,481)</td><td>(59.7%)</td><td>(12,674)</td><td>(55.0%)</td></tr>
<tr><td>Gross profit</td><td>14,516</td><td>40.3%</td><td>10,364</td><td>45.0%</td></tr>
<tr><td>Distribution costs</td><td>(641)</td><td>(1.8%)</td><td>(888)</td><td>(3.9%)</td></tr>
<tr><td>Administrative costs</td><td>(681)</td><td>(1.9%)</td><td>(633)</td><td>(2.7%)</td></tr>
<tr><td>Finance costs</td><td>(495)</td><td>(1.4%)</td><td>(866)</td><td>(3.8%)</td></tr>
<tr><td>Profit before taxation</td><td>12,699</td><td>35.3%</td><td>7,977</td><td>34.6%</td></tr>
<tr><td>Taxation</td><td>(1,292)</td><td>(3.6%)</td><td>(1,447)</td><td>(6.3%)</td></tr>
<tr><td>Profit for the year</td><td>11,407</td><td>31.7%</td><td>6,530</td><td>28.3%</td></tr>
</table>

In addition to the accounting values, there are two columns that express values as percentages. In this example, each line item is expressed as a percentage of revenue.

This reveals, for example, that although the gross profit increased in absolute terms during year 2, it has decreased in percentage terms because the cost of sales, as a percentage of revenue, increased in year 2 as compared with year 1. If the cost of sales could be as well managed in year 3 as in year 1, then profitability could possibly increase further. There may be a good explanation for the relative increase in cost of sales in year 2 but, if nothing else, common size statements can prompt questions about matters that might otherwise be overlooked.

Expressing the distribution, administrative and finance costs in percentage terms reveals that they have all declined relative to revenue during year 2. This suggests that overheads and finance costs have been well managed during year 2 relative to year 1. Although it is not always necessary to express values as percentages to identify matters of significance, the magnitude of the changes is often revealed most clearly when the changes are expressed as percentages.

Bazwaldo Limited
Statement of financial position at
31 December of year 2

ASSETS	Year 2	Year 2	Year 1	Year 1
Noncurrent assets	£	%	£	%
Property, plant and equipment	13,224	33.0%	12,554	38.9%
Current assets				
Inventories	14,332	35.8%	12,852	39.8%
Trade receivables	4,356	10.9%	6,654	20.6%
Cash and bank	8,147	20.3%	194	0.7%
	26,835	67.0%	19,700	61.1%
Total assets	**40,059**	**100.0%**	**32,254**	**100.0%**
EQUITY AND LIABILITIES				
Equity				
Ordinary share capital	1,295	3.2%	1,045	3.2%
Retained earnings	28,332	70.7%	16,166	50.1%
	29,627	73.9%	17,211	53.3%
Noncurrent liabilities				
Loan	6,000	15.0%	8,000	24.8%
Current liabilities				
Trade payables	3,432	8.6%	5,543	17.2%
Taxation	1,000	2.5%	1,500	4.7%
	4,432	11.1%	7,043	21.9%
Total equity and liabilities	**40,059**	**100.0%**	**32,254**	**100.0%**

When expressed as a common size statement, the statement of financial position may reveal interesting changes in the assets, liabilities or equity. For example, trade receivables, as a percentage of total assets, declined noticeably in year 2 relative to year 1. In contrast, the cash and bank is a more significant component of total assets in year 2 relative to year 1. On the equity and liabilities side, retained earnings, as a percentage of total equity and liabilities increased significantly in year 2 relative to year 1, whereas the loan and trade payables have declined in relative significance.

12.3 Illustrative example of the commonly calculated ratios

The preliminary thoughts and conclusions that arise from common size statements can provide a useful basis for further analysis using ratios. Ratios can be classified according to the type of information they provide about the financial health of a business.

12.3.1 Profitability ratios

Profitability ratios provide information about how effectively a business is turning revenue into profits. Profitability ratios also calculate the percentage return attributable to the providers of capital. Commonly calculated profitability ratios and the relevant calculations for Bazwaldo Limited are shown in Table 12.1.

The **gross profit margin**, **operating profit margin** and **net profit margin** provide an indication of how much of the revenue remains after expenses are deducted. The margin calculations for one reporting period are compared with previous reporting periods and/or industry norms in order to conclude on the quality of the margins achieved.

The **return on capital employed** (ROCE) calculation indicates the profitability of investments made by the providers of long-term capital. Capital employed is the sum of owner equity and long-term borrowings. For the ROCE calculation, the profit attributable to these providers of capital is profit before the deduction of interest and tax. The denominator in the calculation is the **average** capital employed.

The **return on equity** (ROE) calculation indicates the profitability of investments made by the providers of equity capital only. The profit attributable to the providers of equity is commonly the profit after the deduction of interest but before the deduction of taxation. The denominator in the calculation is the **average** owner equity.

When the calculation of a ratio includes a value from the statement of financial position, it is preferable to calculate an average value for the whole reporting period. This is because the value of an item on a statement of financial position at the end of the reporting period may not be representative of its value throughout the period. In the case of Bazwaldo Limited, average values for year 2 are calculated by taking opening and closing statement of financial position carrying values and dividing by two.

Table 12.1 Profitability ratios (see 12.3.1 Profitabily ratios, page 135)

Ratio	Formula	Description of ratio	Bazwaldo Limited year 2	Bazwaldo Limited year 1	Industry norm (for comparison)
Gross profit margin	(gross profit/ revenue) × 100	Gross profit expressed as a percentage of revenue	40.33%	44.99%	41.00%
Operating profit margin	(profit before interest and tax/ revenue) × 100	Operating profit expressed as a percentage of revenue	36.65%	38.39%	38.50%
Net profit margin	(profit before tax/revenue) × 100	Profit before tax expressed as a percentage of revenue	35.28%	34.63%	31.00%
Return on capital employed (ROCE)	[profit before interest and tax/ (average owner equity plus average long-term interest bearing borrowings)] × 100	Operating profit expressed as a percentage of average capital employed	43.37%		45.00%
Return on equity (ROE)	(profit before tax/average owner equity) × 100	Profit before tax expressed as a percentage of average owner equity	54.23%		51.00%

12.3.2 Activity ratios

Activity ratios provide information about how efficiently the asset base of a business is utilized. Commonly calculated activity ratios are shown in Table 12.2.

Asset turnover ratios typically express revenue or cost of sales as a multiple of an asset value. An increasing asset turnover ratio is an indication that assets are being utilized more efficiently: each £1 of asset is generating an increasing

Table 12.2 Activity ratios

Ratio	Formula	Description of ratio	Bazwaldo Limited year 2	Industry norm (for comparison)
Total asset turnover	revenue/average total assets	Revenue expressed as a multiple of average total assets	0.996	
Noncurrent asset turnover	revenue/average noncurrent assets	Revenue expressed as a multiple of average noncurrent assets	2.793	
Working capital turnover	revenue/average working capital	Revenue expressed as a multiple of average working capital	2.464	
Inventory turnover	cost of sales/ average inventory	Cost of sales expressed as a multiple of average inventory	1.580	4.71
Days of receivables outstanding	(average trade receivables/ revenue) × 365	Average trade receivables expressed as the number of days of revenue outstanding	55	
Days of payables outstanding	(average trade payables/ purchases) × 365	Average trade payables expressed as the number of days of purchases outstanding	71	
Days of inventory on hand	(average inventory/cost of sales) × 365	Average inventory expressed as the number of days of cost of sales on hand	230	130

amount of revenue. Conversely, a decreasing asset turnover ratio means that assets are not being utilized as efficiently as previously.

The efficiency of working capital management is commonly measured by calculating (i) days of receivables outstanding, (ii) days of payables outstanding, and (iii) days of inventory on hand. In each formula, multiplying by 365 converts the ratio into a number of days.

Days of receivables outstanding is a measure of how long, on average, credit sales are outstanding. An increase in the number of days of receivables outstanding indicates that customers are receiving longer periods of credit than previously. This may be a signal that credit control is not as good as it used to be.

Days of payables outstanding is a measure of the average number of days' credit taken before payment is made to trade payables. An increase in the number of days of payables indicates that longer periods of credit are taken before suppliers are paid. Good working capital management considers the days of receivables and the days of payables in tandem.

Days of inventory on hand is a measure of the average number of days that an item of inventory is on hand before it is sold. Every business that supplies goods to customers must strike the appropriate balance between the cost of holding inventory and the cost of losing a sale if the item is not available when customers demand it. Days of inventory on hand can provide insights as to whether the volume of inventory on hand is excessive and whether business is slowing down (days of inventory on hand increases) or picking up (days of inventory on hand declines).

12.3.3 Liquidity ratios

Liquidity ratios provide information about the ability of a business to meet its short-term obligations as they fall due. As these ratios are based on information in statements of financial position, their usefulness is predicated on the assumption that values taken from a statement of financial position are representative of equivalent values throughout the reporting period. Commonly calculated liquidity ratios are shown in Table 12.3.

The **current ratio** is also called the **working capital ratio**. It expresses total current assets as a multiple of current liabilities. As both are convertible into cash in the short term, the current ratio provides guidance as to whether payment of the current liabilities is likely to be financed by conversion of the current assets into cash. In the case of Bazwaldo Limited, the higher current ratio in year 2 compares favourably with the year 1 ratio and the industry norm. This indicates that Bazwaldo Limited is unlikely to experience difficulties meeting short-term liabilities as they fall due.

The **acid test ratio** is also called the **quick ratio**. It is a more stringent test of liquidity than the current ratio because it excludes inventory from consideration. It assumes that inventory may not be readily convertible into cash and therefore provides guidance as to whether payment of current liabilities can be met from the remaining current assets. In the case of Bazwaldo Limited, the year 2 calculation is higher than the year 1 equivalent and indicates that the

Table 12.3 Liquidity ratios

Ratio	Formula	Description of ratio	Bazwaldo Limited year 2	Bazwaldo Limited year 1	Industry norm (for comparison)
Current ratio	current assets/ current liabilities	Current assets expressed as a multiple of current liabilities	6.055	2.797	4.5
Acid test ratio	(current assets minus inventory)/ current liabilities	Current assets excluding inventory expressed as a multiple of current liabilities	2.821	0.972	3.5
Cash ratio	(cash plus marketable securities)/ current liabilities	Cash plus marketable securities expressed as a multiple of current liabilities	1.838	0.028	2.5
Cash conversion cycle	days of receivables outstanding plus days of inventory on hand minus days of payables outstanding	The number of days it takes to turn an investment in inventory back into cash	210		

current assets, excluding inventory, comfortably exceed the current liabilities. The industry norm, included as an illustrative comparison, is slightly higher, which suggests that Bazwaldo Limited may not be as liquid as other businesses in the same industry.

The **cash ratio** is a more stringent test of liquidity than the acid test ratio because it excludes all current assets from consideration except cash and marketable securities. Marketable securities are short-term investments for which there is a readily available trading market. This ratio therefore includes only cash or assets that are guaranteed to be cash within a very short period. In the case of Bazwaldo Limited, the cash ratio for year 2 is comfortably higher than for year 1. This reinforces the liquidity messages provided by the current and acid test ratios. The industry norm is somewhat higher, which may prompt the owners and managers of Bazwaldo Limited to continue to look for improvement in the liquidity situation.

The **cash conversion cycle** is a calculation of the average number of days taken to convert an initial purchase of inventory into a cash receipt from sale of the inventory. It draws together the activity ratios calculated for days of receivables outstanding, days of inventory on hand and days of payables outstanding. In the case of Bazwaldo Limited, the cash conversion cycle is 210 days. A review of the calculation reveals that the days of inventory on hand is a significant reason for the 210-day cash conversion cycle. No comparative information is available for the purpose of assessing whether this value is normal for Bazwaldo Limited or for the industry. At a minimum, the owners and managers of Bazwaldo Limited should review inventory management policies to assess whether inventory levels could be reduced.

12.3.4 Solvency ratios

Solvency ratios provide guidance on the extent to which a business is financed by debt (as opposed to equity). Commonly calculated solvency ratios are shown in Table 12.4.

Table 12.4 Solvency ratios

Ratio	Formula	Description of ratio	Bazwaldo Limited year 2	Bazwaldo Limited year 1
Interest cover	profit before interest and tax/interest charge	Operating profit expressed as a multiple of the interest charge	26.655	10.212
Gearing	long-term interest-bearing borrowings/ capital employed	Long-term borrowings expressed as a percentage of capital employed	16.8%	31.7%
Debt/ equity	long-term interest-bearing borrowings/ owner equity	Long-term borrowings expressed as a percentage of owner equity	20.3%	46.5%

Interest cover is a measure of the ease with which interest on borrowings is covered by operating profit. The higher the interest cover, the more likely it is that interest obligations can be paid without difficulty. In the case of Bazwaldo Limited, the interest cover increased significantly in year 2 because, as compared with year 1, the operating profit increased and the interest charges decreased.

Gearing is otherwise referred to as leverage. It is a measure of the amount of debt included in total capital employed. Although borrowings can provide necessary capital for a growing business, an excessive amount of debt is harmful to a business because the obligation to repay debt finance can destroy an otherwise successful business. It is helpful to monitor the amount of debt that is carried by a business to ensure that new borrowings will not result in an excessive burden of debt finance.

The gearing and debt/equity ratios are similar measures of the percentage of total capital that is debt finance. In the case of Bazwaldo Limited, the levels of gearing have reduced in year 2 due to repayment of some of the long-term loan and to the increased profits (which become part of owner equity).

12.3.5 Investment ratios

Investment ratios provide guidance on the performance of ordinary share investments. For the purpose of calculating the investment ratios, additional information is as follows:

	Year 2	Year 1
Dividend declared	£2,500	£1,600
Number of ordinary shares issued	1,295	1,045
Market price per ordinary share	£7.50	£4.35

Commonly calculated investment ratios are shown in Table 12.5 (overleaf).

Earnings per share is a calculation of the earnings that are attributable to each issued ordinary share. The appropriate profit figure is after the interest, tax and preference share dividends are deducted. The denominator in the formula is the number of ordinary shares issued (not the nominal value or market value of the shares). The increase in Bazwaldo Limited's earnings per share in year 2 is due to the increase in profits in year 2 that are attributable to ordinary shareholders.

The dividend yield provides an indication of the dividend return that a potential investor could receive if the investor bought shares at the current market price. The potential investor could compare the dividend yield on this

Table 12.5 Investment ratios

Ratio	Formula	Description of ratio	Bazwaldo Limited year 2	Bazwaldo Limited year 1
Earnings per share	profit attributable to ordinary shareholders/ number of issued ordinary shares	earnings attributable to each issued ordinary share	£8.81	£6.25
Dividend yield	dividend attributable to ordinary shareholders/ market value of ordinary shares	ordinary dividend expressed as a percentage of market value of ordinary share	25.7%	35.2%
Dividend cover	profit attributable to ordinary shareholders/ dividend attributable to ordinary shareholders	profit attributable to ordinary shareholders expressed as a multiple of the ordinary dividend	4.563	4.081

investment opportunity with yields available from other opportunities. Some investors prefer to receive a return on their investment in the form of dividends (as opposed to increases in the share price) and would therefore be primarily interested in investment opportunities with higher dividend yields. Bazwaldo Limited's dividend yield declined in year 2 because of an increase in the share price that was disproportionately larger than the increase in the dividend in year 2.

Investors who seek high dividend yields are also interested in the **dividend cover**. The dividend cover is a measure of the ease with which profits cover a declared dividend. It is an indicator of the sustainability of the dividend and whether dividends are likely to increase or decrease in the future. The dividend cover of Bazwaldo Limited has increased due to the increase in profits that are disproportionately larger than the increase in dividends.

12.3.6 What would an analyst conclude about the financial health of Bazwaldo Limited?

Based on the common size statements and the commonly calculated ratios, an analyst might conclude the following:

- Bazwaldo Limited is growing in terms of revenue and is increasingly profitable. Its bottom line profit is 31.7% of revenue in year 2 as compared with 28.3% in year 1.
- The gross profit percentage in year 2 (40.3%) is in line with the industry norm (41%) but lower than the year 1 gross margin (45%). See Table 12.1, page 136. There may be room for improvement in the gross margin in year 3.
- Overheads appear to be well controlled. As a percentage of revenue the distribution and administrative costs declined in year 2 as compared with year 1. Good control of the overheads is a significant reason why the net profit margin was higher in year 2 than in year 1.
- The reduction in the interest charge in year 2 is attributable to the repayment of long-term loans. Bazwaldo Limited reduced its exposure to debt financing in year 2 and the interest charge in year 2 is correspondingly lower. If the directors of the company continue to reduce debt financing, the interest charge will decline further in year 3.
- The company appears to be fundamentally healthy in terms of its liquidity and solvency (See Tables 12.3, page 139 and 12.4, page 140). The liquidity ratios indicate that short-term obligation can be met reasonably comfortably even if, in the case of the acid test and cash ratios, the values are slightly below the industry norm.
- There is some concern about the quality of inventory management. The working capital ratio (6.055) is above the industry norm (4.5) only due to the inclusion of a high level of inventory in the current assets (See Table 12.3, page 139). Furthermore, the inventory turnover (1.58) is well below the industry norm (4.71) and the days of inventory on hand (230 days) is significantly above the industry norm (130 days). See Table 12.2, page 137. The company may be carrying too much inventory for its current stage of development. If the company reduces its levels of inventory and maintains current levels of business, the inventory turnover will increase, the days of inventory on hand will decrease and the cash conversion cycle will decline. A reduction in the cash conversion cycle will free up working capital that is currently tied up in inventory.
- With the exception of the inventory, working capital management of trade receivables and payables appears to be satisfactory (See Table 12.2, page 137), although this will become clearer when trends and comparatives are available.
- In the absence of useful comparatives, it is also difficult to conclude on the total and noncurrent asset turnover activity ratios (See Table 12.2, page 137). There is no reason to think that the company's assets are not

productively utilized but it is not possible to definitively conclude on this without further information.

- Debt, as a source of long-term finance, is a declining component of total capital employed. The gearing and debt-equity ratios are both lower in year 2 in comparison to year 1 (See Table 12.4, page 140). The directors may be pursuing a strategy of financing corporate growth from internal profitability rather than from external debt sources. Although the directors have declared a dividend, the growth in dividends is lower than the growth in profits. If the directors retain a greater proportion of the profits, further reductions in the levels of long-term debt will be facilitated.
- The increase in the ordinary share price (See Table 12.5, page 142) suggests that the stock market views Bazwaldo Limited in a positive light. This profitable company (based on earnings per share) is likely to be most attractive to investors who prefer to obtain a return on their investment through increases in the share price rather than receiving dividends.

12.4 What are the common mistakes made when interpreting financial statements?

In the real world of financial reporting, it is often necessary to take a pragmatic view of the interpretation of financial statements because, notwithstanding the use of mathematical formulae, financial reporting is not an exact science. While ratios help to focus attention on important areas and reveal trends that might otherwise be overlooked, there is no single set of percentages and ratios that will, in all cases, provide a complete interpretation of financial statements. It is necessary for an analyst to be mindful of the following:

- Single calculations are not as useful as a number of complementary calculations. No individual calculation reveals a complete picture. It is preferable to gather complementary evidence from several calculations.
- It is unlikely that perfect information for all ratios will be available. It may be necessary, for example, to substitute cost of sales for purchases because a value for purchases may not be presented in the financial statements. The quality of the analysis may be affected as a result.
- Calculations of ratios and percentages are based on historical information. They do not predict the future.
- Different accounting treatments can distort comparisons. For example, different depreciation policies or the revaluation of noncurrent assets could distort profitability and noncurrent asset turnover ratios.

- Industry norms can be difficult to obtain and the financial health of one business within the industry can be difficult to ascertain as a result.
- Norms differ for different industries. There are no ideal ratios that apply in all circumstances and at all times.

It is as important to be aware of the assumptions and limitations of ratio analysis as it is to be able to undertake an analysis. Mathematical calculations of percentages and ratios are not a substitute for understanding a business and the wider economic environment in which it operates. Percentages and ratios should be viewed as tools that assist a detailed understanding of a business in terms of its performance and position relative to a preceding reporting period or relative to industry norms.

12.5 Summary and conclusions

The interpretation of financial statements involves the calculation and inter-pretation of percentages and ratios for the purpose of gaining insights to the performance and position of a business. The objective is to enable readers to assess the financial health of a business for a reporting period relative to other reporting periods and/or relative to other businesses.

Common size financial statements express all values as percentages of base items (such as revenue, total assets or total equity).

Ratios and percentages are commonly grouped into categories. Profitability, activity, liquidity, solvency and investor ratios interpret financial statements from different perspectives. This is not to suggest, however, that the categories of ratios are mutually exclusive. For example, activity and liquidity ratios have overlapping perspectives, as do profitability and investor ratios.

There are limitations to the usefulness of ratios and percentages. They are use-ful as tools to assist understanding, to form expectations and to identify matters that may require attention from owners and managers. But there are no golden rules of ratio analysis and they are not a substitute for understanding a business.

Test your understanding

The financial statements available for Mousetrap for the most recent reporting period are as follows:

Mousetrap Limited
Income statement for the period ended 31 December 2010

	£000
Revenue	4,865
Cost of sales	(2,944)
Gross profit	1,921
Distribution expenses	(541)
Administrative expenses	(437)
Finance costs	(276)
Profit before taxation	667
Taxation	(311)
Profit for the period	**357**

Statement of financial position at 31 December 2010

Assets	£000
Noncurrent assets	5,805
Current assets	
Inventory	1,552
Trade receivables	397
Bank and cash	858
	2,807
Total assets	**8,612**
Equity and liabilities	
Equity	
Ordinary shares £1 each	575
Retained earnings	2,897
	3,472
Noncurrent liabilities	
8% £100 debentures	4,450

Current liabilities	
Trade payables	350
Tax payable	340
	690
Total equity and liabilities	**8,612**

Additional available information:

Market price of one ordinary share	£5.50
Market price of £100 debenture	£115.00
Dividend declared for the reporting period	£220,000

Required:
   (i) Calculate profitability, activity, liquidity, solvency and investment ratios to the extent permitted by the available information.
  (ii) Comment on the results.
 (iii) Identify the limitations of the analysis.

Further practice and reading

1. http://www.bazwaldo.com

   Insert the following code into the website keyword search option to access practice questions relating to this chapter: *2010chapter12*

2. Thomas, A. and Ward, A.M. (2009) *Introduction to Financial Accounting*, 6th edn, McGraw-Hill

   Chapter 32: The appraisal of company financial statements using ratio analysis

13 Regulatory and conceptual frameworks

You must be able to explain:

○ How accounting techniques contribute to high-quality financial statements
○ The nature of a regulatory framework
○ The nature and content of the IASB conceptual framework

13.1 How do accounting techniques contribute to high-quality financial statements?

Recall the objectives of financial reporting from Chapter 1: to provide useful information about (i) the performance of an organization during a reporting period and (ii) the status of business at the end of a reporting period. Recall the attributes that financial statements should have in order to be considered useful: relevance, reliability, comparability and understandability (collectively referred to as the qualitative characteristics of financial statements).

The techniques presented throughout this text include many examples of how accountants attempt to achieve the objective of providing useful information to a wide range of interested parties:

- Chapter 2 – including comparative period information in financial statements, and distinguishing between current and noncurrent assets and liabilities in statements of financial position.
- Chapter 3 – the logic of deducting cost of sales (rather than cost of purchases or goods available for sale) from income to calculate income statement profit.

- Chapter 4 – including capital expenditure as an asset on a statement of financial position and revenue expenditure as an expense in an income statement.
- Chapter 5 – allocating capital expenditure to income statements on a periodic basis using appropriate depreciation methods and revaluing noncurrent assets when appropriate.
- Chapter 6 – recognizing income as it is earned and expenses as they are incurred rather than as cash as it is received or paid.
- Chapter 7 – including reliable provisions and estimates in financial statements.
- Chapter 9 – presenting relevant information in a statement of comprehensive income.
- Chapter 10 – presenting relevant information in a statement of changes in equity.
- Chapter 11 – presenting the performance of a business from a cash flow perspective to complement the profit perspective presented in an income statement.

The consistent application of accounting techniques such as those explained in this text increases the likelihood that financial statements will provide useful information. High-quality information is therefore predicated on the assumption that everyone prepares financial statements on a comparable and consistent basis, hence the need for regulatory and conceptual frameworks for accounting.

13.2 What is a regulatory framework?

Financial reporting is one of the primary means by which businesses communicate with external parties. For this reason, there must be an agreed basis to accounting for transactions and events. In other words, the process of preparing financial statements should operate within a structured authoritative system. The authoritative system that governs financial accounting processes and outcomes is called a **regulatory framework**. It includes legislation and accounting standards.

Accounting standards prescribe the methods that are suitable for the preparation of financial statements. Financial accounting standards are developed and issued by the International Accounting Standards Board (IASB). The objective of the IASB is to develop a high-quality set of accounting standards for the preparation of financial statements. The standards issued by the IASB are called International Financial Reporting Standards (IFRSs).

The IASB is supported by the IFRS Advisory Council (previously the Standards Advisory Council). Membership of the IFRS Advisory Council comes from a wide range of interested parties. The IASB consults with and is advised by the IFRS Advisory Council on a range of issues that fall within its scope of work.

The standard-setting work of the IASB is overseen by the IFRS Foundation (previously the International Accounting Standards Committee Foundation). The IFRS Foundation is a not-for-profit organization.

The IFRS Interpretations Committee (previously the International Financial Reporting Interpretations Committee) is the IFRS Foundation's interpretive body. It issues guidance when there are conflicting interpretations of IFRSs or when new financial reporting issues arise that are not addressed by existing IFRSs.

An accounting standard is not automatically authoritative merely because it is issued by the IASB. It is given the force of law in different geographical jurisdictions only when formally approved by the national regulatory bodies that have the formal authority to publish accounting standards in their jurisdictions.

In many cases, accounting standards complement national government legislation and stock market regulations. Together, they should provide a robust regulatory framework for financial accounting and reporting.

13.3 What is the IASB conceptual framework?

A conceptual framework sets out a philosophical approach to the preparation and presentation of financial statements. The purpose of such a framework is to communicate the conceptual ideas that underpin financial statements. It is a theoretical position on the best way to produce high-quality financial statements. It is without reference to any particular country, industry or businesses. The conceptual framework document issued by the IASB is the *Framework for the Preparation and Presentation of Financial Statements*.

Conceptual framework documents are useful because there is more than one way in which financial statements could be prepared. Because different people and groups can have different views about what financial accounting and reporting is or should be about, it is necessary for the IASB to make explicit its objectives and ideals so that others can appreciate the particular conceptual framework within which the IASB operates.

A conceptual framework assists the development of consistent IASB accounting standards. It helps to ensure that standards development and accounting issues are consistently addressed with reference to a stated set of objectives. This should help to ensure that accounting standards do not conflict with each other.

The IASB conceptual framework is underpinned by two fundamental assumptions:

- **Accruals basis of accounting**: transactions and events are recorded in financial statements when they occur and not only when cash or its equivalent is received or paid.
- **Going concern**: when preparing the financial statements of a business organization, it is assumed that the business will remain in operational existence for the foreseeable future.

The IASB conceptual framework also addresses:

- The objectives of financial statements.
- The qualitative characteristics of useful financial statements.
- The principles of recognition and measurement in financial statements.
- The concepts of capital and capital maintenance.

Capital, capital maintenance, and the principles of recognition and measurement in financial statements are not addressed in detail in this text.

13.4 Summary and conclusions

The preparation of financial statements is underpinned by regulatory and conceptual frameworks. A regulatory framework sets out the rules that apply to the preparation of the financial statements. Accounting standards provide many of the rules and, depending on the jurisdiction within which a business operates and perhaps the legal form of the business, there may be additional rules set out in government legislation and stock exchange requirements. It is therefore necessary for each business organization to have a full appreciation of the regulatory framework within which it operates.

Accounting standards, which are usually a significant component of a regulatory framework, are likely to be based on an underlying conceptual framework. A conceptual framework sets out the philosophy of accounting that is applied when developing accounting standards. The International Accounting Standards Board (IASB) issues International Financial Reporting Standards (IFRSs) based on its particular philosophical approach to the preparation of financial statements.

Further practice and reading

1. http://www.bazwaldo.com

   Insert the following code into the website keyword search option to access practice questions relating to this chapter: *2010chapter13*

2. Thomas, A. and Ward, A.M. (2009) *Introduction to Financial Accounting*, 6th edn, McGraw-Hill

   Chapter 3: The nature and objectives of financial accounting

   Chapter 5: The conceptual framework of accounting

Appendix: Solutions to Test Your Understanding

Insert the following code into the www.bazwaldo.com keyword search option to access tutorial notes and additional workings for these solutions: *2010solutions*

Chapter 1

1 Option (d) is correct. The assets minus the liabilities equal the equity.
2 (a) False
  (b) True
  (c) True
  (d) True
  (e) True
  (f) False
  (g) False
  (h) True
  (i) True
  (j) False

Chapter 2

1 (a) Noncurrent asset
  (b) Current liability
  (c) Current asset
  (d) Noncurrent liability
  (e) Current asset
  (f) Current asset
  (g) Noncurrent asset
  (h) Current asset
  (i) Current liability

2 Libra

Statement of financial position					
	Day 1	Day 2	Day 3	Day 4	Day 5
	£	£	£	£	£
Current assets					
Inventory		1,650			
Trade receivables			1,650	1,650	100
Bank	3,800	3,800	3,800	2,550	4,100
TOTAL ASSETS	3,800	5,450	5,450	4,200	4,200
Equity and liabilities					
Owner equity	3,800	3,800	3,800	3,800	3,800
Current liabilities					
Trade payable		1,650	1,650	400	400
TOTAL EQUITY AND LIABILITIES	3,800	5,450	5,450	4,200	4,200

Chapter 3

1 Alpha

(i)

	£	£
Opening inventory		12,744
Purchases	30,200	
Purchases returns	(1,023)	
		29,177
Closing inventory		(15,001)
Cost of sales		26,920

(ii)

	£	£	£
Sales		46,552	
Sales returns		(1,925)	
			44,627
Opening inventory		(12,744)	

Purchases	(30,200)	
Purchases returns	1,023	
	(29,177)	
Closing inventory	15,001	
Cost of sales		(26,920)
Profit		17,707

2

(i)

Bookkeeping entries		£	£
dr	Purchases	600	
cr	Trade payable		600
Being purchase of inventory on credit			
dr	Bank	2,500	
cr	Owner equity		2,500
Being investment of new equity capital by the owner			
dr	Trade receivables	1,100	
cr	Sales		1,100
Being sale of inventory on credit			
dr	Trade payable	400	
cr	Bank		400
Being payment to trade payable			
dr	Bank	800	
cr	Trade receivable		800
Being receipt from trade receivable			
dr	Inventory	250	
cr	Cost of sales		250
Being closing inventory at the end of the week			

(ii)

Income statement for the week ending 7 August		
		£
Sales		1,100
Less cost of sales		
Opening inventory	200	

Purchases	600	
Closing inventory	(250)	
		550
Profit for the week		**550**

(iii)

Statement of financial position at 7 August		
Current assets		£
Inventory		250
Trade receivables		300
Bank		6,100
TOTAL ASSETS		**6,650**
Equity and liabilities		
Owner equity at beginning of the week	3,400	
New equity investment	2,500	
Profit for the week	550	
		6,450
Current liability		
Trade payable		200
TOTAL EQUITY AND LIABILITIES		**6,650**

Chapter 4

1 (a) Capital expenditure
   (b) Revenue expenditure
   (c) Revenue expenditure
   (d) Revenue expenditure
   (e) Revenue expenditure

2 (a) Capital expenditure
   (b) Revenue expenditure
   (c) Capital expenditure
   (d) Capital expenditure
   (e) Revenue expenditure
   (f) Revenue expenditure

Chapter 5

1 Caroline

	Furniture	Motor vehicle
31 October 2008	£	£
Acquisition		24,000
Depreciation		(6,000)
Carrying value		**18,000**
31 October 2009		
Opening carrying value		18,000
Acquisition	4,000	
Depreciation	(367)	(4,500)
Carrying value	**3,633**	**13,500**
31 October 2010		
Opening carrying value	3,633	13,500
Depreciation	(400)	(3,375)
Carrying value	**3,233**	**10,125**

Explanation:
Depreciation of the furniture is on a pro rata basis in the year of acquisition. The furniture was on hand for 11 months of the 2009 financial year, hence a depreciation calculation of £4,000 × 10% × 11/12 = £367.

A full year's depreciation is charged on the motor vehicle regardless of the point in time at which it was acquired during the financial year. The charge for depreciation in the 2008 financial year is therefore £24,000 × 25% even though the vehicle was held for only five months.

2 Ruby

(i)

Bookkeeping entries	£	£
dr	Office building : cost	700,000	
cr	Office buildings : accumulated depreciation	320,000	
cr	Revaluation reserve		1,020,000

Being revaluation of office building at 1 July 2009

| dr | Depreciation | 60,000 | |
| cr | Office building : accumulated depreciation | | 60,000 |

Being office building depreciation charge for the 2010 financial year

| dr | Plant and machinery : cost | 180,000 | |
| cr | Bank (assuming the amount due was paid immediately) | | 180,000 |

Being acquisition of new plant and machinery

dr	Bank	75,000	
dr	Plant and machinery : accumulated depreciation	180,000	
cr	Plant and machinery : cost		240,000
cr	Gain on disposal of plant and machinery		15,000

Being gain on disposal of plant and machinery

| dr | Depreciation | 190,000 | |
| cr | Plant and machinery : accumulated depreciation | | 190,000 |

Being plant and machinery depreciation charge for the 2010 financial year

(ii)

Ruby	
Income statement (extracts)	
	2010
	£
Gain on disposal of plant and machinery	15,000
Other income	x
Total income	x
Depreciation	(250,000)
Other expenses	x
Total expenses	x
Profit for the year	x

(iii)

Ruby		
Statement of financial position (extracts)		
	2010	2009
Noncurrent assets	£	£
Office buildings	2,340,000	1,380,000
Plant and machinery	444,000	514,000
	2,784,000	1,894,000
Other assets	x	x
TOTAL ASSETS	x	x
Equity and liabilities		
Revaluation reserve	1,020,000	
Other equity and liabilities	x	x
TOTAL EQUITY AND LIABILITIES	x	x

Working	Office buildings	Plant and machinery
	£	£
Cost at 1 July 2009	1,700,000	820,000
Revaluation	700,000	
Acquisition		180,000
Disposal		(240,000)
Valuation/Cost at 30 June 2010	2,400,000	760,000
Accumulated depreciation at 1 July 2009	(320,000)	(306,000)
Revaluation	320,000	
Disposal		180,000
Annual depreciation charge	(60,000)	(190,000)
Accumulated depreciation at 30 June 2010	(60,000)	(316,000)
Carrying value at 1 July 2009	1,380,000	514,000
Carrying value at 30 June 2010	**2,340,000**	**444,000**

Chapter 6

1

Working	£
Opening accrual	(240)
August 2009 payment	610
November 2009 payment	720
February 2010 payment	870
May 2010 payment	770
Closing accrual (included in statement of financial position)	560
Income statement charge for the year	3,290

2

Working	£
Opening prepayment	12,500
Payment on 1 August 2010	48,000
Closing prepayment (included in statement of financial position)	(28,000)
Income statement charge for insurance	32,500

Chapter 7

1 Jackson

Working			
Calculation of required allowance for receivables	£	£	£
Hugo specific allowance	1,050		
Omo specific allowance	1,250		
			2,300
Trade receivables	63,200		
Irrecoverable debts written off	(9,800)		
Hugo specific allowance	(1,050)		
Omo specific allowance	(1,250)		

Receivable for which general provision is required	51,100
General allowance @ 4%	2,044
Total allowance required	4,344
Existing allowance	7,115
Decrease in allowance	(2,771)

Bookkeeping entries		£	£
dr	Irrecoverable debts	9,800	
cr	Trade receivables		9,800
Being irrecoverable debts			
dr	Allowance for receivables	2,771	
cr	Irrecoverable debts		2,771
Being decrease in allowance for receivables			

Summary of account changes	Given		Adjust		Final	
	£	£	£	£	£	£
	dr	cr	dr	cr	dr	cr
(i) Irrecoverable debts			9,800	2,771	7,029	
(ii) Trade receivables	63,200			9,800	53,400	
(iii) Allowance for receivables		7,115	2,771			4,344

2

Working	
Calculation of irrecoverable debts expense	£
Irrecoverable debts written off	(1,600)
Irrecoverable debt recovered	540
Decrease in allowance for receivables	650
Income statement charge	**(410)**

Bookkeeping entries		£	£
dr	Irrecoverable debts	1,600	
cr	Trade receivables		1,600
Being irrecoverable debts			
dr	Bank	540	
cr	Irrecoverable debts		540
Being receipt of debt previously accounted for as irrecoverable			
dr	Allowance for receivables	650	
cr	Irrecoverable debts		650
Being decrease in allowance for receivables			

Chapter 8

(i)

Ginger	
Income statement for the year ended 31 December 2010	
	£
Revenue	365,200
Cost of sales	(267,460)
Gross profit	97,740
Wages and salaries	(46,160)
Rent	(11,850)
Motor expenses	(3,720)
Insurance	(760)
Irrecoverable debts	(590)
Light and heat	(3,549)
Depreciation	(10,305)
Operating profit	20,806
Profit on disposal of motor vehicle	1,756
Bank overdraft interest	(74)
Profit for the period	**22,488**

(ii)

Ginger			
Statement of financial position at 31 December 2010			
	Cost	Accumulated depreciation	Carrying value
Noncurrent assets	£	£	£
Land	250,000		250,000
Buildings	100,000	(8,000)	92,000
Fixtures and fittings	28,000	(22,400)	5,600
Motor vehicles	16,000	(9,689)	6,311
	394,000	(40,089)	353,911
Current assets			
Inventory		22,680	
Trade receivables	16,950		
Allowance for receivables	(678)		
		16,272	
Bank		7,912	
Prepayment of rent		1,150	
			48,014
TOTAL ASSETS			**401,925**
Equity and liabilities			
Owner equity		225,600	
Revaluation reserve		50,000	
Opening retained earnings	80,358		
Profit for the period	22,488		
		102,846	
			378,446
Current liabilities			
Trade payables		23,004	
Light and heat accrual		475	
			23,479
TOTAL EQUITY AND LIABILITIES			**401,925**

Chapter 9

Bookkeeping journals	£	£
dr Bank account	16,500	
cr Revenue		16,500
Being sale of inventory. Cash receipt lodged		
dr Bank account	3,000	
cr Owner equity		3,000
Being cash investment of new equity by owner		
dr Purchases	7,000	
cr Trade payable		7,000
Being purchase of inventory on credit		
dr Buildings	22,000	
cr Surplus on revaluation		22,000
Being surplus on revaluation of buildings		
dr Insurance premium	800	
cr Bank account		800
Being receipt and payment of insurance premium invoice		
dr Cost of sales	12,400	
cr Inventory		12,400
Being transfer of opening inventory to cost of sales		
dr Inventory	7,000	
cr Cost of sales		7,000
Being recognition of closing inventory		

Cairo

**Statement of comprehensive income
for the period ended 30 September 2011**

	£	£
Revenue		16,500
Less cost of goods sold		
Opening inventory	12,400	
Purchases	7,000	
Less closing inventory	(7,000)	
		12,400

Gross profit	4,100
Expenses	
Insurance premium	800
Profit for the period	3,300
Other comprehensive income	
Surplus on revaluation of buildings	22,000
Total comprehensive income	**25,300**

Cairo

**Statement of financial position
at 30 September 2011**

Noncurrent assets	£
Buildings	50,000
Current assets	
Inventory	7,000
Bank account	18,700
TOTAL ASSETS	**75,700**
Equity	
Owner equity	43,400
Retained earnings	3,300
Revaluation reserve	22,000
	68,700
Current liabilities	
Trade payable	7,000
TOTAL EQUITY AND LIABILITIES	**75,700**

Chapter 10

(i)

Sparrow Statement of comprehensive income for the year ended 31 December 2010	£
Revenue	50,000
Cost of sales	(16,000)
Gross profit	34,000
Distribution costs	(7,425)
Administrative expenses	(15,550)
Reorganization costs	(2,400)
Operating profits	8,625
Finance costs	(800)
Profit before taxation	7,825
Taxation charge	(2,500)
Profit after taxation	5,325
Other comprehensive income:	
Surplus on revaluation of property	6,000
Total comprehensive income	11,325

(ii)

Sparrow

Statement of changes in equity for the year ended 31 December 2010

	Ordinary share capital	Share premium	Retained earnings	Revaluation reserve	Total
	£	£	£	£	£
Opening balance 1 January	8,000	3,000	19,550		30,550
Issue of share capital	2,000	6,000			8,000
Dividends paid			(1,600)		(1,600)

Total comprehensive income for the year			5,325	6,000	11,325
Closing balance 31 December	10,000	9,000	23,275	6,000	48,275

(iii)

Sparrow

Statement of financial position as at 31 December 2010

	£
Noncurrent assets	41,000
Current assets	
Inventory	12,000
Trade receivables	10,000
Cash at bank	16,100
Distribution costs prepayment	575
	38,675
TOTAL ASSETS	**79,675**
Equity and liabilities	
£0.50 ordinary shares	10,000
Share premium	9,000
Retained earnings	23,275
Revaluation reserve	6,000
	48,275
Noncurrent liabilities	
10% loan notes	8,000
Current liabilities	
Trade payables	20,000
Tax liability	3,000
Loan interest accrual	400
	23,400
TOTAL EQUITY AND LIABILITIES	**79,675**

Chapter 11

(i)

Statement of cash flows for the year ended 30 September 2010	
OPERATING ACTIVITIES	£000
Profit before tax	144
Adjust for	
Depreciation	87
Profit on disposal of noncurrent asset	(23)
Income from investments	(4)
Interest expense	21
Change in inventory	44
Change in trade receivables	43
Change in trade payables	129
Change in accruals (w1)	30
Cash generated from/(used in) operations	471
Interest paid (w2)	(48)
Income taxes paid (w3)	(10)
Net cash from/(used in) operating activities	*413*
INVESTING ACTIVITIES	
Acquisition of noncurrent assets (w4)	(280)
Proceeds from disposal of noncurrent assets	98
Interest received (w5)	12
Net cash from/(used in) investing activities	*(170)*
FINANCING ACTIVITIES	
Proceeds from issue of share capital	60
Redemption of 10% loan notes	(50)
Redemption of 5% loan notes	(20)
Dividends paid	(30)
Net cash from/(used in) financing activities	*(40)*
Net change in cash and cash equivalents	203
Opening cash and cash equivalents	(71)
Closing cash and cash equivalents	**132**

w1			
Change in accruals			
opening accruals	33		
attributable to interest payable	(33)		
closing accruals	36		
attributable to interest payable	(6)		
		30	
		30	
w2			
Interest paid			
opening obligation	(33)		
income statement charge	(21)		
closing obligation	6		
	(48)		
w3			
Taxes paid			
opening obligation	(88)		
income statement charge	(22)		
closing obligation	100		
	(10)		
w4			
Acquisition of noncurrent assets			
opening carrying value	510		
revaluation	60		
carrying value of disposal	(75)		
depreciation charge	(87)		
closing carrying value	(688)		
	(280)		
w5			
Interest received			
opening receivable	12		
income statement credit	4		
closing receivable	(4)		
	12		

(ii) The solution is available on www.bazwaldo.com. Insert the following key-word search code: *2010solutions*

(iii)

Analysis of cash and cash equivalents	2010 £000	2009 £000
Cash in hand and at bank	82	4
Short term investments	50	
Bank overdraft		(75)
Total cash and cash equivalents	132	(71)

Chapter 12

(i)

Profitability ratios

Gross margin	39.48%
Operating profit margin	19.39%
Net profit margin	13.71%
Return on capital employed	11.90%
Return on equity (before tax)	19.21%

Activity ratios

Total asset turnover	0.56	times
Noncurrent asset turnover	0.84	times
Working capital turnover	3.04	times
Inventory turnover	1.90	times
Days of receivables outstanding	29.79	days
Days of payables outstanding	43.39	days
Days of inventory on hand	192.42	days

Liquidity ratios

Current ratio	4.07	times
Acid test ratio	1.82	times
Cash ratio	1.24	times
Cash conversion cycle	179	days

Solvency ratios

Interest cover	3.42	times
Gearing ratio	56.17%	
Debt equity ratio	128.17%	

Investment ratios

Earnings per share	£0.62	per share
Dividend yield	6.96%	
Dividend cover	1.62	times

(ii)

- Mousetrap is profitable and generating positive returns for debt and equity investors, particularly the equity investors.
- In the absence of comparable information, it is difficult to assess whether Mousetrap's asset base is being utilized efficiently. However, the days of inventory on hand appears to be excessively high. This may signal an issue with inventory management.
- Liquidity appears to be satisfactory although comparatives would be helpful. The length of the cash conversion cycle is attributable to the length of time that inventory is held.
- Financing debt finance appears to be unproblematic. Interest cover of 3.42 indicates that profits easily exceed debt finance costs. Mousetrap is financed almost equally by debt and equity finance. If this income statement is representative of the underlying profitability of Mousetrap, there is scope for additional debt finance (which is cheaper than equity finance).
- Investment ratios are positive. Comparative or trend data are required to draw final conclusions.

(iii)

- The absence of comparatives and trend data constrains the conclusions.
- There is no information about the industry in which Mousetrap operates. It is not possible to compare calculations with industry norms.
- In the absence of comparatives, the statement of financial position ratios could not be averaged. The resultant calculations may not be representative of Mousetrap's situation. In general, the requirement to use less than perfect information constrains the conclusions. However, this is frequently a practical reality.

Index

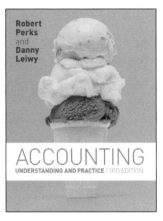

Robert
Perks
and
Danny
Leiwy

ACCOUNTING
Understanding and Practice
Third Edition

Robert Perks and Danny Leiwy

9780077124786 (Paperback)
2010

eBook also available

This book provides a gentle introduction to the complexities of accounting. An evolution of the successful textbook *Financial Accounting: Understanding and Practice*, this new edition has been enhanced to provide more emphasis on Management Accounting topics, with new material that has been structured in line with current teaching in introductory accounting modules. Fully revised throughout, the whole text has been thoroughly updated in accordance with the International Financial Reporting Standards. Ample practice illustrations and examples help present the subject in relation to a business world to which readers can easily relate

Key features:

- An emphasis on understanding and application rather than numerical routines
- Clear explanations and evaluations
- Self test questions with answers provided, challenging discussion questions and group activities

www.openup.co.uk

OPEN UNIVERSITY PRESS
McGraw - Hill Education

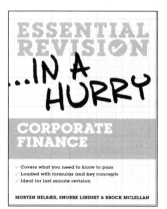

CORPORATE FINANCE

Morten Helbæk, Snorre Lindset
and Brock McLellan

9780335236664 (Paperback)
October 2010

eBook also available

Many topics in finance are hard for students to understand.
Corporate Finance: get it; read it, PASS is a short revision text
presenting the essentials that students have to learn to pass their
Corporate Finance module

Key features:

- Demonstrative examples with complete solutions
- Teaches students difficult theory
- Shows students how to solve challenging problems in an
  effective way

www.openup.co.uk

OPEN UNIVERSITY PRESS
McGraw - Hill Education